THE APPRENTICES

ALSO BY LEON GARFIELD
The Pleasure Garden
The Prisoners of September
The Sound of Coaches

THE
APPRENTICES

LEON GARFIELD

THE VIKING PRESS   NEW YORK

To George Nicholson

First American Edition
Copyright © Leon Garfield, 1976, 1977, 1978
All rights reserved
First published in 1978 by The Viking Press
625 Madison Avenue, New York, N.Y. 10022
Printed in U.S.A.
1 2 3 4 5 82 81 80 79 78

Library of Congress Cataloging in Publication Data
Garfield, Leon. The apprentices.
Contents: The lamplighter's funeral.—Mirror, mirror.
—Moss and blister.—The cloak.—The valentine. [etc.]
1. Apprentices—Juvenile fiction. [1. Apprentices
—Fiction. 2. Short stories] I. Title.
PZ7.G17943Ap   [Fic]   77-21770
ISBN 0-670-12978-X

CONTENTS

A Note About Apprenticeships

In the year 1764, a London evening newspaper reported the case of a Cheapside haberdasher's apprentice—a sober, industrious youth, always polite and quietly dressed—who had embezzled ten thousand pounds (a prodigious sum, equal, perhaps, to half a million dollars) of his master's money. The apprentice had not gambled with it; he had not spent it wildly; he had invested it in sound stock with the worthy idea of setting up in trade on his own when his seven years' apprenticeship should be out.

Seven years is a long time. Apprenticeships were always for seven years; seven years to the trade of surgery, seven years to the trade of rowing a boat. It made no difference. (Except to the apprentice.) Depending on the trade, a child's parents paid a sum of money to a master, who thereafter gave board, lodging, and tuition in exchange for hard, menial work. He also paid a small wage—little more than pocket money. For seven years.

At the end of his time the apprentice became a journeyman—that is to say, he was able to work in the trade for day wages. His only chance of setting up on his own was either by marrying the master's daughter, and inheriting the business, or the master's widow, should matters fall out conveniently. Otherwise he had nothing to look forward to but a life of hard and ill-paid work. The sum of money needed to set up on his own was a dream beyond his reach.

The Cheapside haberdasher's apprentice, however, was plainly no dreamer but a sternly practical soul. He was transported to His Majesty's Colonies in America where, it is to be supposed, his genius prospered, most likely in the banking line. But those who stayed behind, some marrying their masters' daughters, some not, still contrived to live with hope and some content.

L. G.

THE APPRENTICES

THE
LAMPLIGHTER'S
FUNERAL

A T HALF AFTER ELEVEN O'CLOCK (BY THE GREAT BELL OF BOW) of a cold, dark October night, a coffin came out of Trump Alley with six figures in white to shoulder it and a river of fire to light it on its way. Smoke pouring upwards heaved and loitered between the second- and first-floor windows of the narrow tenements, so that those looking down saw, as it were, a thick, fallen sky dimly pierced by a moving crowd of flames.

"It's heathen," said one soul whose parlour had filled up with smoke. "Why can't they go by daylight, like decent Christians?"

Slowly, and with much jolting (the bearers were of unequal height), the coffin turned right and lumbered down St. Lawrence Lane in the wake of the marching fire.

"I wish you long life," said an old Jew to a coffin bearer he knew by sight; and a little crowd on the corner of Cheapside uncovered as fifty lamplighters, all in white jackets and black cocked hats, filed across the road and turned into Queen Street with torches blazing and stinking the night out with fumes of melting pitch.

In accordance with old custom, they were burying one of their number, whose light had been eternally put out two days before in consequence of an inflammation of the lungs. One Sam Bold, lamplighter of Cripplegate Ward, having providently joined the burial club and paid his dues, was now being conducted with flaming pomp to his last snuffing place in St. Martin's Churchyard. Although he had been a solitary man, such was the brotherhood of the lamplighters that any death among them made more than a small hole in the night; their yellowed faces were dull and sad. . . .

One in particular looked sadder than all the rest, not from any extreme of grief, but because, having a chill himself and thinking too much of the fate of Sam Bold, he had taken a good quantity of gin to keep out the murderous cold air. The night had hit him hard, and he felt dizzy. Already the cobbles of Cheapside had almost overturned him; as he got into Queen Street, he caught his foot against a rift in the pavement and went down in a shower of sparks and blazing pitch, like a comet of doom.

A crowd of street urchins who had been following Sam Bold's fiery progress to the grave screamed with unseemly excitement, while the lamplighters tramped grimly on. Then one child—more eager than the rest—darted forward and picked up the still-burning torch. A slender, skinny-fingered child with eyes as round as hot pennies . . .

The torchlight lit his face, so that it seemed transparent with fire and floating in the smoke. The fallen lamplighter gazed vacantly at the apparition; then, overcome with shame at his fall, tried to explain.

"Issa f-funeral . . . muss go on. Respect . . . feel awful. . . ."

The child stared down.

"I'll go. . . ."

"No . . . no. 'S not proper. Wouldn't be 'spectful. . . . Oh I feel awful. . . ."

"I'll be respectful . . . reely."

"You sure?"

"Cross me heart."

"Take me—me jacket, then. Muss wear the p-proper jacket. It's the rule. And me 'at. Proper f-funeral 'at. Give 'em back later. . . ."

The dazed lamplighter struggled out of his jacket; his hat lay in the street beside him.

" 'Ere! P-put 'em on. Muss be 'spectful. Issa f-funeral . . ."

The white jacket engulfed the child and the hat finished him off, so that the lamplighter had the weird feeling he had attired a ghost that had just departed, leaving the empty clothes standing, stiff with terror. A sleeve reached out and took up the torch again.

"I'll be respectful," said the invisible child, and tipped back the hat sufficiently to uncover the seeing portion of his eerily solemn face.

The coffin had already passed on, and the deputy lamplighter had to scamper and run, with flame streaming, till he caught up with the funeral by St. Thomas the Apostle and took his place among the marchers.

At last Sam Bold was laid to rest in St. Martin's Churchyard, and the deputy lamplighter acquitted himself with dignity and respect. He stood stock-still amid the great crescent of fire that lit up the open grave and, with due solemnity after the black earth had thumped down, quenched his torch in the bucket provided—as did all the other brethren of the lamp—with the honourable words: "A light has gone out."

In the oppressive darkness that followed this general putting out, the company of mourners fumbled their way down Church

Lane to where a funeral feast was awaiting them at the Eagle and Child. This was the custom; each man paid towards the coffin, and what was left over provided for meat, cakes, and ale.

The Eagle and Child was an elderly inn that hung over the river like the glimmering poop of a ship that had taken a wrong turn and sailed among houses. . . . One by one the mourners climbed up the wooden steps that led to the overhanging bay where the feast was laid out. Last of all came the deputy, not wanting to disgrace the occasion by hanging back.

The president of the burial club, who collected shillings at the door, held out his hand. For a moment there was a stillness in nature, for to him who expected there was nothing given; the deputy did not possess a shilling. The president frowned, then observing the white jacket and cocked hat, took the occupant of them for Sam Bold's son. The dead man having been of Cripplegate Ward and he of Bishopsgate, they had not been personally known to each other. For all the president knew, Sam Bold had a dozen sons, and this before him was the representative of them all. He withdrew his expectant hand and gestured the orphan through the door. One didn't demand a shilling off a bereaved child.

Inside the parlour, the talk was generally what it always is after a funeral: quiet, with a discreet cheerfulness breaking in; not everyone can be struck to the heart by one man's death. As the ale went down, spirits went up, and there was singing, of a gentle sort . . . nothing rowdy or quick; such songs as "Sally in Our Alley," and "Over the Hills and Far Away."

After a little while, the deputy lamplighter joined in, not wanting to be conspicuous by keeping silent; his voice was high and singularly sweet. Several of the older brethren quietly shed tears, thinking, like the president, that here was Sam Bold's orphan, bearing up wonderfully. None liked to ask where his mother was, for fear of opening old wounds if, as was likely, she turned out to be dead.

At half past midnight there was a commotion on the steps outside, as of many feet struggling against incomprehensible odds. The president went to open the door, and the lamplighter who'd fallen in Queen Street appeared in a dusty and confused condition. After greeting the company, he searched out his deputy and recovered his jacket and hat.

" 'Ad a good feed, lad?" he inquired, gesturing towards the remains of the feast.

The lad, thin and bitterly ragged, looked up and shook his head.

"Not so much as a drop or a crumb," said someone, not understanding the deputizing arrangement and still taking the child to be an orphaned Bold. "It's only to be expected," he went on. "No appetite. Next of kin, you know . . ."

The new arrival—whose name was Pallcat—looked muddled. The child plucked him aside.

"I didn't like to say . . . I didn't have no shilling. . . . And it was only till you came. . . . I'll go now—"

Pallcat, not yet his usual miserly self, felt in his pockets for a coin.

"I don't want nothing," murmured the child awkwardly. "Reely."

Instantly Pallcat took his hands out of his pockets.

"Wodger do it for then?"

"I was sorry for you. . . ."

Pallcat stared down in disbelief.

"What's yer name?"

"Possul."

"Possul? That ain't a name," said Pallcat.

" 'S after St. Thomas the Apostle, where I does odd jobs."

Totally mystified, Pallcat scratched his greasy head, which reeked of the fish oil that supplied the lamps.

" 'Ave a cake," he said at length. " 'Ave a piece of pie and a thimble of ale. 'S all right. I paid me dues . . . and I ain't up to eating meself."

Possul gravely thanked his benefactor and drank and ate. Then there were more songs, and Possul obliged the company with *"While shepherds watched,"* sung solo until he got to *"and glory shone around,"* when the company softly joined in, as became a congregation of lamplighters.

At half past one, the last of the candles supplied by the landlord of the Eagle and Child went out, and the funeral party departed into the moonless night, pausing at the foot of the steps to shake one another by the hand and get their hazy bearings from the watermen's lights that still flickered and danced on the black river.

"Where d'you live, Possul?"

"Over Shoreditch way."

"With yer ma and pa?"

Possul shook his head vigorously, and Pallcat fancied he'd half smiled. (Queer, that, thought Pallcat for a moment.)

"I got rooms in Three Kings Court," he said, blinking to clear his brain. "Just back of Covent Garden."

Possul gazed at him in admiration.

"Two rooms," went on Pallcat, moved to a foolish boasting. "You can come back with me if you like—"

The invitation just slipped out. Pallcat's heart sank as he heard his own voice oozing hospitality. He could have bitten off his tongue. He hoped Possul hadn't heard him. . . .

"Don't want to be a trouble to you."

"No trouble," snarled Pallcat. " 'S a pleasure."

The journey back to Three Kings Court was full of corners

and carpings, as Pallcat roundly cursed the lamplighters of those wards and parishes who'd been too dishonest to fill their lamps to last out the night.

"Issa sacred dooty," he kept saying as blackness engulfed them. "Issa Christian office to lighten our darkness. And it's a wicked 'eathen thing to give short measures and sell the oil what's left."

Pallcat's drunkenness kept coming over him in waves; and whenever it went away he felt very cold and couldn't keep his eyes off skinny Possul, to whom he'd offered a bed for the night.

Why, in the name of all the saints, had he done such a thing? It wasn't like him. What if Possul *had* helped him out and said nothing to the lamplighters about the shameful circumstance that had made it necessary? He, Pallcat, had fed him for his trouble. Surely that was enough? He glared at Possul, whose face was bright with expectation. You ought to be on your knees and thanking me, thought Pallcat irritably.

The smell of ancient cabbage and trodden oranges stole upon the air as they neared Covent Garden. Pallcat had always lived alone and had steadily improved himself by having no other soul to provide for. He worked hard, lighting his lamps at sunset and, thereafter, offering himself out as a linkman to light those who paid him the way home.

Such earning a living by shedding light in darkness gave him notions of great importance about himself; it was hard for him not to think of himself as some kind of judge, dividing light from dark—and choosing where and when to shine.

This, combined with a natural meanness, made men say of him that, when his link went out, he charged for the moonlight —if there happened to be any about.

"Second floor back," said Pallcat as they came to the lofty tenement in Three Kings Court where he lodged.

His room stank so much of fish oil that the smell seemed to

come out and hit the visitor like an invisible fist. Within there was a sense of bulk and confusion that resolved itself, when he turned up a lamp, into all the wild and tattered furnishings he'd bought between the setting and the rising of the sun. Tables, chairs, chests, commodes, pots and jugs, together with a quantity of glass cases containing stuffed birds and cats, were collected in meaningless heaps like the parts needed for the first five days of creation. There was also dust in plenty; it was not hard to believe that Pallcat himself had been formed out of it.

" 'Ome!" said Pallcat, and taking a taper from the lamp, lit another. The oil-stained walls appeared—between obstructions. Possul gazed at them in wonderment. Framed texts hung everywhere; some were burned into wooden panels, some were crudely stitched onto linen, as if by Pallcat himself.

I AM THE LIGHT OF THE WORLD, said one; HE THAT FOLLOWETH ME SHALL NOT WALK IN DARKNESS.

THE TRUE LIGHT WHICH LIGHTETH EVERY MAN, proclaimed another.

GOD SAID, LET THERE BE LIGHT, hung over the foot of Pallcat's bed; AND THERE WAS LIGHT, hung over the head.

HE WAS A BURNING AND A SHINING LIGHT, was propped above the fireplace; and LIFT UP THE LIGHT OF THY COUNTENANCE, was nailed over a mirror that was tarnished like a disease.

"There's a couch in t'other room," said Pallcat. "You can sleep there."

They slept away what was left of the night; they slept on through the grey and rowdy morning. Pallcat awoke sometime after noon. Confused memories kept coming back to him, and he closed his eyes against the daylight that contrived to be as soiled as the windows. He recollected that he had company. Possul's weirdly transparent face, floating in smoke as when he'd first seen it, appeared before his inner eye. Then he remembered that Possul had carried the funeral light when he'd fallen by the wayside; that made some sort of bond between them.

He opened his eyes and gazed at his stuffed beasts, which had been arranged so they might look back at him and reflect himself in their glass eyes. *"All is vanity and vexation of the spirit,"* he mumbled, and pricked up his ears.

The rooms were still. The thought struck him that Possul had already gone and, possibly, robbed him into the bargain. He crawled from the chaos of his bed and poked his head into the next room. Possul lay on the couch, breathing regularly. Being a child, he took sleep in greater quantities than a grown man.

Pallcat felt vaguely displeased; then he felt vaguely disappointed. He'd caught himself hoping that Possul, moved by the kindness and hospitality shown him, would have cleaned the room and prepared a meal while he, Pallcat, slept. But no such thing. The boy was ungrateful, like all boys. His angelic countenance and soft manners were things he'd picked up in the church where he'd worked; they were no more part of his deep nature than would have been a wig or a new hat.

He went out to get some food, determined to make the boy ashamed of himself for allowing a grown man to wait on him. When he came back, the boy was still asleep. Pallcat stared long and hard at his small pale face, and had thoughts about shaking him till his teeth flew out; instead, however, he went into the next room and made a great deal of noise preparing to go out on his duties. He kicked against his oil can, dropped his wick trimmers, and flung the lock and chain that secured his ladder to a banister rail with a heavy crash onto the floor. In spite of this, Possul did not wake up. Pallcat wondered if he was ill. He went back and laid an oily hand on the boy's forehead, and then touched his own; there was no great difference in heat. He bent down and blew gently on the child's face. Possul frowned, stirred, and turned over with a sigh. Pallcat snarled and departed on his sunset task.

His lamps were in the Strand, stretching on either side from Charing Cross to St. Mary's; also there were three each in Bedford and Southampton streets, making four and twenty in all. High on his ladder, Pallcat tended them, filling the tins with oil, trimming the wicks, kindling them, and giving the thick glass panes a dirty wipe before descending and passing on to the next. From each lamp he took the greasy, burnt remainder and afterwards sold it to the bootboys for blacking hats, boots, and iron stoves. In this way he extended his dominion; he gave light by night and black by day.

In itself his task was humble, but when Pallcat was mounted up some twenty feet above the homeward-hastening throng and saw that the daylight was going, he felt as remote and indifferent as the kindler of the stars.

When he returned to Three Kings Court, it was already dark; the kindler of the stars couldn't help feeling warmed by the thought of company. Possul was awake and sitting on the end of his bed; he hadn't so much as lifted a finger to clean or tidy anything. Pallcat put down his empty oil can.

"I'd ha' thought," he grunted, "you'd ha' done *something*— 'stead of just sitting and waiting."

"Didn't like to," said Possul, widening his peculiarly bright eyes. "Might have done something wrong."

"I left food out," said Pallcat, baffled.

"Saw it," said Possul. "Didn't like to eat any though. Just had some water."

"Too idle to eat, even," muttered Pallcat. "You'll 'ave to mend your ways if you stay 'ere."

Possul nodded and mended his ways to the extent of eating

what had been provided. The lamplighter watched him half indulgently, half irritably; the boy ate everything, without asking if he, Pallcat, wanted any. He wondered how much nourishment it was expected of him to provide.

"If you are going to stay," he said harshly, "you'll 'ave to *do* something for it."

Possul, his mouth so full that a piece of jellied veal was hanging out of it, looked up with bright, earnest eyes.

"I'll learn you," said the lamplighter grandly, "to be me apprentice. Now a lamplighter's apprentice is, very properly, a linkboy; that is, a nipper what lights the night folk their way 'ome. I done it meself—and I still do it; it's a 'oly thing to do. *And the Lord went before them . . . by night in a pillar of fire, to give them light.*"

"*The true Light which lighteth every man,*" read Possul, off the wall.

"*Arise, shine; for thy light is come,*" said Pallcat, handing the boy a length of tow that had been dipped in pitch.

"*I was eyes to the blind, and feet was I to the lame,*" said Possul, reading from a text that was still in the stitching stage.

"But not," said the lamplighter, making for the door, "without proper payment. Pitch costs money, and tow don't last for ever."

They went downstairs into the dark, cold court and walked to the Strand and along to the corner of Dirty Lane, where there was a coffeehouse with gambling rooms above. Here Pallcat kindled the torch.

"I'll show you," he said, holding up the burning article, so that his reddened eyes streamed from the sudden clouds of smoke.

Possul gazed at the lamplighter, whose flame-lit countenance resembled an angry planet in the gloom; then his eyes strayed to Pallcat's lamps that winked in the obscure air down either side of the Strand. It took sharp eyes to make them out, they glimmered so feebly within the accumulated filth of the glass that enclosed them. Although they complied with the letter of the law and burned from sunset to sunrise, they mocked the spirit of that law and provided not the smallest scrap of illumination. If ever a world walked in need of light, it was the world under Pallcat's lamps.

"Light you 'ome," shouted Pallcat, brandishing the torch before a gentleman who came stumbling by.

"No—no. I can see, thank you."

"Fall in the river and drown, then," said Pallcat to the gentleman's departing back.

He accosted several other passersby, but none wanted light, so Pallcat damned them all; at the same time he shielded his torch lest a stray beam might have given an advantage not contracted for.

"D'you see? Like this! *Stretch out thine hand . . . that there may be darkness over the land, even darkness which may be felt.*"

At length, three gentlemen came out of the coffeehouse. Their aspect was mellow, their gait airy.

"Light you 'ome?" offered Pallcat.

"And why not?" said one of the gentlemen affably.

"A linkman with his spark!" said another, observing the boy beside the lamplighter. They all laughed and gave Pallcat lengthy directions to their homes.

Pallcat walked on ahead, holding the torch high; Possul took it all in, walking beside the lamplighter and occasionally raising his own arm in what he regarded as a professional way.

Presently Pallcat became aware that they'd attracted a non-paying customer, a wretched, gin-sodden devil who was lurching along, taking advantage of the free light to avoid the posts and projecting steps with which the streets were endlessly obstructed.

"Watch this," muttered the lamplighter to his earnest spark. "This is the way we does it."

Pallcat took off his hat and, waiting for a sharp corner, whipped it before the torch, thus neatly plunging the stinking drunkard into an eclipse. There was a thump and a staggering crash as the wretch collided with a post and fell with a howl of pain.

"Cast out into outer darkness," said Pallcat powerfully; *"there shall be weeping and gnashing of teeth."*

After that they were troubled no more, and each of the three gentlemen, deposited at his home, gave Pallcat a sixpence for the guidance. Pallcat bit the coins and stowed them in a bag hung around his neck; then he and his apprentice went back to the Strand to see out the rest of the night.

Shortly before dawn, when Pallcat's torch was becoming super-fluous, he and Possul returned to Three Kings Court. On the way the lamplighter pointed out those corners and alleys where pitch might be had for a farthing a dip, when a man's torch had burned through.

Before going to bed, Pallcat made Possul a bowl of soup, feeling, at the same time, that the boy ought to be waiting on him. But no doubt that would come in time. Possul was simple-minded; he needed careful training—like a dog. And when all was said and done, he *was* company. . . .

For an hour or so after Possul was asleep, Pallcat stitched away at his unfinished text, which was always his bedtime pleasure and task and somehow made his world seem larger; then he too went down as the blaring sun came up and rendered his room a mad and dirty horror of too-visible confusion.

They slept the day through; Pallcat woke first and went out for food and more oil. When he returned, he found Possul peaceably on his bed, having done nothing but wake up.

"Tonight," said the lamplighter peevishly, "you'll work, my lad."

Possul smiled contentedly and Pallcat could have clouted him with the length of tow that was to be his torch. The boy should have *offered*, instead of just waiting to be told, with his bright eyes going right through Pallcat like a pair of pokers.

"You go where we was last night. I'll go more towards Charing Cross. 'Ere's a penny, 'case you run out of pitch before you gets paid. Remember what I showed you; remember about keeping your light for the lawful customers. Best take me cocked 'at; only don't scorch it."

Possul, feeling immensely important—as became his occupation of linkboy—flamed outside the coffeehouse on the corner of Dirty Lane. The warmth of his torch kept out the bitterness of the night, and his transparent-seeming face made a hopeful island in the black pool of Pallcat's hat.

"Light you home, ma'am?" he called out to a flower-cheeked woman who hobbled the street with eyes like cups of ashes.

"Shove off!" she said, and shrank from the damaging light.

Next, a pair of basket women approached.

"Light you home, ladies?"

They drew near, smiling and shaking their heads.

"Just come for a warm, love."

They held up their hands and drenched them in the heat of Possul's fire. The boy was nonplussed. Light he must not give without payment; but Pallcat had said nothing about warmth. On account of the basket women and several other freezing souls, Possul lost several likely customers.

All in all, he earned but a single sixpence that night—and then spent nearly half of it on fresh pitch for his waning torch. Pallcat was indignant when he'd got over his pleasure and relief at seeing Possul come back. Though he'd never have admitted it, he'd been haunted by the dread of Possul abandoning him as lightly as he'd joined him. He couldn't quite believe that Possul was real; that is, when the boy was out of his sight. . . .

He berated Possul soundly for his extravagance in pitch and warned him to mend his ways. He sent him off to bed with— as the saying goes—a flea in his ear, which doubtless found company in Possul's horrible bed. Then he set about finishing his text and beginning a new one, especially for Possul: *He that toucheth pitch shall be defiled therewith.*

Next night, with many warnings, Possul went out again to set himself up in business on the corner of Dirty Lane. With mingled feelings of suspicion and pride, the lamplighter, who accompanied him as far as the Strand, watched him flame his way towards the coffeehouse. The boy stalked along with such an air of self-importance that one might have supposed he was holding up the sun and moon and all the fledgling stars.

In truth, Possul had a soul no less than Pallcat; the sense of consequence given by being a minister of light had its effect on the boy no less than the man.

"Light you home, sir?"

"Take me to Clifford's Inn, child. D'you know it?"

" 'S off Chancery Lane."

The gentleman nodded and Possul set off. Presently a low noise in a cleft between two houses distracted him. He held out his torch. A woman and nearly naked child were huddled together in an attempt to get warmth from each other. The woman, half blinded by the sudden light, looked savage at the intrusion on her misery. Possul paused, as if to give his gentleman full benefit of the sight.

"Get a move on, boy," he said. "It's no business of ours in there."

Possul withdrew the torch and left the cleft in decent darkness. A little while after, he stopped again. A legless beggar, who squatted on a porridge pot and got about by dragging himself by fist and fingernail over the cobbles, squinted up from the entrance to an alley. Every detail of his misfortune was pitiless in Possul's leaping fire.

"Get along with you," said the gentleman. "Find something better worth looking at."

So Possul looked and found a pair of lovers sitting on a doorstep. Furiously they bade him take his light away—which he did to his gentleman's protesting disappointment.

Just outside the gate to Clifford's Inn, a youngish woman was humped against a wall and crying. Possul lingered, and his torchlight shone on her tear-stained face, revealing harsh bruises and dried blood.

"That's enough," said the gentleman. "When I want to be shown the miseries of the night, I'll employ you again. Till then, my lad, keep out of my way."

He gave Possul only threepence and dismissed him. The linkboy had two more customers that night, and, as if by design (though it was not so at all), he led them likewise on pilgrimages through the horror and despair hidden in the dark.

Even as moths are drawn to a candle flame, so was every cruelty and misfortune drawn into the circle of Possul's torch. Or so it seemed. Consequently, he got a bad name, and all his customers swore they'd never seek his light again. They'd sooner go home in the dark, relying on the lamplighter's feeble glimmers rather than the linkboy's bitter fire.

When he returned to Three Kings Court at dawn, he looked weary, but nothing to worry about. A night's work naturally wore a soul out. Pallcat took his apprentice's earnings, made him soup, and packed him off to bed.

Next night, encouraged by his beginnings, Possul found other customers—and uncannily led them through similar ways, loitering his torch over all manner of luckless sights. Men crying in corners, dead children, thieves lit up in sudden, horrible terror ... Human beings everywhere abandoning themselves to a despair that the darkness should have hid, abruptly seen in their crude nakedness.

Thus Possul's torch shed its light. . . .

Sometimes it seemed that he took pleasure in what he saw; his face was always so earnest and bright. But no one giving him a second glance and catching his eerily solemn eyes could really credit him with so unnatural a pastime.

Although many of the sights he lit up would have been unremarkable enough by day, by night—picked out of the blackness like little worlds of total hell—they were vile and disgusting. The only explanation was that Possul lacked sensitivity and taste.

Pallcat of course knew nothing of this; Possul never talked much—and then only when spoken to. It never seemed to occur to him that he, Pallcat, had ears that liked exercise. Still, the boy breathed and ate so that one could hear him, and he was a living soul in the lamplighter's dingy lodgings. Pallcat even got a contrary pleasure out of feeding him for no thanks and being taken for granted as an ever-present father. If only, the lamplighter thought, he'd flesh out a bit and not look so shamefully skinny and pale. There was no doubt that each dawn when the boy returned, he looked whiter and more transparent, so that Pallcat had the feeling that sooner or later he'd come back as plain bones.

The lamplighter kept his apprentice on the go for a week; then, on the seventh day, it rained, so Pallcat told Possul not to stay out beyond midnight as no one would be about after that.

The rain was not heavy; it was more of a fine drizzle, a weeping of the night air that made the torch hiss and spit and give off smoke in thick bundles. Several gentlemen emerged from the coffeehouse but, having had their bellyful of the loitersome linkboy, waved his offers aside. In accordance with Pallcat's example, Possul wished them in the river. The curse, coming from his soft lips and attended by his bright, earnest gaze, seemed curiously terrible. Yet he uttered it more as if it were a charm to bring him the customers he lacked.

As if in response to this charm, a man came out of the coffeehouse on his own. He'd had no experience of Possul, so he was not driven to choose darkness instead of light. He was a huge elephant of a fellow, untidily dressed and wearing a frown as if he'd bought it as suiting his particular cast of features. He squinted balefully at Possul's fire.

"Light you home, sir?"

The man grunted ill-temperedly, searching his capacious mind, and came out with: *"Take heed therefore that the light which is in thee be not darkness."*

He sniffed and wiped his nose against the back of his hand. "Well?"

"Yes, sir. I'll take heed. Where to, sir?"

"Red Lion Square. D'you know it?"

"Off High Holborn, ain't it?"

"Thereabouts. Lead on."

Possul lifted up his torch and went; the large man lumbered after. The rain, although not increasing, had soaked the streets, so that the torch, reflecting upon the streaming cobbles, ran along like a river of broken fire. Bearing in mind his customer's strict injunction, Possul kept to the middle of the road and watched where his light fell. He could hear the irritable fellow quite distinctly, muttering and rumbling to himself like distant thunder over the trials of a bad night. The linkboy would be lucky to get a penny from such a man. At last they turned into

Grays Inn Passage; the torch flickered across a bundle of rags heaped against a doorstep. As if unable to help himself, the link-boy paused. The huge fellow lurched and swayed to a halt.

"What d'you think you're doing, boy?"

"Nothing—nothing, sir. It's just me torch . . . shining, shin'ng on—" He jerked the light apologetically towards the doorstep. The bundle of rags leaped out of the night; it contained a twig of a woman with arms and cheeks as thin as leaves. She was either dead or so close to it that it would have taken a watchmaker to tell the difference.

Possul remained perfectly still while his torch flames plaited themselves ceaselessly round the melting pitch and fried the soft rain. The huge man's complaints had died away into a heavy sighing; he swayed from side to side as if he found difficulty in managing his bulk.

He carried a stick—a heavy cudgel such as might have been used to beat off a footpad. He poked at the rags with it. There was no response. Possul brought his torch closer to the woman's face. Her skin was blotched and covered with open sores that the rain had made to shine. Her eyelids stirred as Possul brought the fire closer still.

Suddenly a twist of blue flame—no bigger than a finger—danced up above her mouth; then it vanished with extraordinary rapidity. It was as if the spark of life had been made visible, departing.

"Get back," grunted the man, pushing Possul away with his cudgel. "She's full of gin. You saw it? That gasp of fire above her lips. The torch set it off. Get away. It's not for you and me to burn her before her time."

He gave Possul another shove, swore malevolently at the night—and bent down, so that every stitch of his clothing protested at the effort. He picked up the gin-sodden, diseased creature as easily as if she'd been a frayed old coat; then he heaved her on his back.

"Move on," he said to Possul.

"Where to, sir?"

"My house. Would you have me carry this unwholesome burden farther?"

"What will you do with her, sir?"

"Eat her. Plenty of pepper and salt. Then I'll give her bones to my cat."

The creature that was flopped across his back emitted a raucous moan.

"Peace, ma'am, peace. Presently you'll have comfort and warmth. Hurry, boy, hurry, before we're all poisoned by the stink of her gin."

In a moment, Possul's fire broke out into Red Lion Square and cast the large man's shadow with its misshapen double back against the fronts of the stately houses; it seemed impossible for those within not to feel the dark passing. Possul himself, holding the torch, cast no such mark; the intensity of the light seemed to have eaten him up altogether; to shadow fanciers, the lurching monster with the grotesque hump upon its back was quite alone save for a steadily marching fire.

Presently the fire and the shadow halted. Then the shadow grew enormous and engulfed one particular house. . . . Cautiously, and with solemn gentleness, the shadow's owner took off his hump and laid the tattered woman against his front door while he fumbled for a coin to pay the linkboy.

Why was the night suddenly so dark? He stood up and turned. The boy with the torch had vanished. The square was empty and without light. He fancied he glimpsed a flickering coming from the direction of Fisher Street, which was some way off. It might have been the light of a linkboy; then again, it might not.

The woman at his feet moaned again; he banged ferociously and urgently on his front door. He looked again towards Fisher Street, but the light had gone. He shook his head as if to rid it of a memory that was already faltering into disbelief. His front door opened, but before he went inside, he stared upwards as if for the sight of a new star. Nothing . . . nothing but blackness and rain.

Nor was it only from Red Lion Square that Possul had vanished; he disappeared from Three Kings Court, also. The night wore out, and Pallcat waited. Time and again he stirred himself and went down into the rain to search the maze of streets about Covent Garden. It was possible that Possul had got lost. Folk often did, round Covent Garden. He went along the Strand and wasted a whole torch in searching. Possul was nowhere to be found. He went back to his rooms. As he mounted the stairs, his heart beat in expectation; he crept into Possul's room on tiptoe, almost as if he were frightened that, by making a noise, he'd scare off the fragile dream. He needn't have bothered. He might as well have tramped in with iron boots; the room was empty.

Next morning he went outside again, squinting painfully against the cheap, all-pervasive light. He searched, he inquired, he scavenged in lanes and alleys; he went to the church where Possul had worked. The verger remembered the boy but had not seen him for many days. Most likely he was dead; it happened sometimes, and mostly to the gentle ones. . . .

Night came on, and, after tending his lamps, Pallcat renewed his search. He carried his torch through street after street, calling now softly, now loudly, for his apprentice. Every darkened alley might have concealed him, but the numerous stirrings and breathings in the night that Pallcat's sharp ears picked up turned out to be such visions as Possul had lit up, visions of savagery and despair. These hateful and tragic images steadily burned their way into Pallcat's soul, as if the light he served had entered his breast and blistered his heart.

For two nights and days the lamplighter scoured the town; he scarcely dared return to Three Kings Court on account of the sharp pain of expecting, expecting . . . and then finding only filth, confusion, and the emptiness of glass eyes. Possul had vanished, as if off the face of the earth.

At length he went down to the river, which he hated on account of its impenetrable blackness and sense of death. He asked of the waterman if they had seen, had *found*, a boy: a thin boy with bright eyes and a transparent-seeming face. They had not. But not to give up hope. Often corpses took days to come up and be caught under the bridge. . . .

" 'E weren't real," said Pallcat mournfully. He was in the parlour of the Eagle and Child, in company with two lamplighters from Cripplegate Ward. He had given up the river for the night.

On being prompted, Pallcat's companions recollected the boy at Sam Bold's funeral feast, but they did not recall Pallcat going off with him; one thought that the boy had gone off on his own, the other had no clear memories of the latter part of the night.

" 'E never talked much," said Pallcat softly. " 'E were just a—a *presence*. I *felt* 'im when 'e were there; and then when 'e went out I couldn't believe in 'im. 'E 'ad a sort of shining in 'is face. I do believe 'e were a spirit . . . I think."

"What sort of a spirit?" asked one of the lamplighters with interest. "A angel, p'raps? Some'at of that kind?"

"No . . . no!" said Pallcat, with a flurry of indignation. "A dream in meself. Something made up out of me mind. A spirit like—like—"

"Like gin?" offered the other lamplighter humorously.

Pallcat glanced at him, and the man saw with surprise that Pallcat's old eyes were bright with tears.

"It were a grand dream," said Pallcat, half to himself. "I wish I'd not waked from it, that's all."

He stood up and walked to the window that hung over the river. He brooded on the blackness below, seeing his own face, irregular in the rippled glass, like something floating and drowned.

"I wish," he was whispering, "I wish—" when Possul came in.

"*Where you bin?*" screeched Pallcat.

"Found this one with me torch," said Possul, his bright eyes gazing hopefully at Pallcat.

Hanging onto Possul's back, much in the way the wreckage of a woman had hung over the large man's back in Red Lion Square, was an indescribably filthy and gruesome tot—a midget of an infant with a smear of a face and a crust of lousy hair.

"Got him out of the river by Salisbury Stairs. Been looking for his home. Ain't got one—like me. So I thought—I s'posed he'd make another spark?"

Pallcat did not speak, so Possul went on: "I call him Stairs, after what he fell in off. Can he come home with us?"

Still Pallcat did not speak. The thought of providing for yet another was looming large in his mind; nor could he rule out the possibility of others yet to come. He had seen a light in Possul's eyes such as no lamp had ever given. He could not put a name to it; all he knew was that without it the darkness would be frightful. He gave a little moan. He would have to clean up his rooms; no one else would. He would have to create order out of chaos; no one else would. . . .

"I gave you a fine light, Possul," said Pallcat hopelessly. "And look what you done with it. You must have come out of a winder, Possul, and that's where you'll end up. In a church winder, shot full of arrers. That's what 'appens to saints, Possul, and, things considered, I ain't surprised. Come on 'ome—the pair of you."

Possul smiled, and Pallcat wondered, not for the first time, which of them was being created in the image of the other.

MIRROR,
MIRROR

BETWEEN GLASS HOUSE YARD AND SHOEMAKER'S ROW LIES FRIERS
Street, where Mr. Paris's premises occupy a commanding
position on a corner. In the gloom of the November evening his
shop window flares out extravagantly, as platoons of candles
execute various dancing manoeuvres in flawless unison. On closer
inspection, however, they turn out to be a single candle reflected
in a cunning display of looking-glasses. Mr. Paris is a master
carver of mirror frames; golden boys and golden grapes cluster
round the silver mirrors and seem to invite, with dimpled arms
outstretched, the passerby to pause and contemplate himself.

Inside, in the dining parlour, the family is sitting down to
supper: Mr. and Mrs. Paris—a handsome couple who will be
middle-aged when it suits them—Miss Lucinda, their young
daughter, and Nightingale, the new apprentice.

Nightingale has not long arrived. He has scarcely had time to
wash himself before sitting down to table. All day he has been
tramping the streets with his father, a Hertfordshire joiner, and
gaping at the multitudinous sights of the town. All in all, it has

been a solemn day, what with the many unspoken leave-takings between father and son, the looks over the tops of toasting tankards of ale, the deep pressings of hands, the sentences begun and left half finished as the same melancholy thought strikes them both. . . .

They have never before been parted; or at least, not for more than a day. But now the inevitable time has come. Ten pounds have been paid for the apprenticeship, and Daniel Nightingale is to embark alone on the great voyage of life . . . as the village parson had been pleased to put it. Like all such voyages, it is to be seven years long, and the only provisions that the father might properly give his son to take with him have been the wise precepts he himself has treasured up and written down from his own seven years of apprenticeship.

Never come between your master and mistress. . . .

Nightingale looks up the table at Mr. Paris and then down the table at Mrs. Paris; the husband and wife gaze at each other with identical smiles, as if each were the reflection of the other's heart.

Carry no tales or gossip between master and mistress, nor chatter with the servants of their private affairs. . . .

A greasy girl comes in with a dish of mutton and a carving knife. She puts them both on the table with a glance at Nightingale that makes his blood run cold.

Look upon your master as another parent to you. . . .

Nightingale catches Mr. Paris's eye, but finds it altogether too slippery to hold. Mournfully he remembers his own parent; only a few hours ago he was "Daniel, boy . . . Dan, dear . . ." Now that fond distinction has been shorn away and he is plain "Nightingale."

Perhaps now that I'm just a Nightingale, he thinks as a plate is set before him, I ought to sing for my supper? He smiles to himself, not having thought of many jokes before—wit in Hertfordshire being as thin on the ground as turnips are thick. Mr. and Mrs. Paris continue with their own smiles, and the table presents an amiable aspect . . . with the exception of Miss Lucinda, the master's pretty daughter. She dislikes the new apprentice for no better reason than that he has failed to recognize her as the queen of the household. She knows it is every apprentice's ambition to wed his master's daughter, and she cannot endure the notion of being a rung in someone else's ladder to the sky. She is not much beyond fourteen, with fair hair, fair skin, and a general brilliancy about her that suggests she has caught some shining complaint from her father's wares.

"I hope and trust, Master Nightingale," says Mr. Paris, never taking his eyes off his wife, "that at the end of your seven years we will all be as contented and smiling as we are now?"

The apprentice, caught with his mouth full, nods politely. At the same time, mournful thoughts of the day return. Seven years, seven long years . . .

After the meal, Mr. Paris rises and shows Nightingale where he is to sleep. According to usage, the apprentice's bed is made up under the counter in the front room that serves as showroom and shop; thus if dreams come, they are more likely than not to be dreams arising from the day's work, so no time will be wasted. Mr. Paris bids Nightingale goodnight and leaves him with a wax candle which he must be sparing with, as it is to last him for a week.

The apprentice mumbles his thanks and, when he is alone, prepares to say his nightly prayers. He is scarcely on his knees before the door opens abruptly and startles him. His master's daughter stands in the doorway. He has no time to observe her before she calls out, "Nightingale! Catch!"

She tosses something towards him that glitters in the candlelight like a speeding star. The apprentice is too surprised to do more than put out a hand that just touches the object before it falls with a crash to the ground. It is, or, rather, was, a looking-glass. Now, it lies on the floor, shattered into silver knives and slices. Miss Lucinda smiles.

"You've broken a mirror, Nightingale. That means seven years' bad luck."

"You slept well, lad?"

Mr. Paris, smooth and glazed looking from his morning shave, came into the shop. The apprentice—hours of work, six until eight—had already taken down the shutters and swept the floor. Ordinarily as clear and truthful as daylight, Nightingale remembered his father's precept: *Carry no tales.* . . . He nodded in answer to his master's inquiry and said nothing of the sleepless night he had spent, caused by Miss Lucinda's grim prophecy of an apprenticeship that was to consist of seven years' solid bad luck.

He took breakfast with the family while the morning sun streamed into the parlour, enveloping Miss Lucinda and making her hard to look at. At half past seven he went to the workroom, where Mr. Paris's journeyman—an ancient craftsman with the head of a prophet and hands like the roots of trees—was already at work.

"Job," said Mr. Paris. "This is Nightingale."

The journeyman looked up from his carving and smiled at the new apprentice. Everyone in the household seemed to smile . . . excepting the daughter. Nightingale, with the natural confidence of a good-looking youth, felt that sooner or later he would be able to melt her. His heart began to beat more easily.

"Come here, Nightingale," said Mr. Paris. "Tell me what you see."

The master drew a cloth from a handsome mirror that stood upon an easel as if it had been a painting.

"Look closely. Take your time, and tell me what you see."

The apprentice, doing his best to reflect his master's smile, obeyed and looked in the mirror. A soft, blushing face that required shaving but once a week beamed awkwardly back at him.

"Why, me, sir!"

"Indeed?"

Nightingale's heart sank as he heard Mr. Paris's voice take on a decided edge. What *should* he have said? He felt as if he were suddenly standing upon nothing.

"Is it not very vain of you to think, Master Nightingale, that I should keep an image of you in my workroom? Why should I do such a thing? Who would buy it?"

The ancient journeyman sniggered; Nightingale went as red as a radish.

"Job," said the master. "Tell him what *you* see."

Job, still sniggering, presented his own splendid countenance to the glass.

"I see vines, Mr. Paris; and the fruits thereof. I sees naked little boys, what might be angels, a-buttressing the mitres. And at the bottom, finely 'graved, I see 'Josiah Paris, Mirror Frame Carver. Friers Street. Blackfriars.' "

"In a word, Nightingale," said Mr. Paris, "he sees a *frame*. A well-carved frame. He does not see his own image, my lad."

The journeyman smirked and went back to his carving, while Nightingale felt that his seven years' bad luck had begun with a bull's eye.

"In our line of trade," went on Mr. Paris, covering up the mirror, "a craftsman—be he master, journeyman, or apprentice— looks *at* a mirror, not *in* one."

"Yes, sir. I see, sir."

"A mirror," said Mr. Paris, expanding his thoughts and person at one and the same time, "is nothing."

"Yes, sir."

"And yet it is everything. It is like life itself; it gives back only what is put into it. Smile—and you create a smile; scowl and you double the distress."

"Yes, sir . . . I see that now, sir."

"Human life is a mirror," said Mr. Paris musingly, as if his ideas were being reflected off mirrors inside his head. "Thus the idle apprentice who gives his master only a tenth of his time, gets back, from life, only a tenth of its value."

"Yes, sir. I'll always remember that."

"There's much wisdom to be gained from mirrors and the framing of them, Nightingale. It is not for nothing that we say, when a man thinks deeply, he *reflects*."

"He always does that," said the journeyman when the master had gone. "It were the same with the last 'prentice and the one afore him."

"Where are they now?" asked the third apprentice, sweeping wood shavings industriously. "Didn't they stay out their seven years?"

The journeyman's chuckle faded into a remote smile, and he bent over his work.

"It ain't for me to say. Carry no tales is a good rule for journeymen as well as 'prentices."

Soon after nine o'clock the shop bell jumped, and Nightingale was summoned to assist his master. A tall, well-spoken gentleman had called to purchase a looking-glass for his wife. Books of patterns were duly consulted and several samples fetched out for demonstration of their quality. To Nightingale's surprise, the gentleman, who'd been overbearing to begin with, turned soft as putty and easy to please. Although he'd been as awkward as the devil about the patterns, the mirrors themselves had quite the opposite effect. He fixed on a simple oval and made his escape as soon as price and delivery were settled.

Nightingale opened the door and bowed him out and into his carriage.

"Consumed with vanity," said Mr. Paris, handing his apprentice the pattern books and glasses to put away. "That gentleman was eaten up with vanity. You saw how he couldn't bear to look closely at the mirrors? Only a vain man avoids his reflection so very particularly. He has such a fixed notion of his countenance that he will admit nothing that might disturb it. You saw what an ugly hooked nose he had? Most likely, inside his head, that nose was aristocratic. He had a hairy mole above his lip. Most likely he thinks of it as a rare ornament."

Nightingale nodded in a bemused fashion and caught himself wondering if the radiant Miss Lucinda looked much in mirrors, and if she did was it a mark of modesty or was she contrary to all philosophy?

They dined at one: the journeyman in the workroom and Nightingale sitting down with the family after he had helped the greasy girl to bring out the dishes from the kitchen.

"I don't ordinarily take on a lad with an irregular cast of feature," said Mr. Paris, smiling down the table. The apprentice felt his cheeks grow warm, and he tried to absorb himself in the plate before him.

"Nor have you done so this time," said Mrs. Paris, glancing at Nightingale before smiling back at her husband. "You really couldn't say he was wanting in countenance."

The apprentice, though grateful for the compliment, felt his cheeks grow hotter; and Miss Lucinda's eyes seemed to be scraping the skin off his bones.

"In our line of trade," said Mr. Paris to the household in general, "a dropped eye, a marred cheek, bad teeth, or a bent nose are highly disadvantageous. The possessor of such a countenance would not be welcomed in this establishment. Bodily misfortunes we can tolerate, providing they are not exposed. Job has a fallen hip and, I'm told, swollen knees. For my part, I've no objection to a wooden leg, even, if the stump be kept wholesome and clean. But the face must be as Caesar's wife"—here he acknowledged Mrs. Paris with a peculiarly fine smile—"the face must be above suspicion. We must be able to look in mirrors without awkwardness, without shame. A man with a defect of countenance, in such circumstances, might fall into a melancholia and go mad of it. In our line we must be able to endure and endure ourselves with equanimity. I don't say, with pleasure, but with equanimity. It cannot have escaped your notice, Nightingale, that we are a particularly fine-looking family?"

The apprentice looked up and saw his master's daughter sitting on her father's right hand. With every intention of being agreeable, he began to study her features with admiration and zeal. A look of sharp spite rippled across her face as if it had been a reflection in water suddenly shuffled by a wind.

At eight o'clock the old journeyman took his day's wages and holding high his magnificent head, removed his fallen hip and swollen knees into the November dark. As he left, the old man asked the apprentice if he would care to join him for a glass of ale nearby. Reluctantly Nightingale declined; he was weary to the point of faintness from his sleepless night, and he ached for his bed.

He stumbled through the evening meal in a dull silence and afterwards begged to be excused from sitting with the family in the parlour. He was given permission to retire but not without a warning that his candle was to last out the week.

Thankfully he went into the shop and had scarcely taken off his coat when, as on the previous night, his door flew open.

"Nightingale!"

It was Miss Lucinda. Nightingale flinched in the expectation of something else being tossed for him to catch. This time, however, she had come on another errand.

"I want you to come and look at a mirror of mine," she said remotely. "It's upstairs, in my parlour. Come and look at it."

The apprentice, swaying beside his bed as if he would fall asleep before falling down, said, "Yes, Miss Lucinda."

He believed that he must have made some inroads upon her affections and that this was her way of showing it. He followed her upstairs, hoisting himself by the banister rails and counting them to keep awake. She led him into her little room, where, in imitation of her father's workroom, there was an easel on which stood a shrouded mirror.

"I want you to look in the mirror, Nightingale, and tell me what you see."

He was to be tested again. He tried to think. What should he say this time? Should he praise the frame? Or, if she herself was reflected in the glass, should he praise her? What would please her most? Much depended on his words. . . .

He stood before the mirror, preparing himself. . . .

She snatched the cloth away. Nightingale shrieked aloud. A black-socketed skull grinned back at him! He trembled violently, believing, for a moment, that he'd seen an uncanny portent of his own doom. Then he perceived that he'd looked, not in a mirror, but through clear glass behind which had been arranged the death's head.

Miss Lucinda laughed—and he rushed from the room in terror. Downstairs he lay on his bed, sobbing bitterly on account of the fright he'd had, on account of being the object of a hatred he could not understand, and on account of being parted from those who loved him. He felt he could never sleep again. . . .

Next morning he awoke suddenly. Someone wild and amazed was staring him in the face. He leaped from his bed—to discover that a mirror had been set to confront him. He fancied he heard a sound of laughter in the passage outside.

He got through the day in a fog of bewilderment and unhappiness. The shop bell rang and rang; customers came and went; he bowed them in and bowed them out; he swept and tidied and stood stock still whenever Mr. Paris chose to unburden himself of more wisdom than Nightingale thought ever should have been contained in a mortal head; and whenever he was alone, he crouched down behind the counter, held his aching head in both hands, and wept like a child.

"I saw you crying behind the counter," said Miss Lucinda as she passed him in the passage. "And all the street saw you, too."

Filled with a new dismay, he ran back into the shop. High over the counter a mirror had been tilted so that everything was reflected outwards. He climbed up on a chair and took it down carefully, trying to avoid seeing the fear in his own face. After that, he was cautious about every expression and every action; he could never know for certain whether he was being reflected, and watched.

Was it possible that the master knew what his daughter was doing? Perhaps he'd instructed her? Perhaps this was all his testing time? Perhaps it was like those ancient trials by fire and water to temper the spirit and make it worthy? Only his was a trial by mirrors? . . . "A craftsman must endure and endure . . ." he murmured to himself as he sat, absorbed in such fanciful reflections, in the little necessary-house at the end of the yard. He had gone there more to relieve his mind than his body; and indeed, as his thoughts drifted, he did come to a kind of melancholy peace.

He raised his eyes as if to heaven; a shaft of light was shining through the ventilating aperture above the door. It fell upon a tilted square of silvered glass. Miss Lucinda's face was gazing down with a look of disgust and contempt. He cried out—and she vanished. He heard her jump down from whatever she'd been standing on; then he heard her feet pattering away.

He pulled up his breeches and hurried back into the work-room, feeling guilty and ashamed of being alive. He picked up a broom and began to sweep the shavings from round the feet of the ancient journeyman; then he went to fetch Job's beer.

The old man was working on a design of oak leaves and chil-dren's faces; patiently he tapped away with his mallet so that the bent gouge he gripped inquired into the wood like another finger. From time to time he laid his tools aside and set the frame against the mirror it was being carved for . . . and his marvellous prophet's head gazed back with a remote and dreamy rapture.

"Your beer, Mr. Job, sir."

The journeyman nodded. "Lay it on the bench, Master Night-ingale."

The apprentice obeyed and looked again over Job's shoulder at the unfinished frame. The children's faces were sharply defined and were all exactly alike. They were Miss Lucinda. . . .

Nightingale wondered if he dared question the journeyman about their master's daughter. He longed to ask the old man what *he* thought of her. Did she ever speak to him? Did she ever speak to anyone? Even her father and mother never seemed honoured with a word from her; nor, for that matter, did they speak much to her. Was she, perhaps, not their child? Or was she a mad child, suffered to roam the house and never checked for fear of provoking something worse than tricks with mirrors? Surely Job would know what she was.

The journeyman, without taking his eyes from the mirror, reached for his beer.

"Recognize 'em, Master Nightingale?"

"They're Miss Lucinda, ain't they, Mr. Job, sir?"

"And a good likeness, don't you think? They was to have been angels. That's what they are in the pattern book. But I thought Miss Lucinda would be a nice fancy. It'll please the master. And that's what you and me's here for, Master Nightingale. Journeymen and apprentices alike must always please their master. Just as you aim to please your own pa at home."

So she's an angel, thought Nightingale, and found himself left with no choice but to keep at his work and show, by all means in his power, that his chief aim in life was indeed to please his master.

After all, when he came to think about it all carefully, he wasn't so badly off. No one had clouted him; no one had injured him bodily. . . . "Country born and country bred," he muttered with rueful philosophy. "Strong in the arm and weak in the head. And what's wrong with that?" Well, not weak, exactly, but good and solid. Nothing too fanciful. When all's said and done, there's no sense in thinking and thinking about something a country body can't hope to understand. And—and they say worse things happen at sea. So I ought to be thankful I've not been sent for a sailor! Besides, who knows but Miss Lucinda will come to respect me for holding my tongue about her tricks? Who knows but I'll turn out the industrious apprentice yet and wed my master's daughter? They say it does happen. . . .

He pursued this line of comfort, with varying success, for the remainder of the day; whenever he passed Miss Lucinda he endeavoured to express in his smile forgiveness for her cruelty and admiration for her beauty at one and the same time. On such occasions, she did not seem to see him. Then—

"Nightingale!"

Once again she was at his door, demanding that he should come and look in her mirror. He sighed, and steeled himself for another look at the death's head. As he followed her, he even prepared some sort of philosophical remark that he hoped would impress her with his worth.

"Look at yourself, Nightingale," she said. "Look at what you are." She took away the cloth. A pig's head, still bloody from the butcher's axe, peered back at the apprentice.

He tried to laugh, but in truth he felt too sick and frightened to do more than imitate the grin of yesterday's skull. He stumbled out of the room and made his way back to his bed.

On the next day he came upon mirrors laid in different places: mirrors that caused him to fall headlong down a pair of steps outside the workroom, that led him to gash his forehead against an open door, that made him trip over a piece of wood that wasn't there and so to break a costly jug.

There was no mirror any more in the privy, nor was there one above the counter; but that didn't help. He couldn't be easy in his mind that they really weren't there. Indeed, he could not be easy in his mind about anything. . . .

He found himself walking about the ill-lit house like one newly blinded—with hands outstretched, never knowing whether he was coming to a reality or its reflection. His chief hope was for the night; it was only in darkness that he could feel secure and be able to distort his face with weeping and anguish without restraint. Until that blessed time, he did what he could to wear the glazed smile of his master, his mistress, and Job, the lame old prophet in the workroom.

When night did come, he was too sick and giddy in his brain to do more than nod when Miss Lucinda, like a white spirit, came to summon him to her mirror again. Wearily he climbed the stairs to the pretty little parlour. A dead rat. He shrank away. Truly had the country Nightingale flown into a forest of glass and thorn.

In the blackness of his bed he cried out against his father's ambition that had sent him forth on so dreadful a journey.

"I want you to be better than I am, Daniel," he had said. "I want you to be something more than a humble joiner. You shall be a master carver, and, God willing, one day you will be carving cathedral pews and screens and all manner of beautiful things. That's what I want for my son."

"And who knows," said his mother musingly, "but that some-day, like your father before you, you will wed your master's daughter? It's the dream of every apprentice, you know; and the reward for the industrious ones."

"We are making a great sacrifice," said his father.

"But no sacrifice can be too great," said his mother, kissing him. "Always remember that."

Lying in a sea of tears, Nightingale remembered, and feeling his mother's kiss, wondered whether he himself was the sacrifice that could not be too great.

He knew there had been two other apprentices before him. Had they suffered as he was suffering? Had she hated them, too? This possibility gave him a crumb of comfort, and he fell to supposing they'd fled, no matter what the consequences, even though rebellion in an apprentice was reckoned a great sin. He tried to smile. Most likely they'd been town sparrows and knew better ways of the world than did a country Nightingale.

"I think you should know, Nightingale," said Mr. Paris, over the evening meal, "that we are pleased with you." As usual, he smiled down the table at his smiling wife, while on his right hand sat Miss Lucinda, the devil-angel of the household. "I am writing to your father to tell him that we find you courteous and respectful."

Nightingale smiled fixedly down at his plate. A week had passed, and his spirit was broken as surely as the looking-glass he'd dropped on his first day.

He longed to cry out, to protest against the monstrous injustice to which he was being subjected. Every shame, every piece of spiteful humiliation that could be inflicted by mirrors had been daily visited on him, and nightly he'd been condemned to go to bed with an image of himself in a mirror that was no mirror, as something hateful and beneath contempt.

"Look at yourself! Look at yourself! Look at yourself!" Miss Lucinda commanded, standing in her pretty, blue-papered parlour, and uncovering, one after another, the framed sights of worms, a hanged man's head, a broken piss pot with "Nightingale" scrawled on it in black. . . .

"I can tell you now, Nightingale," went on Mr. Paris, cheerfully, "that when I brought you out of Hertfordshire, I had my doubts about country lads. One hears such tales of boys new to the town running after all manner of gaudy nonsense; worshipping the golden calf, one might say. An apprentice, my boy, must put his master above everything else. It's the only way to get through his seven years with honour and profit."

Nightingale said, "Yes, sir," and went out to fetch his master another jug of ale.

"Look at yourself, Nightingale. Look in my mirror. See what you are tonight."

Miss Lucinda stood in her parlour, while the apprentice, already without his jacket—for she'd come to him late—swayed before the shrouded easel. Dully he'd been racking his brains to imagine what she'd concealed this time behind the false glass. What hideous object could she have scavenged this time to frighten him with and to show him what he was?

"Look, Nightingale!"

She took away the cloth. The apprentice felt his head spin and his ears roar. Framed in the glass that faced him was—nothingness. Blackness, a bottomless pit . . .

The extreme shock of meeting with such utter emptiness overbalanced him. He felt himself begin to fall forwards, as if he were actually being sucked into the hole before his eyes. A black velvet bag had been placed behind the glass. . . .

"Nothing," she said. "That's what you are now. Nothing . . . nothing."

What would he be tomorrow, he wondered, as he half fell down the stairs. What was there on the other side of nothing?

It was a damp, misty morning with a cemetery chill on it; Job, who was afflicted with rheumatism in addition to his other bodily misfortunes, asked if the apprentice might be sent to Greening's in Glass House Yard to fetch a mirror that was cut and waiting. It would have been a cruel torment if he'd had to walk there himself.

"Nightingale?"

"Yes, Mr. Paris, sir?"

"Can you find your way to Greening's in the Yard?"

"Yes, sir. Directly, sir."

"Nightingale!"

"Yes, sir?"

"Check the glass carefully. They'll pass off rubbish if they can. No flaws, mind; no cracks in the silver, no spots of tarnish round the edges."

"Yes, sir."

"How will you judge, Nightingale?"

"I—I'll look at it . . . all over."

"And what will you see, Nightingale? Yourself. Much good that will do us, eh, Job?"

The old man rubbed his knees and sniggered.

"The human countenance, Master Nightingale, is no yardstick for perfection, not even yours. Words, lad, that's what's needful. *In the beginning was the Word*, and all that. Here, take this—"

He gave the abashed apprentice a card on which was printed, bold and black, something that might have been Hebrew for all Nightingale could tell.

"Just you hold it up to the glass they give you and read the letters clean and clear. Then you'll be able to see what's what."

Nightingale put on his coat, took the card, and set off. The very idea of going out after his distressful week revived him considerably; he felt, as he shut the shop door behind him, that he was emerging from a peculiarly bad dream. Once outside, however, this comfortable sensation was reversed by the mistiness of the morning that had the effect of rendering the buildings and street indistinct and much more dreamlike than the house he'd just left. Consequently, he was quite unable to throw off the creeping uneasiness of what he might be shown that night in Miss Lucinda's mirror. What was it that could lie on the farther side of nothing?

He walked quickly, without particularly meaning to; the chill in the air forced him to be brisk and vigorous, even though he felt, as they say, distinctly under the weather. He reached Glass House Yard and found Greening's without difficulty.

It turned out to be more of a warehouse than a shop, with tall racks in which white-covered mirrors were stacked like huge, wordless volumes in a library for giants. The air in the beamed and boarded interior was brooding and pensive. . . .

"Mirror for Mr. Paris," said Nightingale to a short, weaselish apprentice who appeared reluctantly from the obscure shadows at the back of the shop.

"Mirror for Paris!" shouted out the weaselish one to the shadows he'd just left.

"Third shelf along on the right. Got his name on it!" came a shout in reply.

The mirror, wrapped in white muslin, was brought down and laid on the counter.

"Sixpence on the clorf," said the weasel hopefully.

"I heard that!" came the shout from the back. "There's nothing to pay and well you know it!"

The weasel shrugged his thin shoulders.

"Got to try and make ends meet," he said amiably.

Nightingale smiled. The apprentice's attempt at sharp practice had been transparent enough even for Nightingale to see through. The other, not at all abashed, beamed over the counter.

"Givin' you a 'ard time, I see."

"What do you mean?" asked Nightingale uneasily.

"Paris and that 'orrible bitch of a daughter of 'is."

"No such thing!" Nightingale shrank in terror from the temptation of pouring out his misery to a stranger. He smiled again, this time with the glazed smile that was the livery of his master's house.

"You look fair worn to the bone," said the weasel with interest.

"Stop gossiping and give him the mirror!" shouted the invisible one.

"Ain't gossiping. Just offerin' comfort to a fellow 'prentice in distress. It's Paris's new one."

There came a thunder of large feet on bare boards and Mr. Greening himself issued from the cavernous depths of his shop. It was not to be wondered at that he kept in the shadows; he was extraordinarily ugly, with a monstrous nose that was afflicted with warts, like an old potato. He pushed his apprentice aside and laid his grey-and-silver-stained hands on the counter.

"You always look as pale as a corpse, son?" he inquired, studying Mr. Paris's new apprentice with small bright eyes that resembled chips of glass.

"It must be the weather, sir," said Nightingale with a pang of alarm.

"How long have you been with Mr. Paris?"

"Only a week, sir."

"God help us!"

"I—I'm quite happy there, sir. . . ."

"As the dying man said when the last drop of feeling left him," remarked Mr. Greening. "Well, well, you'd best take the glass and be off."

Eager to escape, Nightingale took hold of the wrapped mirror.

"Aren't you going to check it?"

Nightingale blushed and remembered the card. He produced it; Mr. Greening nodded approvingly, unwrapped the mirror, and obligingly held it up. Nightingale presented the card to the glass's silver face. The black words leaped out at him:

FOR NOW WE SEE THROUGH A GLASS, DARKLY; BUT THEN
FACE TO FACE: NOW I KNOW IN PART; BUT THEN SHALL
I KNOW EVEN AS ALSO I AM KNOWN.

Mr. Greening put the mirror down.

"All right, son?"

Nightingale nodded, but found himself staring into the air where the mirror had been. The words seemed to remain suspended in nothingness before him. He felt quite dizzy with trying to read them.

"Here!" he heard Mr. Greening say. "Fetch him some brandy and water. And mind—I know just how much brandy's left! Mirrors," he went on kindly, reaching out a hand to guide Nightingale to a chair, "can sometimes unsettle the strongest stomachs."

Nightingale sat down. He couldn't imagine what had come over him. He felt faint and sick. He put it down to the strong smell of polishing oil that suddenly seemed to be everywhere. Gratefully he drank off the brandy and water—which contained less water than might have been expected, on account of the apprentice being generous with his master's property—and rose to go. His legs had gone like water. . . .

"Sit still for a while. Wouldn't do to go dropping that mirror on your way back. Seven years' bad luck, you know. . . ."

Nightingale nodded and shuddered; he looked up at Mr. Greening, whose nose now seemed so enormous that it filled Nightingale's world. The warts were like large bald mountains and the tufts of hair that sprouted from the nostrils were like the forests of the night. Way, way above this fleshy landscape gleamed Mr. Greening's eyes, as distant as the stars. . . .

"I'm going to be sick," said Nightingale.

"Got a bucket here," said the weasel.

"Broke a mirror," confessed Nightingale after he'd brought up his breakfast, "on me first day. That's what done it."

"That's what done it."

"She threw it to me," said Nightingale after a pause. "And that's when it all started."

"What started?"

"Things."

"What things?"

"Mirrors . . . mirrors . . ."

"He's crying," said the weasel brightly.

"Mustn't carry tales," said Nightingale, and hiccupped.

"Won't tell a soul," said Mr. Greening sombrely. "What about the mirrors?"

"Everywhere. Even in the privy. And the one upstairs. That's the worst. . . ."

"Won't tell a soul," said Greening again. "Why is it worst?"

So Nightingale told him. . . .

What with the smoking of countless chimneys and, in particular, the dirty guffaws of the furnaces in Glass House Yard, the mist had condensed into a fog. Mr. Paris's apprentice, emerging from Greening's, had immediately been plunged into the November breath of the town, which smelled as if all the inhabitants had belched after partaking of the same bad dinner.

He was carrying, in addition to the mirror he had been sent for, a wrapped box of about the same size as the mirror but some six inches deeper. It was heavy and seemed to grow the more so as he walked. But the weight of it under his arm was as nothing compared with the weight on his heart.

He had betrayed his sacred trust. How he'd come to pour out all the details of his wretchedness to the ugly Mr. Greening, he would never know. He believed that, somehow, he'd dozed off and talked in his sleep. He looked back towards the strange shop as if for an answer, but the establishment was already lost in the fog. He had a sudden idea of throwing the heavy box away; he did not know what it contained and he was deeply afraid of it.

"It's a sort of mirror, you might say," the weaselish apprentice had said, and grinned malevolently.

Mr. Greening had warned him not to look in it himself. Under no circumstances was he to open it until she, and she alone, stood before it. He was to set it upon an easel, in a good light, and bid her look. The weasel had laughed aloud, and even Mr. Greening had smiled as if in terrible anticipation.

"What is it? What will it do?" Nightingale had asked, trembling with shame over his betrayal and fear for the consequence of it.

For answer, Mr. Greening had rubbed his grotesque nose and recalled the words on Nightingale's card.

"Then shall you know even as also you are known," he'd said, and left it at that.

If the early morning had been dreamlike, the day had now grown up into nightmare; Nightingale wouldn't have been surprised if he'd awakened with a start to find himself under the counter in Mr. Paris's shop. In the past he'd had dreams every scrap as convincing. . . .

A fire came looping at him out of the thick air.

"Light you home, mister?"

The fog had brought out the linkboys with their torches like a plague of fireflies. Nightingale jumped, and stared at the thin, pale child who stood before him, holding aloft a flaming length of tow that really served no better purpose than to draw attention to the evil state of the weather. The light reached no farther than a yard before it came back off the fog and bathed the linkboy in its glow.

"How much?" asked Nightingale.

" 'Pends how far," said the linkboy, blinking away tears brought on by flaming pitch.

"Friers Street. Mr. Paris's shop."

" 'S only round the corner. Off Shoemaker's Row. Cost you a penny."

Nightingale closed with the offer and the linkboy set off, miraculously weaving his way through a nothing that hid countless bulky somethings. Dazedly Nightingale kept his eyes on the streaming fire that superfluously added its own smoke to the atmosphere. He wished he'd got rid of the box before the linkboy had appeared.

"Nothing like a bit of fire for keeping out the cold," said the linkboy, and offered Nightingale a warm.

Although the torch shed no useful radiance in any particular direction, there was no doubt that Nightingale found its presence a comfort.

"Friers Street," said the linkboy suddenly, and waited while his customer searched and found a penny. Then, payment being made, he flickered off and was rapidly extinguished in the premature night.

"And where have you been, Nightingale?" asks Mr. Paris severely.

"I come over all queer at Mr. Greening's," says Nightingale humbly, and means it with all his heart. He has managed to deposit the mysterious box under the counter without being seen, before presenting himself to his master.

Mr. Paris looks closely, then resumes his glazed smile. He believes his apprentice, having satisfied himself that he certainly *looks* queer.

"He was taken over queer at Greening's," he tells Mrs. Paris as they sit down to table.

Nightingale looks up from his plate apologetically—and sees Miss Lucinda staring at him in triumph. He tries, with his eyes alone, to make some sort of approach to her, but without the smallest success.

For the rest of the day he is given only light tasks; Mr. Paris is not an unkindly man when things are brought face to face with him; he is really concerned for his pale, listless-looking apprentice. He begins to wonder if he has been altogether wise in caging a country Nightingale. . . .

Nightingale himself has similar thoughts; he dreads more than ever the coming of the night. Try as he might, he cannot imagine what terrible vengeance on his behalf has been concealed in the box. What if his master's daughter should be killed by it? That would turn him into a murderer!

The ugly Mr. Greening and his weaselish apprentice haunt his mind like a pair of malicious spirits in a darkened room. He resolves he will do nothing with the box. He is quite set on that; he'll not raise a finger to provide either the light or the easel. . . . Then, quite out of the blue, Mr. Paris bids him carry the easel from the workroom into the shop, ready to display Job's frame, which will soon be finished.

Nightingale's heart falters as fate comes in on Mr. Greening's side.

"Candle in the window won't do us much good on a night like this," says Mr. Paris, looking out into the deplorable weather. He glances back at his distinctly frightened and ill-looking apprentice, and then at the gloomy counter under which he is to sleep. "But keep it going all the same. Leave the shutters down and let a little brightness inside for a change, Nightingale."

Thoughtfully he turns the looking-glasses in the window so that they face inwards and reflect the candle quite strongly upon the empty easel in the shop.

Nightingale feels a sense of panic concerning the powers of Mr. Greening as he watches the father unknowingly arranging matters conveniently for the striking down of his own daughter.

At last the apprentice is left alone. He fetches out the box, takes off its outer coverings, and places it on the easel. There is only a thin lid between him and whatever the box contains. He has determined that he will look in it himself. The candlelight, multiplied by the looking-glasses, dances and glitters on the box.

Nightingale reaches out a hand, trembling in every limb at what he is about to behold. Mr. Greening and his apprentice rise up before his inner eye and scream warnings. . . .

"Nightingale!"

It is *she*. She has opened the door and stands just within the room. Her eyes fall upon the easel and the covered object upon it. She sees the apprentice standing before it, pale as death.

"What have you got there?"

Nightingale withdraws the hand that had been about to uncover Mr. Greening's gift.

"A—a sort of mirror, you might say," he answers, helplessly repeating the words of the weaselish apprentice. To his horror, he hears, in his own voice, a reflection of the weasel's mocking tone.

Miss Lucinda hears it, too.

"Let me see it," she says, and pushes him to one side.

He smiles in a dazed, glazed fashion, feeling that it is fate that has pushed him and not Miss Lucinda. She reaches out, but seeing his smile, hesitates.

"You've arranged this, haven't you?"

He does not answer; he does not need to.

"It's your revenge, isn't it?"

"Not mine," mutters Nightingale, thinking of the ugly Mr. Greening.

"You've put something vile in there," says Miss Lucinda, contemptuously, "some disgusting thing out of your own brain."

She lowers her hand, and Nightingale sighs with audible relief. She falls silent, and Nightingale hangs his head in an effort to avoid her brilliant and penetrating eyes. Then he looks up and sees that once more she has raised her hand and now rests it upon the thin lid of the box.

"Your thoughts," she says. "They're here, aren't they? What do they amount to? A toad? A piece of filth? Something dead and rotting? Something so foul and degrading that it's best covered up? Let's see, Nightingale, once and for all, how mean and depraved an apprentice's mind and heart can be!"

She laughs, and before Nightingale can stop her, she lifts up the lid. Light streams into the box, and the lid falls with a clatter from her hand. Nightingale turns away in terror. He waits for some shriek or sound of death, but there is only silence. Fearfully he looks back. She has not moved. A terrible pallor has spread over her face; even her lips, for all their redness, have gone a greyish white. What horrible, deadly thing did Mr. Greening hide in the box?

She breathes deeply as if suffering from an intolerable constriction; and the something so degrading that it should have been covered up gazes back at her. Helplessly she looks, with pitiless clarity, upon—herself.

Mr. Greening's box contains no more than a perfect mirror. Neither ripple, tarnish, nor flaw interposes to alleviate the girl from the image that she herself has so monstrously described.

Her expression, halted by shock, has remained unchanged from the look she'd worn before. Every mark of scorn, contempt, lamed ambition, and cruelty is bloodlessly plain. The very smile of deep pride—that had once lent her a sort of distinction—robbed of its color, has become a dull sneer. The eyes, fixed on the bland surface of the glass, have lost all brightness, all penetration, and become as glass, glass eyes in a glass head. . . .

Filled with guilt and fear, Nightingale approaches to see what it is she has seen. As he moves, she gives a low and anguished cry, which resembles not so much a sound as a shudder made audible, for it is accompanied by a continuous, violent trembling.

She is mortally afraid that he will see what she has seen, that he will see her as she now sees herself. His countenance joins her as she watches it, examines it minutely with ever-increasing agony.

"But it's only glass!" says Nightingale with gentle amazement.

"Only glass," she repeats, finding in the apprentice's face nothing worse than relief and bewilderment. "Quicksilver, lead, and glass . . ."

"That's how they make mirrors, isn't it?" says Nightingale, as if persuading a child out of too strong a dream.

"They put lead, as thin as paper, on the glass and pour quicksilver over it," she murmurs. "I've watched it being done. My father once took me. I'll take you, if you like . . . some day . . . if you like . . ."

Nightingale moves closer. He cannot really help himself. For a moment, their faces are reflected together; then their joined breath mists the glass, obscures them, and dissolves eyes, lips, cheeks, and tears into a strange, double countenance, seen, as it were, in a glass brightly.

But the candlelight, reflecting busily off all the looking-glasses from the window, keeps catching at the corners of Nightingale's eyes, so that he seems to be looking into the heart of a diamond.

He blinks and turns away, glancing, as he does so, from mirror to mirror, in each of which he sees his master's daughter. Sometimes he sees her in profile, sometimes just the coils of her golden hair, sometimes the curve of her cheek and the projecting edge of her lashes, and sometimes, as strange as the other side of the moon, her second profile. . . . He looks and looks, and as far as his eyes can see, his universe is filled with Lucindas. . . .

And she, at last abandoning her reflection to the eyes of another, follows his example and roams the angled mirrors. Everywhere she sees him, but cannot, by reason of the confused architecture of light, make out for certain what it is he is gazing at. She looks and looks, and as far as her eyes can see, her universe is filled with Nightingales . . . and their song is suddenly sweet.

Outside, the fog piles up and rolls comfortably past the window of Mr. Paris's shop; from somewhere in the invisible street, a gentleman curses as he trips over a lamplighter's ladder, and from every darkened corner come the linkboys' eager cries.

"Light you home, mister! Light you home, ma'am!"

MOSS
AND
BLISTER

THERE THEY GO, MOSS AND BLISTER, HURRYING UP BLACKFRIAR'S Stairs and on through the dark streets, under a sky fairly peppered with stars as cold as frozen sparks. Up Coalman's Alley, across Bristol Street . . .

"'Appy Christmas, marm—and a nappy Christmas to you, miss!" bellowed a bellman, coming out of an alehouse and wagging his bell like a swollen brass finger.

"*For unto us a Child is born, unto us a Son is given!*" He hiccupped, and drew out a little Christmas poem of his own composing, while Moss and Blister stood stock-still and listened. Then he held out his hand, and Moss put a sixpence in it, for it was Christmas Eve, and Moss, who was a midwife, felt holy and important.

Ordinarily, Moss was brisk and businesslike to a degree, but on this one night of the year she was as soft as butter and gave her services for nothing. She lived in hopes of being summoned to a stable and delivering the Son of God.

"It's written down, Blister," she said to her apprentice after the bellman had weaved away. "It's all written down. *Unto them that look for him shall he appear the second time.*"

Blister, a tall, thin girl with sticking-out ears and saucer eyes, who flapped and stalked after stubby Moss like a loose umbrella, said, "Yus'm!" and looked frightened to death. Blister also had her dream of Christmas Eve and a stable, but it was not quite the same as Moss's. She dreamed that Moss would be delivering *her* of the marvelous Child.

Naturally, she kept her ambition a deep secret from Moss, so that the dreamy frown that sometimes settled on her face led Moss to surmise that her apprentice was a deep one. . . . Mostly these frowns came in the springtime, for Moss knew it would take nine months . . . which was one less than the toes on both her feet. At the end of every March, she'd lie in her bed, waiting with ghostly urgency for Moss to appear beside her, for Moss had a gift like the angel of the annunciation. She could tell, long before it showed, if any female had a bun in the oven, a cargo in the hold, or a deposit in the vault—depending on the trade concerned.

She'd stop dead in the street, fix her eye in a certain way upon some lightsome lass, dig Blister in the ribs, and follow the female to her home. Then she'd leave her card, and everyone in the neighborhood would know that a happy event was on the way. Truly, the sight of Moss, in her ancient cape that was green with rain and age, was as sure a sign of pregnancy as morning sickness or a passion for pickles.

But she never looked at Blister in that certain way, and every Christmas Eve Blister would grow frightened that someone else had been chosen to bear the glory of the world. The dreamy frown, but now tinged with apprehension and melancholy, settled on her face as she floundered on in Moss's wake.

"Make 'aste, marm!" shrieked out a linkboy, streaking his

torch along a row of railings, so that a fringe of fire fell down and iron shadows marched across the houses like the army of the Lord. "Cat's 'avin' kittens!"

"There's a imp for impidence!" puffed Moss, shaking her fist and making as if to rush upon the hastily fleeing offender. "Just let me catch 'im and I'll pop 'im back where 'e came from!"

"Just let *me* catch 'im!" screeched Blister, shaking her fist likewise, so that midwife and apprentice made a pattern in the street, of wrath in two sizes.

Then Moss gave up and beckoned to Blister; there was no time to waste; they were needed in Glass House Yard, where Mrs. Greening's waters had broken and the whole household was having contractions in sympathy.

"D'yer fink it'll be the one?" panted Blister, swinging her heavy business bag from one hand to the other. "You know. '*Im* what's comin' for the second time?" Her voice trembled, and so did her lip.

"Nar," said Moss. "It's got to be in a stable, Blister. Ain't I told you that? There's got to be a donkey and three kings and wise men with frankincense and—and more."

"Wot's frankincense?"

"It's a sort of fruit. Summat between a orringe and a pommygrunt," answered Moss, who did not care to appear ill-informed.

Blister nodded. They really were pig ignorant, the pair of them; although why a pig, who knows where to find truffles and live the good life, should be put on a level with Moss and Blister, passes understanding. Moss didn't even know that the world was round, while Blister didn't know that China was a place as well as a cup. Moss's arithmetic—apart from counting out her fee, about which she was remarkably sharp—was confined to the natural proposition that one and one, coming together, can make one, or, sometimes, two—twins being the largest number she had ever been called upon to deliver. And Blister was even more ignorant than that.

Although she knew her trade in every particular, and could have delivered a baby as safely as kiss your hand, she'd no more idea of how the seed had been planted than she knew what happened to the River Thames after it went past Wapping. Moss had never seen fit to enlighten her. In Moss's view, all that Blister needed to know was how to get babies out; getting them in was no part of the trade. The nearest she ever came to telling Blister was at Christmastide, when she went on, with a radiant smile, about a woman being with child of the Holy Ghost. This made Blister very frightened; she had nightmares of being confronted, when she least expected it, by something inexpressibly fierce in a sheet.

Presently they reached Glass House Yard, and there was Mr. Greening's shop, leaking light and commotion at every joint. They began to cross the dark cobbles when Moss cried out.

"Stop! Stop!" She halted in her tracks with her arms spread out so that her cape fell down like a pair of mildewy wings. Something had darkened her path.

"Black cat, Blister! Cross your fingers and think of wood— else the baby will be wrong way round!"

Obediently Blister dropped her bag, crossed her fingers, and emptied her mind of everything except a broomstick that stood behind Moss's kitchen door. It was the only wood she knew.

"Done it, mum."

Moss heaved a sigh of relief and advanced upon the premises of Mr. Greening.

"You can't be too careful," she said, giving her famous double knock upon the door. "Not where such 'appiness is at stake!"

"They're 'ere! They're 'ere! Thank Gawd you've come! Mr.

Greening—it's the midwife! Mrs. Greening! It's all right now!
Oh, thank Gawd you're 'ere! They're all goin' off their 'eads! Is
it always like this, marm?"

Mr. Greening's apprentice, who was small and sharp like a
weasel, and who nursed ambitions of becoming one of the family,
was quite beside himself with anxiety and excitement as he admitted Moss and Blister through the trade counter that occupied
the entrance of the establishment. They'll remember this, he
thought to himself as he took Moss's cape and offered to assist
Blister with her bag. They'll remember how I give up me Christmas and worritted myself sick like a son!

Mr. Greening himself appeared. He was an ugly man with a
nose like a warty old potato. He was a silverer of mirrors, which
was an unusual trade for one of his unlucky appearance.

"Thank God you've come!" he cried.

Next came the Greenings' two daughters, young ladies of
twelve and fourteen and quite as ugly as their father.

"Thank God you're here! We thought ma was going to die!"

Then a maidservant looked in, and a neighbour's wife, and
they thanked God for Moss, so that Moss felt deliciously holy
all over. With a wave of her hand she dispatched Blister upstairs
to see how things were proceeding; then she went into the warm,
bright parlour to receive whatever else of respect, gratitude, and
hospitality might be coming her way.

"This way, miss! Do let me carry yer bag. Gawd, it's 'eavy!"
exclaimed the weaselish apprentice as he conducted Blister up
the stairs and towards the room from which Mrs. Greening could
be heard moaning and peevishly inquiring where everyone had
gone. "Wotcher got in it, miss? The Crahn jewels?"

"Instryments," said Blister. "Knives and forksips and fings."

"Gawd," said Mr. Greening's apprentice. "It's a real business,
ain't it?"

Blister smiled proudly, and the weaselish one couldn't help reflecting that the saucer-eyed Blister was a raving beauty compared with the two Miss Greenings at whom he'd set his cap in the hopes of marrying one of them—he didn't care which—and inheriting the business.

"Make much money at it?"

"Not on Christmas Eve," said Blister. "We don't charge then."

"Why ever not?"

"Ain't you 'eard? It's on account of the Son of God might be comin'. It's all written down."

"I never 'eard of that one!"

"You're pig ignorant, you are," said Blister loftily.

"No more'n you. 'Ow would you silver a mirror?"

"Dunno. 'Ow would yer deliver a hinfant arse first?"

"Send for you! What's yer name?"

"Blister. 'S on account of me skin bein' all bubbly when I come out. What's your name?"

"Bosun. It's on account of me family bein' Bosuns."

"I never 'ad a family. I was given to Moss when she delivered me. Sort of present. Moss took a fancy to me, called me Blister, and brung me up."

"Like 'er daughter?"

" 'Prentice. She ain't got a daughter. . . ."

Bosun nodded and, with an affable smile, stood aside for Blister to enter Mrs. Greening's room.

The lady lay in her bed, weeping and groaning that all the world had abandoned her, that nobody cared any more, and that she was going to die.

There was indeed some reason for this latter fear as she was advanced in years and had begun to believe herself past the age of childbearing. Like Sarah of old when the messengers from God had crossed the plain of Mamre to tell Abraham that his wife was with child, Mrs. Greening had laughed when Moss had called and left her card. She'd leaned behind the door and laughed at the stout little angel of the annunciation till the tears had run down her cheeks.

But then, as the days and weeks had gone by, she'd come to laugh on the other side of her face, for Moss had been right and the mirror maker's wife did indeed "have a little reflection in the glass."

"I'm going to die," moaned Mrs. Greening, seeing that her visitor was only the midwife's gawky apprentice. "It's true—it's true!"

"Yus'm," said Blister, who had been taught there were two things in the world that there was no sense in arguing with: bad weather and a woman in labour.

She opened her bag and began to set out the instruments on a table. They were a ferocious assortment: scalpels, cruelly curved bistouries, probes, leathern forceps, scissors, and a bone saw that, from age and infirmity, had lost all but a few of its harsh teeth. Moss had picked them up, as she liked to call it, at various stages in her career when she'd attended in the presence of surgeons. She hadn't the faintest notion what they were for; the only instruments she actually used were her small strong hands and a pair of dressmaker's scissors she'd also picked up and which she kept in her pocket to cut the umbilical cord. Nevertheless, she insisted that Blister always lay out the whole surgical armoury, as she felt the sight of it gave her a real professional standing and the air of one who was not to be trifled with.

Mrs. Greening, watching Blister's preparations, lost her fears in a terrified awe; dying was nothing beside what her imagination had suddenly proposed. Blister, sensing the lady's respect, felt proud, but at the same time she couldn't help wishing the weaselish apprentice outside the door could also behold her in her importance.

She'd been quite taken with Bosun and had been flattered by his admiration for the mystery of her craft.

"You must keep yer mouf shut, marm," she said, loudly enough for Bosun to hear and be further impressed by her wisdom. "Breeve froo yer nose."

"Why must I do that?"

" 'Case yer baby's born wivout sense or soul. Gets out froo yer mouf, marm."

For the time being, Mrs. Greening gave up groaning and shut her mouth.

"That's it, marm," said Blister, and went to unlatch the window. "Mustn't 'ave nuffink shut," she said. "Else yer labour will be 'ard as nails. Winders, doors, boxes, cupboards, drors . . . all got to be open. An' bockles, of course—"

"What?"

"Bockles—bockles! No stoppers or corks in 'em. Anyfink corked up corks up you, too."

"Tell Bosun," said Mrs. Greening feebly.

But there was no need; Bosun had heard.

"Right away, Mrs. G.! Don't you fret, marm! Bosun'll open everything!"

With a sound of thunder, Bosun was off, turning keys, lifting lids, opening bottles, and dragging out crowded, obstinate drawers. They'll remember this, he thought, when I comes to ask for the 'and of one of them ugly girls. They'll remember 'ow Bosun ran 'is feet off like a lovin' son!

"Knots," said Blister. "Mustn't 'ave nuffink tied nor knotted. Twists you up, else. If you got a norse or a dawg, it's got to be untied, else the hinfant won't be able to get out."

All these strange requirements, these pebbles of magical wisdom that were laid up in Blister's head, had been gathered by Moss in her rollings among mothers and grandmothers whose memories stretched back to the beginnings of time. Moss had taken them all in, rejecting nothing, however far-fetched, and passed them on to her apprentice with the deep words: "You can't be too careful; not where such 'appiness is at stake!"

"I think it's dead!" said Mrs. Greening in a sudden panic. "I can't feel it any more! It's dead—it's dead!"

"Yus-m," said Blister, and drawing back Mrs. Greening's bedclothes, bent down and laid her large, sticking-out ear to Mrs. Greening's hugely swollen belly.

Now as no one was talking about Blister, her ears were as cold as ice.

"Mother of God!" shrieked Mrs. Greening, and Blister started in pleased surprise to hear herself thus addressed.

"Yus-m?"

"The pain! The pain!"

Downstairs in the parlour, Moss was sipping port wine, which always imparted a rare skill to her fingers and a brightness to her eyes.

"Never put the stopper on, sir," she said reproachfully to Mr. Greening, and gently but firmly she took the decanter into her own hands and refilled her glass. "Nor clasp your 'ands nor cross your legs, else the baby'll never come."

Mr. Greening compressed his sensible lips and cast his eyes towards the ceiling. Nevertheless, he obeyed the midwife's injunction. Even as he did so, everyone heard Mrs. Greening shriek out, and directly after came Blister's shout.

"She's started! Come on up, marm! She's on the way!"

The mirror maker stared down in bewilderment at his uncrossed knees, and everyone else in the parlour looked terrified, as if they'd just received an inkling of a mysterious web of laws in which they were all caught like so many helpless flies. The neighbour's wife, who had been inclined to regard Moss's superstitions with contempt, now stared at the fat little midwife with a respect that bordered on dread. And so she should have done, for Moss knew very well what she was about and was right to neglect nothing when such happiness was at stake.

Moss finished off her wine and rose to her feet.

"I'll call you," she said, "when it's over."

She left the parlour and briskly mounted the stairs. Outside Mrs. Greening's door, she came upon Bosun, who had gone very white in the face as the cries and grunts from within increased in urgency.

"You must cover up all the mirrors," she told him, "else the baby will be born blind."

Bosun nodded and prepared to fly at the midwife's bidding. She raised her hand.

"And put neither wood nor coal on the fire till the cord's cut, else the baby might be born dead."

"I never knew, I never guessed there was so much to it, marm."

"You can't be too careful," said Moss, sombrely, "where such 'appiness is at stake."

Bosun fled. They'll remember this, he thought. They'll remember 'ow Bosun was a real son to them!

By the time he'd scoured the premises and covered up every last glimmer of reflecting silver and returned to his station outside the bedroom door, matters were far advanced. Panting and gulping, he listened. . . .

" 'Old 'er legs, Blister! Up a bit . . ."

"Yus'm."

"Bear down, mother! Bear down wiv all yer might!"

"I can't! I can't!"

" 'Old your breff when it comes on! 'Old yer breff when you feel it pushin'. . . ."

"It's burning me—it's burning me like fire!"

"Bear down again, mother! Blister! Give 'er knees another shove! Push, mother! Push like ye'r rollin' a cart of 'ay!"

"I can't . . . I—I've no more strength!"

" 'Old yer breff agin! Ah! I can see it! Luvly little thing! Ye'r all but crownin' now, mother!"

"No—no! I don't want to! It's going to kill me! Stop it!"

" 'Eave ho! 'Eave ho!"

But Mrs. Greening was still reluctant to bring forth the little "reflection in her glass," and she began to curse and swear in a way that made Bosun's toes curl up. He'd no idea his mistress knew such words, nor was so wild and abandoned a soul as she sounded.

" 'Eave ho! 'Eave ho! mother," urged Moss, and there followed a most awesome grunting, as of stout hawsers straining when the full tide heaves a great vessel to tug against its moorings.

"Ugh! Ugh! Ugh!"

" 'Eave ho! 'Eave ho!"

"Ugh! Ugh! Ugh!"

"Spread them knees a bit, Blister!"

"Yus-m."

"There ain't nothing knotted anywhere, Blister?"

"Bosun!" screeched out Blister anxiously.

"Yes, miss?"

"Bootlaces! Got 'em undone?"

Bosun looked down. His shoes were tightly laced—and double-knotted. Guiltily he bent down and tried to untie them. Mrs. Greening moaned and groaned; Moss urged her to still greater efforts—and Bosun pulled and snapped his laces.

"Done it—done it, miss!" he shouted in triumph, and Mrs. Greening gave a last mighty cry.

"Clever girl!" said Moss. "Blister! Get me scissors out, there's a dear!"

"Yus-m."

"Look what a luvly little thing it is! All its fingers and toes! Listen—listen! Ah! There it goes!"

Suddenly there came a fragile sound, so thin and winding that it scarcely seemed to make its way through the air. It was the sound of a voice, brand new, never before heard since the beginning of time.

And I done it! thought Bosun, looking down incredulously at his broken bootlaces. Oh, they'll remember this when I comes to offer meself as their son!

"Tell Mr. Greening!" said the mother's exhausted, happy voice. "I want Mr. Greening to come. . . ."

"Bosun!"

"Yes, miss?"

"Go tell 'em it's over and everyfing's all right! Tell Mr. Greenin' to come on up an' 'ave a look at 'is wife an' son!"

They'll remember this, thought Bosun, flying down the stairs, when I'm their SON!

The last word came out aloud, in a dismayed grunt and squeal. A son! But now they'd already got one!

In the twinkling of an eye the apprentice's ambitions tumbled as the tiny creature, which he himself had done so much to deliver safely, usurped his prospects. He saw it all. It would grow and grow and, sooner or later, come to lord it over him; Bosun would count for nothing; the newcomer would inherit the business. . . .

"You got a son, Mr. Greening," he said, entering the expectant parlour and doing his best to keep the dismay out of his voice. "You got a bruvver," he said, gazing mournfully at the two ugly daughters. At least, he thought, he would no longer have to worry which of them would be the least disagreeable to marry. It's an ill wind, he reflected wryly, that don't blow at least *some* good!

Everyone in the parlour exclaimed aloud with joy and began hastening upstairs, while Bosun—passed-over Bosun—went about fastening latches, closing doors, and corking up all the bottles with the vague, melancholy feeling that he was bolting the stable door after the horse had gone. He looked down at his loosened shoes. He sighed.

"And I'll even 'ave to buy meself new laces!"

He peered into the fire he'd just replenished and tried to see castles in the coals. They've forgotten, he thought; they've forgotten all about Bosun now. He shifted a piece of coal to make a roof for what would have been a fine mansion, but it fell through and the walls collapsed into blazing ruins. " 'Ow like life," whispered Bosun. " 'Ow like life!"

"Bosun?"

"Yes, miss?"

Blister had come down; she looked flushed and disarranged from her recent efforts. Even her ears stuck out more than usual; like a pair of cupboard doors, thought Bosun, bitterly. He couldn't help regarding her as partly the author of his misfortune.

"Mr. Greenin' says you're to gimme a glass of port wine to drink 'is son's 'elf."

"Yes, miss."

"An' 'e says you're to 'ave one yerself."

"I ain't thirsty," said Bosun, but nevertheless he joined Blister. There was, after all, no law that could make him drink to the infant who had just done him out of his inheritance.

" 'Ere's to seein' your face in the glass!" he said defiantly.

" 'Ere's to the Son of God!"

"The son of Greening, you mean."

Blister shook her head wisely.

"It's got to come in a stable, wiv' free kings an' a donkey and a special star."

"That'll be the day!"

"It'll come, one Christmas Eve. It's all written down."

"And will you be there to 'elp?"

"I'll be there," said Blister, shutting her saucer eyes tightly and swilling down her wine. "Me an' the 'oly Ghost."

She swallowed and opened her eyes, and the two apprentices gazed at each other over the tops of their glasses: the one mournful, the other still full of hope. In one, ambition had fallen; in the other, it still remained in the skies.

She ain't really such a bad looker, thought Bosun. In a narrer glass you'd never see them ears!

" 'Ave another glass of wine!" offered Bosun, feeling distinctly less careful over his master's property than he would have done half an hour before.

"Yus!" said Blister, thrusting out her long, thin arm.

Bosun recharged the glasses and smiled somewhat crookedly.

" 'Ere's to seein' *your* face in the glass!" said Blister, politely echoing her companion's toast.

"And 'ere's to the Son of God!" responded Bosun. They drank.

" 'Ave—" began Bosun, when there came a loud knocking on the street door. Bosun frowned and put down his glass. " 'Elp yourself," he said. And then added broodingly, "We all got to 'elp ourselves, miss."

He left the parlour and clattered through the shop. Blister felt a gust of cold night air come sweeping in as the street door was opened; she shivered. Bosun returned.

"It's for you. Midwife wanted. In a 'urry. 'Ow did they know you was 'ere?"

"We allus tell a neighbour in Glastonbury Court. They 'ave to know where to find us. Moss!" screeched Blister.

"What is it, Blister?"

"Anuvver call! In a 'urry!"

"Whereabouts?"

Blister looked inquiringly at Bosun.

"Said it were in Three Kings Court."

"Free Kings Court, Moss!"

"*Three Kings?*" Moss's voice took on an edge of excitement. "What 'ouse?"

"New Star public 'ouse," said Bosun.

"The Noo Star, Moss!" howled Blister.

"The Star? The New Star?" repeated Moss, from upstairs. "Christmas Eve, three kings, and a new star? Blister! Come an' fetch yer instryments! Blister! It might be the one! 'Urry, girl, 'urry!"

Blister and Bosun stared at each other. Curiosity and excitement filled the heart of one apprentice; apprehension and dread clutched at the other.

Could it really be the one? thought Blister. Never! Three kings and an inn called the New Star weren't enough. It had to be more than that. Partly relieved, she ran upstairs to collect her instruments.

"Carry yer bag, miss?" offered Bosun impulsively as Blister came down again in the wake of the fat and trembling Moss.

"Wot? All the way to Free Kings Court? Won't they miss you 'ere?"

"Not now they got a son," said Bosun bitterly. "Besides," he went on, brightening a little, "if it's 'im—you know, the one what we drunk to—I'd like to see 'im. Wouldn't want to miss 'im. It'd be summat to remember all right."

"It won't be 'im," said Blister, thrusting out her lower lip. "It can't be 'im. It needs more'n free kings and a star. . . ."

" 'Urry, Blister! 'Urry!" Moss was already in the street. "What if it's reely 'im an' we're too late?"

There they went, Moss and Blister, hurrying by starlight, with Bosun clanking the bag of instruments and keeping a watch for footpads and other demons of the night. They hastened up Water Street and into Ludgate Hill. . . .

"It's got to be in a stable!" panted Blister.

" 'Appy Christmas, 'Appy Christmas!" called out a pair of watchmen on Fleet Bridge who were warming themselves before a brazier of glowing coals that threw up their faces in a ruddy comfort amid the empty fields of the night.

"Look, Blister, girl! Shepherds abidin' . . . and the glory of the Lord shinin' all round 'em! Make 'aste, make 'aste! I reely think it might be the night!"

But it took more than that to convince Blister. She shook her head so violently that tiny drops of salt water flew out of her saucer eyes.

"It ain't the night! It ain't!" she muttered as they passed Temple Bar and came into the Strand. "There's got to be frankincense and—and more!"

"What's frankincense?" asked Bosun, ready to come upon it at any moment if only he knew what to look for.

Blister did not answer; she was in no mood to tempt fate. Moss put on a spurt of speed and scuttled on ahead. Still shaking her head, Blister stalked after, into Southampton Street and Covent Garden. Bosun, burdened with the heavy bag, came panting up beside her.

"And—and there's got to be a donkey," mumbled Blister,

putting yet another obstacle in the way of Moss's heart's desire, "and a wise man from the East."

As they drew near Three Kings Court, her great saucers were awash with new tears. She bit her lip and clenched her fists; and then, wickedness of wickedness, she secretly knotted a corner of her cape and vowed to keep her fingers crossed against the coming, that night, of the Son of God. It had to be she, and she alone, who was to be got with child of the Holy Ghost. She peered furtively up to the stars.

" 'Ere I am," she whimpered. "Blister! It's me you're lookin' for! Me! Down 'ere. Me wiv the big ears . . ."

Thus Blister, in her bottomless ignorance, strove with all her might and main to prevent the second coming on that Christmas Eve. That such an event would mark the end of the world's misery meant nothing to Blister. What would be the good of it? In the middle of all the happiness, she would have remained the one black spot of woe; and made all the darker by the thoughtless brightness all around. Moss would forget her in the excitement; Moss would be on her knees before a stranger, and Blister would be out in the cold. . . .

At last they came to Three Kings Court, where a single lantern lit up the frontage of the New Star Inn. Despite its name, the New Star was the oldest building in the court. It was left over from the days when Covent Garden had been a convent garden and had supplied the palace of Westminster with fruit and vegetables. Since then, however, tall tenements had come crowding in, imprisoning the New Star and taking away its pleasant garden. Only the coaching yard remained to mark its former glory; but even that was a mockery, as no vehicle could possibly have gained entry to the court through the narrow passage that was all that the greedy builders had seen fit to leave as a way in.

There was, in point of fact, a bulky old-fashioned coach still standing, in a corner of the cobbled yard. It was a dreamy, melancholy sight that suggested a great journey abandoned, or a faithful love discarded and forgotten in the haste of new prospects. For a time it had been used as a trysting place, but when the roof had rotted and the seats decayed, it had become a playground for children. . . .

Under the arch that formed the entrance to the yard stood a grimy, oil-smelling lamplighter who lived nearby. It was he who was holding the lantern and swinging it, turning the night into an earthquake of sliding shadows.

"She's in there," he said to Moss.

"Where?"

"In the stable."

Moss turned to Blister and Bosun. Her face was ecstatic.

"It's no good!" whispered Blister. "There's got to be a donkey, too!"

They passed under the arch and crossed the yard. The lamplighter followed them, and his swaying lantern was reflected in the windows of the derelict coach, so that it seemed, for a moment, that the abandoned vehicle had come to life and was inhabited by a procession of spirits bearing candles. . . .

The innkeeper's wife, hearing the footsteps on the cobbles, hastened out to meet the midwife.

"We wouldn't have known a thing about it," she explained. "She came in so quiet. It was only on account of her beast braying out that gave her away. And then we came out and found her. . . .

"Her beast?"

"She came on a donkey. It's in the stable now, eating its head off—"

"A donkey? A donkey! Gawd! Did you 'ear that, Blister?"

Blister heard. "There's got to be a wise man," she moaned softly.

"She's some sort of gipsy," went on the innkeeper's wife. "She's as dark as a nut. Come up from Kent, we fancy, selling apples. They thieve 'em out of barns down there and travel into London on their donkeys like regular apple sellers. She must have been took short in the Strand. She was squatting in the old coach when we found her. At first we though she was just poorly . . . so we took her into the stable, as we'd got no rooms in the house at the moment. Then we saw what it was. She's very near her time. . . ."

Although the innkeeper's wife tried to be casual and offhand in her account, it was plain that she, no less than Moss, was moved by the strange and prophetic nature of the circumstance. Perhaps all this had been in her mind when she and her husband had decided to move the gipsy into the stable? Perhaps this is the way prophecies are meant to be fulfilled? *Seek, and ye shall find; knock, and it shall be opened unto you.*

Two lamps, which had once lit the ancient coach on its way, shed their light now over the stall where the gipsy had found refuge in her distress, and a bucket of burning coals had been placed in a swept corner to give some warmth in the freezing night. The sight thus illumined was old and strange, full of mysterious shadows and still more mysterious light. There was the donkey, half emerging from the gloom and bowing its gentle head to nibble at the straw on which its mistress lay. Farther back, half hidden by the wooden partition, stood the innkeeper and two or three travellers who had been putting up for the night. The dim light rendered their faces intent and profound. . . .

"We've not managed to get a word out of her," confided the innkeeper's wife, "that we can understand, that is. She gabbled away in her own lingo when we took her out of the coach, but as soon as she saw we meant her no harm, she buttoned up her lip, and she's been quiet as a mouse ever since."

The gipsy was dark brown as a nut. Her hair was black and was braided cunningly over her ears, so that her oval face seemed to have been laid in a basket of black straw. Her eyes were as black as her hair and fixed themselves on Moss with a look that was at once suspicious and defiant. Only the drops of sweat that stood upon her high forehead betrayed that she was in any difficulty or pain.

"It's very unusual," murmured one of the travellers, "for any of her race to be abandoned at such a time. She must be an outcast of some description. . . ."

"This gentleman seems to know a thing or two," said the innkeeper's wife softly. "He's what you might call a wise man." As she said this, she gave a curious smile and a little nod to Moss. Blister wept; she stood alone before the inexorable power of fate.

Moss, her joints crackling like gunfire, knelt down beside the gipsy. Reverently she laid a hand, first on the woman's brow and then on her rusty black gown, through which she strove to feel the motions of the child within. She looked up at Blister and nodded. Dully Blister took her bag from Bosun and began to lay out her instruments on the straw.

The gipsy watched the preparation impassively and then transferred her gaze to Blister herself. Hastily Blister looked away. She dreaded that the woman, full of the mysterious gifts of her race, would be able to spy out the devil of jealousy that dwelt in Blister's soul.

The gipsy frowned and bit on her red, red lip. Moss, observing this, drew in her breath sharply.

"Go see nothing's locked nor tied nor stopped up," she murmured to Blister. "I think 'e's comin' and we must make 'is way straight, like it says."

Blister swallowed and retreated from the stall.

"I'll 'elp!" offered Bosun excitedly. He attempted to press Blister's hand under cover of darkness, but Blister shrank away. . . .

"The donkey!" burst out Bosun, coming up upon Blister suddenly. "You forgot it! But no matter—I untied 'im!"

Blister stared at the weaselish apprentice with misery. He departed.

"There was a bit of old 'arness," he said, appearing beside Blister again, " 'angin' on a 'ook. I unbuckled it!"

Blister clenched her fists, and the weasel scuttled busily off.

"There was an ol' bottle in the corner. . . . I took the cork out! Don't you worrit, miss! I'll do what's needful . . . for the sake of *'im*!"

Blister moaned.

"There was a copper pan polished so's you could see yer face in it. But I covered it up!"

Blister snarled, and Bosun, mistaking the sound for anxiety, reached out to comfort Blister.

"Miss—miss! There's a knot got into yer cape! 'Old still and I'll undo it. There—"

Helplessly Blister submitted; she dared not let it be known what was in her heart.

"Blister! Come quick!"

Moss's voice was summoning her. She stared wildly towards the stall. The innkeeper and the travellers had moved back, out of decency and respect. A glow seemed to rise up from where the gipsy lay. Suddenly this glow became fiercely bright!

"I just put a bit of wood on the fire," murmured the innkeeper's wife, "to keep her warm."

"Never do that!" squealed Bosun. "That were wrong!' He rushed inside the stall and, burning his fingers, snatched the brand from the burning bucket and doused it in a barrel of water that stood nearby.

He smiled at Blister as she entered the stall.

"I 'opes," he said, sucking his injured fingers, "that *'e* remembers this when we all come to be judged."

Thereupon Bosun retired to the darkest part of the stable, where, with the innkeeper and the travellers, he awaited the birth of the saviour.

"Blister!"

"Yus-m?"

"Down 'ere! What the matter wiv you, girl? 'Old the lady's knees. Gently—gently, girl! Remember what she might be! Oh, my Gawd! She's all but crownin' and not a word nor a cry! It's a mirricle, all right!"

Blister, leaning forward and pressing on the gipsy's bent knees, put her face close and said fiercely, "Were it the 'oly Ghost? Tell us—tell us!"

The gipsy's dark eyes widened and swam with moisture.

"Blister!"

"Yus'm?"

"What are you on at? Don't fret 'er! It's comin'! I—I can see 'is 'ead! It's 'im all right! It must be! 'E's *shinin'*!"

Bosun, in the shadows, heard the midwife's rapturous cry. The coming of the saviour instantly produced in his mind thoughts of a world where apprentices were level with their masters, where there was no toil to blunt the nights and days.

Moss thought of herself in a stained-glass window, offering the Son of God to the black-haired Queen of Heaven, while Blister, her apprentice, saw herself cast into the outer darkness, despised and rejected alike of the Holy Ghost and Moss and all mankind.

She glared, with fearful desperation, into the gipsy's eyes. She pretended to yawn, stretching wide her mouth. The gipsy looked suddenly frightened; she tried to clench her teeth against the awful power of Blister's example. An expression of terrified pleading came into her eyes as she strained. Blister was the devil, encouraging her to lose her child's soul through her open mouth! A great shudder convulsed her, and she shook her head from side to side.

"Blister—Blister, my love!" Moss was sobbing. "That it should be us . . . together . . . on this night! Oh, Blister, I knew, when I 'eld you in me arms, that you and me would do summat wonderful! Oh, Blister! That were a blessed night when you was born!"

As she heard these words, Blister's heart lifted up. It had been a blessed night when she'd been born! She shut her mouth, and the gipsy bestowed on her a smile of the most wondrous radiance.

"Scissors, Blister! Where's me scissors? Quick, girl! What are you at?"

Bosun, staring towards the stall, believed he saw a radiance rising up as the glorious new life began. Then came the cry, like a thread of gold. . . . Everyone pressed forward eagerly.

"Oh, Blister!" cried Moss, her voice shaking. "Oh, Blister! We wasn't worthy after all! It—it ain't 'im! It—it's a girl!"

Hopes raised foolishly settled into ashes. The travellers went back to their rooms, and the gipsy nursed her child while her donkey nodded and nibbled. The innkeeper's wife, rueful of countenance, bade the midwife farewell, and the old coach in the yard looked deader than ever as Moss, Blister, and Bosun passed it by.

"If only," said Bosun to Blister, "they'd been the other way round. If only there'd been a girl at Mr. Greening's and a boy 'ere! What a night that would 'ave been, eh?"

He sighed and pondered on how nearly he and the world had come to being saved.

"If only it 'ad been a boy!" sniffed Moss, dabbing her eyes.

"We'd never 'ave 'ad to work again," said Bosun.

"There'd be no more dyin'," said Moss.

"There'd be no more rainin' on Sundays," said Bosun.

"There's be no more damp winters," said Moss. "And no more growin' old."

"There'd be strawberries all the year round," said Bosun, "growin' in the streets."

"We'd all be wed," said Moss, "wiv never a death to part us."

"We'd all be beautiful," said weaselish Bosun. "There wouldn't be a ugly face anywhere."

He glanced at Blister, who was gazing up to the stars. Blister alone was neither mournful nor full of regrets. She was smiling, a strange, secret smile. She had not been rejected, not by the Holy Ghost, or Moss, or mankind. She *had* been visited; she knew it. She smiled and smiled at the stars. Bosun continued to watch her and found her mysterious and quite heart catching. Blister, feeling his scrutiny, looked into his eyes.

"All we needed was a boy," sighed Moss.

"All we needed was a boy," repeated Blister, and the two apprentices—the one like a beanpole, the other like a weasel—continued to gaze into each other's eyes.

" 'Appy Christmas!" called the lamplighter, who still stood under the archway that led out into Three Kings Court. *"For unto us a Son is born!"*

"It were a girl," said Moss sadly. "We needed a boy."

"But I got a boy," murmured Blister.

"You got a boy," agreed Bosun, and took her by the hand.

There they go, Moss, Blister and Bosun, hurrying through the dark streets.

"Moss!" called out Blister. "It were *'im*, after all."

Moss turned and looked back at Blister and then at Bosun. She smiled and nodded.

"In a manner o' speakin', dear," she said. "In a manner o' speakin'."

THE

CLOAK

I T WAS NEW YEAR'S MORNING, AND NATURE, IN A BURST OF GOOD resolutions, had decided to begin with a clean slate—or about a million of them: snow had fallen heavily during the night. Everything was white; roofs, alleys, courts, lanes, and streets looked as fresh and hopeful as a clean page awaiting the first entry. . . .

A greasy old lamplighter, high on his ladder in Southampton Street, brooded on it all. He saw his own footprints and the marks made by his heavy ladder as he'd moved from lamp to lamp. Everything showed, even where he'd stumbled. He saw two kitchen maids hastening to fetch the morning's milk. He wished them a Happy New Year, and his voice, floating down through the silence imposed by the snow, startled them. They looked up with bright morning faces, wagged their fingers at the old man, and, laughing, returned his greeting.

The silence was uncanny; folk moved across the white like toiling dreams. A gipsy woman with a laden donkey came down from Covent Garden way as soundlessly as a black thought.

Her face was dark, her hair was wild, and she and her beast

trudged up a little storm in the snow.

"Apples! Sweet Kent apples!" she cried as she saw the lamplighter. "Who'll buy?"

She halted beside the ladder and turned her fierce eyes upwards.

"No teeth," said the lamplighter sadly. He gazed down into the baskets the donkey patiently bore. In one lay a bushel of green and yellow apples; in the other, well wrapped in rags, slept a tiny baby, no more than a week old. The lamplighter grinned.

"But I must say, your little 'un looks soft enough to eat . . . even with poor bare gums like these."

He stretched back his lips in a kindly snarl.

"You can have her for a pound," said the gipsy.

"Nowhere to put her, dear."

"Fifteen shillings, then? Just so long as she goes to a good home."

The lamplighter shook his head. He climbed down from his perch and, dipping his little finger into a tin of blacking he'd been gathering from the burnt remains of his lamps, reached into the basket and marked the top of the baby's head with a tiny cross.

"That's for luck, dear. Lamplighter's blacking, nought shall be lacking."

"That's kind," said the gipsy with approval. "Here's a sprig of white heather for you and yours. Gipsy's heather brings good weather. Where's the nearest pawnshop?"

"That's a bad way to start the new year, dear," said the old man.

"Got to keep body and soul together," countered the gipsy. "Ain't I?"

The lamplighter scratched his head as he considered the problem.

"They won't take apples . . . nor babies, neither."

"Got a garment," said the woman proudly.

"They'll take that. Right off your back, if need be."

"Will they?"

She stared into the lamplighter's cracked and ancient eyes. Suddenly he kindled up and grinned with an air of elderly mischief.

"Drury Lane, dear. Mr. Thompson's."

The gipsy returned the old man's smile.

"Rachel's blessing on you!" she called as she began to continue on her way.

"And a Happy New Year!" answered the lamplighter, watching the woman and her donkey move soundlessly down the street, kicking up the snow in a fine spray so that it seemed they were walking upon a long white sea. It was just five minutes to eight o'clock.

At the southern end of Drury Lane, upon the left-hand side, stood the premises of Mr. Thompson, Personal Banking on Moderate Terms. From a stout iron gibbet above the shop door hung the emblems of the trade: three brass balls that winked and gleamed in the wintry sunshine, beckoning to all in distress. Even on them the snow had settled, crowning them with caps of white, so that they resembled three little round and shining brides of Christ.

Upon closer examination the brass balls did indeed bear vague smudges like countenances, but not of a particularly radiant cast. Long ago, an actor (most of Mr. Thompson's customers were on the stage, or temporarily off it) had climbed up and painted the masks of grim Tragedy on each of them, but time, weather, and the scrubbing brush of Coot, the apprentice, had worn them away to the merest ghosts of grief.

The Cloak

A rigid man was Mr. Thompson (and so was his brother-in-law, Mr. Long, who pawnbroked in nearby Henrietta Street), and he conducted his business on the principle of the iron hand in the iron glove.

"A pawner is a man in difficulties," he always warned his apprentice whenever he was called away and had to leave the shop in that youth's care. "And a man in difficulties is a man in despair. Now despair, my boy, makes a man untrustworthy; it turns him into a liar, a swindler, a cheat. Poverty may not be a crime, but in my experience it's the cause of most of 'em. Poverty debases a man, and a base man is a man to keep a sharp eye on. It tells us in the Bible that it's hard enough for a rich man to enter the Kingdom of Heaven, so think how much harder it is for a poor one and the dishonest things he'll do to get there! He'll swear on his mother's grave that the article he's pawning is worth twice as much as ever we could sell it for. He'll give you his solemn word that it's only a loan and that he'll come back tomorrow and redeem it. We know those redeemers, my boy. Like tomorrow, they never come. So you watch out!"

With these words, Mr. Thompson had left his apprentice as he and his brother-in-law, Mr. Long, had gone off into the country for Christmas and the New Year. Then, recollecting that it was a festive season, he had thought a joke would be in order.

"And if anyone comes," he added, with a grisly twinkle in his eye, "and wants to pawn a soul, you just send him down to Mr. Long's! A Merry Christmas, my boy, and if you watch out, a prosperous New Year!"

Accordingly, the apprentice watched out; he watched out in ways, perhaps, that even his master never suspected.

He was a neat, thin youth of sixteen and was in the fourth year of his apprenticeship. He wore brass-rimmed spectacles (borrowed from stock), which lent him a studious air and enlarged his eyes, which were, otherwise, inclined to be small and furtive.

Although the shop was not yet open, he was already seated on his high stool in a discreet wooden cubbyhole that resembled a confessional, occupied in resting his elbows on the counter and making mysterious entries in a ledger. Beside him was a short piece of mahogany on which his name—Mister Coot—was painted in black; and beside that was a yellowed card announcing that "The House of Thompson wishes all its customers a Happy New Year." It was kept in a small linen wallet and brought out every year.

Presently, having completed his entries, Coot gazed at the festive card and, with a jerk of inspiration, arranged the piece of mahogany over it to produce the heartwarming sentiment that "The House of Thompson wishes Mister Coot a Happy New Year."

He sat for several minutes admiring it, then fished in his waistcoat pocket and came up with a massive silver watch secured to his person by means of a stout steel chain, like a criminal. He flicked up the lid and, observing that it lacked a minute till opening time, he thoughtfully picked his nose. At eight o'clock, Coot-time, he slipped from his stool, crawled under the counter, and unbolted the door, returning with ratlike speed and dexterity lest a customer should catch him at a disadvantage. The House of Thompson was open to the new year.

The first customer was an aging actor, hoping to raise five shillings on a pair of breeches that weren't worth three.

"And—and a Happy New Year to you!" he finished up, leaning over the counter with a mixture of affability and confidence through which despair showed in patches.

Coot smiled his pawnbroker's smile (which was next door to an undertaker's) and silently removed his name from the card, thereby returning the greeting and saving his breath.

He began to examine the breeches with fastidious care.

"Did I leave a guinea in it, old boy?" asked the customer with pathetic jocularity as Coot turned out the pocket.

Coot said nothing; he was watching out. He pushed the breeches back to their owner.

"Ay'm afraid they ain't much use to us. A bit too far gone."

The actor was thunderstruck. He was outraged; he was humiliated; he was bitterly dismayed. He argued, he pleaded, he begged—

"All right. A shillin', then," interposed Coot with composure, when he judged the customer to be sufficiently low in spirits to be agreeable to anything.

"A shilling? But—"

"Try Mr. Long's in 'Enrietta Street. P'raps my colleague, Mr. Jeremiah Snipe, might up me a penny or two. On the other 'and, 'e might down me a sixpence. Go on. Shove off and try Mr. Jeremiah."

The pawnbroker's apprentice stared coolly at the customer, knowing him to be a beaten man. He wouldn't try Jeremiah— never in a month of Sundays! He wouldn't dare risk another such slap in the face. He was done for; he didn't even kick up much of a fuss when tuppence was knocked off his shilling: a penny for receipt and warehousing and a penny for two months' interest in advance.

"Really," he muttered. "That's a bit sharp, ain't it?"

For answer, Coot slid his eyes towards two framed notices that hung on the cubbyhole's wall. Decorated with the emblems of the trade, in the manner of illuminated missals, they set forth the rates of interest permitted by law and the regulations designed to protect both parties, in a lending transaction, from the sharp practice of each other.

Wearily the actor shook his head. There was no sense in wasting his eyesight on the small print. Everything was above-board, and the apprentice was as honest as an iron bar.

"I'll be back next week," he said, taking his tenpence and mournfully patting his pawned garment, "to redeem you, old friend."

"Redeem? You don't know the meanin' of the word," murmured Coot, as the customer departed into the not-quite new year.

Next came a fellow trying to pawn a wig, but the watchful apprentice found lice in it and sent him packing; and after him came a lady with the odd request that the apprentice should turn his back while she took off her petticoat hoops on which she wanted to borrow seven shillings.

"Turn me back?" said Coot, mindful of Mr. Thompson's instruction to watch out. "Ay'm afraid not. You might even nick me timepiece," he said, laying that precious object (which his father had given him to mark the beginning of his apprentice-ship) on the counter. "I'll just sit as I am and not put temptation in your way."

So the lady, with abject blushings, was forced to display her dirty linen and torn stockings to Coot's dreadful smile.

"Why—they ain't even real whalebone," he said when the hoops were offered across the counter. "Ay'm afraid they ain't much use to us. Two shillin's. That's the best."

"You dirty little skinflint!"

"Come to think on it," said Coot, rightly taking the expression as a personal insult, "a shillin' and ninepence is nearer the mark."

He pushed the hoops back. "Or you can try Mr. Long's in 'Enrietta Street. My colleague, Mr. Jeremiah Snipe, might up me a penny or two. On the other 'and, 'e might down me a six-pence. Go on. Shove off and try Mr. Jeremiah."

He stared at her trembling lips and tear-filled eyes. She was done for, all right. She'd not try Jeremiah—never in a month of Sundays!

He was right, of course; he was always right; that was why Mr. Thompson trusted him.

"I'll be back, of course," said the lady, struggling to salvage some shreds of her self-respect, "to redeem them next week."

With that, she snatched up her shilling and ninepence (less tuppence) and departed into the fast-aging year.

Coot smiled and watched her through the window, noticing how her unsupported skirts dragged in the snow and wiped out her footprints even as she made them.

"Redeem?" he murmured. "You don't know the meanin' of the word!"

He sat still for a moment, lost in philosophy; then he slipped from his stool, crawled under the counter, and bolted the street door. Returning, he gathered up the hoops and breeches, ticketed them, and carried them into the warehousing room at the back of the shop.

Here, in a dispiriting gloom that smelled of fallen fortunes, humbled pride, and camphor to keep off the moth, they took their places amidst a melancholy multitude of pledges awaiting redemption. Wigs, coats, gowns and sheets, walking sticks, wedding rings, shoes, and watches waited in a long and doleful queue as, month by month, they were moved up till, at the end of a year and a day, they were sold off unredeemed.

It was a grim sight, but Coot, being in the trade, was not unduly moved by it. He surveyed the crowded racks and pigeonholes and shelves.

"Redeemed?" he whispered. "You don't know the meanin' of the word!"

When he arrived back, he found his cubbyhole as black as

night; in his absence, a shadow, thick as a customer, seemed to have taken up residence.

"What the 'ell—" began the apprentice; then, craning his neck, he saw the gipsy woman at the window, obscuring the light.

She'd got her arms stretched out and was pressing her face and hands against the dirty glass as if to see what was being offered for sale. She gave Coot quite a turn, looming up like that; angrily, he waved her off.

She grinned at him and pointed to the sign that hung over the door. Coot frowned; of all folk, gipsies needed watching the most. Turn your back on them and they'd have the buttons off your coat.

"Shove off!" he mouthed. "And a 'orrible Noo Year!"

But the woman continued to grin, showing a set of teeth much too good for her. She pointed to the sign again and moved aside so that Coot could see her donkey. Vigorously he shook his head.

"No livestock!" he shouted. "Don't take 'em. Try Mr. Long's in 'Enrietta Street!"

Now it was the gipsy's turn to shake her head, so Coot unbolted the door and it opened by a crack. At once a sinewy brown hand came through and grasped the lintel. Coot glared at it and meditated slamming the door hard.

"Rachel's blessing on you, dear!" came the gipsy's harsh voice.

"Wotcher want?"

"Got something to pawn."

"Nicked?"

"You know better than to ask that, dear!"

He did indeed. Nevertheless he had to watch out. Come to think of it, there wasn't much time left for watching out; Mr. Thompson was due back in a couple of days.

"What is it, then?"

"Garment."

Coot snorted. The gipsy stank like one o'clock. He'd not have advanced a sixpence on every stitch she stood up in—including whatever she wore underneath.

"Try Mr. Long's in 'Enrietta Street," he said, and tried to shut the door.

"Real silk, dear," said the gipsy. "Fur collar and all. Worth a mint."

Coot opened the door a further two inches and applied his eye to the gap, taking care to duck under the grasping hand. He saw that the woman was clutching a bundle under her free arm.

"That it?"

She laughed and tossed back a flap of the bundle. Coot saw the top of a baby's head. There was a black mark on it.

"Don't you bring that in 'ere," said Coot nervously. "It's got somethin' nasty."

"But it's cold out here."

"You should have thought on that before. You gipsies ain't fit to 'ave babies. It don't come in 'ere."

To Coot's surprise, the gipsy nodded meekly and returned the baby to its basket. Then she came back carrying a black article that she'd removed from one of the bundles on the donkey. It was silk, sure enough.

"All right," he said, letting go of the door and bolting back to his place with his customary neatness and speed. But as he settled on his stool, he couldn't help feeling that she'd been too quick for him and come in while he was still at a disadvantage.

Silently the garment was passed over the counter and Coot began to examine it. It was a cloak of black silk with a violet lining. The collar was real fox fur, and round the inside of the neck there was some delicate embroidery. It certainly was a handsome article, but nevertheless, the pawnbroker's apprentice knew he had to watch out.

" 'Ow did you come by it?"

"It was my father's, dear."

"Oh, yes. Your father's." Coot grinned knowingly.

"My father's!" repeated the woman, with a touch of anger.

"Where are you from?" pursued Coot. "Got to ask on account of the law."

"Kent."

"That's a long way off."

"T'other side o' the moon!"

"Far enough, eh?" said Coot, meaningly.

The woman nodded. "Far enough, dear."

" 'Ow much was you expectin' on this garment?"

"Two silver pounds, dear."

"And the rest! D'you think I'm off me 'ead? Two pound to a thievin' old thing like you? You're 'avin' me on! Two pound for a bit of furry rubbish like this? Take a look at it . . . take a good look! Moth in the collar like nobody's business! And what about this stitchin'? Won't last out a week! And—and look 'ere! Dirty great stain that won't come out in a month of Sundays!" (There was indeed a rusty brown stain on the violet lining, though it was not a large one.) "And the 'ole garment whiffs something awful. Never get that smell off it! If I was to let you 'ave five shillin's on this, I'd be doin' you a favour and meself an injury."

"Only five shillings, dear? I was hoping, I was counting on more than that. I got my little one to care for."

"Like I said, my good woman, you should 'ave thought on that before. Five shillin's is the 'ouse's best."

"A pound, dear. Make it a silver pound!"

"Why don't you shove off? Try Mr. Long's in 'Enrietta Street. Maybe my colleague, Mr. Jeremiah Snipe, might up me a penny or two. On the other 'and, 'e might down me a sixpence. Go on. Shove off!"

"Ten shillings! Give me ten silver shillings!"

"Five. What would my master say if I was to give you over the odds? 'E'd 'ave me out quicker'n a dose of rhubarb! You want to do me down, you do! Five shillin's—or I send for the constable!"

This was Coot's master stroke. The woman's eyes widened and she began to tremble. He'd got her!

"All right, then—all right!" she muttered. "Give me the five silver shillings and a receipt."

"Receipt? What do you want that for?"

"To—to redeem my cloak. I—I'm coming back for it . . . soon."

"Redeem?" said Coot. "You don't know the meanin' of the word!"

But the gipsy insisted with all the obstinate ignorance of her tribe; so Coot chuckled and wrote out a receipt.

"That'll cost you another threepence," he said, giving her the money and packing her off out of the shop.

When she was safely out of sight, he bolted the door and examined the cloak again. He tried it on, but it was far too big for him, and covered him like a shroud. He tried lifting a corner and flinging it over his shoulder, in the manner of an ancient Roman, but it really wasn't his style. Regretfully he took it off, noticing that the rusty stain was on the left-hand side and would, had he been of a height, have covered his heart; as it was, it rested over his sweetbread.

Thoughtfully he stroked the fur collar and looked again at the embroidery round the inside of the neck. He pursed his lips; then he grinned broadly. The embroidery was not, as he'd first supposed, a pattern; it was instead a line of Gothic letters making up a text.

"*I know that my redeemer liveth*," said the pawned cloak.

"That's what they all say!" chuckled the pawnbroker's apprentice. "But they don't know the meanin' of the word!"

By half past seven in the evening, the brave New Year was torn to tatters. No more snow had fallen, and clean white streets were crossed and double-crossed by the black passing of men and women going about their daily affairs.

Freed from toil, the pawnbroker's apprentice chose to walk where the snow had been well trodden down. He was wearing his best shoes and did not want to spoil them; also, perhaps, at the back of his watchful mind was the thought that it was best to leave no footprints, as his journey would not bear the closest examination.

He walked with a springy step, quite like a young lamb; it was as if all his hours of grimly patient dealing had compressed him like a spring, so that now he leaped forth with a youthful twang. He was done up to the nines, wearing a dazzling waistcoat, a ginger wig, and silken breeches of egg-yolk yellow. He was a butterfly; he was a youth transformed.

Presently he reached Henrietta Street and gave a smart double knock on the door of Mr. Long's (Loans Arranged on Modest Security), and while he waited, winked up knowingly at the three brass balls. Jeremiah Snipe opened the door.

"A 'Appy Noo Year, Jerry!"

"Same to you, Cooty. And with three brass knobs on!"

Jeremiah, who was renowned for his wit, smirked as he stepped aside to admit his colleague and friend. He was a month younger than Coot and of a round-faced, angelic appearance that tended to make his customers feel ashamed of bargaining with him. But there lurked under that soft exterior a spirit every bit as stern as Coot's. Well, perhaps not quite so stern, as he'd been in the trade four weeks less than his friend, but he was catching up fast.

"You've got something, haven't you, Cooty?"

Coot beamed.

"Thought so," said Jeremiah shrewdly. "That's why you're done up like the cat's dinner."

"Take a squint at this," said Coot, ignoring his colleague's wit. "Gipsy brought it."

He produced the cloak. Jeremiah whistled, then crawled under his counter so that he might examine the article from his usual situation. Coot made to follow him when he saw Jeremiah's boot defensively poised, so he stayed the wrong side of the counter, reflecting that, whenever positions were reversed, he defended his own territory in the same way.

"Five pounds," said Jeremiah when he had finished studying the garment.

"Don't you come the skinflint with me, Jerry," said Coot affably. "Make it six."

Jeremiah smiled like an angel in a stained-glass window—a very stained-glass window—and nodded. "Six it is, then."

Agreement having been thus reached, the two industrious apprentices settled down to complete the necessary business of their interesting arrangement. As was required by law, Jeremiah noted down the transaction in Mr. Long's ledger, while Coot did the same in his own ledger, which had nothing to do with the law. Then Jeremiah handed over six pounds of Mr. Long's money, less the cost of warehousing, receipting, and two months' interest in advance, as was permitted by law. This done, Coot handed back to Jeremiah half of the proceeds, as was demanded by the terms of their partnership and the liability of their friendship.

"It's not as if we was thieves," Coot had said to Jeremiah when the idea had first come to him and Jeremiah had cast doubts on its honesty. "We're just businessmen. We ain't reely breakin' the law. You might say we ain't even goin' close enough to touch it! Look at it this way, Jerry," he'd gone on, feeling that his colleague remained unconvinced. "Think of bankers."

"Well?"

"They're lawful, ain't they?"

"According to their lights."

"Well, then—you put your money in a bank—"

"I don't. I keep it in my shoe."

"I was just supposin'. You put your money in a bank, and then the bank goes and does all sorts of things with it. Lends it out, invests it, buys things with it . . . and generally treats it like the money was its own. And that's what we'll be doin'. Folk pawn articles with us, and we pawn 'em again to each other. We're only borrerin' and lendin' out at interest. We ain't stealin', we're just reinvestin'. And as long as nobody catches on, we'll end up in pocket. Bound to."

"But what if they *do* catch on?" asked Jeremiah, filled with something of the foreboding of the ancient prophet whose name he bore.

"It won't 'appen," Coot had said firmly. "Never in a month of Sundays. It'd need more rotten luck than we got a right to expect. Listen, Jerry: in business, you got to take some chances. I'm more experienced than you. Just let me do the worryin' and be 'appy to take the money. That's all I ask."

So Jeremiah, borne down by Coot's arguments, and borne up by the prospect of income, agreed. All this had taken place a year ago, since when the two industrious apprentices had prospered exceedingly, being careful to transact their private business when their masters were out of town. It was for such opportunities that Coot and Jeremiah obeyed their masters more fully than they suspected, by watching out.

The Cloak

"Where shall we go tonight, Coot?" asked Jeremiah when he had ticketed and stowed away the cloak in his master's warehouse room.

"Ay raither fancy the Hopera," said Coot, with extreme cultivation. "So get your rags on . . . and don't forget your claret pot."

The pot referred to was Jeremiah's silver christening mug, which occupied, in his affections, a place similar to the great silver timepiece in Coot's.

At a quarter past eight o'clock the two apprentices left Henrietta Street for their night on the town. They marched in step, as if an invisible band were playing—just for them. They were smart, they were elegant, they were dapper. They gladdened the heart and imparted a youthful gaiety to the precincts of Bow Street. Their eyes sparkled, their shoe buckles twinkled, so there was brightness at both ends, and money in the middle.

To begin with, they took in—as Coot put it—the second act of the opera. They went up into the gallery, where, with footmen, students, and other lively apprentices, they whistled and hooted and clapped, cheered on the lady performers and threw oranges down on bare heads in the pit till they were requested to leave or take the consequences. Then they went to a respectable inn and got mildly drunk on claret and port, after which Jeremiah was sick on the pavement and Coot fell into the snow. Partly recovered, they found a cockfight in Feathers Court and lost ten shillings each on a bird that lay down before it was so much as tickled. Then they joined up with half a dozen weavers' apprentices and had a tremendous time trying to steal door knockers and pelting a pursuing constable with stones disguised as snowballs.

They parted with the weavers' apprentices—who'd run out of money—and took up with a couple of likely lasses who'd caught their roving eyes in the Strand. They told the girls they were soldiers on leave and that they'd been wounded in the foreign wars. They limped a bit to prove it . . . then kissed and cuddled and bought the girls supper in Maiden Lane, lording it over the waiter till the wretched man felt like pouring hot soup over the apprentices' heads.

But he did no such thing, and Coot tipped him well to impress the girls with his careless generosity.

Coot and Jeremiah were firm believers in keeping business and pleasure apart. Though Coot would have fought with a cringing customer to the last breath in his body to beat him down by a shilling, he thought nothing at all of casting such a shilling (and two others like it) into the waiter's greasy palm. And Jeremiah, who, with crocodile tears, would have denied a customer an extra penny, happily filled and refilled his silver tankard with wine, spilling it on the table and in his lap, at threepence a throw.

At last the two bright apprentices tottered back towards Drury Lane, quite worn out from their night on the town. They'd broken windows, tipped an old watchman into a horse trough, and unscrewed a lamp from a standing coach. They'd lost their lasses somewhere round the back of Covent Garden, and they'd not a penny left to bless themselves with, but they were happy and singing, and they kicked on front doors as they passed, with night-piercing screeches of " 'Appy Noo Year!"

"Look!" hiccupped Jeremiah, staring boozily down Drury Lane. "You got a customer, Cooty!"

Coot blinked and stared. Several figures seemed to be outside Mr. Thompson's, and they were on fire; flames were coming up all round them. Coot wiped his eyes and the figures reduced themselves to two: a tall man and a linkboy who had, presumably, guided him there. The linkboy's torch leaped and danced and illuminated the three brass balls in a manner that was quite uncanny; the masks of Tragedy fairly glowered down.

Dazedly, Coot gazed upon the scene, then shouted out, "Shove off! We ain't open till eight o'clock!"

The customer saluted him but did not move, so Coot pursued a winding, uncertain path to confront him and make his meaning clearer. The linkboy, seeing the angry apprentice, bolted and left the street to the feeble memory of his light.

"I told you," said Coot, squaring up to the customer in the manner of a weaving prizefighter, "we're shut. Closed. No business, see? All gone bye-bye. Shove off and come back in the mornin'."

The stranger, who was a good twelve inches taller than the pawnbroker's apprentice, looked down sombrely. There was something nasty about the man; he had a hooked nose like a vulture and eyes that seemed to keep shifting about all over his face. Coot took a step back and bumped into Jeremiah, who had been sheltering behind him.

Suddenly the stranger reached into his pocket, and Coot, who was expecting a knife or a pistol, endeavoured to get behind his colleague. But the stranger only produced a slip of paper.

"Wassat?"

"Don't you recognize it?" inquired the stranger harshly.

" 'Ow can I recko'nize it when you keeps wavin' it about?"

"It's a receipt."

"Really? You don't say."

"It's a receipt for a cloak. You gave it to a gipsy woman this morning. She pawned the cloak with you for five shillings."

"Well, what of it?" said Coot valiantly. Events were moving a little too quickly for him quite to grasp their significance.

"It wasn't hers."

"Nicked? What an 'orrible thing. I'm sorry to 'ear it. Them gipsies! Night-night!"

"It was mine. I gave it out for cleaning. I can prove it was mine. There was a text inside the collar. *I know that my re-deemer liveth.* I am that redeemer, my friend. I want my cloak back. Either that, or I fetch a magistrate to search your premises and examine your books. That's the law, my friend. So bring out the cloak."

Coot felt Jeremiah beside him begin to shake and tremble like a straw in a tempest. Although he couldn't see him, he knew his face had gone dead white and that he was crying; he always did.

But he, Coot, was made of sterner stuff; four weeks sterner. Delay, that was it. Put off the evil hour and it might never come to pass. There was no sense in meeting trouble half way. Far better to step aside and let it go rampaging past.

He informed the stranger that, at that precise moment, the cloak in question was in the firm's warehouse, which, unfortunately, was some distance away. It couldn't be helped, and he, Coot, sympathised with the gent's annoyance. But that was how things were, and nothing was to be gained by crying over spilt milk. He would do his very best to obtain the garment in the course of a day or two. He couldn't speak fairer than that.

Just what was in Coot's complicated mind was hard to say. Perhaps he thought the stranger was a bad dream from which he would awaken if only given the time.

"I want my cloak now," said the stranger, refusing to behave like a dream. "Either that, or pay me the value of the garment. Ten pounds. The cloak, ten pounds—or the law."

At this point, Jeremiah spoke up. His voice fell upon the night like the wail of his namesake, the prophet, deploring the loss of Jerusalem.

"Give him the ten pound, Cooty! For God's sake, give him the ten pounds!"

The worst had happened, like he'd always known it would. The rotten luck that was more than they'd any right to expect had befallen them. They were done for.

"And where am I goin' to get the ten pound?" snarled Coot, turning on his friend, who retreated several paces, weeping bitterly.

"I don't know—I don't know!"

"Pardon me," said Coot to the stranger, who appeared to be relishing the friends' predicament. "Ay wish to consult with may colleague on business."

He joined Jeremiah.

"Keep your voice down!"

"Give him the ten pounds then!"

"Can't. You give 'im the cloak."

"But I lent six pounds on it! How am I going to account for that? Old Long comes back the day after tomorrow!"

"So does old Thompson! And six pound is easier to find than ten."

"But I'll have to find it! You'll just be dropping me in it, won't you, Cooty?"

Coot laid a hand on Jeremiah's shoulder, as much to steady himself as to reassure his colleague.

"We're in it together, Jerry. We'll find a way. You just see if we don't. It'd take more rotten luck than we got a right to expect if we didn't manage some'ow. For Gawd's sake, Jerry, give 'im back the cloak!"

"You'll help, then?"

"I swear it. On me mother's grave," muttered Coot, forgetful of the fact that his mother was not yet in it. He returned to the stranger.

"We are sorry to 'ave hinconvenienced you," he said coldly,

"but the garment was taken in good faith. We—I 'ad no idea the garment was nicked. 'Owever, hunder the circs., we are prepared to return your property at no hextra charge. My colleague and I will—"

"At once!" interrupted the stranger, "or I go for the magistrate!"

"If you was a smaller man," said Coot venomously, "I'd punch you right in the nose!"

"Six pound!" wept Jeremiah. "How are we going to find it?" The cloak had been given up, and the friends were still in Mr. Long's shop.

"Don't you worry, Jerry," said Coot. "I'll come up with somethin'. I've never let you down yet."

"You've never had the chance!"

"Now that weren't friendly, Jerry. But I'll look after you."

"You'd better, Cooty. You'd better!"

"What do you mean by that?"

"If I go to jail, so do you. There's other things, you know. If I get caught on this one, you get caught on the others. Don't you think I'm going down alone. You always said we were in it together."

"That's nasty, Jerry. Particularly as you've always been 'appy to sit back and enjoy the money I thought of gettin'. But I don't 'old it against you. You're younger than me. All I want you to consider is that . . . well . . . what's the sense in both of us goin' down when it need only be one? Wouldn't it be better if one of us stayed safe so's 'e could 'elp the other when the time came?"

"All right. You take the blame and I'll help you when you come out of jail."

"Point taken," said Coot. "But the money 'appens to be missin' from your 'ouse, not mine. Otherwise I'd be 'appy to oblige."

Jeremiah began to cry again; then, seeing that his tears had no effect, he grew exceedingly angry. He made it plain that he did not trust Coot. Coot had got him into it, and Coot was going to get him out. Or suffer by his side.

At last Coot was forced to see how matters stood. Jeremiah was taking advantage of previous acts of friendship and was holding them against him. He just wasn't capable of distinguishing between business and pleasure.

"If that's the way it's to be," he said bitterly, "we got to lay our 'ands on six pounds, and another five shillin's, which is the hamount I'm in to Mr. Thompson."

"And before the day after tomorrow," said Jeremiah, anticipating any attempt to delay.

"Six pounds ain't a fortune," went on Coot, ignoring the interruption. "As I see it, there's reely only two ways of gettin' it. We could either borrer it—or nick it."

"I ain't stealing," said Jeremiah quickly. He felt that it was in Coot's mind for him, Jeremiah, to do the nicking. "You can get hung for that."

"Point taken," said Coot. "No nickin' on account of the risk. Although—"

"Any stealing you can do yourself, Cooty."

"Like I said, no nickin'. That leaves borrerin'."

"Who'd lend us six pounds, Cooty?"

"Good question. What about pawnin' more of the stock to each other?"

"I've had enough of that. We're sure to get found out."

Coot sighed and stared at his overcautious associate. His eye fell upon Jeremiah's christening mug.

"All right," he said slowly. "Seein' as 'ow you've taken things out of my 'ands, you can do somethin' yourself for a change. 'Ow about pawning' that pot of yours?"

Jeremiah began to cry again. Tears ran out of his eyes as fast as melting snow. Contemptuously Coot waited.

"You're a pig, Cooty," said Jeremiah at length, still sobbing. "Take it, then, and give me six pounds!"

"Six pounds?" said Coot. "Ay'm afraid," he began from force of habit, and then corrected himself. "Climb down a bit, Jerry. You know I daren't make it six. Old Thompson goes through the books like a dog through a dust 'eap when 'e gets 'ome! 'E'd never stand for six pound! Not for an old piece of Sheffield plate with scratches all over it!"

"It's not plate! It's solid silver! I wasn't christened in plate!"

"Tell us another, Jerry! Look at it! Copper showin' through everywhere, plain as a baby's bum. Two pound is the very best. Solid silver my eye!"

"You're a dirty rotten liar, Cooty! Make it four pound, then?"

"I daren't, Jerry. It's more than me place is worth. Tell you what though. I'll make it two pound ten shillin's and that'll only leave you three pound ten to find. There, now, don't say I ain't comin' up trumps. That's what I call real friendship!"

"And that's what I call dirty swindling, Cooty. You're not leaving here till all the money's made up. If you do, you'll be right in it alongside of me. You can pawn your watch. . . ."

"Me timepiece?" cried Coot, shocked to the core. "But it's a valuable hobject. No . . . I couldn't do that."

"Then it's jail for the both of us."

"Do you know you're bein' very nasty, Jerry? And 'ard. I never thought you was so 'ard underneath."

"Your watch, Cooty. Come on. Let's have a look."

Silently Coot withdrew the gleaming article.

"This 'ere timepiece is worth—is worth fifteen pound if it's worth a penny," he said sorrowfully. "You're takin' an 'ammer to crack a egg, Jerry."

"Pass it over, Cooty."

Coot released his treasure from its chain and laid it on Jeremiah's counter. Jeremiah fell to examining it closely.

"Fifteen pound? Oh dear me, no! Old Long would have me committed for life if I was to go along with that," said Jeremiah. Like Coot, he had good reason to fear his master's scrutiny of the books, and, also, he was still smarting under Coot's treatment of his christening mug.

"If I was to give you two pounds, I'd be stretchin' it, Cooty."

"Two pound? You dirty little skinflint!" shouted Coot, banging on the counter so that the watch jumped in alarm. Jeremiah folded his arms.

"To begin with," he said, "it ain't silver. It's only pewter. And what's more, it's stopped ever since you dropped it earlier on. And it's all scratched and dented like a tinker's spoon. That there chain's worth more than the watch."

"That there timepiece was give me by my pa!" said Coot savagely. "I wouldn't be pawnin' it but to 'elp *you!* Come on! Give us twelve pound!"

"You'll take two pound ten shillings," said Jeremiah coldly. "Just like me."

"You lousy rotten stinking little skinflint!" raged Coot, attempting to regain possession of his watch. "I'd sooner rot in jail than be treated like this! Oh, for Gawd's sake, Jerry, make it nine pound and call it a day? Please, Jerry! It's me pa's watch! It's valuable to me . . . It—it's all I got in the world!"

"Two pound ten," said Jeremiah. "Less warehousing, of course."

"You're cuttin' off your own nose, Jerry. You're cuttin' your own throat."

"And yours, Cooty," said Jeremiah, not without satisfaction.

"What about the other pound and five shillin's?"

"I'll take your weskit for half of it; and you can take my new coat for the rest. That's fair."

"Your coat, Jerry, it pains me to tell you, ain't worth more'n two shillin's. I'll 'ave your best shoes, too!"

"I don't like you, Cooty."

"Nor me you, Jerry. And I never 'ave."

Following on this frightful revelation, there was a pause.

"But it's been worth it," said Jeremiah finally. He had been brooding on how he might display, even more crushingly, his contempt for Coot. "Yes. I don't begrudge the experience. It's shown you up, Cooty. I'm glad to have paid to see you, really to see you. I've had a narrow escape, Cooty. I might have turned out like you if I hadn't seen what you're like underneath."

"Likewise," said Coot, determined to outdo Jeremiah. "And what's more, I'd willin'ly 'ave paid out double to see what I 'ave just seen. 'Orrible. Made me sick to me stomach. You're the sort, Jerry, what gets 'uman bein's a bad name. Thank Gawd I found out in time."

Jeremiah, who could come up with nothing better for the moment, opened the shop door and indicated that his colleague's presence was no longer welcome. Breathing heavily, the two apprentices stood in the doorway. Coot thought of punching J. Snipe in the face. He shook his head. He recollected, *Vengeance is mine; I will repay, saith the Lord.* He stared up and saw the weighty emblem of Mr. Long's trade poised above Jeremiah's head. Go on, God! he thought. Fix 'im! But the three brass balls remained stolidly in the air.

"And don't you go sending me any of your customers any more," said Jeremiah, having thought of something else. "Because I'll tell them what a grinding little skinflint you are. I'll show you up. If you send them to me, I'll give them what they ask for."

"And I'll give 'em more!" said Coot furiously. "Just for the pleasure of hexposin' you! I wouldn't send a dog to you, Jerry!"

"If I could find that gipsy," said Jeremiah, stung to the quick, "I'd get down on my hands and knees and thank her for letting me see the truth."

"I might remind you," said Coot loftily, "that I'm the one she came to. I'm the one what was chosen to be redeemed."

Jeremiah breathed deeply.

"Garn!" he said. "You don't know the meaning of the word!"

Slowly Coot made his way back to Drury Lane. A church clock began to strike midnight; the New Year was past. Unthinkingly Coot fumbled for his watch to see if the church was right. No watch; no waistcoat, even. He shivered as he felt the cold strike through.

Snow had begun to fall again, tiny flakes that pricked and glittered as they passed through the feeble rays of the street lamps. Little by little, as the snow settled, the black scars and furrows that marked the road lost their sharpness and seemed to fade. Presently they were reduced to smudgy ghosts, like rubbed-out entries in a ledger.

By the time he reached Drury Lane, the snow was fairly whirling down and he was as white as the street. The flakes kept stinging him in the eyes, so that he could scarcely see where he was going.

It was under these circumstances that he saw the apparition; and considering how much he'd drunk and what he'd been through, it wasn't surprising. He saw the Holy Family.

Out of the snow they came: the laden donkey, the radiant mother, and the tall, saintly man beside her. Coot crossed himself as they drew near.

"Buy an apple, dear!" called out the gipsy woman. "Buy a sweet Kent apple for good luck!"

"A Happy New Year! A Happy New Year, my boy!" called out the man by her side.

He was the stranger, the hook-nosed stranger, stalking along in his treacherous, ruinous black silk cloak!

They'd been in it together—the pair of them! They'd done him! They'd swindled him! They'd stripped him bare! The thieves! The rogues! The rotten, crafty swindlers! They were all in it . . . most likely the baby and the donkey, too!

Coot stood as still as a post, and then began to shake and tremble with indignation. Helplessly he watched them pass him by and then vanish like a dream into the whirling curtain of snow.

Then he gathered together his tattered shreds of self-respect and reflected on many things.

"I suppose it were worth it," he whispered. "All things considered, I suppose it were worth it in the end."

With aching head and shaking hands, he unlocked the door of Mr. Thompson's (Personal Banking upon Moderate Terms) and let himself in.

He leaned across the counter, staring into the dark emptiness, which was his place in life.

"If anybody comes in to pawn a soul," he whispered, remembering his master's little joke, "just you send 'em down to Mr. Long's! But what if," he went on, smiling mournfully to himself, "they comes in to redeem one?"

He went to the door again and opened it. He stared out into the teeming weather. Although the little family had long since gone, he fancied he saw them imprinted on the ceaseless white. He tried to recollect their features—the man, the woman, the tiny child. But they were just shapes, haunting shapes that left not footprints; all that remained was a vague perfume of apples and spice.

"Try my colleague in 'Enrietta Street," he called softly into the night. "Go on; try Mr. Jeremiah Snipe, my friend."

THE VALENTINE

NOT VERY FAR FROM JESSOP & POTTERSFIELD'S, IN LITTLE Knightrider Street, is St. Martin's Churchyard, where wicked children hide among the headstones, waiting to nick any wreaths and sell them back to the undertakers. Horrible, unfeeling trade! But even in the midst of death life must go on!

One cold, bright morning in February (it was the fourteenth, but they didn't know it), three such shrunken malevolents played and darted among the dead, like apprentice spooks. . . .

"Look out—look out! There's summ'un comin'!"

Instantly they vanished behind the tombs and crouched, trembling in the freezing grass, as the Lady in Black drifted towards them over the green. They quaked. What was she? Was she a witch, a spirit, a ghost? . . .

They'd seen her before; she haunted the churchyard, and one grave in particular . . . the one under the shadow of the bent elder tree. They'd heard that every St. Valentine's Day she brought a wreath of flowering ivy and wild garlic.

Sure enough, they saw she carried a wreath, and their interest quickened. She was deeply, impenetrably veiled, and only the dim sparkle of her eyes could be seen as she approached and paused by the graveside, glancing first at the overhanging bough, and then down to the smooth coverlet of grass. Quickly she knelt and laid the wreath against the headstone.

"Get a move on!" muttered the tiny watchers, perishing from stillness and cold. "Get a move on, can't yer?"

But the Lady in Black remained in her prayerful attitude for several minutes, as if longing to be translated into stone and stay for ever by the grave under the elder tree. Only a faint trembling of her veil betrayed that she was still alive; she was whispering to the sleeper under the grass.

At length she rose and drifted out of the churchyard with a step as silent and light as thistledown. The wreath remained behind. . . .

"Quick!"

"What if 'e's watchin'?"

"Oo?"

" 'Im, down under!"

"Garn!"

"Look! The grass moved!"

"It were the wind."

"But what if it were *'im,* turnin' over?"

"All right, I'll ask 'im. Did yer turn over, mister?"

The three demons held their breath, and one of them pressed his ear to the ground. There was no answer.

"Don't you mind us, mister. It's nuffink personal. It's just that we got to live anyways we can."

Six feet below, Orlando Brown, who had been taken from this life in his sixteenth year, deeply loved and much missed, held his tongue as his lonely tribute and remembrance went the way of young flesh and was heartlessly nicked. . . .

Jessop & Pottersfield's had buried him on St. Valentine's Day, just five years before. They'd done it handsomely and tastefully . . . which was a sight more than Alfred Todds's would have done had the business gone its way; but luckily that was before Mr. Todds's had employed the odious Hawkins.

Hawkins was a nothing, a nobody, a lean, scraggy undertaker's lad so anxious to get on in life (which was comical considering his trade!) that he made himself ridiculous in the district—ridiculous and dreaded!

The very sight of him in his outgrown blacks (he seemed to keep on sprouting like a stick of starved celery), hanging about at street corners, eavesdropping on gossip, and following physicians and midwives, made cold shivers run up and down your spine. He made folk uneasy, especially the old and the sick. He was like a gleaner in the cobbled fields, waiting for the Grim Reaper so he might gather in the fallen sheaves.

His eager knock and his low, horribly respectful voice—"Mr. Todds tenders his sincerest condolences, and might he have the honour of furnishing the funeral?"—made you sick that anyone could stoop so low in the way of business.

These were the feelings of Miss Jessop, lovely daughter of the proprietor of Jessop & Pottersfield's. She loathed and despised Hawkins, who, despite his undeniably dreamy eyes and long poetical hands (with fingernails permanently wearing the livery of the trade), was coarse and pushing and always picking up custom where he had no right to.

The Lord alone knew where Todds's had found him—on some rubbish heap, most likely—but he'd taken to the trade with a passion and zeal that were quite unnatural. He'd worked his fingers to the bone (and they looked it!) for Todds's, scrubbing their dreary yard, washing the customers, running errands for their drunken joiner (who couldn't put a screw in straight to save his life), polishing the lamps on the hearse, and then managing to turn out in time for the funeral, glossy as a beetle in his working blacks. At first he carried a branch of candles; but then when he kept sprouting, he took a turn at bearing. You could always pick out his spiky shanks, coming and going under the pall.

"That lad's a gem," boasted Mr. Todds to Mr. Jessop. "Mark my words, he'll go far!"

And he did go far. In fact, he went right to the confines of Little Knightrider Street and poached trade right out of Jessop & Pottersfield's very pockets. Sometimes Miss Jessop felt that were her ma and pa to drop dead tomorrow, Hawkins would be at the door within the hour, murmuring, "Mr. Todds tenders his sincerest condolences, miss, and might he have the honour of furnishing the funeral?"

So strongly did Miss Jessop feel this that there were times when she almost exploded with fury. The worst of it was that people, good, ordinary people, really were taken in by the loathsome Hawkins and his "sincerest condolences." They stopped their dazed weeping for long enough to nod and leave everything to Todds's, without a thought for the fact that they might have done better elsewhere. It's a melancholy truth that in times of bereavement, when the undertaker ought to come into his own as he is the only one standing upright while others are lying distraught upon couches, nobody thinks of asking a friend or a neighbour, "Is he the best to be had?"

Recommendation goes for nothing. Alas, it's not a trade like butchery or haberdashery that enjoys a regular family custom. Generally speaking, folk only get buried once and are in no situation to praise or complain about the service.

Consequently—and thanks to Hawkins' pushing ways—Todds's now furnished nine out of every ten funerals in the district, while Jessop & Pottersfield's, discreet, courteous Jessop & Pottersfield's, languished in circumstances that daily grew as straitened as the sides of a coffin.

Little by little, economies were forced upon the once well-to-do household: servants were let go, and Miss Jessop herself had to give up music, painting, needlework, and French. Then even the outside boy was discharged. Miss Jessop was deeply sorry to see him go. He promised to write to her, but he never did; instead he bequeathed her the odious tasks that had once been his. To her now fell the disagreeable lot of intruding on other folks' grief in order to get their business.

Dressed in her father's solemn livery, she'd wait, day after day, outside houses where there was known to be sickness. Anxiously she'd watch the windows, waiting for the blinds to be drawn. But more often than not, she was too much of a lady to be in at the death, as they say, with the vulgar promptitude of a Hawkins. With an aching heart she heard, "I'm sorry, miss, but we're already suited. Mr. Todds is looking after us."

"Pray—pray accept our sincere condolences," she'd murmur with a rueful nod, indicating, perhaps, more sorrow for the family's choice than for their loss. Then she'd hasten away to the sympathetic accompaniment of: "Lovely lass, that. What a pity she's in the undertaking line!"

Yes, she was only an undertaker's daughter, but she wore her blacks with a difference. They became her like the night. Yet she was neither betrothed nor even courted. Hers was a trade in which she was fated to blush and bloom unseen. An undertaker's circle of friends is sorely limited: a joiner or two, an unlucky physician, a sexton, and maybe a dusty old monumental mason; so the beautiful Miss Jessop walked alone and ate out her heart with tears and a strange, fantastic dream.

"*O death, where is thy sting?*" she wept into her pillow each night. "*O grave, where is thy victory?*"

Then she'd dry her eyes as her aching bosom made answer: "In St. Martin's Churchyard. Under the elder tree."

She was in love with Orlando Brown, who had entered her father's shop one February 13, and had gone out of it on St. Valentine's Day, never to return.

It had happened in the days of prosperity, long before the appearance of Hawkins, when Miss Jessop had been a tempestuous eleven, much given to moods, passionate affections, and violent disagreements with the household.

It had been following one such disagreement, when she had been confined to her room without supper until she saw fit to beg her mother's pardon, that she had grown so excessively hungry that she risked her father's anger and crept forth to visit the solemn front parlour, which, ordinarily, she shunned like the plague.

This parlour, with its mahogany side table, its massive candelabra, and its black velvet curtains, served as a Chapel of Rest for those who, for one reason or another, were not to be buried from their own homes. Often busy tradesmen did not care to keep a departed one on the premises with customers continually coming and going, so at night a long black cart (which Miss Jessop always remembered as having a disagreeable smell) called at the bereaved's and returned to Jessop & Pottersfield's.

She knew there were often biscuits and wine in the parlour to sustain any mourners who called to make their last adieus. It was the thought of this that gave her the necessary courage.

She stiffened her sinews, clenched her fists, and pushed open the door. Within, all was bright with candlelight. She saw, with pleasure and relief, that there were honey cakes in little black paper cups laid out on a pewter dish on the side table; but at the same time she saw that there was a coffin upon trestles in the middle of the room.

The draught from the open door disturbed the candle flames, so that everything in the room seemed to be moving. Resolutely she averted her eyes from the coffin and fixed them on the side table. But it was no use; she couldn't help seeing, out of the corner of her eye, that the coffin was open and that there was *someone* inside it.

Seized with a wholly unreasonable fear, due, most likely, to her feelings of guilt, she paused. Then carefully marking the direction of the side table and honey cakes, she shut her eyes as tightly as she could and began to fumble her way across the room.

Presently she felt the side table press up against her. She sighed with relief. She reached forward, stretching out her fingers to feel the cold edge of the pewter plate. Where had it gone? Slowly she lowered her hand. Ah! Something cold . . . something very cold.

She opened her eyes; and try as she might, she could not shut them again.

She was not leaning against the side table, nor was she touching the pewter plate. She was pressed against the coffin, and her hand was resting upon the waxy white fingers of Orlando Brown!

The dancing candlelight played uncanny tricks with his quiet eyelids and his grey lips. He was smiling at her. . . .

Miss Jessop screamed and snatched back her hand. She forgot the honey cakes, she forgot everything, and rushed from the parlour, consumed with sickness and dread.

She reached her room and plunged into her bed, where she lay, entirely under the covers, as still as Orlando Brown himself. But it was no use; neither sheets nor blankets, had they been a mile thick, could have shut out the image of the dead youth's face. Orlando Brown kept smiling at her from every corner in her head; he kept smiling gently, gravely. . . .

"No—no—no! Go away from me!"

Her fingers could still feel the icy touch of his; she rubbed them fiercely against the sheets. She began to imagine that he'd actually *held* her, that he'd been reluctant to let her go, and that she'd actually had to *drag* herself away from him!

At last she fell asleep, and he followed her into the house of dreams. Only now he looked dreadfully sad, as if he were reproaching her for having fled from him and leaving him in so grim and lonely a place as a coffin.

"No—no—no!" she wept. "Go away from me, please!"

But he would not; he came to her each night, with his sad, grave smile and his pale hands extended as if for a grave embrace. So gentle did he seem that she lost all fear of him, and by the end of a week Miss Jessop was hopelessly, despairingly in love with Orlando Brown. Never was there a stranger love awakened in a young girl's breast; it was a love that could neither live nor change nor die.

On the first anniversary of his funeral, among the many tokens of loving remembrance that were laid upon the grave under the elder tree in St. Martin's Churchyard, appeared a wreath of flowering ivy and wild garlic, bearing a black-edged card on which was written, rather badly—"Be my vallintyne."

By the second anniversary, however, both the writing and the spelling had improved, for Jessop & Pottersfield's was still prosperous enough to afford a tutor for Miss Jessop.

"Be my valentine," pleaded the card in the ivy wreath to the youth who slumbered below.

Then, that very year, Hawkins was taken on by Alfred Todds's, and Jessop & Pottersfield's fortunes began to decline.

Mr. Jessop's solemn countenance, long dignified by the custom of loss, became a little frayed at the edges by the loss of custom. He took to fault finding, particularly with his daughter, whose reluctance to enter wholeheartedly into the trade had not escaped him. But Miss Jessop, anxious to lay the blame where it really belonged, tossed her head and declared, "If only it had been that Hawkins who'd passed away instead of some others I could mention! *That's* a funeral I'd have been happy to furnish, Pa! Not that," she went on, "*we* would have buried him! More a job for a gardener, I'd say!"

"Go to your room, miss!"

"I'm not a child, Pa. If I go to my room, it will be because I choose to."

She went; after all, there was always Orlando Brown. She was now fourteen and catching up with the dead youth fast. When first they'd met, so to speak, in the front parlour, he'd been a quiet and serious sixteen and she a timid, childish eleven. The gap between them had seemed enormous. But now it had narrowed and they were almost on a footing.

This strange circumstance both frightened and fascinated her, and she couldn't help wondering how she would feel when they were both the same age. Would her love suddenly become mature? There was no doubt that, as time passed, she felt her affection growing deeper and more settled. He was such a comfort and he was always *there*, waiting for her. Everything else might change, but he was constant. Not so much as by the flicker of an eyelid did he alter from that first wild vision of him. He was . . . eternal.

Which was more than could be said for Hawkins. When she, Miss Jessop, was fifteen and looking like a lily opening, Todds's apprentice was already seventeen and ageing as noticeably as a leaf in autumn. Withering, one might almost say. In a year or two, he'd be an old man, while Orlando Brown would still be a smiling sixteen, smooth as candle wax!

Sixteen! It seemed impossible, and yet it must come. How

would she feel about Orlando Brown, who'd once seemed so unattainable?

At last the miracle happened. She was sixteen, and he was sixteen—still. It was as if he'd paused to wait for her, had held back time itself. She imagined him to be standing at the end of a corridor of months and years, with his fine transparent hands outstretched, watching her through closed eyes and smiling his grave smile as she stumbled on towards him, forever catching her hastening feet against the sharp stones of childhood. She blushed as she remembered grubby bandages round barked shins and grazed knees. . . .

"Be my valentine," she inscribed with loving care on the back of one of her pa's trade cards, and pinned it in the middle of the ivy wreath.

On the bright cold morning of February 14, she hastened to St. Martin's Churchyard with the strangest of forebodings. She knew that something must happen to her, but she could not say what. Although one part of her knew that her dream life was no more than an idle phantom, another, deeper part kept urging upon her a sense of terrified expectation. Was this day to be an end—or a beginning?

Reason told her that Orlando Brown, waiting in the corridor of time, must inevitably dwindle into yesterday as she passed him by, but her heart cried out fiercely that this must not be so.

As she entered the precincts of the cemetery, St. Valentine's sun peered over the tops of the neighbouring roofs and strewed the grass with long shadows. All the headstones seemed to be wearing black streamers, as if a great concourse of mutes had laid their stone hats on the ground and gone off into the bushes and behind the yew trees for a quiet repast.

Miss Jessop, deeply veiled in fresh black muslin, walked uncertainly across the grass towards the grave beneath the elder tree. Although she was alone in the churchyard, she felt that eyes were watching her from everywhere. The feeling was so strong that she had to pause and gather up her courage. It was, as nearly as she could remember, exactly the feeling she'd had as she'd pushed open the door of the front parlour at home, so long ago. Were the same eyes watching on this day of days?

She reached the grave and looked up at the overhanging bough of the elder tree. Was there some mysterious emanation of him, drawn up by the tree's roots and dwelling in the knotted wood itself?

She knelt down and laid the wreath against the beloved stone.

"Be my valentine!" she murmured to the grass. "Oh, my dearest darling, you've waited for me so long! Never let me pass you by . . . please!"

Tears flooded her eyes as reason—hateful, horrible reason!—told her that she *must* go on and leave the youth behind. He was rooted to his place as surely as the elder tree was rooted in his heart. From this day forward, she could only look back and look back; and each time she turned, he would have dwindled a little more until at last he would have disappeared altogether.

Then the winds would blow cold across her; they would shake her limbs and break her bloom till the sixteen-year-old Orlando Brown would never even have recognized her. . . .

She stood up. She'd lingered long enough. She knew she must go back to Little Knightrider Street and to the quarrelsome misery of a home growing poorer by the week and day. Then she would have to go out again to Shoemaker's Row, where old Mrs. Noades was dying. She would have to accost the physician, beg a word with the servants, watch with straining eyes for the drawing of a blind . . . and pray that Hawkins didn't get there before her.

If only one could leave a card without causing offence! But that was impossible. What a vile trade it was in which ordinary businesslike prudence—such as anyone might employ—earned you nothing but horror and contempt! A sweep—a common chimney sweep—might call upon a house in high summer and offer to sweep the chimneys before the winter's need of fires. But should an undertaker knock at a house and offer his services, perhaps no more than a single day in advance, he'd be kicked down the stairs like a dog!

She left the grave and drifted silently across the grass. She could still feel eyes upon her, eyes filled now with longing and regret. Even so, she must not look back; reason told her it would be madness. . . .

She came to the lych gate. Surely, after all these years, she and he were entitled to one last look upon each other? Just one brief look?

She turned. She saw the grave. Her heart leaped and danced! The wreath had gone!

She shut her eyes tightly and turned away. She'd made a mistake, of course. The wreath *must* have been there—most likely it had slipped down onto the grass. That was it! Her eyes had deceived her.

Reason bade her look again; but this time her heart was adamant. She could not bear to look again and destroy the sudden wild thought that somehow *he* had risen to claim his tribute.

She returned home with scarcely an idea of how she had found her way. Her eyes were shining like stars. Mr. Jessop, however, was not disposed to take this into account when he berated his daughter for her absence.

It seemed that old Mrs. Noades had passed away and Todds's was furnishing. It was no trifling affair. The Noadeses were a large family with many friends. Was Miss Jessop aware that it meant half a gross of pairs of black shammy gloves, the same of mourning rings, white hatbands—to say nothing of crepe, silk, and best scarves and hoods at ninepence apiece?

"Thanks to your dreamy negligence, miss, we have now lost upwards of three hundred pounds! I hope you are satisfied!"

"You hate me! I know you hate me!" cried Miss Jessop, who could think of no other defence, and she rushed from the house in a storm of sobs and tears.

"Everybody hates me!" she panted, whirling through the streets like a wind-blown black bloom. "Everybody except—*him!*"

She rushed towards the churchyard. She had to go to him. She'd always known that this day would have to be fatal to one of them. Now she understood that he and she must be together for ever. The vanishing of her wreath had been a sign that he accepted her.

But how was it to come about? Various fearful thoughts intruded upon her. She thought of the bough of the elder tree; then she thought of twisting up her veil into a thin black rope and hanging herself above his grave. They'd find her, swinging like a broken blossom, and then they'd be sorry!

She reached the churchyard and gazed towards the grave that was so soon to be her own.

"No—no!" she cried. "It cannot be!"

The wreath was still there. Either her eyes had deceived her, or even *he* had turned away from her.

With bowed head she trudged towards the grave, even though there seemed little point now in hanging herself over someone who had, after all, ignored her tribute.

Mournfully she stared at the wreath propped up against the headstone. Her eyes widened and she caught in her breath. It was not the same wreath! In place of ivy and wild garlic was now an offering of dark holly, speckled with berries bright as blood!

And the card? Even that was changed. Now it read: "I will be your valentine."

"Orlando—Orlando Brown!" she cried; tears rushed from her eyes and caught in her veil, where they sparkled like dew on a web. "I *will* be your valentine!"

With shaking hands she took off her veil and began to twist it fiercely, pulling at it every now and then to make sure it would be strong enough to bear her weight.

Now she stood on tiptoe and secured the black cord she'd made to the bough of the elder tree. She dragged on it several times, and the whole tree shook with grief. She began to make a noose. . . .

"Miss Jessop, Miss Jessop!"

She released the cord and whirled round. Wild love and despair gave way to indignation and fury. Hawkins was standing there! Odious, horrible Hawkins, glossy as a slug in a new suit of blacks. Even his boots shone like coffin handles. He looked more got up to kill than to bury!

What did he want? Sincerest condolences, miss, and might we have the honour of furnishing your funeral? Ugh! One couldn't even hang oneself without Hawkins getting the trade for Todds's!

"Wh-what are you doing here, Mr. Hawkins?"

She could feel herself shaking all over with anger.

"I—er—was just visiting, Miss Jessop."

The smartly dressed undertaker's apprentice was quite taken aback by Miss Jessop's annoyance. If there'd been words on the tip of his tongue, he seemed unable to shake them free. He looked unprofessionally dismayed. . . .

Miss Jessop, seeing this, pushed home her advantage by declaring that it was a pity he was just visiting and hadn't come to stay. She made her meaning as plain as she could by glancing across the sunswept garden of graves and scraping the grass with her own neat black shoe.

For a moment Hawkins' dreamy eyes flickered angrily; then he compressed his lips and sighed. The undertaker's apprentice and the undertaker's daughter stood silently, breathing deeply.

"I'm sure, Miss Jessop," said Hawkins, relaxing into a rueful smile, "that were I to come here to stay, your pa—Mr. Jessop— would furnish the occasion 'andsomely."

"Nothing would give us greater pleasure, Mr. Hawkins."

"Likewise for you, Miss Jessop. We—Todds's—would leave no stone unturned to inter you like a queen. White 'atbands and shammy gloves all round. Though in honest truth, I'd sooner such a piece of business went to your house before ever coming to ours."

Miss Jessop scowled as she unravelled Hawkins' gallantry, which had been delivered with solemn charm.

"Friend of yours, Miss Jessop?" murmured Hawkins, nodding down towards the grave beside which they stood. His eyes lingered on the wreath. "A dear departed, was he? Taken when 'e was six- teen. That's a year less than me. . . . He's grassed over well; but then it's five years and the soil's good in St. Martin's. . . ."

Hastily Miss Jessop looked away. Something black was flicker- ing out of the corner of her eye. With a start she realized it was the veil from which she'd meant to hang herself. It was still tied to the bough of the elder tree.

"I—I never knew him," said Miss Jessop awkwardly. "It was just an occasion we—we furnished . . . a long time ago. It's no more than that."

"Yes, miss. As you say. Only I supposed"—he indicated the twisted veil—"that it was a favour, a love ribbon, in a manner of speaking . . . like round a mute's wand. I thought to myself, that's a beautiful, poetic idea . . . making mutes of the trees. I was going to ask you if we—Todds's—might adopt it . . . that is, wherever there's a suitable branch, of course! I hope, Miss Jessop, you wouldn't take it amiss if we—Todds's—was to do something in the same line? We could call them Jessops, if you like. . . ."

All Miss Jessop's anger returned with a rush. It was intolerable that the insufferable Hawkins should turn even the evidence of her despair to his own business advantage. She didn't want to look at him. She reached up to untie her veil, which had become ridiculous and humiliating in her eyes. Hawkins, unaware of her feelings, came courteously to her assistance. He smelled of varnish and aromatic herbs, and his nose was as smooth as marble.

Briefly his hand touched hers over the knot in the veil. Miss Jessop snatched hers away in instinctive horror, remembering other hands she'd touched. She felt she'd betrayed the sleeper under the grass, who lay so quietly, listening and watching. . . .

Surreptitiously she wiped her fingers clean as Hawkins untied the knot, smoothed out the delicate muslin, and returned it to her.

"It's a nice stone, Miss Jessop," said Hawkins, looking down at the grave again. "They don't do them like that any more. They never do the inscription as deep. Sometimes it's not much more than a scratch."

"Mr. Jessop has always been very particular about the stone."

"And well known for it," said Hawkins gravely. "Even Mr. Todds used to say that when his time came he'd as soon Jessop & Pottersfield's furnished him as anyone else in the trade."

"Really?" said Miss Jessop, taken off guard and warmed by the unusual tribute from a rival. "Did he really say that?"

"Oh, yes, indeed!" said Hawkins eagerly. "Good taste, he always said. That's what Jessop & Pottersfield's have. Impeccable taste. Do you know, in the old days—"

"Yes! In the old days!" interrupted Miss Jessop bitterly. "But things are very different now! We've not furnished anybody for a month, Mr. Hawkins! A whole month! Did you know that? Of course you did! But can you know what it means to *us*, Mr. Hawkins?"

Hawkins looked momentarily guilty and distraught; then with an impulsive gesture, he clasped Miss Jessop's hands.

"Things will look up, Miss Jessop! Please don't you worry! Everything will be all right! It—it's only the season. Come March and a cold snap and before you can say *dust to dust*, there'll be bereavements and funerals left over and to spare! Mark my words, Miss Jessop, you'll not be able to move in the shop for coffins and hatbands and shammy gloves! Oh, the good times are coming back, Miss Jessop!"

"Are you sure of it, Mr. Hawkins?" asked Miss Jessop, undeniably touched by the stately youth's concern for her.

"As sure as we're both standing here in the churchyard!" cried Hawkins, clasping Miss Jessop's hands even more tightly. Gently she freed herself, and Hawkins took off his shining black hat to reveal a pale brow, bright with perspiration.

He closed his eyes and tendered his sincerest apologies for having taken such liberties with Miss Jessop. He did not wish her to think him lacking in sympathy or respect; it was just that he had been borne away by the sight of her distress. . . .

She accepted his apology, and Hawkins, with immense relief and dignity, proposed a stroll among the sunny tombstones to refresh them both. So they walked, side by side—the funereal youth and the funereal girl—pausing by stones and monuments and sombre urns, criticizing this and admiring that, for it was their trade.

Many of the sleepers had been laid to rest by Jessop & Pottersfield's; Miss Jessop remembered them all and talked of the lively times of her pa's heyday. She found herself recollecting the old mutes of her childhood—tall, sad fellows decked with crepe weepers like melancholy maypoles—who'd made her laugh with strange jokes when she'd cried over a dead mouse or a broken doll. . . .

They read the inscriptions as if turning the pages of an old stone album: "Deeply loved . . . deeply missed . . . we will be together again . . . loving . . . loving . . ." Love was everywhere, and the crisp grass rustled and sighed.

"Is this one of yours, miss?" asked Hawkins, pausing beside a simple grey headstone that marked a newly grassed grave. Miss Jessop shook her head.

"Samuel Bold," read out Hawkins. "Lamplighter late of Cripplegate Ward. *To them which sat in the shadow of death, LIGHT is sprung up.*"

"Very suitable," said Miss Jessop.

"If I'd furnished 'im," said Hawkins softly, "I'd 'ave advised a monument, Miss Jessop."

"What sort of a monument, Mr. Hawkins . . . bearing in mind the circumstances of the bereaved?"

"An angel, Miss Jessop. A boy angel, holdin' a torch. Might I show you, Miss Jessop?"

She nodded, and the undertaker's apprentice, with graceful decorum, laid a white handkerchief with a black border at the foot of the grave. Then, placing his hat beside him, he knelt.

At first Miss Jessop was inclined to smile . . . until she saw it was no smiling matter. The youth, upon one knee, had lifted up his arms and was holding them out towards her. His long fingers trembled, and on his face was an expression that would have melted the finest Aberdeen granite. Beloved . . . loving . . . dear one were carved all over it till there was no room left to end it even with a date.

"Would you—would you care for a monument like this?"

"Mr. Hawkins!"

"Please, Miss Jessop! Tell me—"

"I—I don't know . . . I can't say. . . . You must get up, Mr. Hawkins. . . . The grass is chilly and damp. You will catch cold . . your death of cold. . . ."

"And if I did, would you put such a monument over me?"

"I don't know—I don't know! B-besides, Todds's would—would be furnishing you . . . I'm sure they would! And—and in any case, Mr. Hawkins, you wouldn't look half so fine in stone!"

"I love you, Miss Jessop! I've always loved you," whispered the youth, his eyes shining and his face pale with hope.

"Please don't say such things, Mr. Hawkins! You can't mean them. . . ."

But he assured her that he did. Still kneeling, he went on to tell her how, when he first came into the trade, he'd admired her, longed for her, and dreamed of her. He told her, shyly, of how, in the early days, he'd carved her name on every coffin lid and scratched it on headstones where none but he could see it. He told her how he'd vowed to make himself worthy of her. He'd prayed for strength to work and work to make something of himself so that he could approach her. Every funeral he helped to furnish had been a step nearer. . . .

"Oh, stop, stop!" cried Miss Jessop. She was immeasurably distressed and ashamed to hear that all Hawkins' industry, which had ruined her family, had been only for her.

"Everything has been for you," said Hawkins, rising to his feet and standing so close to her that she felt dizzy from the smell of varnish and herbs.

"And now," he murmured into her ear, "the time 'as come, Miss Jessop."

He went on to tell her, with mingled modesty and pride, that

Todds's was opening up in Queen Street and that he, Hawkins, was to manage.

"Though I'm still only a 'prentice, miss, Mr. Todds 'as promised me the management. He only told me yesterday, Miss Jessop ... and my 'eart sang like a nightingale. I knew my St. Valentine's Day 'ad come round at last. That's why I came here, to find you. . . ."

"You came here for me?"

Miss Jessop trembled and blushed deeply as she recollected what she'd been doing when Hawkins had found her . . . the dreadful preparations she'd been making.

"I—I wasn't going to ... really ... I wasn't ..." she stammered, clutching her veil and wishing it would vanish away.

Hawkins smiled and shook his head. A natural compassion for distress prevented him from telling her how panic-stricken he'd been as he'd watched her about to make away with herself. Suddenly his smile broadened as he realized how his impulsive saving of Miss Jessop's life had deprived the new premises of a client. Mr. Todds would not have been pleased with him. . . .

"Why are you smiling, Mr. Hawkins?"

"Pleasure, Miss Jessop, at being with you."

She accepted his explanation, even though she felt it to be not entirely true. The undertaker's apprentice bent to pick up his hat and his black-edged handkerchief. He asked if Miss Jessop would honour him by visiting the new premises? It was very close, he assured her, no more than a walking funeral off. . . .

He extended his arm to Miss Jessop, and together they strolled from the lamplighter's grave.

"We're opening up day after tomorrow, Miss Jessop. With old Mrs. Noades."

She bit her lip with a sudden pang of envy.

"We're making a real occasion of it," went on Hawkins

proudly. "We're donating ten yards of black silk to the church at our own expense. There'll be four mutes with white 'atbands and weepers on their wands done up with black love ribbons. Six branch boys with real wax candles and shammy gloves all round—even for the servants. No 'orses, of course, as she'll be going from Queen Street, but there'll be a featherman—"

"What's that, Mr. Hawkins?"

"Ah! It's the newest thing. French and very smart. It's a tray of black ostrich plumes carried on the featherman's 'ead. Works out at two shillings. . . ."

"It sounds very handsome—"

"Would you care to see it, Miss Jessop? If you are not otherwise engaged, would you attend the occasion as my guest? It would be a great compliment, and I can't think of anything that would set off a furnishing to better advantage than your presence, Miss Jessop!"

"Why, thank you, Mr. Hawkins."

"The repast is to be at the Eagle and Child, on the river."

Miss Jessop inclined her head. "In the old days, Mr. Hawkins, we used to have little honey cakes in black paper cups. They made a very good impression. . . ."

"I'll order them directly!"

They paused by the lych gate.

"I told you," said Hawkins, so softly that she could scarcely hear him, "that I love you, Miss Jessop, and that, for me, the time 'as come."

He put his hand upon hers, where it lay in the crook of his smooth black elbow like a bouquet of lilies.

"In two years I'll be out of my apprenticeship and will be of a man's estate. . . ."

She began to tremble violently; her heart fluttered and she could only draw breath with difficulty. She knew he was about to make her an offer . . . that he was on the point of asking her to become Mrs. Hawkins.

Her mind, confused by the profoundest agitation, struggled for words to reject the youth. She had no choice but to reject him. Her heart was already given; and how could she, in the twinkling of an eye, turn from hanging herself for a dead love to accepting the advances of a brand-new live one? It was too much to ask! She could never, never be wife to one who had never been her valentine. There had to be a springtime of love before its summer. And besides . . .

"Will you—will you accept my sincerest affection and become my wife?" murmured the funereal lover in tones that would have done credit to a parson.

Alas, poor Hawkins! He was too conscientious an apprentice to quite cast off the quality of his trade! Decorum and respect were instinctive to him in the presence of an occasion, and what greater occasion had he ever faced than this present one of declaring his lifelong love?

"Will you marry me?" he repeated, bowing his head.

Miss Jessop, no less conscious of decorum and respect—and admiring them in their proper place—turned her head away and gazed, with anguish and pleading, towards the grave under the elder tree. If only *he* could help her . . . if only *he* could send her a sign!

Her eyes widened. The wreath—his wreath—had gone! What did it mean?

"Will you be Mrs. 'Awkins?"

"The wreath . . . it—it's gone!"

Hawkins somewhat dismayed by this reception of his addresses, followed the direction of Miss Jessop's gaze. He frowned; he scowled; he muttered something under his breath. With an unaccustomed agitation he freed her arm from his.

"It's not gone far," he said, and began to walk, at first slowly and reverently, among the headstones, apparently bowing to each loving memory as he passed.

Suddenly there was a quicker movement among the tombs. Something small and earthy scuttled out. It might have been a large rat. Then it squealed, "Look out! 'E's arter us!"

Two similar creatures emerged from concealment and began to fly, with screams and shrieks, before the advancing figure that, they sensed, was bent upon vengeance.

Hawkins' pace quickened; he broke into a long-legged, dancing run. His hat tumbled off and his fair hair flew out like an unquenched candle. The demon children squealed with terrified delight and went zigzag among the dead. Hawkins, with coattails flying, leaped the graves, swung on the iron railings that enclosed the monuments, and vaulted the "loving memories" and "deeply beloveds" as lightly as a bird.

Miss Jessop, standing by the lych gate, looked on, half in terror and half in fascination as life sprang up among the meek and helpless dead; how it danced and scampered, squealed and shouted, and became, at length, a wild, fantastic game in which the silent sleepers under the grass played the only part they could —by offering their "loving memories" as obstacles, concealments, refuges, and, ultimately, stepping stones for the triumph of—

He'd caught them! He'd stalked them round a black marble monument to the memory of a clockmaker and his wife, and trapped them against the railings! Miss Jessop heard his shout of triumph and the children's wail of dismay. What would he do with them? Nothing. He laughed and let them go. Wrath and sternness were no part of Hawkins. . . .

He returned to Miss Jessop, panting and bearing the now battered circlet of holly.

"Here!" he said. "They nicked it. They nicked yours, too,

earlier on. They brought it to me in the shop. I paid them and—and put this one in its place."

"And—and the card?" murmured Miss Jessop, overcome with remorse and confusion. "Did you put that there?"

"You read it then?"

She nodded.

"Will you be my valentine?" asked Hawkins, flushed and weary from his wild pursuit. "Will you, my love?"

"Yes," said Miss Jessop, who could not find, either in her mind or in her heart, the words to reject him. "I will be your valentine!"

They walked from the lych gate and left the churchyard behind them. They strolled into Queen Street to view the new premises, twined in each other's arms. People smiled as they passed, and an old lamplighter, dragging his ladder, recollected that it was St. Valentine's Day and, remembering an ancient custom, mumbled, "There they goes: the ivy girl and the holly boy."

LABOUR-IN-VAIN

"**M**Y MA," SAID GULLY TO HIS FRIENDS, "LOOKS AFTER OUR family leather business. In quite a big way, y'know. Old-established premises in one of them quiet parts off Old Change."

He himself was apprenticed to Noades's, the bucklemakers in Shoemaker's Row, where he worked in brass, plate, and pinchbeck with chips of Bristol stone sparingly cemented into the more fancy styles.

"My son," confided Mrs. Gully to a new neighbour, "works in the jewellery line. 'Andles pearls and diamonds as if they was as common as them black beads you're wearin'. Meanin' no offence, of course. . . ."

She lived in Labour-in-Vain Yard, where, with the help of an ancient journeyman, she kept a small dark cobbler's shop that always reeked of leather and feet.

"I once worked for a lady what had a real diamond brooch," murmured the neighbour, forlornly fingering her beads. "It was in—"

"My Gully don't go all that much on diamonds," interrupted Mrs. Gully, raising her voice as the journeyman started hammering in the workroom next door. " 'E thinks they're a bit common nowadays."

"She used to wash it in buttermilk!" shouted the neighbour anxiously.

"Sometimes 'e's brung me things on Motherin' Sunday," howled Mrs. Gully, "that wouldn't disgrace 'Anover Square!"

"The lady what I worked for lived in—"

"The Lord God Almighty," bellowed Mrs. Gully when the journeyman's hammering stopped, leaving her voice exposed as a raw, passionate shriek, "knows what 'e'll bring me next!"

They were a proud dynasty were the Gullys, and rising in pride with every generation. But this same pride, which might have united them, divided them in the cruellest way. Although, as the crow flies, it was less than half a mile from Shoemaker's Row to Labour-in-Vain Yard, as the proud apprentice walked, it might as well have been a thousand. Gully visited his ma scarcely one Sunday in a month; and even when he did, it was with feelings of awkwardness and distress.

Being in the buckle business, which, by its very nature, was some inches off the ground, he felt himself removed from the odious trade of feet entirely. He didn't care to think of it at all; and particularly he didn't like to dwell, in his mind, upon his ma's dingy workroom, where the old journeyman sat with his bunioned toes exposed and stinking like the old soles he patched.

So he covered it up in his heart and referred to "the family leather business," in tones of immense refinement. In consequence of this, he couldn't help feeling angry and bitter whenever he called and saw that his ma was making a liar of him.

Similarly, Mrs. Gully resented her son, not because of *his* pride, but because of her own. Having represented him as being in the jewellery line, she was offended that he never brought her the gifts that would have been proper to that exalted trade.

Nevertheless, she felt a certain regret, and, with the approach of each Mothering Sunday, she felt a warmth coming on and made sundry vows to herself that, this time, "things would go better."

" 'E'll be comin' tomorrer of course," said Mrs. Gully, with a sudden rush of gentleness that encouraged the new neighbour.

"The lady what I worked for—"

Then the hammering started up again, and Mrs. Gully had to shout.

"Tomorrer! My son! For tea!"

"Tomorrer!" swore Gully to himself as he stalked along Shoe-maker's Row on the Saturday morning. "Tomorrer I'll reely try to make things go with a swing!" He, too, couldn't help feeling sorrow for the rift between himself and his ma.

"Yes," he murmured as he turned down Puddle Dock Hill in order to avoid passing too close to Labour-in-Vain Yard, "to-morrer I'll reely go out of me way!"

He was on an errand to Janner's of Trig Lane to buy some silver thread and was dressed in his best clothes and wearing his new black shammy gloves. They'd been given to him (together with a black silk hatband which he'd given his ma) last month when he'd gone to old Mrs. Noades's funeral, and every time he put them on, he thought of deaths of mothers and resolved, before it was too late, to heal the breach with his own.

For this good intention he'd even bought her something— something he knew she'd like. Every year, on the Friday before Mothering Sunday, Mr. Noades put up a notice in the work-room reminding everyone of the custom of taking gifts to their mothers and offering, at greatly reduced prices, various items of stock that had been hanging fire on the shelves. Gully, at considerable expense, had bought a pair of pinchbeck buckles ornamented with brilliants that, in the gloom of the cobbler's shop, could have passed as gold and diamonds. They'd been made up into the initial of a lady who'd never come back to claim them; and although they were plainly D's, Gully felt that it was not beyond human ingenuity to represent them as an elegant form of G's.

"Tomorrer," he repeated as he turned into Trig Lane, "things will reely be good!" He thrust his hand in his pocket to feel the sharp little parcel, and he smiled so that his plain, small-eyed face looked almost handsome.

He was still smiling when he stopped outside the silver-thread spinners.

"Went to Janner's, yesterday, Ma," he rehearsed to himself, knowing how she liked to hear about the noble metals. "You know . . . in the precious line. Gold an' silver 'eaped up with no more regard than you'd 'ave for old boots!"

He went into the shop and stood politely before the trade counter.

"Six ounces of silver thread for Mr. Noades's of Shoemaker's, miss."

It was Miss Janner herself who greeted him. She did not look pleased. She had been told to work on this Saturday morning, and she was nursing a strong sense of injury. She compressed her lips and sniffed.

"You can go and ask my pa. First floor. Workroom. I'm not a servant in this house."

Gully went, feeling in his present mood not a little shocked by this sample of a child's pride.

He climbed the stairs and, reaching the workroom door,

knocked. There was no reply, so he knocked again and began to turn the handle.

"Come in quick and shut that murdering door!" shouted an angry voice. "Before you blow me bankrupt!"

Used to folk in a big way, Gully made himself as thin as a piece of paper and slipped inside.

The workroom was tremendously long and low, extending the whole width of the house. At one end it was lit by a window and at the other by the red, watchful eye of a fire.

Nor was the fire the only watchful thing. Mr. Janner himself— a bulky, long-limbed person—stood in the middle of the room with a look that crawled unceasingly along the shimmering threads that were stretched between the spindle women by the window and the silver women by the fire. His was the voice that had greeted Gully, but after one hasty glance he paid no further attention to him. His eyes returned, with a mixture of hunger and dread, to their previous scrutiny.

As the spindle women turned their wheels and drew the valuable thread towards them, he sucked in his lips warningly; and as the silver women at the other end of the room paid out their silk, deftly binding it with wisps of silver as fine as hair as it passed through their palms, he blew out his lips menacingly as if to say, Watch it! Watch it! I know you're trying to nick me silver; but just you try it! That's all—just you try it!

Gully stood stock-still. The atmosphere of suspicion, watchfulness, and value in the long room was the most solemn thing he had ever known; he was in the presence of many hundreds of pounds. It was another world. He struggled in his mind to come to terms with it and find the words that would conjure it up for the pleasure of his ma in Labour-in-Vain Yard.

But it was quite beyond him, and, try as he might, the only image that came into his head was the eerie, slightly unpleasant one that Mr. Janner looked like an enormous spider in the midst of the silver strands, brooding hungrily on the seven or eight pitiful female flies that were trapped in the suburbs of his web.

"What is it, lad?"

"Six ounces of silver thread for Noades's of Shoemaker's, if you please, sir. The lady downstairs—"

"I know."

Mr. Janner frowned and nodded, then left his web by way of holding down the threads and climbing over them with his long, flexible legs—which made him look more like a spider than ever. He had very small feet and wore buckles that, by daylight, looked brass and, by firelight, gold.

He went to a shelf, while the threads continued on their ceaseless, quivering journey from the light of the fire to the light of day. A vague sensation of easing and murmuring sprang up at either end of the travelling threads.

"I'm watching you," said Mr. Janner, beaming round suddenly at the spinners. "I'm still watching you, ladies!"

He beckoned to Gully.

"Here, lad. Come over here and take a look at the back of me head."

Gully obliged.

"Now—you tell them ladies what you can see."

"I—" began Gully.

"That's it!" cried Mr. Janner triumphantly. "Eyes! Eyes in the back of me head! So watch out, ladies! Just because I turn me back, it don't mean I can't see you!"

Then he murmured to Gully, "Watch 'em for me, lad. Make sure they don't wet their hands!"

With this curious injunction, Mr. Janner turned his back and, visibly trembling with anxiety, lifted down a spindle and began to weigh out the precious thread.

"Don't take your eyes off 'em, lad," he muttered. "Watch what they do with their hands. It's all right if they warm 'em . . . to keep 'em dry . . . but nothing more than that. There's eyes on you, ladies!" he shouted out. "There's eyes everywhere!"

Obediently, and with a sense of the trust put in him, Gully watched the spinners as, with dull faces and incredibly rapid fingers, they continued their glittering toil. Then once again an eerie image drifted into his head, and he couldn't help thinking how strange it was that flies should be set to spinning the spider's web for him.

Little by little, as he watched—for Mr. Janner was taking his time and weighing was a tedious business—he found his gaze drifting helplessly from hands to faces, and to one face in particular till it was fixed upon it to the exclusion of everything else.

It was the face of the girl who stood closest to the fire, and such was the illumination that she seemed like a flame herself; her hair was reddish and her eyes flared and sparkled as she turned her head.

Then, suddenly, one of these little blazes seemed to be put out as she winked at Gully. Eagerly he winked back. She smiled, and he smiled back. She blew him a quick, secret kiss, and he blew one back.

On the way out of the workroom, after his business was concluded, he managed to linger by her.

"When d'you finish?"

"Dark."

"Doin' anything tonight?"

"Maybe."

"Meet me outside?"

"Maybe."

"Go on!"

"All right, then. Outside—at dark."

The kiss! Gully couldn't get over it. It had happened so suddenly: the raised hand, the lowered face, the pursed lips, the quick, fiery smile—and then, puff! Though it had been lighter than the wisps of silver that rustled through the girl's hands, it had struck Gully with the force of a cannonball and blown a hole through his head and heart.

He was fifteen and she was fifteen and she was his first real girl. He went back to Shoemaker's Row like a lad apprenticed to the trade of sky and stars.

"I thought you mightn't come," she said. She'd been waiting for him in windy Trig Lane, with a wild yellow cloak blowing all round her as if she'd brought an unwilling friend. She looked agitated.

"And there was me thinkin' *you* mightn't," said Gully, which really didn't do justice to the heartaching fears and doubts he'd gone through during the long afternoon.

"I *said* I'd come, didn't I?"

"So did I."

They began to walk down towards the river. She told him her name was Daisy LaSalle. . . .

"That's French, ain't it?" he asked, a shade uneasily. Anything French he knew was costly, and the buckles he'd bought his ma had left him in reduced circumstances.

"From Spitalfields, where the weavers live," explained Miss LaSalle. "You know, them huge knots."

Gully, not knowing that this was Miss LaSalle's effort at "Huguenots," nodded in a baffled fashion.

"Me ma was an actress."

"I s'pose it was your pa what was in the rope business," said

Gully, dimly pursuing the notion of knots.

It turned out that Miss LaSalle wasn't any too sure about her pa. So far as she knew, he'd been either a beadle or a lamplighter from Bishopsgate who'd been very sweet on her ma and had told her he'd never lit lamps half as bright as her eyes.

"I expect it was 'im," said Gully—and meant it. Miss LaSalle really looked luminous in the dark March night. Gully could have walked by the light of her anywhere.

"Where are we going?"

"I thought we might 'ave a bite of supper at the Three Cranes."

"I don't want you to spend all your money on me," said Miss LaSalle, giving his arm a quick squeeze and, at the same time, bestowing on him a nervous smile.

"That's all right," said Gully, and went on to explain that, although he was only Mr. Noades's apprentice, his ma looked after the family leather business and was in quite a big way. . . .

"Making shoes?"

"N-not reely," said Gully, thinking of the ancient journeyman and his shameful trade. "We don't 'ave much to do with—with feet."

Miss LaSalle gave his arm another squeeze, and Gully, over the worst, went on to say that his ma didn't actually work herself, but looked after the staff.

"They've been with 'er a long time, of course. It's a real family trade. Old-established, y'know . . . in one of them quiet parts off Old Change."

They came to Trig Stairs, from where Gully insisted they take a waterman's boat to the Three Cranes. A friend of his—a clockmaker's apprentice from Carter Lane whom he'd consulted —had advised this. He always did it himself when he'd got a new girl, and he wasn't sure if the game would turn out to be worth the candle.

The river unsettled their stomachs, so they didn't want to eat much. Under the influence of the wind, the water turned out to be choppy enough to slice onions. They both started off cheerfully enough, with Gully waxing expansive about his ma's circumstances, when, after a dozen black and awful yards, he found he had to shut his mouth to stop everything inside him coming up and flying out. By the time they reached the Three Cranes, Miss LaSalle had to help him disembark and, to his dazed shame, pay the waterman herself, as he was too ill to do more than moan.

The landlady found them a table in a corner, removed from all sight of the river.

"Brandy and port wine," she said, eyeing Gully sympathetically. "That'll settle his stomach. Just half a pint taken straight off; then he'll be fit and ready for mutton chops and kisses for afters, eh?"

She proved only partly right. He drank down the potion, and, sure enough, he fancied kisses for afters and made several attempts to claim them, but he couldn't quite manage to keep down the mutton chops. Repeatedly he slumped back in his corner; he was a much divided apprentice: his heart was in the right place, but his stomach was most definitely not.

Nonetheless, as long as he stayed perfectly still and didn't breathe too heavily, he felt quite well. He was with his girl and she was shining in front of him like all the lamps in the Strand. Carefully he told her over and over again about his ma, as, somehow, she seemed interested and he felt it peculiarly important for her to know.

"We're reely in a big way, y'know . . . leather an' all that. . . ."

"I suppose you'll be taking it over when—when your ma gets too old? You'll be following in your pa's footsteps. . . ."

"I thought I told you," said Gully carefully, "that we don't 'ave all that much to do with feet."

They left the Three Cranes at ten o'clock and walked arm in arm along the river, back towards Trig Lane. Gully was feeling much, much better. The worst of his experience was over, and he felt only a little lightheaded. He assured Miss LaSalle that there was no need for her to walk nearest the river, as he was in no danger of falling in. He was, he said, as steady as anything. . . .

Just to prove it, he managed to kiss Miss LaSalle three times; but on the third occasion he was dismayed to feel that her cheek was salty and wet with tears.

"I—I ain't 'urt you?" he asked anxiously.

"N-no. Not really."

"Was I 'oldin' on to your arm too tight?"

"N-no. It wasn't that."

"Was it—was it the mutton chops and . . . and all that?"

" 'Course not!"

"Was it—was it me kissin' you so soon?"

" 'Course not!"

"Then what is it? I ain't done nothing else!"

"It's just that I lost me place. At Janner's. I've been turned off."

"Was it on account of me? Was it because I talked to you?"

"Not really. It was . . . that kiss I blew you. He saw me. I'll swear he's really got eyes in the back of his head! He saw it. He shouted and swore I'd licked me hand. Came up and felt it just after you'd gone. It was wet all right. I was sweatin' with fright!"

"But what was wrong in that?"

"Wet hands. It's a trick of the trade. That's why we got the fire . . . to keep drying ourselves off. If your hands are wet, you can damp the silk and make it weigh right. Then you can nick his silver and no one finds out till it's too late. But there's not much chance at Janner's. He's that careful he won't drink a drop all day, 'case he has to go out for a pee. He'll die in that there silver harness of his . . . and his last words will be, 'I'm a-watching you, ladies!' That's why he's in such a big way. . . .''

Gully stood as still as nature would let him, while the black winds roared down the lanes and alleys that led to the river and threatened to topple him over the low embankment. He was deeply moved by Miss LaSalle's tale, and he was even more moved by her wondrous beauty. He screwed up his face as he thought of avenging his girl by squashing the spidery Mr. Janner with a huge cobbler's hammer.

"You shouldn't have had that mutton chop," said Miss LaSalle with concern. "Put your head down between your knees and you'll feel better. Honest, you will. . . .''

"It—it's all right," mumbled Gully. "Reely."

"Go on. I won't watch, if you like."

She turned away, and her yellow cloak blew out and smacked Gully in the face. He tottered and sank down till he was able to rest his cold, wet forehead against the cold, wet stones.

"Feeling better, now?"

He opened his eyes and saw Miss LaSalle's worn old shoes shifting in front of him. He stared at them as if with deep interest. . . .

"I've had 'em a long time," she said awkwardly. "They was my ma's. They used to have pretty buckles. . . .''

"I got something," said Gully impulsively. "Specially for you."

He stood up and fumbled in his pocket.

" 'Ere," he said. "They got D's on 'em. D for Daisy."

He brought out the little parcel containing the pinchbeck and brilliant buckles and tore it open.

"Oh! Oh! You shouldn't!" cried Miss LaSalle. "You shouldn't spend your money like that!"

"Don't you like 'em?"

"Oh, yes, yes! They're beautiful! They ain't gold, are they?"

"They're for you," said Gully, declining to commit himself.

"I could wear them as brooches," said Miss LaSalle, crying and wiping her eyes on her cloak. "It seems a shame to put 'em on me shoes where nobody can see 'em."

"Yes," agreed Gully. "In our line, we don' go much on feet."

"I'll wear them tomorrow!"

"Tomorrer?" repeated Gully with the vague chill of half remembering something.

"When—when we go to see your ma," went on Miss LaSalle, breathing rapidly and holding on to her young man's arm with a fierce, despairing grip.

Gully stared at her in terror.

"It's all right, ain't it? I can come?" pleaded Miss LaSalle, her voice trembling. "It's just that I was wondering, hoping you could ask your ma if—if she'd let me work for her . . . in the leather line. I'm very good with me hands, and everyone says I'm quick to learn. I did a bit of leather stitching before I went into the spinning line. Only—only you see, after tonight, I got nowhere to live. So I thought, seeing how your ma is in a big way, she'd give me a chance?"

Before he could answer, she leaned over and kissed him on the cheek.

"Light you 'ome, young lovers?" came the sudden cry of a linkboy as he loitered past. Gully turned, his eyes streaming from the torch's smoke. The flame and the lamplighter's daughter seemed to be composed of the same destructive substance.

" 'Ome?" he mumbled, shaking his head. " 'Ome?"

"I won't be no trouble," said Miss LaSalle anxiously. "Really I won't. I'll do whatever you say and I won't put a foot wrong."

"Feet!" groaned Gully, thinking of the shame that gnawed at his soul. "Christ! All them . . . feet and—and *'IM*."

That night, after he'd got back to Mr. Noades's and sprawled somehow onto his bed under the counter, Gully had a horrible dream. He dreamed that he'd given away the buckles he'd bought for Mothering Sunday and that he was going to take Miss LaSalle to the evil-smelling cobbler's shop in Labour-in-Vain Yard. Furthermore, he dreamed that he was actually walking along Shoemaker's Row with her on his arm and that he was stark naked.

He awoke with a terrible cry and it was morning and he was safe in his bed and not on the open street at all. For a moment he felt a great flood of relief . . . and then he remembered that the nightmare lay, not behind him, but ahead. True, he wouldn't be walking down Shoemaker's Row stark naked, but there were worse things than that. The nakedness of the spirit was more shameful by far than the nakedness of the body. The thought of the exposure that lay ahead caused him to shrink into his bed-clothes and wish he'd never been born.

All that morning he prayed with all his might that Miss La-Salle wouldn't come, that she'd forgotten or that some accident would prevent her. But it was no use. At three o'clock in the afternoon she was waiting outside for him, her yellow cloak flapping and her eyes bright with hope.

"Look," she said. "I'm wearing your present!" She lifted up her skirts and displayed her feet, explaining that the buckles had been too heavy for her dress and had dragged it down. "So I put them on me shoes," she went on, "and shortened me skirt so's everyone can see."

Gully, who was always embarrassed by the sight of feet, turned away and entertained the pathetic hope that Miss LaSalle hadn't meant what she'd said about losing her place and wanting to ask his ma for work. But she had meant it; in fact, she'd brought all her possessions done up in a neat bundle of brown paper, inscribed JANNER. TRIG LANE.

"I'd nowhere to leave it," she said, and squeezed Gully's arm till he felt his fingers would drop off.

"We'd best go along Carter Lane," he said, taking the bundle as if he wanted a visible burden to balance the unseen one that was crushing him down. He felt cold and lonely and frightened.

His friend, the clockmaker's apprentice, who was leaning against the shutters of his master's shop, waved and whistled as Gully and his girl passed by.

"Have a good supper!" he called out. Gully managed a feeble snarl.

"Oh, my!" said the clockmaker's apprentice, with exaggerated deference. "We mustn't talk to common 'prentices now we're going a-mothering!"

Gully's face grew white. . . .

"I suppose I should have brought some flowers or cakes for your ma," murmured Miss LaSalle apologetically. "But I put on some scent specially." She skipped round the other side, for the bundle had come between them. "D'you like it?"

She put her head close to his; she smelled sweet and warm—like burnt sugar. Gully thought of the foul-smelling shop towards which they were walking, as straight as the flight of a crow. Hastily he turned off Carter Lane and, in an extraordinary mood of cunning and desperation, began to lead his girl through a maze of irrelevant little streets. He was hoping that either they'd lose themselves and not arrive at all, or that she'd be muddled into thinking that the distance between Shoemaker's Row and Labour-in-Vain Yard was really terrific.

"Why, we're almost in Trig Lane!" exclaimed Miss LaSalle in surprise. "You never said your ma lived so close!"

Labour-in-Vain Yard gaped in front of them; it was a melancholy pocket off Fish Hill, stuffed full of rubbish by the wild

March winds and dirty passersby.

"It's reely," said Gully defensively, "quite fashionable when the wind don't blow."

He paused, as if giving Miss LaSalle a chance to change her mind and escape.

"Shall I take me bundle now?" she asked. "Your ma won't think it nice, your carrying it."

He shook his head, and he and his girl advanced timidly towards the cobbler's shop. It looked meaner and more wretched than ever as it crouched down between its grimy neighbours as if they'd been beating it. And there was no mistaking it, either: GULLY was painted in large uneven letters across the parlour window.

"It goes back a long way," said Gully hopelessly, "be'ind. You'd be amazed 'ow spayshus it reely is . . . inside."

"Fancy having your name painted up like that!" said Miss LaSalle, and Gully couldn't help feeling gratified by the sigh she gave. He glanced at her quickly. Sunlight, finding its way somehow into the Yard, seemed to be setting her red hair on fire. For a moment one pride gave way to another as Gully stood and admired his girl; then the door of the cobbler's shop opened, and his ma was revealed.

"Why, it's Gully!" she said loudly. "And *walkin'* in all this blowy wind! Why didn't you come by 'ackney carridge, dear?"

She's got a visitor! thought Gully with a rush of relief. That means the workroom'll be shut and 'e won't be about! So we'll all be able to be'ave natcheral.

He gazed at his ma with approval. She'd done herself up quite grandly, with a great deal of embroidery and white edging, and she was wearing a smart little black cap she'd run up out of the silk hatband Gully had given her. In a way she reminded him of old Mrs. Noades's funeral cake. . . .

His eyes lingered on his ma's, and a mysterious flicker of understanding passed between them, as if each were admitting to a loving conspiracy. . . . Then Mrs. Gully's eyes fixed themselves upon her son's female companion.

"This is Miss LaSalle, Ma," he said. "She's in the silk an' silver line, y'know."

"Come inside," said Mrs. Gully, smiling. "I got company."

He saw at once that the workroom door was shut as tight as if it had been nailed and that there was not a boot or a shoe or anything to do with feet to be seen anywhere in the parlour. Even the visitor, who sat creaking in a corner chair that was closely guarded by the table, seemed to end up in nothing. . . .

"This is Mrs. Joker," said Mrs. Gully.

"With a *a*," said the new neighbour, creaking forward as much as the furniture allowed. "Joaker with a *a*."

She was an anxious, respectable-looking soul, with black beads and a battered silver brooch.

"Mrs. Joaker used to live in 'Anover Square."

"Just orf it, reely. . . ."

"You don't say. This is Miss LaSalle."

"French?" inquired Mrs. Joaker learnedly.

" 'Er ma was a 'uge knot," said Gully, smiling proudly at his ma.

Mrs. Gully nodded. "Reely? I suppose 'er pa must 'ave been in a big way, too?"

"In the oil an' ladder business," said Gully, avoiding the bright eyes of the lamplighter's daughter.

"Is that so? Mrs. Joaker 'ere was tellin' me that she knew someone in the diamond line. . . ."

"Well, only in a manner of speakin'," said Mrs. Joaker awkwardly, and scraped her chair back against the wall.

"Of course, Miss LaSalle 'ere is in silver. That's right, I believe?"

"Oh, yes, ma'am!" said Miss LaSalle, eager to be obliging and on a level with the company. "Look!" She held out her hands to show the thin black lines that marked her palms and that came from the constant passage of the noble metal.

Mrs. Joaker inspected them with interest.

"That lady I was tellin' you of, yesterday, Mrs. G., used to wash 'er silver in winnygar."

"We—that is, Mr. Janner, always uses 'monia. But it makes you cry like anything."

"My son," interposed Mrs. Gully, feeling that the two outsiders had conversed sufficiently between themselves, "won't never bring me silver, just on account of that. The blackenin', you know. It reely 'as to be gold. 'E won't stand for nothing less. Ain't that so, Gully?"

Gully agreed. The feeling in the little parlour was remarkably pleasant. He smiled gratefully at his ma, and once again the secret flicker passed between them.

"Gully never stints me," she said. "And why should 'e, bein' in the line 'e is?"

Gully nodded earnestly. He was feeling cheerful and airy, almost as if he were dancing on a web. Everything was turning out far better than he'd hoped; even the sun was coming into the parlour as if it had been invited. It shone respectably through the sign-painted window and wrote GULLY in long black letters across the bread-and-butter-laden table and fixed a cake with a cherry on it in the fork of the Y.

Gully chattered on about the grandeur of the Noades's funeral and then about his visit to Janner's, who, as everyone knew, was big in the gold and silver line. . . . He stole a glance at his girl; she shifted and blazed up suddenly in the sunlight. He felt momentarily uncomfortable and paused.

"Them's pretty buckles you're wearin', miss," said Mrs. Joaker, who had been creaking sideways in her chair as if searching for some way, however unlikely, into the conversation.

"Gully give them to me," said Miss LaSalle proudly, and held up her feet as high as she could. "Look! They're D's. That's for Daisy. It's me name."

Gully's discomfort increased. Something he'd pushed to the back of his mind nudged its way forwards.

"That lady I was tellin' you of," went on Mrs. Joaker eagerly, "was called after a flower, too. Marguerite . . ."

"My son's always buyin' presents," said Mrs. Gully, silencing the new neighbour with a look. "Expense 'as never been a object with Gully. 'As it, dear?"

She glanced coolly at Miss LaSalle's exposed feet and then to the floor beside her son.

"W-what was that, ma?"

"I said you was always buyin' presents."

Gully grew red. He had remembered what he'd tried to forget; and his ma had remembered, too. It was Mothering Sunday. After all his resolutions, he'd come empty handed and betrayed his ma and shamed her before Mrs. Joaker. . . .

Mrs. Gully smiled encouragingly at her son. He avoided her eyes and stared bleakly at the floor.

"Ah!" said Mrs. Gully, rising and coming towards him with a rattle of disturbed cups. "Did you think I'd forgot? Dear Gully! Look at 'im, blushin' all over 'is face!" She kissed the air affectionately about an inch above his head. "Tried to 'ide it from me, didn't you? Wanted me to think you'd forgot! But I saw it! I saw it as soon as you come in, dear . . . your present for Motherin' Sunday! My son," she said, turning to Mrs. Joaker, "never forgets them old customs. I wonder what 'e's brung me this time?"

"Ma!" cried Gully in sudden terror, but he was too late. Mrs.

Gully had bent down and taken, from the floor beside him, the neat little bundle of Miss LaSalle's possessions!

Gully saw his girl's hand reach out—then vanish like a flame extinguished. A sensation of fearful cold engulfed him, and he began to shiver violently. He thought he was going to have a seizure.

"The lady I was tellin' you of," said Mrs. Joaker, eyeing the bundle with painful curiosity, "used to get buttons. Real pearl buttons. One every year . . ."

"Buttons?" murmured Mrs. Gully, admiring the bundle before clearing a place and depositing it in the middle of the table. "Fancy that!"

"But then," said Mrs. Joaker, twisting and turning in her chair in order to examine the bundle from all sides, "she 'ad almost everything else. And buttons always comes in 'andy."

Gully and his girl sat in terror and stared at the bundle as if it were a severed head.

"Janner. Trig Lane," mouthed Gully, reading the inscription on the brown paper. For a moment he entertained the forlorn hope that the bundle might contain a quantity of nicked silver, but the glimpses he kept catching of Miss LaSalle showed a different sort of fear from guilt. In a strange way he felt she was frightened, not *of* his ma, but *for* her.

"Shall I open it now, or after tea, dear?"

"It—it—" began to plead Miss LaSalle, when suddenly the little parlour shook as in an earthquake and the tea things jumped in agitation.

A loud, insistent hammering had begun from behind the closed door of the workroom. In Gully's ears it sounded as grim and threatening as the fist of the angel of doom.

"It's *'im*," said Mrs. Gully, nodding towards the thin partition that divided the workroom from the parlour. " '*E* wants '*is* tea."

She never referred to her journeyman by name, but always as *he* or *him*, and in tones of sombre mystery.

The hammering ceased, and a silence fell upon the parlour. Everyone stared uncomfortably towards the closed door. Gully felt as if he were really going to faint. He put out his hands to hold onto the table. Already, in his mind's eye, he could see the workroom door opening and the dark, brutish place within being exposed. He could see the ugly, ancient man who lurked there, spitting on his hands and, as usual, missing them and spattering his knees and the floor . . . the old, old man with his rheumy eyes, his boiled nose, and his hideous bunioned feet. Already the stink was in his nostrils. . . .

"I'd ha' thought," he whispered miserably, "that it bein' Sunday—"

"You know what *'e* is," said Mrs. Gully malevolently. "But this time *'e*'ll 'ave to wait!" She shouted out this last sentiment loudly enough for the journeyman to hear. "*'E*'ll 'ave to wait till we've 'ad our tea and I've opened me present what Gully's brung me for Motherin' Sunday!"

She was answered by two bangs, denoting either impatience or assent.

She ignored them and began, with elaborate courtesy, to offer round tea and cake. But no one—not even Mrs. Joaker—had any appetite. As usual, *he* had spoiled things, and it was impossible for conversation to return to its previous refined level; not with *him* grunting and shifting and banging about next door!

There was no help for it but to do without tea and take everybody's mind off *him* by opening up the present Gully had brought. Mrs. Gully stood up and cleared a space round the bundle.

"It's all right, dear," she said as Miss LaSalle stretched out a trembling hand. "I can manage the knot meself."

"They used to come in little velvet boxes," said Mrs. Joaker, dragging her chair until she was pressed tightly against the table.

"What did?"

"Them pearls I was tellin' you of."

"Oh, them buttons."

"Well, they 'ad to be buttons, seein' as 'ow she 'ad a pearl necklace what was give 'er by the gentleman."

"One button a year don't seem much for a mother to get," said Mrs. Gully, loosening the knot that secured the bundle. "At that rate she'd be in 'er grave before she 'ad any use of 'em. My Gully's got a bit more pride than to bring 'is mother . . ."

She pulled away the cord and let it fall. Miss LaSalle bent to pick it up—and remained half under the table. Gully could see her red hair smouldering near his feet.

"It's well done up," said Mrs. Gully, delicately lifting up a torn shift and shaking it. "Whatever can it be, Gully dear?"

She pulled out a filthy petticoat; Miss LaSalle's dismissal had been too sudden for her to have time to wash her belongings before packing them.

"Where is it, Gully?" asked his ma, coming upon a pair of stockings that were as thick with grime as they were thin with holes. She held them up and shook them in a puzzled kind of way, as if her gift might have been caught up in them. A singularly stale smell spread across the table.

She found a bodice, frayed and stained with grease, and then other items of such humble and pitiful aspect that no one should have seen them, let alone held them up to a neighbour's fascinated view.

"They—they're mine!" sobbed Miss LaSalle, lifting her face to the level of the table, so that Gully saw it was shining with tears of shame.

"Reely?"

Mrs. Gully had begun to gather the articles together. Blindly she included a plate. . . .

"Ma!" moaned Gully.

"Yes?" said Mrs. Gully, as if surprised that anyone in the present company should address her so familiarly.

She had completed her packing up and was now grasping the bundle with hands in which the veins and sinews stood out like seams in leather.

"Get out of 'ere," she said quietly. "Get out."

Then, with a movement so unexpected in its rapidity, that Gully had no chance to defend himself, she flung the bundle in her son's face.

"Get out!" she screamed. "Get out—get out of my 'ouse!"

Gully, half blinded by his girl's ramshackle belongings, made a stupid, clumsy effort to save the plate.

"But Ma—"

"Don't you dare to call me Ma!" shrieked Mrs. Gully, her fists clenched and her eyes blazing. "You proud little wiper, you!"

"But me—"

"Look at 'im standin' there!" raged Mrs. Gully, and then, heedless of the onlookers, began to call upon the ceiling, it seemed, to witness the scorn and disgust, the vile ingratitude, and even the hatred that she saw, like running sores, in her son's eyes.

Gully shrank back as his ma's words poured over him like a burning torrent. He actually felt them scald and sting. Fearfully he raised his hand. . . . "For Gawd's sake, Ma—"

"What do you know about Gawd? Motherin' Sunday, is it? More like Murderin' Sunday! Look at 'im, I say, standin' there with 'is fancy girl! And 'er as filthy as a rubbish 'eap!"

Gully saw his girl shudder and her face twist up in pain.

"Shut your mouth!" he shouted. "Shut your 'orrible mouth!"

"Gully, Gully . . . please!" moaned Miss LaSalle, swaying like a flame about to go out.

"I told you, I ain't your ma no more!"

"Then good riddance!"

"I 'ate you for your snaky pride!"

"And I 'ate you for everythin' else! I 'ate this place and I 'ate this Yard—"

"Labour-in-Vain Yard!" screamed Mrs. Gully in terrible triumph. "And labour in vain it was to bring you into the world!"

"And labour in vain it's been to live in it!" howled Gully, and smashed down the plate he'd still been holding.

Then the sky fell down—or so it seemed. There came a violent crash from the workroom that shook the whole house! It was followed by a sharp grunt of pain.

"It's *'im*," muttered Mrs. Gully, recovering herself a little and panting heavily.

"What's *'e* done now?"

"Knocked something over. Just like *'im*."

There came now from the workroom a moan of intolerable agony.

"Christ!" said Gully. "*'E*'s 'urt *'imself*."

"I'll go—" began Gully's girl, for neither the mother nor the son seemed able to move.

Gully stared at her in bewilderment, then he turned back to his ma. The look that passed between them was stripped of all its secrecy now. Together they rushed to the workroom door.

"Can't do nothing right, can *'e*!" cried Mrs. Gully.

"And on a Sunday, too!" screeched Gully, dragging open the door so wildly that the thin partition shook like the walls of Jericho.

The old familiar smell came rushing out and engulfed the parlour like a great warm garment. Gully and his ma went into the dark room, where a single candle burned on the cobbler's bench and cast a subdued radiance on the racks of worn tools.

Shadowy boots crowded the shelves round the walls, and a beggar's host of them stood patiently in a corner of the floor, as if listening to a sermon. Wrinkled and broken, they reeked horribly, with their uppers displaying every deformity of leather, reflecting the ways in which men and women walked the world. The cobbler's workroom was like a dim graveyard of feet, awaiting the resurrection of soles.

The old man himself was lying on the floor and crying with pain. Somehow the heavy cobbler's last had fallen over and crushed his naked, bunioned foot.

" '*E* must 'ave done it '*imself!*" wailed Gully, and knelt beside the old journeyman.

"Pull it off, pull it off!" urged Mrs. Gully, crouching beside her son and holding onto his sleeve.

Very gently, Gully lifted up the last, and his ma moved the candle to examine the injured foot. It was a frightful bruised and bloody sight; the toes had been crushed, and the old man moaned and moaned.

"Bring some warm water!" called out Mrs. Gully. "From the tea."

Miss LaSalle ran to fetch the jug and the cleanest rag from among her scattered belongings. Gully took them and, with great care and tenderness, began to wash the blood from the old man's foot.

"Thank you . . . thank you," he mumbled, and, looking up at Gully's girl, smiled painfully. "And you too, miss."

"Do it—do it 'urt much?" asked Mrs. Gully, nervously patting the old man's hand.

"Not too bad . . . not now you're all 'ere."

" 'Ow did it 'appen?"

"I got frightened with all that shoutin'. And when I 'eard a plate breakin'. . . ."

"It weren't nothing, reely. It weren't anything worth men-shunning."

"Reely?"

"On me honour. Ain't that so, Gully, dear?"

Mrs. Gully looked at her son. They both nodded earnestly and smiled. The old man seemed reassured.

"I like what 'e brung you for this Motherin' Sunday," he mumbled, twisting his head and peering about him.

"Oh, that," said Mrs. Gully uncomfortably. "It weren't nothing, reely."

"Oh, but it were!" He was looking now at Gully's girl, and his watery eyes were blinking as if before too bright a light. "I never see'd a present so pretty. And French, too. You made a good choice, Gully. Your ma and me is reely proud!"

"It—it's me pa," said Gully softly, as if his words might have blown out the candle. "Miss LaSalle, this 'ere is Mr. Gully. Me pa."

As he spoke, a limitless happiness suddenly flooded Gully's soul. The weight he'd lifted from his father's foot was as thistle-down beside the weight he'd lifted from himself. He wanted to dance and sing; he wanted to rush out into Labour-in-Vain Yard and shout his good news to the sun and sky. He wanted to embrace and kiss everyone, even perfect strangers who might be passing up and down Fish Hill!

But he had to content himself with reaching out for Miss LaSalle's hand and explaining, "Me pa, 'ere, mends soles, y'know. We're only in a small way, but we're a 'appy little family, reely."

He felt his girl's grip answer his own and squeeze and squeeze till it seemed she'd never let go. Then Mrs. Joaker managed to edge her way into the room, and the candle flame flickered so that all the boots and shoes seemed to dance for the old cobbler and his wife.

"I'd best bandage up *'is* foot," said Mrs. Gully with a touch of her old gentility. "It do look a ugly mess!"

"Oh, no!" put in Mrs. Joaker, who had been pew opener at the church in Hanover Square. "*'Ow beautiful are the feet of them that preach the gospel of peace!*"

The old cobbler nodded and smiled with rare contentment. . . .

THE
FOOL

"**B**UNTING! BUNTING, MY OWN DEAREST DARLING!"

Bunting, taking down the shutters of Israels', the clockmaker's in Carter Lane, slowly looked up to the first-floor window for Rachel, his cousin and latest love.

"April Fool!" screeched Rachel, a lovely, dark-eyed girl, and emptied a jug of dirty water down on his upturned face.

Mr. Israels, who was Bunting's uncle, stared through the window at his sodden apprentice.

"It don't take April the First to make such a fool!" he muttered. He knew he ought to have gone upstairs and reproached his daughter, but he really couldn't find it in his heart to blame her.

Although Bunting had been in the business for only a year, he had already done enough damage for a lifetime; and Mr. Israels, who rarely spoke Yiddish, felt himself driven to it.

"Schlemiel!" he said as Bunting lumbered inside the shop and leaned the shutters against the wall in such a way that they fell over almost at once. It was really the only expression that summed up the extraordinary mixture of clumsiness and beaming stupidity that was his sister's child.

Bunting picked up the shutters and went to change his shirt and wash his face.

"Schlemiel!" repeated Mr. Israels as he heard his nephew's large feet clump into the workshop. If Bunting hadn't been his sister's child—his own flesh and blood—he'd have thrown him out long ago; as it was, he could only compress his lips and put up with the great blundering cuckoo among his clocks. It was a bitterness to the master clockmaster that Time, with its beautiful, ticking precision, should have Bunting muddling it.

But today was the Eve of Passover and not really the time for disagreeable thoughts. The shop would be shut for two days, and that night there would be the cheerful family festival to celebrate the Exodus from Egypt with wine and song and Mrs. Israels' stuffed carp. His lovely daughter, Rachel, would be sitting up till late in her new dress, and being the youngest at table, she'd be asking the Four Questions in her uncertain Hebrew, and everyone would smile and laugh and congratulate her. It was a pleasure for which the master clockmaker could scarcely wait.

Last year, he recollected, with a slight frown, as a favour to his sister, Bunting had asked the Questions; and there was a large wine stain on the Passover cloth to mark where he'd sat. The boy's mother had offered to buy a new cloth, but Mrs. Israels had said, "No—no! It was an accident!" and Mrs. Bunting had taken her at her word and done nothing.

Mr. Israels struggled to put from his mind the undeniable fact that his own sister was a mean and selfish woman, who, in addition to everything else, had saddled him with the biggest idiot it had ever been his misfortune to come across . . . in a lifetime of trading.

Bunting, on the other hand, regarded his uncle with enormous admiration and respect. The old boy was a wizard with wheels and was, moreover, the father of the lovely Rachel. . . .

Unable to find a clean shirt, Bunting put the dirty one on again, inside out, and sat down to collect his soaked and shaken thoughts.

He scratched his head and sighed. It wasn't as though he didn't think at all; it was just that he thought slowly. Often, he knew, he was having quite large thoughts, but there never seemed time to consider more than a piece of them. Everything went past so quickly, and it was next week before he'd finished digesting yesterday.

A tree might have thought as Bunting thought, as he sat, rooted in the clockmaker's workshop, while round about, the multitudinous tread of minutes and seconds as they tramped and scampered round the hanging clock faces tried to tell him that time was passing by.

At length he stood up and stared into a clock glass, seeing not the evidence of flying minutes, but his own unchanging, amiable face. He smoothed down his hair and reflected ruefully on how pleasant it would have been to be out and about with the beautiful Rachel, who was the very brightest ornament of the spring; instead, alas! he was shut up in a ticking factory with springs of a very different nature—springs that snapped and stung like vipers whenever he so much as touched them.

He sucked his fingers and dreamed of being a sailor, with a Rachel in every port; but here he was, a clockmaker's apprentice with no time for dalliance but between sunset and ten o'clock of a Saturday night.

It wasn't so bad in the winter, when the sun set early; but in spring and summer—the very seasons for love—the sun set cruelly late, and his time out was cut down to a shred.

Saturday after Saturday he'd pleaded with his uncle, but it

was out of Mr. Israels' hands. Saturday was the Sabbath day until the sun set, and if the Almighty saw fit to shorten Bunting's night out in the warm weather, then the Almighty knew what He was about.

"Listen to me, Bunting," Mr. Israels had said. "In dealings between man and man, time goes by the clock; but in dealings between man and the Almighty, time goes by the sun. So please don't argue."

Bunting buttoned up his coat and went outside again to clean the shop window where the dirty water had splashed. Cautiously he looked up.

"Rachel!"

She came to the window and looked out. This time she threw down only the light of her eyes. Bunting surveyed her and marvelled. Time had sped by so quickly. Only last year she'd been a skinny nothing; now she bloomed like the Rose of Sharon. Eagerly he looked forward to sitting next to her at the table that night; he imagined holding her hand under cover of the cloth, and perhaps—who knew?—after several glasses of Passover wine, she'd let him kiss her! He waved up to her with a flourish, as if he'd doffed a large feathered hat, and bowed. His bottom butted a passerby.

"Schlemiel!" said Rachel, and laughed like tinsel.

Bunting apologized to the basket woman he'd knocked over and helped her gather her scattered wares; then he resumed wiping the window and whistling the latest street song but one.

He wasn't really downhearted by Rachel's treatment; he felt that she was just a little quicker than he was. Sooner or later he'd catch up with her, and with the world in general. . . .

"Time for sale! Time for sale!"

Bunting jumped as the high-pitched, nasal voice, floating down Carter Lane, broke so aptly into the pattern of his thoughts.

He looked eastwards and saw that an ancient, bearded man in a tall black hat was beating his way against the hurrying crowds and sometimes helping his progress with a stout, knobby stick.

It was not Father Time, but old Levy, wearing his long blue coat that flapped open to display a heavy cluster of watch seals dangling from under his crumpled velvet waistcoat. Behind him came his lame boy, with a large mahogany cupboard case strapped to his back. They were at once a pathetic and disturbing sight.

Old Levy bought and sold watches in the streets of most of the towns in the kingdom, and nobody knew for certain how much money he was worth. It was thought to be a great deal, for the old fellow never parted with anything for nothing—not even the time of day. When he did business, which he began by unlocking and opening his boy's cupboard case to display his stock of time-pieces, it was seen that every watch told a different time; you had to buy one to find out what was the right time.

"Buy a watch!" wailed old Levy. "Be the master of your time!"

Rachel came to the window again—as did daughters up and down the street, till fair heads mingled with the shop signs like blossoms among the creaking, swinging leaves. Handkerchiefs fluttered and shrill voices called for their Toms, Dicks, and Harrys to hurry outside, for old Levy sometimes had trinkets from Birmingham, cheap enough for apprentices to tempt their masters' daughters with—and since the beginning of time, girls have loved to yield to tempters. . . .

"Good morning, Mr. Levy!" called out Bunting, bursting to distinguish himself upon this shining April morning, with all the world looking down.

"Morning—evening? Who knows for certain till they buy a watch?" said old Levy cunningly.

He tottered up to the clockmaker's shop and observed with

interest the metal scroll upon the doorpost that denoted a Jewish home and, therefore, a friend in Egypt.

"All right. It's morning. That much I'll give you. And maybe it is a good morning for you. You've got your health and strength and are looking forward to a Passover night with singing and wine and stuffed fish. But I'm an old, old man, and my boy here is lame. The Almighty, in His wisdom, has made one of his legs shorter than the other."

"But He's made the other one longer!" piped up the boy with a brightly martyred smile.

"Schnorrers!" muttered Mr. Israels, who was watching through the window. Again he was driven into Yiddish; for what else described the disagreeable mixture of wheedling, whining, and ingratiating begging that was old Levy and his boy? Besides, he felt it an impertinence for the old wretch to be hawking his wares outside a craftsman's shop. It implied a kinship. . . .

"Careful, Mr. Levy, sir!" cried Bunting, winking up at Rachel. "Your shoelace is undone!"

"My shoe?" exclaimed Levy, and bent his withered back to examine his feet.

"April Fool!" shouted Bunting triumphantly, and lumbered out of range of the knobby stick.

But old Levy made no attempt to raise his weapon. He remained bent almost double. He groaned in agony and slowly fell to the ground, flapping out his coat like a damaged bird.

Bunting looked on; he was still grinning triumphantly. Everything had happened so quickly that he was still with his joke, even though calamity had overwhelmed it.

"My back! My chest . . . my heart!" moaned old Levy. "I can't move. . . . Moses, my boy, help me! Carry me inside! It—it's the Almighty's will . . . and God be thanked that it should happen outside a Jewish house! At least I can die among Jews . . . and on the Passover! Moses, Moses . . . go to the synagogue in Magpie Alley! Fetch the rabbi. . . ."

The boy Moses, who was blessed with one of those extraordinarily transparent and beautiful faces often seen among cripples, hopped about in piteous anxiety, begging someone to free him from his rattling mahogany burden so that he might run, as fast as his lame legs would carry him, to Magpie Alley.

A crowd quickly gathered round the moaning old man, and there were exclamations of, "Shame!" and, "Poor old devil!" and the luckless Bunting found himself being pushed and buffetted and roundly abused. He didn't know what to do until Mr. Israels came out of the shop, called him a schlemiel, and sent him off to Magpie Alley, as lame Moses would have taken all day.

Only too thankful to be removed from the disaster he'd brought about, Bunting lumbered off and ran all the way to Magpie Alley, where the rabbi lived at the back of the synagogue.

He thumped and thundered till the door was answered, and the rabbi, a sensible man, told him to come in and sit down and get his breath back, as it was impossible to understand what he wanted. So Bunting sat down on a chair in the hallway and explained more slowly. The rabbi listened and nodded.

"So it's that schnorrer Levy," he said. His voice and manner seemed altogether more composed than Bunting felt the extreme urgency of the situation required.

"Do you know, my boy," he went on, observing Bunting's anxiety, "why tonight's festival is called the Passover? It's because on this night the children of Israel in Egypt were commanded by the Almighty to smear their doorposts with the blood of the paschal lamb so that the angel of death would pass them over as he smote the first-born of the Egyptians. It was the tenth plague. Well, Levy is the eleventh plague. And the Almighty, blessed be His name, has not told us to this day what we must smear on our doorposts so that the schnorrer might pass us over!"

But the rabbi had been too subtle, and Bunting's anxiety was increasing visibly.

"Do you think you could hurry, sir?" he said.

The rabbi looked at him closely and framed the word "Schlemiel!" Nevertheless, he put on his coat and went with the boy to Carter Lane. After all, he thought to himself, quickening his pace, old Levy was more than ninety, and it was just possible that his hour had struck. On the other hand, he thought, slowing down a little, old Levy had had mortal illnesses before, and they always tended to strike him down on feast days outside a Jewish home. It was really rather fortunate that the two schnorrers hadn't got as far as Magpie Alley. . . .

They reached Carter Lane to find that the crowd had dispersed and that the old man had been taken inside, where he was lying on a couch in Mr. Israels' parlour. He was moaning loudly and attempting to lay his skinny, mittened hands on Moses' glossy black curls, as if to bless him.

A doctor had been called but had been unable to discover anything, as old Levy had howled in agony at the very thought of being examined; so he'd gone away after diagnosing that the old man must have been as fragile as a dried stick and that it was probably wisest to leave him where he was.

The rabbi gazed thoughtfully down at him.

"Shall I pray for you, Levy?" he asked rather dryly.

A superstitious gleam flickered in Levy's bleary eyes.

"Oy—oy—oy!" he moaned.

The rabbi shrugged his shoulders.

"I'll come back again when he's made up his mind," he said to Mr. Israels, and went on to console the master clockmaker by saying that it was a worthy and righteous thing to take in the needy and the unfortunate, especially at the time of the Passover.

"The needy—yes! The unfortunate—yes! But the schnorrer—
no! I'd have taken in any poor man from the street and fed him
till he burst—even as the Almighty tells us. But now I have a pair
of schnorrers in the house . . . thanks to that schlemiel Bunting!"

This was said in the hall, out of Bunting's hearing. He had
been left in the parlour with old Levy and his boy, and he gazed
in unhappy fascination at the tragedy he'd so unthinkingly
brought about.

Curiously the old man and the boy watched him, while the
mahogany cupboard case, propped up in a corner, emitted a
rapid, insectival ticking, as if mocking the stillness of the room.

"I—I'm sorry, sir," muttered Bunting. "I never meant anything."

"Oy—oy—oy!" said old Levy, and his ragged beard twitched
and shifted as his unimaginable lips made a smile. "We are all in
the hand of the Almighty. . . ."

"Blessed be His name," added Moses, dragging and limping
to his master's side.

He smiled his bright martyr's smile at Bunting, and his full
red lips moved in what Bunting took to be a Hebrew blessing;
but to someone quicker than Bunting might equally well have
been, "April Fool!" But Bunting was slow, so he took the
blessing.

The sun had set and, in strict accordance with holy law, all
manner of work was put aside. As Mr. Israels was a clockmaker,
the clocks had been stopped; now was the time of the Almighty.

In the oily, gleaming workshop, poised pendulums shivered in
the tickless air, and the clock faces stared at one another as if expecting a judgment.

Bunting, scraping an egg stain from his velvet cap, felt uncanny
without the remorseless hammering of seconds to fix and rivet

him. His mind peered about in surprise as huge fragments of thought rolled through it—of Rachel, of his stern uncle, of his father and mother, who'd already arrived in a frantic bustle of belongings. His mother had anointed him with scented affection, and his father had given him the shilling he always gave on Passover night. Then they'd whisked away to their room, and all had been uproar. . . .

More than ever Bunting felt like a tree that is condemned to watch men twinkling through their lives while it yawns and stretches and climbs out of bed an inch a year. His thoughts roamed over past Passovers . . . and they all seemed like a watch in the night, coming and going in the blinking of an eye.

He picked up his gold-tooled Haggadah, and a loose page fell out, together with crumbs of last year's unleavened bread, which somehow had found their way inside the book.

He bent to retrieve the page on which were the quaint coloured drawings of the four sons to whom the good man must, each year, tell the old, old story of the escape from the taskmasters of Egypt.

He gazed at them: the wise son looked older than his father; wisdom had aged him frightfully. The wicked son, beetle-browed and moustachioed, was dashingly depicted as a soldier. Bunting had always had a soft spot for the wicked son. Then there was the son who was too young to ask questions, and he looked like a chamber pot in wrappings. Last of all was the foolish son, with hands raised in perpetual amazement. Someone—and it wasn't hard to guess who—had written "Bunting" underneath. He sighed and wondered if Rachel would have liked him better as a soldier.

His thoughts rolled on to old Levy and the lame boy and how angry everyone had been over the way it had all happened. Again and again he'd tried to explain to his uncle and aunt, but they wouldn't listen, and they pushed him aside while old Levy had been carted upstairs and laid in Bunting's room. He'd been told to sleep under the bench in the workshop until the smelly old schnorrer should recover or die. There was no doubt he did stink —of old clothes, old food, old sweat, and old age. . . .

So Bunting, motionless in the silent workshop, with his velvet cap perched on his head like an egg cosy, brooded away. Solemnly he tried to assemble all the fragments of his thought, even as a philosopher might seek to construct the curve of the world from a flowerbed in his garden. . . .

"Bunting!"

He jumped with alarm as his uncle's voice shouted from the dining room.

"What are you doing, boy? Hurry! Must you keep even the Almighty waiting?"

The company was all seated and impatiently waiting to begin the prayers. A host of flushed faces turned to regard him, but the long, gleaming magnificence of Mrs. Israels' Passover table quite obscured them.

It was like a vessel—a white and silver vessel—floating in candlelight. Tall silver candlesticks stood up like masts, and bright wine glasses stood by rolled napkins like angel gunners waiting to discharge their pieces at the moving shadows on the walls.

Sweet and sharp savours hovered in the air, filling the nose and pricking the tongue with countless dreamy memories. . . .

"Sit down, boy! Don't just stand there. Sit down."

Mr. Israels was frowning impatiently from his place at the head of the table. He was fidgeting among an immense pile of cushions; for was it not commanded that on this night all must eat at their ease, in memory of the escape from the house of bondage?

Mrs. Bunting looked at her son from under lowered lids as he took his place, but Bunting's pa beamed like a quarter to three, for he had been sampling the Passover wine.

The other places at the table were taken up by two neighbours from Shoemaker's Row, and by Mrs. Israels' sister and her husband, who was a respectable broker in Cheapside. And there was, of course, the empty chair for Elijah the Tishbite—if he should come.

The broker and his wife were not staying for the night. They had employed a linkboy to light them home after the ceremony and had left him at a nearby inn. They were paying him by the hour, and the broker kept looking critically at Mr. Israels, who, he felt, ought to be getting on with the service. One had to bear in mind that, however pleasant the circumstance, time was money.

At last Mr. Israels opened his book; the broker sighed with relief, and Mrs. Bunting said importantly, "Ssh!", which was her chief contribution to the festivities, as the Passover cake she'd made had been unaccountably left behind in the rush of getting to Carter Lane in good time.

Mr. Israels drew a deep breath and launched the Passover service at a rate of knots that warmed the broker's heart; if he kept it up, and if there were no interruptions, they'd be away by ten o'clock. . . . Little Moses, who had been placed next to Rachel, helped her to follow the text, while Bunting, who sat on her other side, gazed hopelessly into space. His eyes drifted towards the empty chair. What if Elijah did come that night? What would the mysterious prophet say after all his wanderings over the face of the world in search of the open door to announce the Messiah?

"Schlemiel!" whispered Rachel. "It's time to drink the wine!"

Bunting blushed and reached for his glass. There was a moment's silence round the table.

"Oy—oy—oy!"

Quite distinctly, the moan came floating down from aloft. It was quite amazing that old Levy's voice should carry so well. Little Moses smiled pleadingly round the table and asked if he might take a glass of wine up to his old master so that he, too, might join in celebrating the Passover.

There was no gainsaying the little schnorrer when he turned his brightly suffering face to each of the company in turn. Some children are gifted in music, some in painting; little Moses was gifted in the art of begging. He had a real genius for it.

The broker frowned, but like everyone else he had to sit and wait while the lame boy ticked and tocked up and down the stairs like a pendulum out of balance.

Bunting tried to hold Rachel's hand under the table, but she was exceedingly angry. She would not be allowed to ask the Four Questions—for which she was to have been given a present—as little Moses was now the youngest at the table. She dug her nails fiercely into Bunting's finger, so that he squealed in fright and pain.

"Ssh!" said Mrs. Bunting, and Moses came back, full of smiles and apologies, to ask, in his slightly stammering Hebrew, wherefore this night, with its unleavened bread, its bitter herbs, and its enforced reclining at table, was different from all other nights.

Scarcely were the words out of his mouth than Mr. Israels was off again, trying to make up for lost time. He prided himself in knocking minutes off anyone else's time for the service and felt it a point of honour not to depart from his own high standards.

The broker noted with approval the diminishing number of pages ahead, while Bunting struggled in the rear and was, in fact, still laboriously reading the Four Questions to himself, long after most of them had been answered. He raised his eyes, and there was the empty chair for Elijah, and Bunting wondered if the prophet was as far behind as he, and was that why he'd never yet turned up to announce the coming of the Messiah?

At last Mr. Israels arrived at the mention of bitter herbs, which stood for the days of bitterness in Egypt; he pointed jovially at his wife, and that was considered something of a humorous peak in the evening and always made Mr. Bunting laugh.

"Ssh!" said Mrs. Bunting, after which everyone was given a helping of the bitter herb—which was not really bitter at all but was horseradish agreeably flavoured—on a small piece of un-leavened bread. Time went backwards as the children of Israel in Carter Lane partook of the bitter herbs and the bread of affliction like their forebears in the house of bondage.

"Very nice," said Mrs. Bunting, and old Levy, smelling the pleasant aroma through two closed doors, moaned loudly.

"Go see what he wants now," said Mr. Israels to Bunting, whose presence, he felt, could most easily be dispensed with.

Bunting, his eyes watering from the horseradish, rose slowly. He was reluctant to leave Rachel to the charms of little Moses.

"Hurry, my boy!" urged the broker. "The old man may really be in need!"

Bunting went and mounted the stairs, though his heart re-mained below. He entered what had been his own room, and the oppressive smell of the eleventh plague smote him.

Old Levy, still in his stained blue coat and old boots, lay stretched upon Bunting's bed. His sharp features, half buried in the tangle of his dirty beard, looked worn and anxious.

"Oy—oy—oy!" he said.

"What's wrong, sir?"

Old Levy groaned again and lifted up his head.

"Tell me—tell me, my boy . . . are we still in Egypt? Are we still slaves with the whips on our backs? Ain't the Almighty brought us forth yet from the house of bondage?"

He panted for breath, and Bunting wondered if he'd gone off

his head and was imagining himself in ancient Egypt.

"Oy—oy—oy! Let me live long enough on this Passover night to come to that blessed time! Don't let me die in the darkness of Egypt. Don't let me pass away before I've tasted Thy blessed manna, O Lord, and Mrs. Israels' stuffed fish! Tell me, my boy, did I smell horseradish?"

Bunting nodded. "We've just got to the bitter herbs. Would you like some, sir, on a piece of matzo?"

"Schlemiel!" muttered old Levy; then he smiled sadly. "Bitter herbs are to remind us of a bitter time. What need have I to bring into my mouth what already plagues me every night of the year? And matzo! The bread of affliction. Ain't I afflicted enough with sore gums and no teeth? Oy—oy—oy! Still, he's got to the bitter herbs at last—thank God! Maybe I'll be spared long enough for the stuffed fish?"

"I'll bring you some, sir—"

"With a little horseradish!" croaked old Levy anxiously as the boy departed. "I want to remember again my days in the brick-yards with the taskmasters' whips on my back!"

Downstairs, the feast was already on the table, and the shadows were dancing on the walls as everyone leaned this way and that to admire the splendour of Mrs. Israels' stuffed carp.

"It's like a whale!" exclaimed Mr. Bunting, and the neighbours from Shoemaker's Row wondered where such a fish had been caught.

It had been stuffed to suffocation with raisins, chopped herbs, and hard-boiled eggs, and reclined, in an exhausted fashion, in a plated tureen from which its head emerged to rest upon the rim, with the expression of one who has just awakened to its nightmare plight.

Bunting, his attention divided between the radiant Rachel and the immense fish, passed on old Levy's requirements and waited to be given the old man's portion. Mr. Israels told Bunting to stop staring and sit down.

"I rather fancy," he said, with a dryly ironical smile round the table, "that the Almighty will spare Mr. Levy till we've finished our meal. Time enough, my boy . . ."

Bunting sat down, shaking his head. What if the old man should really die before he was out of Egypt that night? He glanced towards little Moses, but the lame one was too busy fascinating Rachel to think of anything else. He looked at the empty place. What would Elijah the Tishbite say if he should come? He looked at the carp, and the carp looked at Bunting, and its open mouth framed the single word, "Schlemiel!"

Accompanied by laughter and a joyous jingling of spoons and forks, the great fish began its last journey round the table, and deep inroads were made in its shining flanks. It came to little Moses, and the lame boy's eyes sparkled with merriment as he performed a clever conjuring trick and seemed to draw, from the carp's gaping mouth, a pretty trinket on a thin silver chain.

Rachel cried out in admiration and delight, and everyone praised the little schnorrer's skill. Indeed, it had been so well done that Bunting couldn't help poking his finger into the cold wet hole when the fish came to him to see if anything else might be found inside.

He drew out half a hard-boiled egg and looked so surprised that everyone glanced expressively at one another; but no one said anything, and the meal proceeded in the utmost good humour.

At the head of the table, according to custom, the gentlemen disputed keenly on details of the Passover and went pretty deeply into history.

"How long would you say it was?" asked Mr. Bunting, smiling intelligently down the table at his wife as if to say, You see, I know how to conduct myself on such occasions! "How long would you say we were in Egypt? I mean altogether . . . since the days of Joseph?"

Mr. Israels frowned, trying to remember. "I believe it was a little more than four hundred years."

"You surprise me," said Mr. Bunting. "I'd no idea it was so long. Time goes by so quickly. Four hundred years!"

"Four hundred years," said the broker meditatively. "Have you ever thought that if one of Joseph's children had invested, say, a shilling at two per cent per annum, compound interest, there would have been a nice nest egg for the family? A very nice nest egg . . ."

"Do it again! Do it again!" said Rachel, giggling, to the little conjuror, and longed to be given the trinket. "Once more!"

"Ssh!" said Mrs. Bunting. "Listen to what's being said. Learn something from your uncles and your father!"

'Several millions of pounds, I shouldn't wonder," said the broker, and wondered how much he already owed the linkboy and whether the lad would have been drinking and unfit to guide them.

"That's astonishing!" said Mr. Bunting. Only a shilling, and in four hundred years. "Did you hear that, my son?" he called down the table. "Your shilling in four hundred years might be worth . . . millions!"

Bunting nodded vaguely. He had heard but, as usual, had not understood. His thoughts were elsewhere. He'd put aside a portion of fish for old Levy on his own plate. All he longed for now was for the meal to end so that he could go upstairs again. He'd heard no further sound from the old man and he was worried.

He became aware that his mother was pointing reproachfully at his plate and asking why he'd taken a second helping and wasn't eating it. He tried to explain, but she lost patience and turned away. The only creature in the room that still seemed interested in him was the carp, now reduced to a ruin of its former self. And its head, lying in the tureen, still said, "Schlemiel!"

I know . . . I know, thought Bunting wearily. But what if he should really die? It could happen, you know. . . .

At last the meal came to an end, and Bunting stood up.

"Where are you going, my boy?"

"To take Mr. Levy some fish—"

"I rather fancy," said Mr. Israels, with another ironic smile round the table, "that he can wait for Elijah. After all, we are all waiting for Elijah, so I'm sure the Almighty will spare Mr. Levy for a little longer, eh?"

Everyone laughed appreciatively over how neatly Mr. Israels had brought in the solemn occasion that was still to come; only Bunting gazed at the empty place and wondered what the ghostly prophet would have said.

Grace was said, and the Cup of Elijah was filled to the brim with the dark Passover wine and put before the empty place.

"I hope," said Mr. Israels, pointing to the large pewter goblet, "that Elijah has a good head for wine!"

He said this every year, and it was considered the second peak of humour of the evening.

"And how long would you say it was that Elijah kept the widow's cruse full of oil?" inquired Mr. Bunting, smiling again at his wife.

"I'm not at all sure about that," answered Mr. Israels slowly. "Perhaps two or three days?"

"Of course," said the broker, "it would depend on how much oil she had to begin with, before one could calculate how much actual money had been saved."

He thought about the linkboy and frowned.

"There was the barrel of meal as well," said Mr. Israels, anxious to defend the prophet against the charge of meanness.

"Naturally that makes a difference. But supposing it was a matter of, say, four hours," went on the broker, obsessed with his evening's expenditure, "then that must be taken into account. Let's say it was five hours—"

"If it was only five hours, it would hardly have counted as a miracle! It must have been at least a week. . . ."

Bunting listened in bewilderment and agitation and wondered if the dispute would ever end. What if Elijah, at that very moment, was driving down Carter Lane?

"Well," said Mr. Israels at length. "We mustn't keep the prophet waiting!"

He raised the second ceremonial glass of wine, which was the Cup of Redemption, pronounced the blessing, and drank.

"Open the door, Bunting, my boy. Open the door for Elijah!"

Awkwardly Bunting struggled to his feet and rested his hand affectionately on Rachel's shoulder, so that he felt its fragile boniness and realised with a shock how young she really was. She glanced up at him, then, tossing her head, went back to begging little Moses for the trinket.

Bunting went out into the quiet, dark hall and listened for a moment for the old man's moaning. Silence.

"Is the door open, my boy? Or are you waiting for Elijah to knock?"

This was a new joke of Mr. Israels', and Bunting heard his father laugh. Then he opened the street door and gazed out into the quiet immensity of the spring night.

There was no prophet in the street, so Bunting looked up. A great white moon swam in the dark heavens, like the eye of the biggest stuffed carp in the universe. As it was Passover night, Bunting supposed the angels had eaten the rest, for he could see no mouth that said, "Schlemiel!"

Presently he thought he heard a sound from upstairs. He left the open door and went to the foot of the stairs and listened carefully. Nothing.

"Bunting! What are you doing out there? Come back. . . ."

He went back into the dining room, where the Passover table was littered with nuts and grapes and all the cheerful confusion of a feast. He stared at the brimming cup set for Elijah, and a silence fell upon the room as the night air swept in. The candle flames, now sunk deep in their waxen sepulchres, ducked and bowed, and the shadows on the walls suddenly loomed upward, like a phantom company arising to greet the coming of their phantom king.

Involuntarily everyone looked towards the open door, as, at this moment, they always did. What if Elijah the Tishbite, in all his robes and with all his ravens, should really come? What if his fiery chariot was, at this very moment, galloping down Carter Lane?

Rachel began to giggle, and Mrs. Bunting said, "Ssh!" Mr. Israels drew in his breath, but no words came. He seemed to remain expanded, and full, as it were, of holy air. Even the broker was struck dumb, for there was a strange, fiery radiance creeping across the polished panel of the open door.

Leaping flames were reflected, and there came a hissing and cracking sound, as of unearthly harness straining and burning wheels whirling through the streets of the air.

"It's Elijah!" murmured Bunting, and then the broker's link-boy, with torch smoking and blazing, crept cautiously into the room. In addition to the smell of burning pitch, there was also a distinct smell of gin.

"I was jes' wonderin' 'ow long you'd be, sir," he mumbled, blinking round at the company, who stared back at him with mingled outrage and disappointment. "The door was open so I—"

The Fool

Whatever else he had to say was lost in a hoarse and fearful shriek that was accompanied by a loud clatter of feet descending the stairs.

Bunting caught a brief glimpse, through the open door, of a tremendous, almost spectral sight. There was old Levy, his long coat flapping and his watch seals dancing, galloping across the hall on his way out of the street door!

The old schnorrer, wearied of waiting for his supper and thinking he'd been forgotten, had crept from his deathbed onto the landing from where he'd intended to moan loudly enough to disturb everyone. Then, finding the house in silence and seeing the reflection of flames and smelling the fire, he had been seized with a ghastly dread that the house was burning down and everyone had left him behind to perish.

"Save me! Save me!" he howled, and, skinny and jingling, capered frantically down Carter Lane.

"Mr. Levy!" cried Bunting. "Your fish—"

"What are you doing? Come back with that plate, you schlemiel!" he heard everyone shouting as he rushed out after old Levy with his portion of stuffed fish.

Although Bunting must have realised that he'd been taken in by the old villain and that everybody had been right while he, as usual, had been wrong, his mind had been so firmly fixed on old Levy's dying happy that it was impossible for him, in so short a time, to rearrange his thoughts and behave sensibly.

"Mr. Levy, Mr. Levy! Here's your fish—"

Old Levy had not gone far; he and his crooked shadow had collapsed, puffing and panting, on a high doorstep at the corner of Creed Lane. His wind and panic spent themselves together, and, somewhat apprehensively, he crouched down and awaited the coming of the schlemiel, who had been his only ally in the household on which he had imposed himself.

It was possible that he felt a pang of regret for having exposed the fool so openly and that he was sorry for what he might have lost in the fool's heart. But who could say what a man as ancient as Levy, the watch seller, really felt?

"Oy—oy—oy!" he said as Bunting came near.

"Why did you run away, sir?"

"It was the fire. I smelled it . . . and the Almighty gave me strength. . . ."

"It wasn't a fire, sir. It was only Elijah—I mean, it was a boy with a torch. . . ."

"Elijah? So . . . so, the Almighty has pulled my old leg—even as He once pulled little Moses' young one. He's lame, you know. . . . Oy—oy—oy!"

"I brought you the stuffed carp. . . ."

Old Levy squinted up at the schlemiel in the moonlight and marvelled at the way he shone. He took the plate with trembling fingers.

"So . . . so Elijah came at last," he mumbled, and began to cram fragments of the fish into an opening in his beard. "And where's the horseradish?"

Before Bunting could reply, the old man raised his hand. There was a ticking and a tocking in the empty street. It was little Moses, hopping and limping under his cupboard case like a large beetle or a child carrying a child's coffin. He halted at the sight of Bunting, then came on as he saw his ancient master eating.

"Tell me, Moses," whined old Levy, putting down his plate and clutching Bunting's sleeve, "*wherefore is this night different from all other nights?*"

Moses chuckled happily as old Levy began to ask the Four Questions in the high, lisping tones of a pretended child.

"*On all other nights we eat either sitting upright or reclining; but on this night we all recline.*"

The Fool

He dragged in his coat to make a space for Bunting to recline beside him, while Moses crouched down and leaned against his cupboard case, which ticked away as if exasperated by not being on the move.

Bunting sat, or was rather dragged down, for the old man had not let him go. Old Levy's bones were miserable to lean against, and his buttons and watch seals dug into Bunting's side.

"We were Pharaoh's bondsmen in Egypt, and the Lord our God brought us out therefrom with a mighty hand," piped the crippled Moses to the deceitful watch seller and the clockmaker's foolish apprentice.

"Have a little stuffed carp, Moses," urged old Levy, "for has not the Almighty brought us out once more from the house of bondage?"

Moses leaned forward and his cupboard of watches chimed faintly as a timepiece struck a meaningless hour.

"I must go back!" cried Bunting suddenly.

"A little longer!" whined old Levy, who liked company. "Stay another minute! How much longer will the Almighty spare me? Who knows. Come—let's sing, *"Only one kid"* and then we'll part . . . till next year in Jerusalem, eh?"

He hung onto Bunting's sleeve despairingly, and began, in his horrible wheezing voice, to hum and chant the last of the Passover songs:

> *"Only one kid,*
> *only one kid*
> *that my father bought for two zuzim. . . .*
> *Then came a cat*
> *And ate the kid*
> *That my father bought for two zuzim,"*

sang Moses, in his high, stammering voice; and his eyes were bright both for the cat and the kid.

"Then came a dog
And bit the cat
That ate the kid
That my father bought for two zuzim,"

joined in Bunting, who loved the old song dearly.

"Only one kid, only one kid."

They all joined in the refrain, and even as they did so, a bright and burning light came along the street, scouring out the shadows and reddening the fronts of the houses till they seemed to run with blood.

"I knows that chune," said the linkboy, who had been sent to fetch Bunting and the plate. "It's Free Blind Mice, ain't it?"

He came and, with his torch held high, watched in puzzlement as the three children of Israel croaked and sang of an ancient deliverance under the many-chimneyed sky.

"Then came a stick
And beat the dog
That bit the cat
That ate the kid
That my father bought for two zuzim!"

"Only one kid . . . only one kid!"

"Then came a fire,"

cackled old Levy, pointing at the linkboy's torch,

"And burned the stick
That beat the dog . . ."

He began to clap his hands in time to the nursery song, and little Moses, with his box of watches rattling and jingling like timbrels, began to dance on his lame feet.

"Then came a fire . . ."

The link boy grinned and, creeping and hopping in Moses's
wake, waved his blazing torch in time to old Levy's rhythmic
clapping.

> *"Then water came*
> *And quenched the fire*
> *That burned the stick . . ."*

Old Levy blew his nose and water flew out; the fire jumped in
fright, and little Moses, with his burden of time, capered away
like King David of old, while the stony-faced houses trembled in
the hopping light.

> *"Then came an ox*
> *And drank the water*
> *That quenched the fire . . ."*

Up lumbered Bunting, and, clumsy as the ox in the song, joined
in with the nighttime dance.

> *"Only one kid . . . only one kid!"*

> *"Then came the slaughterer*
> *And slaughtered the ox*
> *That drank the water . . ."*

screeched out old Levy; and he, too, with his long coat flapping
and his watch seals jingling, linked himself into the leaping
chain, while Pharaoh in his houses twitched the curtains and
stared.

> *"Only one kid . . . only one kid . . ."*

> *"Then came the Angel of Death*
> *And slew the slaughterer*

> *That slaughtered the ox*
> *That drank the water . . ."*

chanted little Moses, for it was his turn.

At once, a chill wind swept down Carter Lane, tearing the torch flame from its roots. Old Levy clutched his chest and stumbled till—thank God!—Bunting came in with the last verse.

> *"Then came the Almighty, blessed be He,*
> *And smote the Angel of Death*
> *That slew the slaughterer*
> *That slaughtered the ox*
> *That drank the water*
> *That quenched the fire*
> *That burned the stick*
> *That beat the dog*
> *That bit the cat*
> *That ate the kid*
> *That my father bought for two zuzim!"*

"Only one kid . . . only one kid!"

The danger was past, and the old man breathed again; it was indeed a Passover night! At last the dancers swayed to a halt and sang the last refrain while the torchlight enveloped them in a fiery garment. Smoke billowed out and made them a concealing tent in the wilderness of Carter Lane.

It was possible that Elijah the Tishbite, passing by in his robes and with all his ravens, had not seen, in all his wanderings, anything half so fine as the ancient man and the three children, escaping from the bondage of time.

"Next year in Jerusalem, eh?" said old Levy to Bunting as the apprentice prepared to return to the clockmaker's shop.

Bunting nodded seriously and, with the timeless song with its immense chain of consequences deep in his heart, went back to the Passover table in Carter Lane.

"Why were you so long?" whispered Rachel, pinching him sharply as he sat down.

"I was only gone for a minute," said Bunting, and then added softly, as if in expiation of his fault, *"A thousand years in thy sight are but as yesterday when it is past, and as a watch in the night."*

Rachel stared at him.

"What sort of a watch is that?" she asked cleverly. "Schlemiel!" and everyone laughed.

ROSY
STARLING

ROSY STARLING, THE BIRD-CAGE MAKER, PRETTY AS A PICTURE and blind as a bat, came out into Drury Lane and felt light and warmth upon her face.

"It's a grand sunny day!" she said to the invisible world.

"Sun? Day?" jeered a linkboy. "It's four o'clock in the mornin', miss, and black as soot! It's me burnin' torch! Can't you smell the pitch?"

"And there was me thinkin' it was you smellin' so horrible!" said Rosy pertly, and longed to put her tongue out, even though she had always been told never to make faces or folk would think her simple as well as blind.

She was apprenticed to Mrs. Berry, a basketmaker in Feathers Court, and she made cages out of willow wands for canaries and linnets that were suitable as presents for children and sold at sixpence apiece. She carried a bundle of them over her arm, tied together with a plaited straw chain.

"You got anuvver free hours beauty sleep," said the linkboy, letting his light fall inquisitively on Rosy's eyes, which were like bricked-up windows.

"Then what are you doin' up so long after your bedtime?" inquired Rosy. "And what's all the bangin' and shoutin' about?"

"They're puttin' up the maypole, and all them sweeps and their little sootikins are gettin' ready to go a-Mayin'. But they ain't washed yet, so they're all as black as me 'at. There's nothin' worth seein' . . . even if you could!"

"Bleedin' sauce," said Rosy haughtily, "to mock me disability!"

She began to move, lightly and hesitantly—like a dandelion clock in ruffled air—towards Maypole Alley. As she brushed and knocked against passersby, she turned and bade them, in no uncertain terms, to watch where they were going.

Rosy Starling had a tongue in her head all right, even though she had no usable eyes; and Mrs. Berry, meaning for the best, had always encouraged her sharpness.

"You're as pretty as a picture, Rosy," she kept telling her. "So you got to watch out . . . in a manner o' speakin', that is. This wicked world's full of villains what'll take advantage else!"

Mrs. Berry said this in good faith; it never crossed her mind that, perhaps, she herself was taking advantage by building such a cage of suspicion round her clever and industrious apprentice that no one was likely to get the chance to tempt her out of Feathers Court.

Presently Rosy felt the tall, close buildings recede, and she knew she must be in the open space where Maypole Alley joined Little Drury Lane.

"Watch what you're doin'!" she kept calling out, feeling bustle and activity and heavy feet all round her and fearing that she was in danger of being tripped and strangled by the ropes employed in raising the maypole.

"Rosy Starling!" someone cried. "You'll get that pretty head knocked off!"

She felt her cages gently tugged, and she herself conducted to a doorstep from where she might watch the May Day preparations in safety.

Watch? Oh, she knew very well what things looked like; Mrs. Berry had told her, and, in addition, her own skilful hands presented to her imagination a wondrous variety of shapes to which were attached sounds and smells and those ghostly emanations given off alike by poles, posts, doors, and villains out to take advantage.

"It's goin' to be a grand sunny day," she said as she seated herself and rested her cages in her lap. "That is, if it don't rain."

"Rosy Starling," said the female who'd helped her, "you're as pretty as a picture!"

"I wish," said Rosy, feeling her cheeks grow warm, "I could say as much for you."

Not knowing how to take the blind girl's reply, the helper departed, and Rosy spread her skirts and laid out her wares so that nobody should sit near her and spoil her pitch. Then she took a piece of bread and cold sausage from one of her cages and settled down to enjoy her breakfast, and to listen, between munchings, to the cheerful uproar that attended the erection of the maypole.

It had first been set up by a farrier, by name of Clarges, to commemorate the wedding of his daughter, a humble sempstress, to the Duke of Albemarle; and every May Day thereafter, Little Drury Lane had been sacred to the high hopes of lowly lasses on the lookout for wandering dukes.

Even Rosy Starling, in spite of her caution and suspicions, couldn't subdue a prickling of excitement as the morning crept on and more and more pairs of brisk young feet tapped on the cobbles and passed her by. Many paused briefly; perhaps they smiled? She couldn't tell. . . .

"But anyway, you're too tall," she said to herself. "And you're

too short for me! And as for you—why, you want to get them
shoes mended and cleaned, too, I daresay, before you come
courtin' me!

"Get a move on with you!" she cried aloud as a pair of feet
shuffled and loitered longer than she liked, and she felt watchful
eyes upon her. "Ain't you never seen a blind lady eatin' before?"

"Sorry, miss . . . sorry."

Fiercely she smoothed down her skirt and tucked the hem into
her shoe buckles so as not to display her ankles unwarily; then
she made sure her little lace cap was pinned at a fetching
tilt. . . .

"Now where's me last bit of bread gone?" She felt beside her.
"Come on—who's stole it?"

"Sparrers, miss. Little thievin' sparrers."

"Sauce!" said Rosy. "And me with me cages all shut up!"

She laughed and, unlatching a cage, inserted her neat, white-
gloved hand and fluttered her fingers temptingly.

"Come along with you! Come inside me little Newgate for yer
sins!"

She heard folk chuckle, so she smiled and raised her face and
silenced them with one look of her bricked-up eyes. Not that
they were at all shocking or ugly—any more than the coloured
stones children play with are shocking or ugly. . . .

Presently the commotion round the maypole died away, and
there was a noise of creaking and straining. This was followed
by anxious shouts of "To me! To me!" and finally by a groaning of wood and an almighty thump that shook the very doorstep
on which Rosy Starling sat.

Everyone stamped and cheered, and Rosy Starling knew that
the maypole was up. Carpenters' hammers banged and children
shrieked, while Rosy Starling, very ladylike, clapped her hands
and called, "Well done!"

She began to hum a tune Mrs. Berry was fond of, but of which she didn't know the words.

"La—la—la!" she chanted, gently nodding her head. "La—la—la!"

> *"Bobby Shafto's gone to sea,*
> *Silver buckles at his knee . . ."*

"Who's that? Who's singin' me song?"

> *"He'll come back and marry me*
> *Bonny Bobby Shafto!"*

The voice faded and was soon lost in the general hubbub. It had been a light and airy tenor; Rosy judged the singer to have been young and perhaps three fingers taller than herself. His voice had trembled slightly, but there'd been so much noise going on that, with all her sharpness, Rosy Starling had been unable to tell for sure if it had been a tremble of laughter or villainy.

She bent her head low and continued listening, trying with all her might to unravel the tangled skeins of sound, for she hated a mystery. Impatiently she waved off neighbors and street traders who kept wishing her good morning and asking after Mrs. Berry; they distracted her and broke up her patterns. But it was no use; the voice had gone.

Little by little the air grew warmer and full of the sensation of real sunshine; it seemed to clothe her and hold her in a soft, enormous hand. She wriggled her shoulders luxuriantly. She could smell onions and veal pies and the brown nutty sting of strong ale. The food stalls were opening for business.

She sniffed harder and made out oranges and new bread, and— and there was another smell that she couldn't quite put a name to; it was a most curious and haunting smell that seemed to be made up of opposites: rosewater and vinegar, and with something of chestnuts, too. It was quite near. . . .

> "Bobby Shafto's bright and fair
> Combing down his yellow hair . . ."

"So it's you!" said Rosy Starling. "Come back again and smellin' like an old bathhouse!"

"Good morning, miss."

"Any fool can see that!" answered Rosy coldly, and averted her face. The voice had been too shaky by half and, more than ever, Rosy Starling suspected a villain.

"Mind if I sit down next to you, miss?"

"Suit yourself," said Rosy Starling offhandedly. "It ain't my doorstep."

She shrank aside as she felt the air disturbed and waves of the curious smell coming over her. She heard clothing creak and rustle and she heard the clink of metal on metal. Could he be a soldier, with flashing eyes and teeth and wearing his sword? One and all they were villains, Mrs. Berry said; break your heart and leave you as soon as spit! So just you watch out, my girl. . . .

"You're—you're as pretty as a picture," he murmured in her ear.

Rosy Starling nodded and, smiling, turned to show him her stone-dead eyes.

All the dainty colours and tinsel ribbons of the little May Day fair spun and jostled past the doorstep like torn-up wedding paper as the apprentice, Turtle, shivered and stared into the bewitching face that framed the cold, milky-marble eyes.

"What are you gawpin' at? Ain't you never seen a blind lady before?"

He grew as cold as ice, then as hot as fire. The sudden look, which was not a look at all, had unnerved him. He felt frightened and guilty, and, as he continued to look at her, he was seized by an uncanny sensation that the blind bird-cage seller was watching him from some invisible vantage point inside her head.

Rosy Starling shrugged her shoulders and turned her back with a rush of her marvellous reddish gold hair. She was divided between fear and fascination; Mrs. Berry's warnings shouted urgently in her head, but the tales of May Day dukes also whispered in her heart. He was still there and watching her; she could feel his eyes, like fingers, touching her hair. . . .

The apprentice was indeed staring at the blind girl's hair; he couldn't keep his eyes off it. Since he'd come into Little Drury Lane, he'd been absorbed by it. He'd measured it in his mind from crown to tip; he'd weighed it and graded it and coveted it as a madman covets a sunbeam. It was the very perfection of his trade, and his soul ached to possess it. He was a hair merchant's apprentice on the lookout for stock.

He worked a little way to the north, for Mr. Delilah of Martlet Alley. Delilah was not, of course, his master's real name; it had been bestowed on him in recognition of his skill in charming the hair from the heads of the canniest milkmaids and barmaids as far afield as Birmingham, and selling it to wig makers for Hanover Square: Delilah being generally considered the chief practitioner and patron saint of the trade. It was his way to lay his victims low with compliments and port wine before begging a lock of their hair as a keepsake; after which, as he put it, he'd crop 'em closer than a nag's tail.

But even a Mr. Delilah must grow old; the merchant's eyes were dulled and his amorous chatter had a weary ring. So he'd taken unto himself an apprentice—one Turtle, by name.

Patiently he'd trained him up in the business. He taught him how to grade hair according to shade, weight, and fineness. He showed him how to comb it with a hackle and rid it of nits and the eggs of lice by passing it between thin needles and then washing it in weak vinegar; and he expounded the mysteries of steaming curls in a saucepan and dyeing them with green chestnuts, logwood, and alum.

"But first you need to lay your hands on it," he'd say, smiling at his apprentice as a thousand soft and curly memories floated through his mind. "And hair that's worth the getting takes a sight more than a pair of sharp scissors and a shilling! Yes, it takes charm, my boy."

Here Turtle, who'd been assured by his ma and aunts that he possessed charm enough to fetch the birds out of the trees, would look earnestly and admiringly at his master as if he'd never seen anything, in all his born days, as charming as Mr. Delilah. How was it possible? How did he do it?

"It's my eyes, my boy. It's all in the eyes," said Mr. Delilah modestly. "When I lays in a compliment, I keeps my eyes on the lass. Like this." He stared with eyes somewhat moist and squinting at his respectful assistant. "You see? There's a language in eyes. It's a language that every lass understands."

Turtle, who possessed the brightest and most *speaking* eyes his ma and aunts swore they'd ever seen, nodded in wonder; and Mr. Delilah, much gratified by his apprentice's attitude, gave him the day off to go down to Little Drury Lane on May Day with five shillings and a pair of scissors.

"There'll be lasses by the dozen," he said, "with new-washed heads and on the lookout for husbands. Use your eyes, my boy, and fetch me back a head of hair fit for a duchess!"

"Cat got your tongue?" said Rosy Starling to the silent, scented presence beside her.

The apprentice Turtle, of the speaking eyes and amazing

charm, blushed and tried to prevent the scissors and shillings from clinking together and betraying him. How in God's name was it possible to charm a lass when, for all she knew, he might have been as ugly as a toad? Of course, he could ask her outright to sell him her hair, and that would be an end of it. But what if she refused? Turtle was in a quandary. . . .

"If you can't talk," said Rosy Starling, sniffing out an advantage and longing to use it, "why don't you sing again?" She began to plait her hair into an ingenious golden rope down which the sunshine raced. "Go on! Where did Bobby Shafto go and what did he do after he combed his yellow hair?"

"I—I don't know any more of that song," said Turtle awkwardly. He was beginning to wish he'd never sat down on the doorstep. There was no doubt that the blind girl, with her lack of admiration for his good looks, undermined his confidence grievously.

"Then sing the first part again," said Rosy Starling.

"Not here, sitting on the doorstep in the street! Folk would stare like anything!"

"Then shut your eyes and come into the dark with me!" said Rosy sharply. "If that's all eyes can do for you, you'd best go home and put them out with a poker!"

Turtle shivered.

"Well?"

Turtle began to sing very softly:

> *"Bobby Shafto's gone to sea,*
> *Silver buckles at his knee . . ."*

"Louder! Louder!"

> *"He'll come back and marry me,*
> *Bonny Bobby Shafto!"*

Some grinning idiot—whom Turtle could cheerfully have strangled—threw him a bent penny, and an urchin loudly offered to stand in for the blushing bride's father and give Turtle away when Mr. Shafto should present himself, while another, less generously and more shrilly, opined that Mr. Shafto was well out of it and unlikely to return.

Rosy Starling turned her face away and smiled maliciously. Idly she unravelled her hair, shook out the bends and folds left by the close plaiting, and began to weave it up again, her cotton-white fingers making airy incantations over the gold, as if she were bending sunbeams. . . .

He'd stopped singing. Someone was coming. . . .

"Buy the pretty lady a watch, then she'll never be late for lovers' meeting! Buy a watch, young sir, or a pretty brooch?"

It was some ancient dirty peddler. She could smell him; she wrinkled her nose.

"Ah! Here's the very thing! A real Spanish comb for that lovely hair!"

Turtle scowled at the old peddler, who, with his tall black hat and long blue coat, seemed like some devilish wizard bent on betraying him. How could he buy the girl a comb when he was dead set on cropping her closer than a nag's tail? He shook his head violently.

"Or a pretty Liverpool watch?" pleaded the old villain, dragging forward a thin, lame boy who carried his box of wares.

"You're wastin' your time, mister," murmured a woman who'd paused to stare. "A watch wouldn't be much use to her. She's blind."

"Oy—oy—oy! What a shame!"

Turtle looked gratefully at the woman and waved the old man away; but he, feeling he'd gone to some trouble in displaying his wares, wasn't so easily got rid of.

"Look at this, young sir! I can see you're a young man with kindness in your heart. Buy her this! It'll make her happy and it'll feel so good round her neck. Believe me, young lady, it'll suit you a treat. Just try it. The young man here wants to buy you something. I can tell by the way he's looking at you. Here! Feel the quality! Better than gold, on my life and soul!"

The old wretch winked at Turtle and offered a cheap brass chain such as might have secured a Bible in a country church.

Rosy Starling stretched out her hand. She was both confused and delighted. Did he really want to buy her something, or had it been just peddler's patter? She took the chain and nervously held it up against her neck.

"Pretty as a picture, my dear," said the old man. "Like a duchess, by my life!"

"No!" said Turtle suddenly—and Rosy's heart sank. "That silver one. Let her have that!"

It turned out to cost three shillings, which was a fortune to Turtle. He paid for it with shaking hands, and wondered why. Brass would have done as well as silver for her. She'd never have known the difference. . . .

"That first one," said Rosy Starling softly. "It wasn't as good as this one, was it?" She played with the cool silver necklace and pushed back her hair to display it better.

"How did you know?"

"It was the way you said, 'Let her have that,' " answered Rosy. She smiled wisely, and Turtle became suddenly afraid of the uncanny girl with her power of dark sight that could spy into the farthest corner of his heart. He tried to fix his mind on her hair, which was, after all, what he really wanted; he must beg a lock of it as a keepsake. . . .

"I like silver," murmured Rosy Starling. "It's the moon, ain't it?"

"No, not really," said Turtle, somewhat puzzled. "The moon's more white, if you know what I mean. . . ."

"Of course I know! But white's clean and cold. White's nothing at all!"

"Black is nothing—"

"That's what you think!" Rosy Starling laughed, shutting her eyelids and letting Turtle imagine for himself the richness of her dark. "What colour are your eyes?"

"Grey."

"Grey? But that's old and sad. Grey's dusty and dead."

"I'm not old!" said Turtle indignantly. His eyes were his best feature, even if she couldn't see them. "And I'm not dusty, either."

"But sad? Are you sad?"

Turtle thought hard; he smiled and shook his head.

"No . . . no . . . I'm not sad."

Rosy Starling laughed again.

"Then you must be yellow, like Bobby Shafto's hair! That's sunshine and daffodils. What colour are you wearing?"

"A blue coat, with brass buttons . . ."

"Blue's sleep, and the sky."

"But there's clouds in the sky," said Turtle, his voice darkening as he stared at the blind girl's hair, which she'd woven and plaited into a sparkling prison of sunlight. She raised her hand to it, and Turtle was put in mind of when he'd first spied her at a distance, fluttering her white fingers inside one of her cages to tempt the birds.

"For that matter, there's dreams in sleep," said Rosy Starling, sensing her companion's uneasiness and longing to use her powers to dispel it. "I dream a lot, you know."

"What can you—what do you dream about?"

"Oh, trees and rivers, and meadows and rainbows and sunshine on the sea!"

"But you've never seen them! How do you know?"

"And how do *you* know about—about what's inside?"

"It—it's dark, isn't it?"

"No! No it isn't! It's light! It's as bright as day all the time! It's full of—of green smiles and brown sighs, and silver voices and golden laughter! It's full of shapes, like cats and donkeys, and little things with wings—not birds, but more like children that smell of lilac and orange!"

She paused with a look of blind triumph and pride, as if challenging Turtle, with all his grey eyes, to put forward anything half so rich and fine.

"You smell a bit orange," she said.

"It—it's my trade," said Turtle quickly.

"Sellin' oranges?"

"No. I'm an apprentice. I—I work in a shop in Martlet Alley."

Rosy smiled ruefully; in spite of everything, she had rather hoped for something more in the way of a duke.

"And there was me thinkin' you might have been a soldier," she said at length.

"Would you have liked me better?" said Turtle, wishing, at that moment, that he'd been apprenticed to any trade other than that of buying hair.

"No. If you'd really been a soldier, you'd have been in red, and that's a colour I hate."

"Why?"

"Red's for pain. Red's pricked fingers and scrapes and wounds. I'm glad I can't see it."

"But there's more than that! The setting sun is red—"

"I know—I know! Bleedin' all over the sky!"

"But red's the colour of—of lips and—and the colour of love!"

"Gold's the colour of love," said Rosy Starling obstinately, and began to play yet again with her reddish gold hair. Her fingers encountered the necklace she'd been given. "Or maybe silver," she added, with a quick, mischievous smile.

Turtle felt a rush of pleasure that drove tears into his eyes. He turned away and stared foolishly at the painted maypole and the lively crowd that jigged and jostled about it. Any moment now the sweeps would be coming out of the dark alley for their grand dance, and all the busy little fair would explode like the bursting buds of May.

He caught sight of a girl he knew being chased in and out of the throng by a most determined lover. He'd catch her all right; he was as quick as a flea. Now they were going round the maypole. She'd put on a tremendous burst of speed, and her green and yellow ribbons were fairly flying. She was the faster, and the distance between the pursuer and his girl stretched out; but at the same time, as they raced round and round, that other distance, between the girl and her pursuer, diminished as the pair of them both won and lost the race. Who had been chasing whom?

As he watched, a great bewilderment and an unaccustomed tenderness filled Turtle. He blinked to clear his eyes, for the scene was becoming no more than a misty sea of colours. . . .

"What is it?" asked Rosy Starling suddenly. "I felt you jump. You're trembling, aren't you? What's wrong?"

"Nothing . . . nothing at all!"

"Are you feelin' ill? Do you want to be sick?"

"It's nothing, I tell you!" answered Turtle almost savagely.

He was lying. He was feeling sick. He had just seen his master, Mr. Delilah!

The aged charmer of Martlet Alley, neat as a pin and somewhat flushed with wine, had been overcome by the thought of lasses on the loose and had come down to Little Drury Lane to try his shaky hand once more at cropping closer than a nag's tail.

Turtle stared at Rosy Starling, whose telltale glory blazed above her blind face like a beacon for the wickedness of the world. His master couldn't fail to see it; he'd go mad for it! He'd never forgive his apprentice if it didn't end up on a shelf in Martlet Alley. He'd have to slip away before his master saw them together; if he was quick and quiet about it, she'd never know. . . .

"He's goin'!" thought Rosy Starling in a panic. "What have I done? He's leavin' me!"

Turtle sat down again, shaking like a leaf. He was too late; Mr. Delilah had seen the pair of them. He'd winked and shaken hands with himself; he'd pointed to his own sparse head and snipped at it with his fingers. The hapless Turtle nodded.

He's stayin'! thought Rosy Starling, her heart beating wildly. He's not leavin me! Oh, Mrs. Berry, Mrs. Berry! How wrong you was about the world!

Turtle began to fumble for his scissors. Mr. Delilah, full of purpose, was coming towards him. He was pushing his way through the crowd. He'd got a girl in tow; she wasn't much of a catch, but then neither was Mr. Delilah in bright sunshine. Nevertheless, Turtle owed his master a duty, and it wasn't up to him to choose where and when to perform it—however disagreeable it might turn out. But if only she wouldn't keep *watching* him!

"What are you doin' now?" asked Rosy Starling as Turtle gripped a blade of his scissors almost tightly enough to cut off his fingers.

"Your hair," he muttered, making his final choice. In spite of the gaily crowded sunshine, he felt lonely and cold, and wished the ground might swallow him up.

"What about me hair?"

If only she could really see him, she'd understand. If only, for a single instant, she'd be granted the gift of sight so that she'd *know* how he felt, how bitterly he hated the harsh neccessity of making a living. Surely all this must show in his face . . . even as the peddler seemed to have seen more than he himself had guessed. Oh, God! Let her *see* me!

"Go on! What about me hair? What colour is it?"

"Red!" whispered Turtle in anguish.

Rosy Starling's hand flew to her lips. She went terribly white, so that, with her milky-marble eyes, she was all stone.

"No . . . no! It's gold. It's really gold!" said Turtle; and then the sweeps' apprentices came out of dark Maypole Alley, brisking the air with their garlanded brushes and shaking long-handled shovels for pennies.

Darkness to light! Creatures of the flues and tunnels and the black interstices of every habitation came tumbling out into the sunshine as if a sudden exhalation of a laughing god had blown them out of all the chimneys in the town!

Some were in rags of satin; some wore crowns of gilt paper; some waved handkerchiefs black as pirates' flags and bowed to the children of day. Then three fiddles and a tambourine struck up a tune, and the sweeps began to dance!

Cheers and clapping filled the air, and shrieks and screams echoed and echoed from the confines of the surrounding houses as pretty girls, hoopla'd by infant sweeps with old petticoat hoops, were dragged out to join the dance.

The crowd rose up on tiptoe, jumping and hopping for a better view, and cast its shadow on the doorstep where the blind girl crouched.

"Dance!" she muttered to her unseen companion. (Was he still there?) "Go on! Leave me! Find someone else to dance with!"

"No."

He *was* still there! She reached out to touch his sleeve.

"Are you—are you feelin' better now?"

He put his hand over hers and held it tightly.

"Come and dance with me!"

"You're mad! How can I dance?"

Although she scowled and shook her head, there was no mistaking the eager trembling of her voice. The rhythmic uproar of the dance was invading her, and she wondered, with exquisite agony, what it would be like to fly in the dark.

"I'll hold you! I'll not leave you for an instant!"

"I'm frightened. You don't know what it's like!"

How was it possible to tell him of the terrors of her world . . . of the mindless, sightless violence that existed all round her?

"Trust me, please!"

"I'll fall—"

"You'll fly!"

He pulled her to her feet. How strong he was! He must be a regular Samson. . . .

"Me cages!" she cried out. "Someone will pinch 'em!"

"Who'd steal from *you?*" said Turtle wryly. "Come and dance!"

He led her through the crowd.

"Look! Look at that!" exclaimed voices. "She's going to dance! That blind girl's going to dance! Fancy that!"

"Ain't it a bleedin' wonder!" said Rosy Starling scornfully. "And me with me disability!"

She tossed her head and leaned, lightly as a feather, on Turtle's strong left arm.

He watched, with infinite care, the ground before her feet; he guided her away from the looser cobbles; he wove her in and out of the moving dancers, drawing her away from the wilder ones and taking her gently into the current of the maypole dance.

She followed as effortlessly as his shadow.

"Quicker, quicker!" she whispered. "I can go quicker . . . only, only just keep hold of me hand!"

Turtle obeyed. He danced well, and he knew it. Music of any description excited and exhilarated him, but he had never before felt it so strongly as now when he moved to the ragged banging and scraping of the sweeps' three fiddles and tambourine.

"Like King David before the Ark of the Covenant," muttered the ancient peddler to his boy as they watched from the fringe of the crowd. "By my life and soul!"

Turtle was indeed dancing with a rare skill and ecstasy as he stared and stared at Rosy Starling, who seemed insensible to his tethering hand and flew like a bird.

Walls were melting before her and crowding bars were proving no more substantial than bad dreams. The darkness was expanding and stretching till it was an infinite green space through which, she felt, she could dance and fly for ever. There was no loneliness in it, no red of pain nor white of death; all was green as far as the inner eye could see.

"On me own! On me own! Let me try! Let me spin!"

Turtle hesitated, then let her go. She swayed a little, then she began to turn. Every part of her expressed amazement and delight. Turtle stepped back, as did other dancers till there was a moving circle of space about her. Everyone felt the strange nature of the blind girl's escape into space.

"Got to have it! Just got to have it, my boy!"

Turtle groaned in dismay as he heard his master's eager, straining voice in his ear. Mr. Delilah had joined the dance. He'd failed in his own quest, had drowned his grief in more wine, and was now resolved to forestall his apprentice.

He had his scissors out most dangerously. God knew what injury he might inflict in his drunken passion to crop Rosy Starling closer than a nag's tail!

"Come away! Come away, sir!"

"But—but that hair! Did you ever see a finer mop? Got to have it!"

"No—no! Leave her!"

"Sentiment, my boy! 'S'all sentiment! Just lemme get at her! I'll show you!"

"For pity's sake, sir!"

"Pity? Pity?" mumbled Mr. Delilah, and then, in the manner of all drunkards, he succumbed to a sudden terrifying vision of life's sadness and began to cry.

"Pity . . . pity . . . p-pity . . ." he wept as his apprentice led him, unresisting, away.

Turtle looked back again and again at the dancing girl with the marvellous reddish gold hair. She was spinning on air, it seemed, and Turtle kept catching glimpses of her strange fixed eyes, which formed an unearthly contrast with the wild animation of her limbs. At each turn he felt they watched him, and his heart stung and ached.

"This way—this way, sir," he mumbled, and helped his master out of Little Drury Lane.

"Where are you? Where are you?"

Rosy Starling had halted. She was laughing and swaying and feeling the air with her cotton-white hands.

"Where's 'oo, miss?"

"Him. The one I was dancin' with."

"What's 'is name, miss?"

"I—I don't know. Bobby Shafto, it might have been. Bobby Shafto! Bobby Shafto, come back and—and—"

She faltered as she became aware that the music had stopped and that she was an object of general compassionate interest.

"What were 'e like, miss?"

Her questioner was a diminutive sweep's boy, who, with his long-handled shovel, resembled an imp, late for hell and with no excuse but the sunshine. He stared up at the lost blind girl. Dark to dark. Instinctively he put out his hand and she, feeling the smallness of it, clasped it tightly.

"His name was Turtle, miss," said another voice. "Works for Mr. Delilah, the hair merchant in Martlet Alley. The pair of them went off together."

"A hair merchant?" inquired Rosy Starling, uncomprehending.

"You know, miss. They buy hair. They go up and down the country buying lasses' hair and making it up into wigs for the gentry. They got quite a name. It's said they could charm the hair from off the Queen of Sheba if they set their mind to it! It's a marvel yours ain't gone!"

"I knew he worked in a shop," said Rosy quietly. "But he never said more than that."

She let go of the small hand she'd been holding and clenched her fist.

"He did ask about me hair. He just said, 'Your hair.' And I asked him, what about it? But he never said. I suppose he was waitin' till he got me on me own. Of course it was me hair he wanted. I—I knew it all the time!" she said with a sudden burst of defiance. "I weren't *that* blind!"

The walls had grown up about her again; they were pressing in everywhere, imprisoning her till the slightest movement of her head, her hand, her foot was fraught with danger and pain.

Of course she'd lied about knowing. Really she'd been quite taken in! One had to admit that he'd been clever. Neither her sharpness nor the strength of her remaining senses had been able to warn her. Turtle . . . Turtle . . . "So that's the name I have to give it!" She meant the image or sensation of an image that had been created in her mind.

But it turned out that he'd done her a service. He mightn't know it, but he'd done her a real favour. Now she was armoured against everything, against *everything*! It was light that was dangerous, not darkness.

"I thank me lucky stars I couldn't see his face!" she said harshly, and began to walk away.

"I thank me lucky stars I can't see any of your faces!" she shouted. "For all I know or care, you're all as ugly as toads!"

She stumbled, and a child laughed. Someone went forward to help her. She shook off the kindly hand.

"And what do *you* want? I got no money. Are you after the dress off me back?"

"He—he wasn't that ugly, miss. And he was cryin' as he went."

"Any fool can cry," said Rosy Starling contemptuously. "I can do it meself."

She found her doorstep, gathered up her cages, and counted them fiercely before hanging them over her arm. Then she made her way back to Feathers Court. Although she walked slowly and hesitantly, she held her head high, as if to display to all who were interested, her stony, joyless eyes.

"Sell anything, Rosy?" asked Mrs. Berry out of the black smells of home.

"No."

"It's a mean world, wastin' your time like that!"

Rosy didn't answer.

"Where did you get that silver chain?"

"It was give me."

"Who give it to you?"

"I never saw his face," said Rosy, with weighty sarcasm.

"You want to look after it," said Mrs. Berry in admiration. "It's a good 'un. He didn't take advantage, did he?"

"He never took nothing."

"What was he then? A bleedin' duke?"

"He was—he was just a 'prentice . . . like me," said Rosy Starling.

"Some girls have all the luck!" said Mrs. Berry, and Rosy Starling's darkness emptied as her mistress went away.

"He was just a 'prentice," repeated Rosy Starling, remembering the singing voice and the dance. She touched her necklace and raised it to her lips.

"I like silver," she whispered, and then cried out, in aching gratitude, for her day: "Bobby Shafto, Bobby Shafto! Come back—"

She was gone. Turtle, having left his master in Martlet Alley, had returned to the fair. It was fly blown and tawdry. In spite of all its blaring colours, it was grey, which was sad, dusty, and dead.

He found the doorstep. Two pairs of lovers were squeezed up on it. He stared down at them bleakly till they asked him if he'd know them again if they should meet elsewhere, and if they did, they'd black his prying eyes and generally render him unrecognizable to his own ma.

He trudged on through the crowd and knocked over a pie stall, for which he was roundly abused. He bent to pick up the pies and was contemptuously kicked by the small son of the establishment.

A girl made eyes at him; her hair was as coarse as a goat's. A friend shouted and waved to him several times, and then was forced to give up under the mortifying reflection that Turtle didn't wish to know him, or, more acceptably, he'd been struck stone blind.

In a sense, Turtle *was* blind, inasmuch as he couldn't see what he most wanted. A dozen times he'd been on the point of asking if anyone knew the blind bird-cage seller? He realised that she wouldn't be hard to discover, but somehow he couldn't bring himself to pursue her into her darkness once she'd chosen to vanish into it.

He left the fair and walked among the courts and alleys that abounded in that part of the town. As he walked, he sang, regardless of the impudence of street boys,

> *"He'll be mine for ever mair,*
> *Bonny Bobby Shafto!"*

His mind was filled with a thousand romantic tales of minstrels singing under castle walls to discover a prisoner. He looked up at all the windows, and down into all the gratings that covered the half windows below ground, but they were all blind, blind as stones. From none of them did he receive that feeling of being watched that he'd felt so strongly in her presence.

"But she wasn't watching me!" said Turtle suddenly. "I was watching myself!"

He shivered as if May had slipped on sudden ice into January, and he knew, in his heart of hearts, that the blind girl was lost to him for ever.

He went back to Martlet Alley. Mr. Delilah—a tousled, somewhat sheepish Mr. Delilah—was sitting behind the counter of the shop.

"And who," said the forlorn charmer, eyeing his bleak-looking apprentice, "has put out the light in them bird-charming eyes?"

Turtle shook his head and sighed.

"I don't think I'm really cut out for the trade, sir."

"More charmed than charming, eh?" pursued the master, not altogether displeased to see his apprentice discomfited. Turtle had gone out in the morning like a young lion; he had come back like a shorn lamb.

"However, all ain't lost. While you've been out, we had a stroke of good fortune." He began to fumble under the counter. "A remarkable stroke, I might say."

He drew out two thick plaits of reddish gold hair. Turtle stared at them in grief and horror. There was no mistaking them. There was no other such hair in all the world.

"She—she brought them in herself," said Mr. Delilah hastily, fearing an unmannerly attack from his trembling and white-faced apprentice. "I swear it! I never laid a finger on her! She cut them off with her own hands!"

"Why—why did she do such a thing?"

"She said to give it to you."

"Did you—did you buy it from her?"

"She didn't want anything. She said it wasn't much to give for what she'd got. She said she knew all the time it was what you really wanted."

Sadly Turtle took the fine soft hair and held it between his hands. It was the first time he had touched it, and as he did so, her voice came back to him, offering him the richness of her strange dark world; he seemed to feel once more the mysterious touch of her hand as she'd danced.

He shook his head. "She didn't know. She really didn't. I could see that."

He laid Rosy Starling's hair down on the counter. As he did so, he closed his eyes and Mr. Delilah couldn't help being affected by the transfiguring nature of the smile that suddenly lit up his apprentice's face.

"But it will grow again!" murmured Turtle. "Of course—of course! It will grow again!"

Mr. Delilah looked on in silence as his apprentice left the shop.

He watched him through the window hastening away in the direction of Drury Lane and, doubtless, the remnants of the fair.

He shrugged his shoulders and winced, as his head was tender. He took up the hair from the counter, stroked it, and then stared back at the window and the darkening alley down which Turtle had sped, full of hope for—

"Let it not be that outward adorning of plaiting the hair," he murmured, and felt pleased by the aptness of the text.

He sighed, put the hair away, and gazed with melancholy interest at his own reflection in a glass showcase. Even though the light was already dim, it still proved unkind. He should really never have gone out in broad daylight.

A pang of envy struck him as he remembered young Turtle sallying forth in the morning, proud as the son of light. Yet even that son of light had met his match—in a daughter of the dark.

That made one think, and was worth bearing in mind for an aged charmer whose eyes were now like broken eggs. Yet within? . . .

"Let it be the hidden man of the heart . . . which is not corruptible," murmured Mr. Delilah, and prayed that he, one day, might be looked at by the eyes of the blind, and be transfigured, as his apprentice, Turtle, had been.

THE
DUMB
CAKE

MIDSUMMER EVE, WHEN HERBS AND BRIMSTONE TURN IN THE
dish and show their darker side, when milkmaids prepare
to shudder in churchyards and bakers' daughters gather their
friends to make the dumb cake and see the phantoms of their
lovers chasing them up the stairs, when spinsters wash their night-
gowns and scour the town for hemp seed for a midnight sowing,
when linkboys dip their torches in blue-burning sulphur to hunt
the fern seed that will make them invisible, and when St. John's
Wort, Vervain, Trefoil, and Rue sell like hot cakes to every lass
anxious to avoid the evil eye and encourage the glad one.

It is eight o'clock in the morning, and Parrot, youth of today
but man of tomorrow, the future author of *The Chemistry of
Thought*—perhaps the most profound work on the nature of
existence ever to appear in print—takes down the shutters of the
apothecary's shop in Portugal Street and frowns on a world that,
one day, will venerate his memory.

Of this he is entirely convinced, for he has the good fortune to
be apprenticed to T. W. Chambers and has been for the past
three years. He glances up at the gilded sign as if to reassure

himself of the fact before retreating from the Midsummer sunshine into the dispensary at the back of the shop.

Mr. Chambers is a scientist to his violet-stained fingertips, just
like Parrot. Mr. Chambers is a man who believes in nothing
that cannot be weighed and measured, and if he were to meet
with a Midsummer hobgoblin or any other such nonsense, he
would kill it and bottle it in Spirits of Wine. He is a soldier in
the small but shining army of Truth, just like Parrot, and together they march forward under the banner of Experiment and
Doubt.

Their patron saint is that Thomas who thrust his scientific
fingers into the wounds of Christ; but Parrot and Chambers
would not have left it at that: they would have prescribed an
ointment.

"Shop!"

Parrot thrusts out his lower lip and wipes a spatula on his
apron before marking his place in Cheselden's *Human Anatomy*;
then he goes to see who the devil is interrupting him.

"If you please, Mr. Parrot, I would like an—an ounce of Syrup
of Spearmint and—and an ounce of Orchis in Wine."

A female. One Betty Martin, friend to his sister and enemy to
science and the thinking man. A remarkably silly cow.

"Leaf, flower, or root, miss?"

"Oh—oh! I've no idea! Which is best, Mr. Parrot?"

Sunshine, streaming into the shop, mysteriously explodes into
blue, green, yellow, and red as it strikes through the four great
flasks in the window. Parrot, pacing behind the counter, becomes,
though he does not know it, a Joseph in a coat of many-coloured
light—a master of Midsummer dreams. One moment he is bright
green, then yellow, then a deeply philosophical blue.

"Depends what for," says the master of dreams, regarding his
customer with ill-concealed contempt. He halts in the red, like

a flame wearing an apron. "Earache, headache, vomitin', broad worms, long worms, obstruction of the bowel, passin' blood in the water, stones, neck sores, the bloody flux—or bad breath?"

"Jesus preserve us! It's—er—for me ma! Honest, Mr. Parrot! She needs it for a—a salad!"

You silly cow, thinks Parrot, resting his hands on the counter and leaning forward with a courteous smile. What kind of a fool do you take me for?

"Cross me heart and hope to have me tongue split if I tell a lie!" swears Betty Martin, crossing her fingers, her toes, and her legs in case some malign spirit has its beady eye on her. "We're having folk in to dinner. . . ."

Parrot studies her carefully; sunbeams go clean through her paper-thin dress and show her up like two sticks of celery, deceitfully crossed.

"*Reely?*"

Betty Martin lowers her eyes, and Parrot observes, with scientific detachment, that she has gone red in patches. He ponders the arrangement of vessels under her skin that has produced the phenomenon. She might cut up into something quite interestin', he thinks, and allots her a footnote in *The Chemistry of Thought:* "Martin, Betty. See the Author's classic dissection, now preserved in the College of Surgeons."

He thrusts out his lower lip again (which is a sure sign with him that he has completed some line of reasoning) and retires to the dispensary, where he fills two vials from jars on a shelf and labels them carefully with both name and date—not that such refinements matter to a fool like Betty Martin. He knows perfectly well what she's up to, and it ain't cookery!

He returns to the shop. "That'll be a shillin', miss."

"Cheap at the price!" she says, and throwing the money on the counter, rushes off like a mad thing, clutching the vials to her bosom. Parrot cannot help noticing that the fingertips of her pink-gloved hand were sodden from biting and chewing.

"MARTIN, Betty. See the Author's famous lecture on Primitive Superstition and Midsummer Madness in the Young Female."

Thankfully he returns to the dispensary and *Human Anatomy*, in which all the secrets of life are laid bare in a hundred and fifty full-page engravings.

But he cannot rid himself of a certain irritation that distracts his study. "Love potions!" he mutters angrily, staring down at a diagram of the heart—that imaginary seat of mortal folly—in which the great vessels are shown as sprouting everywhere, like rhubarb. "Silly superstitious cow! MARTIN, Betty. See the Author's justly celebrated account of Orchis and Spearmint, bought by uneducated Females for use as love potions on Midsummer Eve."

He can't help wondering if she's going to dose the pawnbroker's boy from Drury Lane whom she goes out with on Saturday nights. He compresses his lips as he thinks of her slipping the mixture into his drink while he's not looking, and then making cow's eyes (for which she's well equipped) at him till he's either sick from love or, more likely, from what he had drunk. "MARTIN, Betty. See the Author on a Case of Ritual Poisoning."

"Shop!"

This time it's the other cow: his sister. He serves her with Garlic Root and dried Vervain as if she were a stranger. She goes out and doesn't bother to shut the door, which is a sign, if ever he needed one, of her bad breeding. He marvels that he can be related to a family as ignorant as his own.

His pa is a drapery and inn-sign painter in Russell Street who had once nourished hopes of his clever son following in his footsteps, but Parrot's feet—thank God!—had proved too large for such a mould.

"Clumsy" and "clodhopping" had been the terms applied at the time, and Parrot had been undeniably offended; but that was a long time ago, and Parrot is no longer distressed at having been once accused of having no talent. The years have taught him that a prophet is not honoured in his own country, so it follows that the country shall not be honoured in the works of the prophet. His family are not even distinguished by a footnote in *The Chemistry of Thought*.

"Parrot!"

"Here, Mr. Chambers! I'm in the dispensary, sir!"

Parrot's heart warms with pleasure as his master slops in and perches himself on the high stool before the chemical scales.

Mr. Chambers is a large, untidy man, reeking of brimstone and cloves. In spite of a rosy complexion and strong appetite, however, he is by no means a well man. He suffers from internal disorders, some of which, he has confided to Parrot, are likely to prove fatal.

This is a great source of worry to Parrot, who cannot help fearing that one terrible morning he will be left masterless and stark alone in the world.

"I'm afraid it's me spleen that's playing me up," says Mr. Chambers mournfully. "You'd better pour me out a drachm and a half of Camomile in White Wine, Parrot, my boy."

Anxiously Parrot dispenses the decoction, and Mr. Chambers drinks it off with a grimace that is followed by a pained but courageous smile. Parrot breathes a sigh of relief and hands his master a calf-bound notebook about the size and thickness of a Bible. The apothecary broods for a moment, and Parrot, thrusting his lip out, thinks: "CHAMBERS T. W. See the Author on A Rich Mind in a Poor Body."

Mr. Chambers opens the notebook and, heading a new page with the date, inscribes a precise account of his morning's symptoms, not overlooking the state of his tongue—which he verifies in a small physician's mirror—and the slight adhesions that often trouble his eyes. This he follows by a record of his pulse and of the remedy he has just taken.

He sits back against the scales and, moistening his forefinger, leafs back through several closely written pages, murmuring, "Yes . . . yes . . . it's honest, at least, and true. And what more can I give you?"

He shuts the book and returns it to Parrot, who replaces it on its shelf with the melancholy reverence due to a bequest, which, in a way, it is—but of a peculiarly precious kind. This stricken giant, this martyr to most of the ills in *The English Physician*, is actually bequeathing to his apprentice the most vital part of himself. Not only is he doing his ordinary duty in confiding the various mysteries of the trade—the secrets of distillation, sublimation, and fulmination, the arts of simples and compounds, of linctus and tincture, of troche and electuary—he is, day by day, putting into his apprentice's hands a scientific account of bodily misfortunes unequalled anywhere outside the Book of Job. Every twinge, ache, palpitation, sudden shooting pain, or cloudiness of the water that afflicts him is carefully set down, together with the numerous remedies (usually in wine) that he takes for relief.

It is a unique heritage, and Parrot vows inwardly that it will have an honourable mention in *The Chemistry of Thought*.

Parrot will publish, thinks Mr. Chambers, observing his apprentice's thrust-out lip, for he also nurses a strong desire to appear in print and would have done so had not ill health held him back. Yes. Parrot will publish. *His Name Endureth For Ever: A Life of T. W. Chambers*, by his apprentice, Parrot.

Unfortunately, Parrot is Mr. Chambers' only hope. He has no children of his own, so it's only Parrot who stands between him and oblivion, which Mr. Chambers visualizes as a faded shop sign, banging in the wind of Portugal Street.

He blinks and hastily engrosses himself in a diagram of the liver, having just felt some twinges where he supposes that organ to be.

"It's swelled," he says, unbuttoning his waistcoat and cautiously feeling his side. "Me liver. It's up by two fingers under me rib. Pour me out an ounce of that fresh Tincture of Aloes and Cinnamon, dear boy."

"Shop!"

Parrot frowns and ignores the call till he has dispensed the tincture, which, he makes sure, has stood for the required nine days in gin.

He is some little while gone, and when he returns, he finds Mr. Chambers sitting in his place and suffering from a touch of the dropsy, which he has diagnosed from an engraving of the Abdomen with all its Contents.

The suffering apothecary takes two ounces of Gentian Root and Cochineal in Brandy and feels much better. His eyes brighten, and soon he's fit enough to take a turn at stirring wax and turpentine into a mortar of ointment, while Parrot keeps off the flies. After a little while, they change about, and so the morning proceeds with the steady compounding of remedies for the ills of a world that really prefers magic to medicine.

"Shop!"

But Chambers and Parrot are faithful scientists; as long as they have each other to sustain them, they are content to labour in private for the public good and dream in footnotes to *The Chemistry of Thought* and Parrot's *Life of Chambers*.

"Shop—shop!"

The Midsummer madness grows apace, but it will never pass the dispensary door. The infected females who buzz and creep in and out of the coloured sunshine for their sprigs of this and that against the coming midnight are of no more account to Chambers and Parrot than the flies who ceaselessly try to get into the ointment. The dispensary remains a sanctuary of sanity that revives Parrot's soul every time he comes back into it.

The presiding genius, however, still gives Parrot cause for concern. At about half past eleven, Mr. Chambers is stricken by a sudden obstruction of the upper bowel, for which he has to take three ounces of Devil's Bit in Rectified Spirits of Wine. Parrot records the transaction in the calf-bound notebook, as Mr. Chambers is afflicted with a tremor of the hands that prevents his writing intelligibly. At present he cannot discover the cause, but does not see that another ounce of Gentian and Cochineal in Brandy can do him any harm.

"Shop!"

At one o'clock Mr. Chambers goes out for some food and returns, bringing Parrot an apple and a piece of pie. Parrot eats and Mr. Chambers watches him indulgently.

"He was more than a father to me. See Parrot's *Life of Chambers.*"

A mood of deep but melancholy affection now overtakes the apothecary as he reflects inwardly on his childless state. Parrot is good, no doubt about that. One glance at his shining, studious face is enough to confirm Parrot's loyalty and excellence. But . . . but Parrot is not—*Chambers*. He does not have, in the last resort, Chambers' blood in his heart. What ought to have been, so to speak, a chamberful, is, ultimately, an alien vessel. He does not even *look* like Chambers. . . .

"Your eyes are watering, sir," says the observant Parrot.

Mr. Chambers examines them in his physician's mirror, dragging down the lower lids till they resemble frayed pockets too full of eye.

"Kidneys," he says. "Four ounces of Wintergreen in Wine."

Parrot pours, and Mr. Chambers rises to reach for the notebook, but is overcome by a sudden giddiness that causes him to sit down again.

"Shop!"

Mr. Chambers bravely conceals his new disability until his apprentice has departed.

He rises again, and, to his relief, all seems well. It was undoubtedly the liver that was to blame, and there exists no more efficacious remedy than brandified Gentian and Cochineal.

He doses himself liberally, and then moves accurately to the bench on which the mortar of ointment stands. He takes off the cover and pours in another ounce of turpentine, which he proceeds to stir into a slow, greyish white whirlpool.

A fly, perceiving only one guardian over the feast, rises from a shelf and buzzes reflectively. Mr. Chambers beats it off. Briefly it retires to the brown ceiling; then it returns, and Mr. Chambers is shocked to see how bloated and venomous looking it is. It has a positively goblin aspect and appears to have more than one head.

Seeking to entrap and destroy it, Mr. Chambers baits a small glass dish with a fingerful of ointment, and then, with pestle concealed behind his back, waits.

There is a terrible crash, and Parrot, fearing the worst, rushes back into the dispensary. He finds Mr. Chambers seated at the table and breathing heavily. There is a quantity of broken glass on the floor and a large fly twitching in the mortar of ointment.

"It's me damned kidneys again," says the apothecary heavily—and has some more Wintergreen in Rectified Wine.

"Shop!"

Parrot hesitates; he does not want to leave his master in his present distressed state. Mr. Chambers also does not want his apprentice to leave him alone. He is desperately worried. He has just begun to see things—things for which he can find no rational explanation. He has seen his apprentice's phantom, or double; in fact, he is seeing most things double, including a mysterious creature with pointed ears and a potbelly that has slipped in through the dispensary door.

"Shop—shop!"

Reluctantly Parrot goes, and Mr. Chambers stares gloomily round the sanctuary of science. They've got in all right. Midsummer hobgoblins mock him from the bellied flasks and swing, like the wraiths of hanged children, on the chemical scales.

"But I have no children," mumbles Mr. Chambers desolately. "And *there's* the fly in the ointment!"

Meanwhile, in the shop, Parrot attends the customers: a stubby midwife and her vacant, bag-carrying girl. The shop is sombre, for the sun has long passed its prime. The apprentice is a shade among shades, and the customers are but shadowy figures, touched round the edges with faint coloured light.

The midwife has a client, a mother down the road, "what is stopped up tighter than a drum." Already she has tried everything she knows, from Hog's Fennel to sitting the mother over a bowl of steaming Betony water; she's opened all the windows and door, but it seems that nothing short of a charge of fulminating powders will shift her and bring her to bed of an heir.

Parrot frowns and thrusts out his lower lip, when there is a stumbling sound from the dispensary, followed by a strong recommendation.

"Shyrup—I mean, Syrup of Shage—that is, Sage and Honey, ma'am. Try it. And two pills of Ginger and Spikenard. Try 'em. . . ."

The midwife listens and nods her fat little head. Chemistry is all very well, she grants, and she's the last one to leave any stone unturned. But what about the hobgoblins, eh?

There's a moment's silence, then an angry cry of "Don't you talk of—goblins in this shop, ma'am! I won't have it!"

The midwife nods again. She respects Mr. Chambers' chemical feelings, but surely he must know that it's Midsummer Eve when queer things are bound to happen? Therefore, ain't it possible that the invisible ones are as much to blame as chemistry for the stopped-up condition of the mother down the road?

So, taking all into account, she'll have six ounces of the Sage and Honey, a dozen of them Ginger pills, *and* a sprig of St. John's Wort and Rue to hang round her neck. Many's the child that's been born under the strength of such herbs. And who but a fool would take such chances when such happiness was at stake?

Parrot watches the midwife and her lanky girl hurry down Portugal Street and vanish. He shuts the door, and the darkness in the shop unaccountably oppresses him. Despite the warmness of the weather, he shivers and hopes he is not getting a fever. Defiantly he thrusts out his lower lip and returns to the dispensary, where Mr. Chambers has lighted another candle.

"They're gone, now, sir."

"Who? Who?"

Mr. Chambers glares round at the flasks and scales as if in panic.

"The midwife and her girl."

"Oh."

"Can I—can I get you some more medicine, sir?"

"Why?"

"You—you look a bit flushed, sir."

Mr. Chambers hastily fishes out his physician's mirror and examines himself.

"It—it's only the candlelight. I'm all right, Parrot! Perfectly all right. Never felt better!"

He tries to get up but cannot keep his balance.

"I think, perhaps, I'll go and—and lie down."

"Let me help you, sir!"

"Only—only to the door. Mrs. Chambers will come. My wife . . . my wife . . ."

Parrot supports him. He feels the large man trembling, and a multitude of apprehensions and fears overwhelms the apprentice.

"You can lock up, Parrot. Go out and—and enjoy yourself, my boy. I—I'll go to—to bed, I think. . . ."

"Mrs. Chambers! Mrs. Chambers!" calls Parrot urgently. He opens the door from the dispensary into Mr. Chambers' home.

"Mrs. Chambers!" echoes the apothecary.

He sways round to dismiss his apprentice . . . and Parrot is suddenly transfixed with horror!

Round his loved and honoured master's neck, just above his loosened cravat, is hanging, for the world to see, a bundle of dried St. John's Wort and Rue. Parrot feels the blood in his veins turn to burning acid and eat a hole in his heart.

Mr. Chambers, seeing the look upon Parrot's face, does not fully understand it; he tries to laugh but is too drunk to manage more than a guilty hiccup.

Parrot retreats. "You!" he mutters. "T. W. Chambers! Why . . . why you're no better than—than the rest of 'em! You . . . you . . ."

Mr. Chambers, sobered a little by the accusation, extends a fat hand, much stained with Gentian and Cochineal.

"It—it's a joke, really! It's nothing, my boy! Only—only I was thinking . . . she said—the midwife said it was—was wrong to take chances when such—such happiness is at stake. That's all! That's why. And—and after all, where's the harm in it, Parrot?"

Parrot does not answer.

"It'll always be you, Parrot!" goes on Mr. Chambers anxiously.

"You're more than a son! Much, much more! You'll have me book! I promise you! Even if—if I was to have a son of me own— tonight—it won't make a drachm of difference . . . to us! It's all for—for Mrs. Chambers! I swear it, my boy! It'll always be you and me . . . Chambers and Parrot!"

"Never!" says Parrot harshly, and strikes all mention of his master's name from *The Chemistry of Thought*.

"Parrot!" moans Mr. Chambers, seeing all too clearly: "*A Faded Sign: Death of an Apothecary*, by Parrot."

Then he totters through the doorway, calling, "Mrs. Chambers! Mrs. Chambers . . . Sarah, my love!"

Midsummer Eve, when landlords polish their pewter ware and hang Garlic Root and Rosemary on the taps of the sherry firkins —for goblins are well known to be demons for the drink.

"Why, if it ain't young Mr. Parrot from down the road!" says a landlord conversationally as the apprentice slumps in at the door. "Tell us, lad, with all your chemical learning, what's a good balm for a bleedin' heart?"

"Cut it out," says Parrot. "With a surgeon's knife."

Parrot means it. His master's treachery has struck deep. Although he has tried to persuade himself that his anger is because of Mr. Chambers' shameful betrayal of truth and science, he knows the blow to have been bitterer than that.

Plainly, the wretched man had wanted a son of his own so much that he'd thought nothing of betraying everything Parrot held most sacred for the stupid hope of a magical Midsummer begetting.

Parrot wasn't good enongh for him—Parrot, who had tended and even worshipped him more than any son would have done! Was it for this that he'd uprooted his heart from Russell Street and planted it in Portugal Street? The soil is poisoned everywhere! Despised and rejected of men, Parrot leaves the inn for such comfort as there's to be found in the darkening streets.

Midsummer Eve, when apprentices and their girls foregather in St. Mary's Burying Ground to light the bonfire that will bring the phantoms of dead lovers from their graves to marry again under the haunted porch.

"Look! Look! There's Johnny Parrot from the apothecary's! Come over here and tell us a good ointment for a burnin', blisterin' love!"

"The bite of an adder," says Parrot. "That'll put out the fire!"

He leaves them to their shallow madness and reflects, as he crosses the Strand, that a wise man must always be lonely in a world of fools.

Midsummer Eve, when watermen's boats on the river are hung with sprigs of Rosemary, Eyebright, and Lily of the Valley —all of which are sovereign against lovers' forgetfulness.

"Ain't you the 'pothecary's lad from Portugal Street?"

Parrot nods.

"That's a bit of luck! Come and tell us of a potion or a syrup that'll teach these old bones to remember what it's like to be young!"

"That black syrup there," says Parrot to the waterman, and points to the dark, flowing river. "That's a good remedy for all aches and pains."

Parrot sets no store by memory. It's memory, not wisdom, that makes him so lonely. Every back is turned on him, and he walks in the valley of the shadow.

Midsummer Eve, and Miss Kitty Parrot—just seventeen and pretty as paint—has two best friends home to Russell Street for the desperate purpose of baking the dumb cake; two to make it, two to break it, and one to hide the pieces under the pillows for dreams of lovers to come. On such a night, nobody wants to be left on the shelf.

Betty Martin, a pastrycook's daughter, has brought the ingredients, and Sally Brown has brought the dish. Miss Parrot herself has supplied the basin and spoon, and her ma has lit the oven fire. They are all in the kitchen, and Mr. Parrot, drapery and inn-sign painter, is engaged in sketching the curious scene.

"Ssh! Not a sound, boy! Can't you see that they're making the dumb cake?"

Parrot, having fled from one silence, now finds himself unhappily in another. He thrusts out his lower lip with savage contempt. Betty Martin catches his eye and goes red again in patches. But Parrot no longer wants to cut her up for the benefit of science; he wants to cut her up because he hates her and the whole stupid pack of them.

His misery has, by now, passed through a cold fire and emerged as a finely tempered dislike for the whole human race. He feels that the world would be a better place without them. He would like to be the destroying angel, killing and killing until, high on some lonely mountaintop, he'd survey the bloody wreckage and empty out the last of the vials of wrath.

Unaware of this, Sally Brown holds the basin, and Kitty Parrot, her sleeves rolled up to her elbows, stirs.

"Just like your shop," whispers Mrs. Parrot to her son.

Sally Brown and Kitty Parrot change about, biting their lips the while so they won't utter a single whisper, which would spoil the spell. Betty Martin, wearing a white shift, newly washed and inside out—for that's important—looks on, and Mr. Parrot catches exactly the expression of rapt attention in her cowlike eyes.

Parrot cannot stand it any more. He leaves the hell's kitchen, dragging his feet in the hopes his sister will break her silence, even if only to abuse him. But everyone ignores him, so he wanders into the parlour, where his father's ugly daubs of Kitty Parrot disfigure the walls. There's Miss Parrot as Spring, there's Miss Parrot as Summer, and there's Miss Parrot combing her hair. She's all over the house; the only likeness of her brother is at the age of three months—a nameless, faceless lump of dough in his mother's arms. Mr. Parrot had never painted a wise thing in his life.

Parrot finds a piece of charcoal in a box on the sideboard and gives his sister a beard and blacks out both her eyes; then he goes back into the kitchen, where the cake is already in the oven and the three Midsummer maidens are preparing to go out into the backyard and sow hemp seed. Sally Brown and his sister glare at him balefully as they sweep past on their way upstairs to put on their shifts, which they hadn't wanted to dirty while mixing the cake.

Betty Martin stays behind and watches the oven, in which all their hopes of future happiness are steadily browning and giving off a strong smell of cinnamon and mint.

Mr. Parrot catches her attitude down to the smallest detail of the tip of her tongue poking out between her teeth.

"It's a gift!" murmurs Mrs. Parrot in admiration. "A gift from God!"

Parrot considers the proposition that God must be something of a miser; then Sally Brown and Kitty come downstairs, looking like bundles of washing. Silently the three girls go outside into the yard, carrying a bag of hemp seed and a little brass fork and trowel.

Parrot watches them dimly flitting about in the darkness. He sees them bend down with their silly heads together. The fork and trowel flash in stray starlight . . . and in goes the enchanted seed.

The maidens, white as marsh wraiths, rise up and walk backwards to the house. Not a word is spoken, not a guiding look is cast. Betty Martin trips on her shift, and Parrot laughs loudly, but none of them can be tempted to break the spell. Any moment now, they will see, rising from the newly sown seed, the ghosts of their future lovers, following on with outstretched arms.

As they pass him by, their eyes are shining brightly, as if they'd really seen more than the broken fence and their own bare, muddy feet.

Mr. Parrot sketches them being pursued by three spectres, part earth, part air. . . .

Still in their secret, hugging silence, they go to the kitchen. Betty Martin opens the oven door and a great deal of smoke comes out, for someone has left a piece of brown paper inside, and it has got burnt. But no one dares to cough.

Sally Brown—who is the strongest—takes a cloth and lifts out the iron dish, which she puts by an open window to cool. Who, when the time comes, will break the dumb cake? Why, Betty Martin and Kitty Parrot; it's all arranged. And who, when no one's looking, will steal the pieces and hide them under the pillows upstairs? Sally Brown, of course!

Then she who's destined to be married will have, this night, sweet visions of her lover; but she who's doomed to be left on the shelf—to live and die alone—will have no such luck. Either she'll dream of nothing or of new-made graves into which she falls, she'll dream of winding sheets that tangle her limbs and of rings that fit no finger, or, if by force, they do, they'll straightway crumble into a grey dust.

The three maidens gaze somewhat nervously at the blackened cake that is now out of its dish. In their heart of hearts, they are inclined to shrink from it, but, having gone so far, none of them has the courage to draw back.

So Kitty Parrot and Betty Martin score the cake with a knife and snap it into three—for it's overdone and as crisp as a dried twig. They turn their backs, and Sally Brown, solemn as an owl, creeps upon tiptoe, steals the pieces, and flits from the kitchen with startled eyes.

While she's gone, Mr. Parrot draws Betty Martin with a dream coming out of her head, like smoke from a haystack. Sally Brown comes back, looking pale with fright, as if she'd stolen a march on her companions and already laid her head on her pillow and seen something she hadn't bargained for.

Now is the most solemn time of all, for it is almost midnight. The three maidens, quiet as mice, are to walk backwards up the stairs to their beds. They are to stare fixedly, looking neither to the right nor the left, and, if all is well, they will see the shades of their lovers hastening after them. But then they must hurry, for under no circumstances must such unnatural beings catch them on the stairs! They must pin up their shifts so that they can really scamper like the wind into the safety of their beds. Never, never must the pursuing shadows touch them and plant their grisly kisses on their pale lips!

But there still remains something important to be done, for during the strange, backward journey there must not be a sound in the house that has not been made by ghosts, for phantom lovers, sometimes in default of actually appearing, announce their presence by knocking, rustling curtains or scratching at a wainscot.

Therefore, in order to guard against mistakes, the three maidens leave the kitchen and begin upon their silent rounds. They move from room to room, fastening loose cupboard doors and closing windows against any misleading draught. Miss Parrot puts out the cat—who's not sorry to go—and hangs a black cloth over her canary's cage. Then, with a look of mingled pity and dislike at her brother, she and her white-gowned companions prepare to mount.

Their shifts are pinned up and their slender legs and garden-grimy feet give them a curious uprooted appearance, like mandrakes. Mr. Parrot sketches them rapidly, for everyone knows that once they've begun to mount, no one but the mysterious spectres of Midsummer Eve must be present to watch.

"Come along, boy. Into the kitchen with you. Don't always spoil things for everybody. Use your imagination, for once. . . ."

Parrot glances at his father's drawing, thrusts out his lower lip—which always annoys everyone—and goes. He feels as cold as ice. He is on the mountaintop and ready with the last vial of wrath. He slams the door. His mother and father shrug their shoulders and retire to the parlour. They had intended to join their son in the kitchen, but they have no inclination to put up with bad temper.

The hall is now cleared of all save the three Midsummer maidens. They station themselves at the foot of the stairs and clutch one another fiercely by the hand. Then they draw in their breath, and with shaking knees and pins and needles in their toes, they take the first upward step.

They pause. Was that a scratching? They look mutely at one another and ask with their eyes alone. One by one they shake their heads and take another step. Was that a knocking? Surely that was a knocking! No . . . no . . . Two further steps are accomplished, and Betty Martin gasps and bites her lip, for she's trodden on something sharp. But she didn't utter a word; she shakes her head to prove it; the spell is still intact.

Something rustled! It was absolutely distinct! The three maidens hasten up still farther and fix their enormous eyes on the darkened pathway of stairs they've already mounted.

A church clock—St. Clement's, in point of fact—begins to chime the midnight hour. They tremble in the sudden and appalling certainty of imminent pursuit by phantoms! The very shuddering of the air tells them that ghosts are about . . . for have not the mysterious requirements of the haunted time been obeyed in every particular? Since a quarter to eleven, the maidens have maintained a strict silence . . . and it has been a perfect torment. They have sown the seed and washed their shifts, which are still uncomfortably damp.

It would be cruel indeed if, after all this labour, none of them saw her lover's shadow; it would be crueller still if only one of them was so blessed!

Hemp seed we've sown,
Let our crop be mown!

"Ah!" shrieks Betty Martin. "He's come! He's there!"

She points to the foot of the stairs. Sure enough, a ghastly apparition has manifested itself and with waving arms is giving every evidence of instant pursuit!

"I'll kill him!" screams Kitty Parrot, recognizing the apparition in spite of the mask of flour with which he's whitened his contemptuous face. It is her brother, Parrot.

The future author of *The Chemistry of Thought* laughs with a loud and bitter mockery as the three foolish females glare down at him; then the church clock tolls the last stroke of midnight, and Parrot's laughter dies on the air.

The three harmless girls in their shifts on the topmost stair have vanished! In their place are now three demons whose eyes are burning with all the fires of hell!

"I'll kill him!" repeats the one who had been his sister. "So help me, I will!"

Her hair is wild, and her raised fingers are armed with ten terrible daggers. Parrot stands stock-still, then gives a startled cry and bolts for the kitchen as the three furies rush suddenly down upon him.

He slams the door, but before he can secure it, it bursts open and strikes him a violent blow on the side of the head.

He staggers back and sees the demons standing in the doorway before him. There is a haze of madness in their eyes and the threat of mutilation in their eager hands.

In a flash, he sees himself all over the kitchen table and floor, a twitching, bloody index of all the hundred and fifty engravings in *Human Anatomy*. He shrieks with terror and goes through the back door like a dose of Epsom Salts.

He travels at immense speed down Russell Street, unable to determine whether the sounds of pursuit are in his mind or in the actual air immediately behind him. There is no way of confirming this save by looking back, and that he dares not do for fear of losing whatever advantage he might have.

His chief hope lies in finding company, but both Russell Street and Bridges Street are horribly empty. Then he sees ahead, reflected in the sky above the crippled crowd of chimneys, the glow of the bonfire in St. Mary's Burying Ground.

He turns sharply into Russell Court, bruising his shoulder on a projecting piece of brickwork. Heedless of the pain, he runs fiercely towards the lych gate, which has been hung with a confused variety of branches as a protection against the more disagreeable powers of the night.

As he passes under it, he experiences the wholly unreasonable hope that it will put paid to his pursuers. Nevertheless, he does not relax his pace and runs fleetly towards fire.

"A—ah!" he shrieks as the soft ground suddenly opens and departs from beneath his feet. Monuments, headstones, and all the sober furniture of the graveyard rush upwards on either side of him, like the promised end of Babylon. Then they vanish, and Parrot lies on his back, staring at a rectangle of reddened sky.

He has fallen into a newly dug grave. Terrible thoughts suddenly visit him, of heedless gravediggers crashing a black coffin down on his upturned face and filling him in. He shouts and begins to struggle up . . . when a strange blue flame comes dancing towards him and hovers round the edge of the grave.

It is a linkboy with a brimstone torch. Searching for midnight fern seed, he has heard the despairing cry. Now, looking down, he sees Parrot's flour-white face and his clawing, grave-filthy hands.

"You're dead," he pronounces, and the dripping blue flame gives his face the aspect of a goblin judging the damned. " 'Ave you woke up to get wed under the porch, mister?"

Parrot's brain, shaken by his fall, cannot comprehend the ambiguity of his situation. He groans.

"They'll be comin' to wed yer," says the blue goblin, looking about him with relish and then bending low so that the shadows stretch his eyes and nose unnaturally upwards. "All in their windin' sheets!"

Parrot struggles and falls, then struggles again, and by means of clawing at projecting roots, emerges from the grave, in which, contrary to popular supposition, he has found no rest.

"Look! Look!" howls the goblin, between terror and delight. "You got three of 'em, mister!"

Parrot turns. In spite of the protection hanging on the lych gate, the three furies are now standing on the other side of the grave.

" E's dead—'e's dead!" screams the goblin malignantly as Parrot runs for his life. "I see'd 'im come out o' the grahnd! Catch 'im! Catch 'im afore 'e goes back into 'is grave!"

It is when he hears this terrible cry—this pronouncement that he is dead—that Parrot loses his only hope. He knows, too well, that to be diagnosed as dead *is* dead; he himself would not have given half a drachm of limewater for anyone after such a diagnosis.

"Catch him! Catch him! Catch him!"

Now all the Midsummer madmen and fools in the churchyard, the gatherers under the porch and the dancers round the fire, take up the linkboy's cry. They scream with laughter and try to prevent Parrot's escape, and Parrot knows, in his heart of hearts —which does not figure in *Human Anatomy*—that he has emptied the last vial of wrath upon his own head.

Hands clutch at him, feet interpose themselves between his racing legs. Fools, fools! They don't know that the three furies in their winding sheets really mean to tear him to pieces before their very eyes! Fools, fools! They have been playing at magic without realizing the terrible fact of it!

At last Parrot, by violence and desperation, manages to flee the burying ground and escape into White Hart Yard. From thence he rushes across Drury Lane and is quickly swallowed up in the odorous gloom of Clare Market, where the stink of butchers' meat serves only to sharpen his expectation of dismemberment.

He runs and staggers round the confines of the market, vainly seeking a way out. He is weeping now because his head aches, his bruised shoulder aches, and the palms of his hands are grazed and bleeding from his struggle in the grave.

Never has there been such a martyrdom as Parrot's on Midsummer Eve, and the worst of it is that he no longer can be sure whether he's being martyred for the truth or the lack of it.

Suddenly he becomes aware that he is surrounded by stillness. Black pools of blood and gnawed bones glimmer among the cobbles, as if other furies had found other victims and then passed on. Parrot peers at the melancholy spectacle in pity and awe; then he begins to regain command of himself as he realizes that he has outdistanced his pursuers. He wipes his eyes on his sleeve and, with a sense of unutterable relief, makes his way cautiously to Portugal Street.

He reaches Mr. Chambers' shop and, still unable to believe his good fortune, lets himself in. He rests for a moment against the door and then, hearing nothing from the street outside, goes into the dispensary and lights a candle. It's over! He's escaped—

"Shop!"

"W-who's there?"

"Shop—shop!"

With a sudden palsy that Mr. Chambers himself might have envied, Parrot goes to the herb drawers and takes out a Garlic Root and a Sprig of Rue. He has no idea whether they are the best herbs for his particular situation, but surely they are better than none? He tucks them inside his shirt, next to his icy skin, and goes to see who has summoned him.

A wraith, a phantom, a white-gowned omen of disaster, stands in the darkness before him. He clutches at the herbs and raises his candle. His customer is Betty Martin.

She stares at him, not uttering a word. Her eyes, in the quailing light, seem to be trying to swallow him up.

"You're shaking," she says at length. "Like a blooming leaf!"

"It—it's me spleen," mumbles Parrot, thrusting out his lower lip. "It's playin' me up again."

"Ain't there something you can take for it?"

"I—I s'pose so. Camomile in White Wine. That's the thing. I'll go and take an ounce right away."

He goes back into the dispensary, and Betty Martin follows him.

"I'll pour it out for you," she offers. "Your hands are shaking fit to spill the lot. Here, let me do it!"

Helplessly Parrot slumps into his seat and secretly touches

his herbs, while Betty Martin, rustling in her crisp shift, dispenses.

"Drink it up," she says softly, handing him a beaker. "Every last drop!"

She perches herself on the high stool in front of the chemical scales, so that her shadow stretches up the wall and looms over him from the ceiling like a menacing cloud.

He drinks.

"W-what is it? What have you given me? You—you've poisoned me! What did you put in me drink?"

Betty Martin smiles demonically, and Parrot's blood congeals. He knows now that he has chosen the wrong herbs, and Betty Martin knows it, too. She fixes him with her enormous eyes.

"W-what did you give me to drink?"

"Don't you know? It was Syrup of Spearmint and Orchis in Wine, of course!"

She slips from the stool and moves closer and closer till her wild hair and brooding face fills Parrot's world. He drops the beaker. . . .

"Ssh!"

"I feel sick. . . ."

"That's it!" murmurs Betty Martin triumphantly. "It's working! It's love—"

"No!"

"Oh, yes. It's the potion."

"But—but why me?" says Parrot, thinking of the pawnbroker's boy from Drury Lane, who, surely, had been the intended victim.

"Because it's Midsummer Eve, and it was you I saw on the stair. We made the dumb cake and it just had to be—like this. What would have become of me else? I'd have been left on the shelf. I'd have been an old maid. We all agreed it had to be. Kitty couldn't have you . . . and Sally didn't want you. But I do,

Johnny Parrot, I do! Why did you run away?"

"MARTIN, Betty," thinks Parrot, dazedly. "See the Author . . . oh, just see the author now!"

Upstairs in his bed, Mr. Chambers snores gently with his fat arms going almost half way round his portly wife; his coloured fingers peep at her waist like posies of flowers. There is a serene smile on his puffing lips as he dreams of children—countless little Chamberses—and the great calf-bound, gold-lettered volume of his *Life*.

"Parrot will publish," he mumbles in his sleep. "No doubt about that." And he lapses into the silence of divine content.

Downstairs in the dispensary, the candle has gone out. There are sundry strange noises, as of Midsummer goblins laughing and tinkling the chemical scales; then there is an almighty thump, as of *Human Anatomy* falling to the floor and *The Chemistry of Thought* being slammed shut. There is more soft laughter and an anxious murmuring.

"Ssh!"

"Why? It's not still the dumb cake, is it?"

"Ssh! Or you'll break the spell!"

"What spell?"

"Don't you know? Don't you know?"

"Tell me . . ."

> *"Hemp seed I've sown,*
> *Now the crop's to be mown!*

"But dumb . . . dumb . . . dumb . . ."

"Yes," says Parrot after a little while. "I think I see. *There was silence in heaven about the space of 'alf an hour.*"

"What's that?"

"Revelations," says Parrot mysteriously. "And his name was John, too."

TOM TITMARSH'S DEVIL

MISS SPARROW WAS A PRINTER'S DEVIL—AND TOM TITMARSH'S, too. She taunted him and haunted him and, in the end, tempted him into eating of the forbidden fruit.

"Yes!" mourned the bookseller's apprentice, one morning in July. "She's destroyed me! I never ought to have listened to her. Never, never, never!"

Miss Sparrow's complexion was of a streaky, Satanic black, like an old boot or a burnt tree. This was as much from trade as from nature; she was so liberally daubed with printer's ink that if you'd put her in a press, you might have had fifty clear impressions without the need for re-inking her once.

She'd got it on her nose, her cheeks, her brow, her small, firm chin, and even in her ears; her hands were ten thin slices of the night, and the glimpses she permitted of her flying ankles showed *them* to be pitch black, too—although, in fairness, this might have been due to stockings.

She flew importantly about the town in a filthy brown apron and an old green dress, carrying proofs for correcting to booksellers and authors, whom she held in equal contempt: the former for selling rubbish, and the latter for writing it. She was as critical as the Father of Lies himself.

Tom Titmarsh had not been two months into his apprenticeship when he came across her for the first time. His master, Mr. Crowder of Crabtree Orchard, had just stepped out and left him to mind the shop.

The new apprentice, immensely proud of this trust, tiptoed up and down and along the avenues of shelves, soothing the books with a duster that would scarcely have awakened a fly.

Crowder's was a quiet brown world of infinite retirement, monkish in its peace and scented with leather, glue, and a touch of good quality snuff. From time to time, the whisper of a page being turned, somewhere out of sight, increased rather than broke the silence; and through the latticed window, the noiseless vision of the street, gesturing and arguing and hastening on its ceaseless way, charmed the reflective mind without disturbing it.

Then, at half-past eleven, in burst Miss Sparrow like a bat out of hell! She gave a wild screech of *"Printer's!"* and flushed out all the moths and browsers from where they'd been slumbering, mind out of time. Books were dropped, faces raised, and a sound like many serpents filled the air.

"Ssh!"

Tom Titmarsh, when he'd got over his shock, raised a finger to his lips and glided to his private nook at the back of the shop, where he slept, ate, and learned the trade. Miss Sparrow clattered in his wake.

"Proofs of the pudden', boy!" she said, slapping down her smeary sheets on his one o'clock pork and pickles. "And if I was you I'd eat 'em. I never read sich rubbish in all me born days!"

"I don't think that's your place to say, miss," murmured Tom Titmarsh, looking uncomfortably into the body of the shop. He had been brought up as cautiously as truth from a well, and he shrank involuntarily from the shiny blackness of the printer's devil.

Miss Sparrow stared at him with a mixture of incredulity and contempt.

"Oh, my!" she said at length. "I'll bet you piss rose water!"

She laughed shrilly and left him, with a red face and shaking the crumbs off the proofs and apologizing to Mr. Crowder for the pickle stains.

Luckily Tom Titmarsh's master was a sensible, fatherly man who took his duties towards his apprentice seriously, and was prepared to stand in the place of a parent. He advised Titmarsh to have as little as possible to do with Miss Sparrow. Tom Titmarsh was only too happy to agree, and did his best to wipe the she-devil out of his thoughts, where she seemed to have settled like a blot of ink. Somehow, he really couldn't get her out of his mind's eye, or, rather, the corner of it, so that she was always lurking somewhere.

For instance, he found out without trying that she worked for Gardiner's of Angel Court, which was nearby; and when she came back during the following week for the corrected proofs, he heard himself neglecting Mr. Crowder's advice to the extent of making a little joke about a devil working in such company.

At once she looked at him sharply and made him feel uncomfortable.

"Now, don't you go forgetting, boy," she said, "that it's the devil what keeps all the angels in business. So I'm bleedin' well entitled to a share in their profits, ain't I?"

She grinned, and before he could move, she'd tapped him on the forehead with the rolled-up proofs and clattered noisily out of the shop.

Titmarsh rubbed his forehead and stared at the still shaking door. The remark about sharing in the profits of the angels had really disturbed him, so that he wished he'd taken his master's advice and had nothing to do with the printer's devil.

Mr. Crowder said she was born to be hanged and he couldn't understand why a respectable house like Gardiner's kept her on; Titmarsh couldn't understand it either, and he tried so hard to rub her out of his mind that he almost wore a hole in it.

Miss Sparrow—Cleopatra to her friends, of whom, temporarily, she had none—was a bewildering mixture of impudence, ink, and information. The impudence was her own property; the ink and information she got from Gardiner's.

Sparrow by name and sparrow by nature, she picked up every crumb of the trade that fell her way. She'd stand over the compositor, breathing down his red and bristly neck, and try to make out the print backwards as he laid it in his stick; then she'd fret the pressman by risking her nose and fingers in her efforts to read the printed pages as they flowed from the press.

"Take 'em to so-and-so's," she'd be told, and off she'd go like a streak of blackening to the nearest alehouse, where she'd finish her reading over a glass of gin and water.

With furrowed brow and grubby finger, she'd trace her way through every scrap of print she could lay her hands on, though God knew what she made of it all! If the curl of her lip while she was reading was anything to go by, she made rather less than its author might have hoped for, but every once in a while she'd come across a piece of writing that would cause her to wriggle her toes and exclaim aloud, "Now that weren't half bad! You can take me word on it. Truly!"

But more often than not, she'd just look up and say, with an inky smile, that she'd seen paper put to better use in a bog house.

"It's a wonder you don't need spectacles, miss," said Tom Tit-marsh, forgetting his master's advice yet again in his awe at the extent of Miss Sparrow's reading.

It was a fine day, but the summer sun, never very strong in Crabtree Orchard, seemed in need of spectacles itself as it came in hazily through the window. The shop was deserted save for a tall thin gentleman in black who kept looking up and round as if a shadow had tapped him on the shoulder. He was waiting to see Mr. Crowder and would not confide in the apprentice.

"It comes to me from me pa," said Miss Sparrow confidentially. She perched herself on a stack of sermons by the Bishop of South-wark that were newly in from the binders. "Me wild, consumin' passion for readin', I mean; not me good looks."

She began swinging her legs and glancing inquisitively at the stranger, who looked away with some embarrassment. Miss Spar-row's gaze was both shameless and penetrating.

"Me pa's a schoolmaster down Eastcheap way, and he's that fond of books that when me ma ran off with a tinker, I don't think he noticed for a week. Every night he used to stuff me pillow with pages what had come loose, and when me bed broke, he propped it up with old books. There was books every-where, like mice, and whenever I put out me hand for a bun or a penny to buy one with, he'd put a book in it and say, 'Fruits of the Tree of Knowledge, miss. It'll do you more good!' "

She paused and helped herself to a piece of Titmarsh's pie.

"He always used to say," she went on, speaking with her mouth full besides dropping crumbs everywhere, "that the Bible was all wrong about Eve and the serpent and the Tree of Knowledge. It never was the serpent what tempted Eve; it was the other way round. She tempted him. If she hadn't been so bloody ignorant and ripe for spoiling, it wouldn't have happened. . . . I mean, death, disease, and the poor and all that sort of thing."

She was talking quite loudly and Tom Titmarsh noticed that the stranger was listening. He had a smile on his face that was more like a snarl, and he kept feeling in his pocket. Titmarsh wondered uneasily if he'd been stealing books while Miss Sparrow had been chattering.

He really ought to have kept the printer's devil at a proper distance instead of encouraging her to make herself at home. After all, it wasn't as if she fascinated him; nobody in their right mind could have considered Miss Sparrow to be fascinating. It was just that, in the strangest way, Titmarsh got the impression that *he* fascinated *her*.

She was always calling in with excuses that plainly she didn't expect to be believed, and engaging the bookseller's apprentice in conversation. She was definitely interested in him. She asked him about his schooling and what subjects he'd liked best. She wanted to know what line his pa was in, and why he'd put Titmarsh into bookselling. Had he shown a particular genius for it?

Undeniably flattered by such interest, Titmarsh told her that his pa was a master joiner in Hackney who made bookshelves, so it had seemed a natural step to take.

Miss Sparrow nodded; Gardiner's had printed a book about joinery, so she knew a great deal about it. In fact, she knew a great deal about everything and kept tantalizing Titmarsh with amazing scraps of knowledge, which she kept stored in her head like apples in an attic. Once she started to tell him the History of the World, but Mr. Crowder came back and Miss Sparrow scampered off in a hurry.

Titmarsh had thought she'd looked guilty, and when Mr. Crowder warned him, quite severely this time, to have no more to do with "that one," he promised himself he'd obey.

But most mysteriously (and Tom Titmarsh couldn't understand how it had come about), here she was again, sitting on the bishop's sermons and scuffing her feet against the bindings, as if she'd been asked.

He was on the point of coming to his senses and bidding her to be off, when she gave him her most Satanic smile and asked, "Sold any good books lately?"

"Why, them you're sitting on, miss," said Titmarsh, surprised, "are selling very brisk. Very fine they are, too."

Miss Sparrow sniffed and, lifting her skirt, stuck her head down between her knees in order to read the title.

"I've seen," she said, coming up with a grimy grin, "paper put to better use in a bog house."

She slid off her perch, wiped the seat of her skirt with fastidious hands, and clattered out of the shop. Titmarsh, catching sight of the waiting stranger's snarl of amusement, thought that whatever Miss Sparrow had inherited from her schoolmaster pa was nothing beside what she'd got from the Prince of Darkness, who, when he fell from heaven, was well known to have splashed down into a vat of printer's ink.

He busied himself in wiping the mud off the bishop's sermons until his master returned.

"This gentleman to see you, sir," he said quickly, and was glad that he wasn't obliged to confess to Miss Sparrow's visit.

"The name is Match, sir. Match," said the stranger, dragging his hand out of his pocket and offering it to be shaken.

He was fearfully thin, and his skin, stretched over his joints, shone as if, like his clothes, it had been worn threadbare. He turned out to be an author with a manuscript that he pulled out of his pocket and offered to the bookseller. He smiled as he did so, and Titmarsh saw that the snarling effect of his expression was due to the general tightness of everything that covered his bones.

Mr. Crowder, who could hardly refuse the ragged notebook

without letting it fall, opened to the first page.

"*Thine Is the Kingdom*"! cried Mr. Match eagerly, before Mr. Crowder had had a chance to read. "That's the title, sir! *Thine Is the Kingdom*! A good one, don't you think? From the Gospel of St. Matthew, of course!"

Mr. Crowder nodded and closed the book.

"Won't you read it, sir? Please read it! You must read it!"

"We're in business here," said Mr. Crowder wearily, "to sell books, not to read 'em, Mr. Match."

Mr. Match snarled and laughed, but he was remarkably persistent. He wouldn't take the book back, and Titmarsh could see that he was really quite desperate. He kept clutching at his narrow chest and revealing wrists and arms like old bleached sticks.

Patiently Mr. Crowder explained that, although he was sure Mr. Match's work was worthy to appear in print, a small edition of it, bound in cloth, would cost somewhere in the region of fifty pounds; and, as Mr. Match was, as yet, unknown—

"But I'll pay!" cried Mr. Match eagerly. "I'll pay for the printing myself, sir! I was quite prepared for that! I understand it all. I'll pay every penny!"

Mr. Crowder compressed his lips and examined the book again. He believed the cost would be nearer sixty than fifty pounds. It was possible that he felt sorry for Mr. Match and hoped to put him off throwing his money away, but the author, who didn't look as if he had two pennies to rub together, closed with the bookseller instantly. He shifted his ugly boots as if he were about to dance with delight. He was enormously grateful.

"Will it come out quickly, sir? It must come out quickly. You see, there's topical matter here that will lose by delay. I beg of you, sir, bring it out quickly!"

"Topical matter, eh? Are you going to set the town on fire, Mr. Match? Ha ha!"

"That's right! That's exactly right!" cried Mr. Match, snarling and laughing. "The town on fire! Everybody will be reading it! But only if it comes out quickly! Please, sir!"

"I'll send my boy here round to the printer's today," said Mr. Crowder indulgently. "If it's as topical as you say, we mustn't lose a minute, sir!"

When Titmarsh came back from Angel Court, where he'd taken the manuscript, he was still out of breath.

"You needn't have run so, my boy," said Mr. Crowder, patting him on the shoulder. "There wasn't that much of a hurry. *Thine Is the Kingdom*, indeed. Now what can be topical about that? Authors are always the same, Titmarsh. They'll say anything to get their work out quickly. And shall I tell you why? They're consumed with an absolute terror of dying before they've had a chance to become famous. It's a kind of madness they have. Poor devils! Sometimes I think they'd be better off if they did die before seeing their masterpieces end up as wrapping paper for cheese!"

Titmarsh blinked and nodded. He felt an enormous pity for the starved looking Mr. Match, who was prepared to sacrifice everything he had in the world for *Thine Is the Kingdom*. He prayed with all his heart that somehow the book really would "set the town on fire," and that, above all, the sharp and biting Miss Sparrow would be prevented from reading it and summing up Mr. Match's eager dreams with, "I've seen paper put to better use in a bog house."

"Printer's!"

Titmarsh jumped in alarm and crept away from the shining shelves towards his brown nook. Miss Sparrow, fierce and filthy as ever, came clattering after.

"Proofs of the pudden', boy!" she said, and slapped down the first proofs of *Thine Is the Kingdom* on Titmarsh's plate of chopped ham.

She paused, and Titmarsh flinched in expectation.

"And if I was you, Tom Titmarsh, I'd read it. It weren't half bad. You can take me word on it. Truly!"

Titmarsh gaped. In a moment all the melancholy thoughts he'd been harbouring during the past week, of Mr. Match hanging himself on account of his book's failure, melted away. He felt so happy and relieved that had Miss Sparrow been cleaner he might have embraced her! He thought her to be the best judge of a book to be found anywhere in the town.

Miss Sparrow, happily unaware of the narrowness of her escape, lifted up the sheets and picked at the chopped ham beneath.

"Fruits of the Tree of Knowledge, Tom Titmarsh. That's what I'd call it. Do you a sight more good than—" she said, making a wry face as she swallowed her mouthful, "—this!"

"I'll tell Mr. Crowder," said Tom Titmarsh cheerfully. "I'm sure he'll want to read it!"

"That'll be the day!" snorted the printer's devil. "There never was a bookseller yet what read more of his stock than the title!"

She stalked out of the shop, pausing only to shout that she'd be back in three days to pick up the corrections.

"Well, Tom Titmarsh? Didn't I tell you it weren't half bad?" said Miss Sparrow, returning on the third day.

"I—I've not had time to read it yet, miss," said Titmarsh, defensively. "But I will. I promise I will."

"You can read, I s'pose?"

"You've got to be able to read in this trade, miss."

"When will you read it then?"

"When—when it comes back from the binders."

"Word of honour?"

"Oh, yes. After all, it's not a very long book."

"Christ!" said Miss Sparrow. "I don't know why I bother with you!"

To be honest, Tom Titmarsh didn't know either, but he couldn't help feeling a little hurt that Miss Sparrow had actually said so. Nevertheless, he resolved to keep his word at the first opportunity.

The printed sheets were promised for the first week in July, and, most unusually, Gardiner's was prompt in its delivery. Mr. Crowder had never known anything like it, and said so.

It was raining quite heavily when the cart arrived, and Titmarsh saw that Miss Sparrow had taken off her apron and laid it over the sheets to keep them dry. She managed to squeeze Titmarsh's hand meaningly while Mr. Crowder was signing for the delivery, and the apprentice nodded in confirmation of his promise.

"What's that you've got on your hand, my boy?" asked Mr. Crowder curiously as Titmarsh began stacking the sheets in a corner for the binder to collect.

Titmarsh looked down. Black as Satan's shadow, the printer's devil had left her mark. Her inky fingers had streaked the back of his hand.

"It—it must have come off the paper, sir," lied Titmarsh, and was ashamed to see how readily he was believed.

During the following week Miss Sparrow called at Crabtree Orchard twice. Titmarsh noticed that she'd cleaned her shoes and had sewn up the trailing hem of her dress. He flattered himself that she'd done it on his account, and he responded by taking an extra pride in his own appearance. He bought a pair of stockings with green silk clocks; but she didn't notice them, so Titmarsh grew gloomy and supposed her improvement was on account of the book she esteemed so highly. Either that, or some-where she had found another friend.

She barely exchanged half a dozen words with him, so that Titmarsh found himself unwillingly obeying his master by having nothing to do with the printer's devil. He tried to swallow down his disappointment and derive some pleasure from being able to face Mr. Crowder with a clear conscience.

Plainly Mr. Crowder appreciated this, and he treated his young apprentice with exceptional kindness. Several times he urged him to take advantage of the sunshine in the middle of the working day.

"Take a walk round Covent Garden, my boy," he'd say, with his fatherly smile. "Buy yourself some fruit. It'll do you more good than books, Titmarsh."

Indeed, the weather was outstandingly fine, and the whole world went about strawberry-cheeked and apple-eyed. Titmarsh walked among the flowers, bought peaches and apricots . . . and wondered about Miss Sparrow and *Thine Is the Kingdom*. He wished he could be thoroughly happy, but somehow that was denied him, and he obscurely felt that the sunshine couldn't last.

On July 10 the binder's boy delivered twenty gilded presenta-tion copies of the Bishop of Southwark's sermons—and the first two hundred of *Thine Is the Kingdom*.

Mr. Match came in almost at once. Titmarsh wondered if he'd been waiting in the street all night. He stood and gazed at his printed work with tears streaming down his cheeks. Then he shook hands with Mr. Crowder and with Titmarsh. He had been sweating so much that the apprentice felt he'd shaken hands with a drink of warm water.

"I hope it goes well!" he muttered. "You see, I've put so much into it! It's very important to me. . . . It's my heart and soul . . . in print!"

He took away six copies, and Mr. Crowder remarked that authors were always their own best customers.

"And sometimes," he added, with a melancholy smile, "they are their only ones."

Titmarsh hoped, from the bottom of his heart, that this would not be so. He felt in the strangest way that Mr. Match desired something more than fame: he longed to give rather than receive. The apprentice was profoundly moved, and when the Bishop of Southwark called in to sign his own presentation copies, he took the liberty of recommending *Thine Is the Kingdom* with great warmth.

The bishop shrugged his broad shoulders. The work of other authors did not really interest him. Nevertheless, he accepted a copy of Mr. Match's book and promised to give his opinion on it. Titmarsh felt that Miss Sparrow would have been proud of him.

"You've not read it?" asked Mr. Crowder when the bishop had gone.

"Oh, no, sir!" said Titmarsh, and, for the last time felt able to look his master straight in the eye.

That night, with beating heart and carefully shielded candle, Tom Titmarsh settled down to keep his promise and read *Thine Is the Kingdom*. Even before he had opened the book, a feeling of intense secrecy overcame him, so that several times he had to creep out of his brown sanctuary to make sure that the slight sounds of the night were not his master's slippered footfalls approaching to find out what his apprentice was doing.

Then he began to read . . . and the warm night seemed to grow cold about him, so that he actually had to put on his coat and breeches to stop himself from shivering.

Very quickly he understood why Miss Sparrow had been so deeply stirred, for the book enshrined her own words about the devil sharing in the profits of the angels—not that there was anything in the least angelic about it. It was a frantic and nightmarish book, and it seemed unbelievable that it had sprung from so frail a man as Mr. Match. It was a wild and savage book that made Titmarsh's eyes smart and burn as if from smoke.

It was about a walk the author had taken one black night, from London Bridge to Covent Garden. Everything was described in the sharpest detail, so that the reader was forced to believe in every word.

For a penny the author had had the light of a linkboy's torch to guide him through the night, and as he'd walked he'd seen such sights thrown up out of the darkness that he'd screamed out, in his heart of hearts, and cursed the first day of creation that had brought light into being and so revealed the agonies of hell.

He had seen, in a lane off Fleet Street (everything was named and described), a woman running from a house with blood pouring from her cut throat; he had seen a family of beggars (in an alley that Titmarsh knew well) eating a dog that was scarcely dead; he had seen a strangled baby lying outside the very church where Titmarsh worshipped every week. He had seen a dozen other sights, no less monstrous and no less precise, until at last he'd come to Dorset Street, where he'd begged the linkboy to halt awhile, for his soul ached as if it had been put through a mangle.

They stood outside St. Bridget's; a brown light gleamed from the church windows, and the soft, gentle sounds of a service could be heard.

"Our Father which art in Heaven," chanted the clergyman, and the unseen congregation followed suit.

"Hallowed be Thy name . . ."

"Hollowed be Thy name," said the congregation.

"*Hallowed! Hallowed!*"

"*Hollowed! Hollowed!*" echoed the congregation.

"*Thy kingdom come . . .*"

At these words, there was a noise in the churchyard, a straining and a grunting that caused the linkboy to lift his torch and push it inquisitively through the iron railings.

At first it seemed that the motion of the light was causing the shadows to move and swim among the tombs; then Mr. Match saw, to his creeping terror, that the stones themselves were shifting. Slowly and inexorably they were being shrugged aside by some commotion in the ground beneath. He supposed it to be an earthquake until he saw what seemed to be a host of pale mushrooms sprouting from the disturbed earth.

But they were not mushrooms. They were the seamed tops of skulls. The dead were rising up. Bony and splintered by the torchlight, they clawed their way up the sides of their own headstones and glared eyelessly into the night, as if astonished to find the world still standing.

With open-work arms akimbo, they leaned and looked until, with an angry rattling of jaws, they fell aside; for others were rising up. More and more they came; many generations had been buried at St. Bridget's, too many, indeed, even for standing room. They began to jostle one another with a dreadful snapping and clicking. Presently they began to climb on top of each other, bone fitting into bone as if mortised.

Higher and higher grew the pile till it formed a kind of spire, level with the church's and closely cobbled with polished heads. Indeed, it was a church itself—a church of bone.

"Care to go inside?" said the linkboy, pushing open the gate as if what had happened were the most natural thing in the world.

Helplessly Mr. Match nodded and followed, picking his way across the upturned earth.

"Forgive us our trespasses," came the clergyman's voice from St. Bridget's, and Mr. Match and the linkboy went inside the bone church as if for the last Sunday of the world.

It was bitterly cold within, and rags and dusty sinews hung down from the lofty vaulting of ribs and spines like a host of battle honours. Mr. Match looked up, and the dead looked down, and one of them began to preach a sermon. He never knew which one, for all their mouths were open, and all their eyes were wide.

"In the beginning," whispered the preacher, "in the very beginning, that is, God made the devil, and that was His greatest creation. When He made the devil, He made Himself, because before there was the devil, there was no god. Before there was evil, there was no good. Then He made darkness to make light, because without darkness, there can be no light. Nothing can exist of itself alone.

"He thought of guilt, so that He might create innocence. He caused Cain to kill Abel; he caused Judas to betray Christ. Without Cain, there is no Abel; without Judas, there is no Christ. Without guilt, there is no innocence; without agony, there is no joy. . . ."

So the sermon went on, heaping paradox on paradox, even as the dead were piled on top of one another, while the author, by these strange and wayward means, struggled to answer the questions in his own tormented heart. He was trying as best he knew to come to terms with all the cruelties and miseries he'd seen in the night. He was trying to begin again and see which way reason had really gone, and whose was the kingdom.

At last, Titmarsh finished the book. He closed it with shaking hands, and a feeling of unutterable distress filled him, together with a sense of shame. The shame was because he had read the book in secret and did not want his master ever to find out the thoughts it had put into his head. He lay down but did not go to sleep. He was too frightened of the dreams that might visit him.

"Printer's."

Miss Sparrow crept in at the morning door. She'd washed her face and combed her hair, so that she looked vaguely familiar rather than instantly recognizable. She came quietly into Titmarsh's sanctuary and gazed at the bound copies of *Thine Is the Kingdom*.

"Well?" she asked. "Did you read it, Tom Titmarsh?"

"Yes, miss."

"And what did you think of it, Tom Titmarsh?"

"Like you said, Miss Sparrow, it was fruits of the Tree."

She frowned as if not entirely satisfied by the apprentice's answer. She sensed an evasion. She helped herself to one of his apricots.

"Well, then, which part did you like best?"

He'd dreaded such a question. He'd hated the book and never wanted to talk about it again. He didn't answer her and, most unwisely, tried to avoid her eye. Instantly she flounced round to confront him.

"You didn't understand one bloody word of it!" she cried angrily. "You're a fool, boy! An ignorant fool what's not worth bothering with!"

She threw her half-eaten apricot on the floor and left the shop like a whirlwind.

Dully Tom Titmarsh watched her pass by the shop window with her black hair tossing. He felt a pang of bitterness and jealousy for Mr. Match and his devilish book, and he wished the pair of them had never seen the light of day. Unhappily, he'd been no match for Mr. Match, who'd plainly stolen Miss Sparrow's heart and head away.

He picked up *Thine Is the Kingdom* again, not with any intention of rereading it, but because it was the key to something that quite suddenly he wanted very much. More than anything in his present world, he wanted to win the approval of the devil from Angel's Court. . . .

"I want to see your master! At once! At once!"

Titmarsh dropped the book in fright. The Bishop of Southwark had come into the shop and was standing in front of him. He was white with anger.

"I—I'm sorry, sir. Mr. Crowder is out. Can I—?"

"This—this book!" said the bishop, holding out *Thine Is the Kingdom* with a shaking hand. "It's nothing more than blasphemous, godless rubbish! I don't know what Crowder was thinking of to have it in his shop! You may tell him from me that he hasn't heard the last of it. I'll see to it that it's burned by the public hangman! And I'll have its miserable author put in the pillory! I forbid you to sell so much as a single copy of this—this monstrosity! I forbid it!"

Titmarsh had never seen anyone so angry before. His Grace, who was ordinarily a calm gentleman, had been quite transformed. Mr. Match had indeed set him on fire, although perhaps not in the way he'd intended.

When Mr. Crowder came back, Titmarsh, trembling with fright over the whole affair, told him of the bishop's visit. Mr. Crowder listened very seriously. Although privately he resented the bishop's high-handed attitude and the fact that he'd plainly distressed the gentle apprentice, he could not afford to offend so valuable a customer. He told Titmarsh to put Mr. Match's work in a dark corner, out of everyone's way, until the case should be decided.

Titmarsh did as he was told, but couldn't help thinking all

the while of Miss Sparrow and what *she* would say if she knew
how he was treating the fruits of the Tree of Knowledge—no
matter how sour they'd turned out to be. He pushed them behind
a pile of the bishop's sermons . . . and then he found himself
thinking about the pinched, starved-looking Mr. Match, whose
very book looked poor and thin beside the good fat leather of
the sermons. He thought about the luckless Mr. Match, bruised
and bloody in the pillory . . . and he thought again about Miss
Sparrow and what *she* would say and feel. He thought a good
deal more, in fact, about Mr. Match than he did about his book;
and he thought a good deal more about Miss Sparrow than he did
about either.

"You're looking very pale, my boy," said Mr. Crowder in the
middle of the afternoon. "Forget about His Grace and take a
stroll round Covent Garden. Here, buy yourself a peach."

With tears in his eyes, Tom Titmarsh thanked his master, but
at the same time he felt horribly guilty because he knew he intended to deceive him.

He took the money Mr. Crowder gave him and ran, not to
Covent Garden, but to Drury Lane, where Mr. Match lived above
a pawnbroker's. He was going to warn him of the bishop's violent
intentions and beg him to escape. This was the least he could do,
and he hoped it would reinstate him in Miss Sparrow's eyes. But
Mr. Match wasn't there. He had not been back for days.

Sick at heart, Titmarsh began to make his way towards the
market, where the last of the day's fruit was going cheap. Clutching his master's money, he stepped carefully, as the cobbles were
treacherous and slippery from squashed apples and plums, while
the air was thick and heavy with the sweet smell of rotting.

He looked everywhere to find some peaches, but they were all
gone, so he had to make do with a pound of black cherries from

a barrow woman who was sitting on the arm of her barrow in a narrow alley. She'd pulled open her bodice to feed her filthy baby and told Titmarsh to help himself, as her free hand was engaged in dismissing the flies that competed with her child for milk at her breast.

Titmarsh left the market and began to make his way back to the shop. He passed the entrance to Angel's Court, and there was Miss Sparrow, coming out of Gardiner's. Her hair was wild and her face was newly inked. She was whistling.

He shouted to her eagerly. She turned and saw him, and shook her head.

"Can't stop now, boy!" she called back. "Proofs to deliver."

He ran after her, pushing aside all who stood in his way. Foolishly he held out the bag of cherries.

"What do you want, boy?"

Breathlessly he told her of the bishop's anger and honourably blamed himself for everything, as he'd urged the bishop to read the fatal book.

"You recommended it?" she said with interest.

"Yes, miss."

Miss Sparrow took a cherry from his bag, and Titmarsh understood he'd been partly forgiven. His heart beat rapidly, and he went on to tell her that he'd been to Drury Lane in the hope of warning Mr. Match. . . .

Miss Sparrow took another cherry and squeezed Titmarsh's hand, so that he knew he'd been forgiven altogether.

"What's to be done now, miss?"

"Can't do nothing about the books," said Miss Sparrow mournfully.

"But him? Mr. Match?"

"I'll tell him. Don't you worry."

"Do you know him then?"

Miss Sparrow took a whole handful of cherries and grinned her grimiest.

"Course I know him! His name ain't Match. It's Sparrow. He's me pa, Tom Titmarsh. He's me pa!"

As he walked back to Crabtree Orchard, people turned and stared at him. He stumbled into obstructions as if he didn't see them or feel the pain they must have inflicted. His eyes were full of tears and his face was as white as a bone.

She'd deceived him right from the beginning! All the interest and concern he thought she'd had for him had been for her accursed father! Everything had been for her father, and she'd had no more care for Titmarsh than she'd had for the birds of the air.

A dark hatred rose up in his heart for Miss Sparrow and her devious ways. He hated her for entrapping him into reading her father's nightmare of a book. He hated her for filling his head with her own blackness as well as her father's. Everywhere he looked inside his mind, he saw her blackened face, and his hand prickled and burned from the last pressure of her night fingers.

From now on, he would never be able to sleep without the most horrible dreams; he would not be able to talk without stammering and being afraid the wrong words would come; he would not be able to be alone without the constant dread of being spied upon. He knew that nevermore could he meet his master's eye without a morbid terror that Mr. Crowder could see what was in his mind.

"Yes! She's destroyed me!" mourned the bookseller's apprentice. "I never ought to have listened to her. Never, never, never!"

On the afternoon of July 13, Mr. Crowder came into the shop and told his apprentice that *Thine Is the Kingdom* had been prohibited from further sale and that first thing in the morning the public hangman would be calling to collect the entire stock for burning. The Bishop of Southwark, using all his considerable influence, had struck like a thunderbolt.

Eagerly Tom Titmarsh dragged the volumes out of their dark corner to make the hangman's task easier. Such was the bitterness he still harboured against Miss Sparrow and her father that he could scarcely wait for the morning and the fire.

He rose early the next morning and paced the shop, going frequently to the door to look outside. He'd never to his knowledge seen a hangman before, and he pictured someone stern and brutish, with a face of implacable stone. Although he shrank from the very idea of such a personage, he couldn't help feeling a gruesome fascination at the thought of such a man's hands.

At about half-past six o'clock, there came a grumble of wheels turning into Crabtree Orchard, and Titmarsh unfastened the door. A moment later a youth, not much older than Titmarsh himself, came into view, dragging a black-painted cart. The hangman had sent his apprentice.

The youth, seeing Titmarsh's strained white face, halted.

"This 'ere Crowder's place?"

Titmarsh, suddenly unable to speak, pointed up to the shop sign.

"Well? Is it or ain't it?" inquired the youth, grinning amiably. "You'll 'ave to come out with it an' tell us. I can't read."

Titmarsh stared at the hangman's apprentice. His face was simple rather than brutish; his eyes were lustreless and his mouth was large and loose. He might almost have been a baby, stretched out to fill his coarse brown clothes.

"This is Mr. Crowder's," whispered Titmarsh.

"Thank Gawd! I come fer some books!"

Suddenly Titmarsh began to feel sick, not because the youth

was so horrible, but because he was not. One might have passed him in the street without knowing; one might have shaken him by the hand without suspecting. Titmarsh stared at his hands. They were strong and firm and freckled by the sun, for his was open-air work. There was a puckered scar on one of his wrists. . . .

"I got that on me first day," said the hangman's apprentice, observing Titmarsh's look. "I was jus' steadyin' 'im fer the drop, when 'e turned an' bit me like I was a pie or summ'at. Christ, but I yelped! Since then, I've learned to be a bit smarter, I can tell yer!"

Titmarsh trembled but could not tear his eyes away from the youth's hands, which were so ordinary, in spite of what they had done.

"Them books, mate. Show us where they are."

Titmarsh pointed to the corner at the back of the shop.

"Don't s'pose you'd lend a 'and?"

Titmarsh did not answer, and the hangman's apprentice grinned good-naturedly. His was a lonely trade and he was used to it. He clumped past Titmarsh and presently returned with a stack of books that obscured all but his ragged hair and his full, dull eyes.

"These the ones, mate?"

"*Thine Is the Kingdom*," whispered Titmarsh, all bitterness and anger leaving him as he contemplated the youth's stubby fingers, which might have been a sailor's, so naturally did they curl, as if about a rope.

"That'll be the day!" chuckled the hangman's apprentice, unloading his burden and going back for more.

"Comin' along to watch?" he asked, when he'd finished and all the books were on the black cart. "Outside Newgit. Debtor's Gate. Nine o'clock. Be 'appy to see yer, mate."

He glanced at Titmarsh half shyly, and the bookseller's apprentice perceived the appalling loneliness of the hangman's apprentice. He nodded, and the other looked as pleased as Punch.

"Will you—will you read it before you burn it?" muttered Titmarsh as the youth raised the arms of the cart.

"Told yer, mate; can't read."

"But your master?"

"Can't read neither. Don't 'ave to in our line. Were it a good book, then?"

"Oh, yes. Very, very good."

It was with some reluctance that Mr. Crowder gave his apprentice permission to watch the public burning. He was surprised, and said so, that such an occasion should attract a gentle soul like Titmarsh.

"But if you should see our Mr. Match there," he added as Titmarsh was leaving the shop, "tell him I'm sorry. I wouldn't want him to think that I was to blame."

Although the sun was as bright as blazes and cold pies were on sale, there wasn't much of a crowd outside Debtor's Gate. Perhaps fifty people had gathered to see Mr. Sparrow's heart and soul out of the world and give the hangman his customary cheer.

The books had been torn into fragments for easy burning; in his mind's eye Titmarsh saw the stubby fingers hard at work. They'd been stuffed into an iron cage that was suspended from the gallows' bar, and a gaoler stood on each side of the platform, as if to prevent any last minute attempt to rescue the condemned print.

Titmarsh, his heart thundering with apprehension, pushed his way through the meagre crowd. He had seen Miss Sparrow.

She'd washed her face again and tied up her hair with black ribbon, as if in mourning for *Thine Is the Kingdom*. She was crying, and Titmarsh would have given anything to make her smile. He reached her side.

"I—I've got some plums here, miss. Will you have one?"

She looked at him in silent misery, and shrank away.

Now the hangman, a square-built man with silvery hair and light-blue eyes, came out of the prison gate and everyone cheered and called to him by various familiar names. He smiled and waved and rubbed his hands, and Titmarsh found himself thinking, with a thrill of horror, that he was the living image of the Bishop of Southwark.

"Go on, miss," urged Titmarsh, holding out a plum to the sobbing devil by his side. "It'll do you good."

"Christ!" she said. "Don't you *care* what they're doin' down there?"

The magistrate's clerk, all in Sunday black, came out and read the order, condemning *Thine Is the Kingdom* to be burned to the public shame.

"They're ripe and sweet, miss," said Titmarsh; Miss Sparrow turned and spat in his eye.

At last the hangman's apprentice came out holding a blazing faggot, and everyone cheered again. He handed the faggot to the hangman, then, seeing Titmarsh, grinned and waved. Titmarsh waved back, and Miss Sparrow, with all her strength, stamped on his foot.

Then the hangman, who was so like the bishop that Titmarsh could hardly believe that it wasn't the same man, and shuddered accordingly, pushed the faggot between the bars of the cage. For a moment it seemed that the fire had gone out, but this was because of the strength of the sunshine. In moments the fire blazed up and a great black column of smoke waved up to the blue sky. The bars grew red hot and all manner of castles and figures appeared in the heart of the flames.

"Thine Is the Kingdom!" wailed Miss Sparrow as the flames slowly died in the cage and the paper within shrivelled to a cob-

webby nothingness. "For never and never, Amen!"

Then she broke down and cried so passionately, and with so little restraint, that she didn't care who led her away from the pie-strewn, ash-infested place where her beloved pa had gone up in smoke.

"Come back to the shop, miss. Rest awhile and I'm sure you'll be better for it."

She looked up at Titmarsh, whose arm was about her shoulders. Her face, in the sunshine, blazed with tears.

"That book. It were all the world to us. All the world, Tom Titmarsh. We'd talked about it . . . and—and dreamed about it. It were everything we felt about things. And now—and now—?"

"Yes, miss. I know. But you'll feel better when you've had a rest and something to eat."

"Christ!" said Miss Sparrow. "I don't know why I bother with you!"

They came to Crabtree Orchard, and Tom Titmarsh went into the shop while Miss Sparrow waited round the corner. Mr. Crowder, seeing something like a smile on his apprentice's face, raised his eyebrows.

"Well?"

"All burned," said Titmarsh, and Mr. Crowder, with a vague air of disappointment, left the shop.

Titmarsh who had recently learned guile, listened carefully, then, assured that his master was not coming back, poked his head outside the door and whistled. A moment later, a tearful and bedraggled Miss Sparrow crept in.

"Printer's," she wept, from force of habit, and just in case the bookseller should return.

Gently Titmarsh led the unhappy devil to his sanctuary and sat her down.

"I think," she said, "I'll have a plum now."

"Here, miss," said Titmarsh, lifting a book from a pile on the floor and handing it to her. "Fruits of the Tree of Knowledge. It'll do you more good.

She gazed at him with eyes that seemed to have swallowed up her face. She opened the book, and Titmarsh felt she was opening his heart. Slowly her eyes moved across the page, then they stopped. Her hands began to shake so much that the print must have danced.

'But—but it's *his*!" she whispered, peering about her as if she feared that stern gaolers would come and tear the book away. "It's the book! It's *Thine Is the Kingdom*!"

"Yes, miss. Like I said, it's fruits of the Tree of Knowledge."

"But I thought . . . I saw . . . I watched it being burned!"

"No, miss."

"What—what was it then? What was it, all torn and hanging in the iron cage on the gallows?"

"Very sad thing, miss. Unfortunate mistake. The hangman's apprentice—him I waved to—couldn't read. So he took—"

"What did he take, Tom Titmarsh?"

"He took the Bishop of Southwark's sermons, miss. All the presentation copies, signed with his own name, and half the new printing besides."

"And—and the hangman burned them?"

"Every last word. Burned in public by the hangman at Debtor's Gate. Religious works like that. Shocking."

The printer's devil drew in her breath and stared.

"Oh, Tom Titmarsh, Tom Titmarsh! You ain't no tomtit at all. You're an eagle, that's what! A bleedin' eagle!"

Then, as the full enormity of what had happened, and whose soul had gone up in smoke, came home to her, she began to laugh and laugh till her eyes streamed, and Titmarsh had to support her, as she was in danger of falling off her perch.

"But why—why did you do it? You never liked pa's book . . . so why, why?"

"You liked it," answered Tom Titmarsh steadily. "That's why I did it."

"Christ!" said Miss Sparrow, dabbing her eyes on her apron. "Why did you ever bother with me? Was it for me looks?"

"No, miss."

"The name," said Miss Sparrow, biting her lip and not exactly knowing what to feel, "is Cleopatra."

"And I'm not surprised," said Titmarsh, who had perceived in the inky devil a fascination that glowed like fire in a dark place.

She smiled contentedly, and a perfume of printer's ink assailed Titmarsh, so that, for ever after, it was always in his memory as being sweeter than roses.

He picked up the book she'd let fall. He opened it but did not look inside.

"*Thine Is the Kingdom*," he mused, and gazed into the devil's eyes.

"No . . . no," murmured Tom Titmarsh's devil. "For better and for worse, it's ours."

THE
FILTHY
BEAST

HALF PAST FIVE OF A WARM AUGUST MORNING AND THE TOWN was bright and still. A profound silence inhabited the valleys between the buildings, and the rooftops locked in sleep. Here and there steeples pointed upward like sharpened fingers: "Ssh!"

Suddenly something moved. Horribly high up, across the frontage of Martlet and Peabody, silk mercers, a small figure floated magically upon the air, and a whisper drifted down into the neighbourhood of Amen Corner.

> "With a one! And a two!
> And a one! And a two!"

It was not the wandering angel of the City, nor even the drifting spirit of the town; it was Shag, walking his narrow plank as if it were as wide and safe as the Strand.

Arms outstretched and jerking his hips and knees like a cockerel, Shag strutted along what, in the early light, looked to be no more than a darkened strip of nothing. It was a queer, breathless, and private sight.

"With a one! And a two!
And a one! And a two!"

He came to the eastern extremity of his perch and nodded familiarly to the dome of St. Paul's, which rose into the sky with a huge, dim shine, as if it were still wet from the sunken tide of the night; then, pivoting deftly on heel and toe, Shag flapped his stumpy arms and proceeded westward with an elegance not to be denied.

"With a one! And a two . . ."

He snapped his head from side to side, staring alternately at the filthy peeling wall of Martlet and Peabody and over Smithfield way, where, among the sea of tumbled roofs, slept the tattered giant of Bartholomew Fair. He grinned in confident expectation and continued on his secret dance to the marvellous morning.

"With a one! And a two!
And a—"

He halted. He was being watched. A scowl darkened his face, and he congealed into his well-known imitation of a gargoyle.

A thin grey cat had crept out onto a neighbouring roof and was staring at him. With infinite caution Shag reached down into the pocket of his apron and drew out a bottle of ale.

"Puss, puss!" he muttered benevolently, and taking a deep swig, projected his mouthful across the gap between the buildings in a pursed-up jet of immense force.

He missed the cat—which hissed and departed—but was rewarded by a startled shriek from below.

"You dirty beast up there!"

Gleefully Shag skipped along the tottery plank until he was

able to peer down into the valley of the shadow and triumph over his chance victim.

"You dirty beast dahn there!" he mimicked, and a spattered kitchen maid in her shift, who had nipped out into the alley for private reasons, shook her fist and vanished in an angry flurry of grey and pink.

Shag beamed and remained brooding over the silent valley, thinking his gargoyle thoughts . . . which were not so much thoughts as sensations that inhabited Shag's head.

Presently his patience was rewarded. Out of the blind end of the alley there came swinging and looping a bent, ragged figure on three legs—two of iron-tipped wood and one of dirty flesh and bone.

It was Creeping Jesus, out and about early to occupy the best begging pitch in Smithfield and, if necessary, defend it to the death against all his mutilated rivals, chief of whom was Tom-in-the-Pot, who had one leg less than Creeping Jesus himself.

Shag cried out shrilly and, as the cripple looked up, gave his well-known imitation of a lad about to fall from the scaffolding. Creeping Jesus shouted in alarm and, in his haste to avoid injury from the plummeting boy, caught his crutches in the cobbles and went arse over stump in the dirt.

"You stinkin' beast up there!" he howled, and Shag grinned down on his second victim of the day.

Shag watched with interest as Creeping Jesus cursed and writhed and struggled to regain his human posture; then he capered along the plank until he came to a window and rapped smartly on the glass.

"Get away from there, you dirty little beast!" came a shriek from within, as a female, tousled from sleep, lifted her head from her pillow and beheld Shag peering malevolently in.

At once Shag gave his well-known imitation of mortal panic

and vanished from human sight. The female, thinking he'd slipped and gone to his death on the ground beneath, rushed to the window—and up popped Shag's face to frighten the wits out of her with its mixture of suddenness and diabolical delight.

Nobody knew why Shag did these things, least of all Shag himself. They gave him pleasure, and that was reason enough. He was made that way, and if it was really God who made him (as He's supposed to have a hand in all of us), then someone must have jogged His elbow while He was at it.

At six o'clock Shag, keeping a sharp lookout on the quickening street below, caught sight of his master, Mr. Howie, striding along and looking up. Hastily Shag gave his well-known imitation of an apprentice who has been hard at work since half past five. He slapped a brushful of biscuit-coloured paint across the face of Martlet and Peabody, wiped his brow—and rested.

Mr. Howie, who had been an apprentice himself, was not taken in. He knew that Shag was a lazy, idle good-for-nothing; the only reason he put up with him was because Shag, though he lacked every human virtue, had a good head.

This had nothing to do with the appearance of Shag's head, which was dull and brutish, nor did it refer to what was inside it, which was meagre and chiefly bad; it meant that Shag had a good head for heights.

In his time, Mr. Howie had lost two apprentices to the perilous trade of house painting: bright lads who'd fallen, like doomed angels, from the tops of houses to the hard ground beneath. They had been better workers than Shag, but, thought Mr. Howie as he stared up at the little monster in his employment, there was no doubt that an apprentice still on the scaffolding was worth a sight more than two in the grave.

He shouted up that he'd be back in half an hour and would expect to see some progress, and Shag shouted back that, as God was his witness, he'd already been working so hard that his eyes were nearly falling out.

Mr. Howie called him a bleeding little liar and went off to a job of interior painting in Paternoster Row. Shag began slapping paint energetically in all directions over Martlet and Peabody's, and hoped that the force of gravity would spread it before his master returned. This took him until a quarter to seven, when Mr. Howie, in a white apron and paper hat, came back and had the rare good fortune to catch his apprentice actually at work.

"Good lad!" he shouted, in pleased surprise, and Shag took another rest.

At seven o'clock exactly, Shag was disturbed by a loud scraping and banging from below. Inquisitively he peered down to the front of the shop and saw, bobbing and bowing, the top of the well-brushed head of Piper, the silk mercer's apprentice, who had stepped out to take the shutters down.

Now Piper was exceptionally smart in a green coat and brown breeches with knee buckles like tin daisies. Piper was the good, industrious apprentice, the real angel of Amen Corner, who came at customers like an anxious butterfly.

"Can I help you, ma'am? Allow me . . . oh, allow *me!*"

Piper opened carriage doors as if they were jewel caskets, and handed out the rustling, perfumed contents with a courtesy that had to be seen to be believed.

"Careful, ma'am . . . careful! I just washed down the pavement and it's still a bit wet!"

Nothing was too much trouble for Piper, who wanted to get on in the world. He was on the go from seven till seven, and walked so airily that it was a marvel he'd not been blown down the end of Warwick Lane.

Thoughtfully Shag loaded his brush and, taking exquisite aim, let fall a gobbet of paint. He missed Piper by no more than an inch, but the paint splashing on the pavement spattered Piper's striped stockings.

"You filthy beast up there!" shrieked Piper, and skipped inside the shop for turpentine and a rag to repair the damage.

This was the only communication between the two apprentices, who were divided by five and forty feet of air and united by the Law of Gravity alone. Shag dropped—and Piper suffered. Shag danced with pleasure—and Piper danced with rage. To Shag, Piper was no more than the top of a head, created by Providence, for aiming at; to Piper, Shag was no more than a pair of patched boots above which lurked the spirit of the devil.

Piper, who went to church on Sunday, had come to have strange, heretical thoughts. He believed that the world was upside down and that hell was really in the sky. Everything pointed that way. Did not all goodness, nourishment, and beauty come up out of the soil, while filth, beer swill, cheese rinds, and disfiguring, biscuit-coloured paint rained down on him ceaselessly from on high?

Since the coming of Shag, Piper, who took a virtuous pride in his appearance, had fairly reeked of turpentine, and, though he drenched himself with a strong floral scent bought from Chambers of Portugal Street, he succeeded in smelling not so much like flowers as a painting of them.

Shag also smelled like a painting—but not of flowers. Shag smelled like a painting of half-eaten apples, old cheese, and fish. Unlike Piper, Shag did not go to church unless Mr. Howie sent him there to paint something; consequently, he had no thoughts of God or the devil, heretical or otherwise. He liked the sun and feared the slippery rain, and took no other interest in the sky. After all, you couldn't drop things upwards. So Shag also found heaven below, by way of dropping things on Piper's well-brushed head.

The Filthy Beast

And there it was again! The industrious apprentice's head had bobbed into view as Piper set about sweeping the pavement in front of the shop.

Shag rubbed his hands together and, poking out his tongue for greater concentration, bided his relentless time. Piper bobbed and dodged until at last, overcome by honourable weariness and the heat, he rested on his broom. And paid a frightful penalty. A pint of dirty water came down like a bomb and exploded on his bright green sleeve.

Shag heard the angels singing, and he clapped his hands in triumph and joy; Piper screamed and rushed back inside the shop.

His coat—his best coat! The filthy beast had ruined it! He knew he never ought to have put it on till evening, but the sun had been shining and he'd felt so happy. . . .

He stumbled past bales of flowered satin and rosy tiffany like a broken greenfly. He was weeping with pain and rage.

"Please, God, strike him down!" wept Piper. "Smash him all over the ground!"

He leaned against his master's soft, expensive merchandise and soaked a corner with his tears till, hearing sounds from upstairs, he swallowed down his sobs and pulled himself together.

He wouldn't let that swine aloft destroy him as if he were no more than an ant. It wasn't fair—it wasn't fair!

He hung up his coat to dry, and by the time Mr. Martlet came downstairs, he was once more in command of himself. He was the industrious apprentice, willing and eager, forever carrying bales of taffeta and watered tabby from the storeroom to the window space and laying them down as if they were Infant Christs; he was at everyone's beck and call and waited on his master and mistress with a devotion that bordered on the holy.

"Piper, do this! Piper, fetch that! Piper, the window! Piper, the door!"

"Oh, yes, sir! Directly, ma'am! No trouble at all!"

He who pays the piper calls the tune was a saying most deeply engraved on the virtuous apprentice's heart.

Outside, in the hot sun, the other apprentice, Shag, sat on his high place, gnawing an apple and swinging his legs, and waiting on the reappearance of Piper's well-brushed head, of whose complicated contents he'd neither a thought nor a care in the world. Sometimes he amused himself by daubing rude pictures as far across the frontage of Martlet and Peabody as he could reach; sometimes he'd just sit and stare and pick his nose till he'd catch sight of Mr. Howie, striding along and looking up. Then he'd work like a demon to render his enormous, biscuit-coloured bosoms and bottoms unrecognizable to his master's suspicious eye. All the rest of mankind worked hard to be noticed for it; Shag only worked hard when he didn't want to be noticed.

Down below, at the other end of gravity, honest Piper continued to work his fingers to the bone and his soul to ashes in his efforts to please. He darted in and out of the shop, opening carriage doors, bowing and scraping and dancing attendance, and pausing only to wipe the sweat from his brow. He carried huge bundles, he cleaned up after pet dogs, he swallowed down insults and lapped up contempt, and, in general, he spread his spirit on the floor for customers to walk upon. There was a lady who trod on his finger as he was rubbing a paint spot from the hem of her gown. He smiled and begged her pardon for causing an inconvenience.

Perhaps somewhere in the wide world other worms might turn, but here, in Amen Corner, the silkworm—never!

So Piper endured all that life, and Shag, could drop upon him, and he turned the other cheek so often that even Father Time—

unchristian though he was—took pity on him and at last, at long last, struck seven o'clock.

Piper's day was done. After he'd put up the shutters, swept and tidied the shop, stacked the tumbled bales in the storeroom, and danced a last attendance on his master and mistress, he was free. Free!

"And where are you off to, Piper, in such a hurry?"

"To the Fair, sir! To Bartholomew Fair!"

All day he'd been longing for it with a passion that no one would have suspected. Sometimes he'd felt terrified and sometimes exalted to the skies at the thought of what the Fair might bring. A thousand times during the day he'd drawn back—only to be pricked on, in the very next moment, into a wilder, fiercer resolve. What was his secret? It was too deep for words; even in the looking-glass, he hid it under a dangerous, silky smile.

"The Fair again, Piper? But you went yesterday, and the day before."

"Yes, sir. So I did."

"I would have thought you'd been often enough, Piper."

Piper said nothing; the only answer he could have made lay far too deep for words.

"Take care of yourself, Piper. Keep out of mischief."

"Yes, Mr. Martlet, sir," said Piper, and found himself thinking, unaccountably, of lions tearing him apart and wild bears paddling in his vitals. "I'll take good care."

But he knew he would do no such thing. All his day's waverings were at an end. He was now fixed so firmly on his course that not even death could have stopped him; his disconnected soul would have gone marching, pale and eager, to the Fair.

White as a sheet, he put on his stained green coat and left the shop with an airy skip that contained the ghost of a stumble.

Outside, a sudden dread of something unspeakable falling on

his head and ruining him beyond all hope caused him to halt. He winced and looked up. Shag's plank was empty and the scaffolding was bare. It really seemed as if God had put the devil to flight and come into His own.

Piper breathed again and whispered to himself, "*The Lord is my shepherd!*" and went on towards the Fair.

Giltspur Street was in an uproar; from earliest morning it had been an impassable battleground of barrows, stalls, beggars, and children as savage as wolves. A cannon might have cleared a path, but Piper was unarmed, so he had no choice but to step aside and go into the alleys that led, a long way roundabout, to Cow Lane and the Fair.

These alleys were steep and narrow, and the evening sun turned them into dark cracks down which the sounds of the Fair echoed like lost laughter and music in a shell. Piper hastened, for suddenly he was alone and sorely afraid.

A swarm of Bridewell boys—those turbulent charity apprentices all in penitential blue—had watched him daintily avoid the crowds. They'd taken it as an insult and had followed him into the alleys. At first they'd crept in a menacing silence, but now they began to mock and mimic him, dancing devilishly in his wake and greeting each turn of his dead white face with fists that would have squashed his nose and shattered his teeth.

Please, please, God! screamed Piper in his heart. Smash 'em! Smash 'em down into pieces with Thy strong right hand!

Even as he gave his prayer silent words, a parish constable, huge and full of beer, came out of a court, and the Bridewell boys scattered like puffs of dirty smoke.

The Lord is *my shepherd!* thought Piper, with immense relief. I do believe He really is!

The colour came back into his cheeks and the skip into his

step as he hurried on to the Fair. At last he came out by the sheep pens, and there before him stretched the furious, shrieking heart of Bartholomew Fair.

All the world filled up the open space and threatened to boil over, and the hot sun, acting on hanging meat and old sausages, provided a rich, heavy stink that wobbled the exhausted air.

Everything seemed to be shaking and trembling, like those glimpses of a gaudy heaven—the real heaven—he'd sometimes caught sight of on the other side of his father's eyes. The very screams and shouts were no more than pictures of shouts, hung up like an exhibition of dreams.

"Walk up! Walk up! See the transparent child!"

"Nuts and damsons! Golden pig and honey!"

"Walk up! Walk up! See the Resurrected Man! See the mare with five legs!"

"Peaches and pomegranates! Best Kent cherries of the year!"

"Walk up! Walk up! See the mermaid in a bottle! See the girl born back to back with a bear! See the Nottingham Giant! See the Brussels midget—not eighteen inches high! Walk up! Walk up and see all the wonders of the world!"

"Fried apples and raisins! Peacock pie!"

"Tickets for the lottery! Win a prial of diamonds! Win a ruby ring! Win a golden timepiece! Win a coach and pair!"

"Walk up! Walk up and see the burnin' of Sodom and Gomorrah! See old Noah's Flood!"

> *"See the savage lion!*
> *See the dancin' bear!*
> *See the pussy with two 'eads!*
> *See the lady all covered with 'air!"*

All hope and amazement, all eagerness and eyes, the virtuous apprentice passed into the throng like a soul into the forecourt of heaven, for here were the riches of creation, poured out with an unwithdrawing hand.

Here were marvels, not monsters, as terrific deformities became objects of wonder and applause. Maimed creatures, the offspring of disaster, who'd hidden for a year in shadows from the workaday world, now flaunted their extra limbs and feet with fifteen toes; and Creeping Jesus and Tom-in-the-Pot—who had but one leg between them—fought and banged in the dust over a shilling, rolling over and over like upturned beetles, waving their stumps as more and more money showered down, untainted by the pale stain of pity.

"Walk up! Walk up! See King Solomon and 'is lovely daughter! See 'em caper! See 'em dance! See Princess Betty dance on the slack rope till your 'earts come out of yer mouths!"

Piper halted. The sweat ran down his back; he felt cold as ice.

"Walk up! Walk up, young lovers, all! Walk up and try yer luck! Sixpence to come in, and a shillin'—only a shillin'—to try fer the best prize of all! Win two pound, or a night with the princess 'erself!"

Piper began to move towards the rope dancers' tent with stiff strides, as if moved by a force beyond his will. A huge painting was flaunted on the wall of the tent, a painting of King Solomon's daughter in all her glory. She was all the wild, tender world, at once shy and alluring, at once frightened and frightening.

Nearer and nearer drew the virtuous apprentice; his eyes were bright with tears. This was the secret that lay too deep for words. He was in love. He was desperately, wildly, passionately, frantically in love with King Solomon's daughter. He would have given his life itself for—

"A night in Paradise!" shrilled the tiny boy who'd been shouting on a platform in front of the tent. He beat on his drum, and his voice squealed in ecstasy.

"Where are you, young lovers? Walk up! Walk up and try yer luck!"

Piper walked up. Though he'd only seen her twice in the flesh, he'd seen her since in every turn of his mind's eye. He'd seen her in every pile of tumbled silks; he'd seen her in every reflection that passed the shop window; he'd seen her in the sky and in the darkened corners of the storeroom; he'd seen her in carriages and glimpsed her hastening down every street. If he'd been able to sleep, he would have seen her in his dreams; but all his life had become a dream, and he saw her always in the absolute blackness that reigned when he pushed his knuckles into his screwed-up eyes.

"Come along, young lover! You got a lucky face!"

Once more, the forces that moved Piper took command, and the silk mercer's apprentice paid his sixpence and went inside the tent. At once he felt as if he'd entered the setting sun. There was a melting heat, and everything, the earth, the sky, and the pushing, shuffling throng, was of a golden brown. The very air was brown, and Piper's bright green coat lost all its colour, though not its ugly stain.

He pushed his way forward until he stood before the dancing rope, which was stretched between two poles some twelve feet high. To one of the poles was fixed a Jacob's ladder, up which Piper had seen an angel pass, yesterday and the day before.

Outside, the drum rattled and the tiny boy shrilled on, with his monotonous invitation to come and behold the Princess Betty and for young lovers to try their luck. The crowd grew greater, and Piper, gazing up at the rope, felt that he was going to faint. He closed his eyes and swayed; then the drum rattled in his very ear. He opened his eyes and saw that the tiny boy had come in and was half way up the ladder and beating his instrument with one hand.

He begged for silence for His Majesty, King Solomon, the greatest performer on earth—the only crowned head that had performed before Europe, and fresh from triumphs in Japan. Another roll on the drum and out from behind a tattered curtain scampered King Solomon, in taffeta and brown plush. He wore a tipsy tin crown and carried a sceptre as tall as a door.

He was old, very old, and as he bowed in all directions, he seemed in danger of breaking in two. The boy came down, and King Solomon went up the ladder on twinkling, skinny legs. He swung and swayed and heaved himself up on the rope. Then, balancing with his sceptre, he scampered back and forth, twelve feet in the air.

He was an old, old man, and maybe a king in Israel; it was a wonder he was still alive. Yet everyone longed for him to fall and break his scraggy neck. Three times over he performed his perilous journey, till it seemed the most tedious thing in the world; at last the king came down, and the boy went up and danced like a monkey while Solomon beat on the drum.

Then both were down and bowing and smiling and waving all round. They ran back and forth between the poles, swinging the ladder and pointing, pointing to the tattered curtain that had begun to shiver and bulge as if with child.

"We gives you—we gives you, young lovers all, the lovely, the beautiful, the talented, the marvellous, the soul-eatin' Princess *Betty!*"

There was a roar, as if from the throats of ten thousand lions, as from behind the curtain came the absolute darling of the Fair.

She sparkled, she glittered, and beams of devouring fire flashed from the sequins glued to her eyes. She neither curtsied nor smiled, but, with a toss of her golden head, she flew up the ladder and danced along the slackened rope.

She had long, thin white hands that twisted and turned and

seemed to catch the air for support when she needed it. Sometimes she'd fling them out in a strange, embracing gesture; sometimes she'd flutter them at this young lover or that; sometimes she'd clasp them over her head while she marched—with high, uplifted knees and delicate naked feet—contemptuously above the fascinated throng. She'd jump—and everyone would cry out; she'd swing from side to side—and everyone would sigh.

With every sound that reached her, she turned and stared with a look of unchanging contempt. Who could fathom her? Who could plumb her uncanny depths? Not King Solomon in all his glory. He, like the others, watched and gaped. Only a lover, then . . .

Piper's heart thundered within his neat chest as he remembered that yesterday—only yesterday—she'd seen him looking up and had seemed to smile. Could he be her destined lover—he, Mr. Martlet's good apprentice?

She danced to the middle of the rope, swinging, swinging . . . and the crowd went mad! Each time she swung towards them and soared aloft, she flounced out her skirt, and a storm of pink paper, cut up like rose petals, flew out from underneath and fluttered down. She was all flowers, and Piper could smell roses in the air.

There was a great rush forward as everyone scrambled for the paper petals; Piper secured a whole handful and furtively kissed them. He felt she saw him, for she seemed to nod. Or had he been mistaken? Was she nodding to King Solomon to tell him she'd finished her dance? She flew to the ladder and dropped lightly down.

Now came the moment that Piper had been waiting for, the moment that had caused him so many terrors and determinings throughout the day.

The old man took his daughter by the hand and cast down the challenge to "Young lovers, all."

"Walk up! Walk up! 'Oo'll try fer a shillin' to walk the tight-rope and win a darlin' prize? Win two pound—or a night with the Princess Betty! Can I say fairer than that? Up the ladder and across the rope—and the lovely lady's your'n!

> *"Lovers old and lovers young!*
> *Come set yer foot upon the rung!"*

He clasped her hand in both his own and held it up to the audience, so that, for a moment, she seemed like a marvellous waxen doll. She looked across the rows of faces, and once more Piper felt that her eyes lingered longest on him. He made to step forward, but somehow his legs were imprisoned. He couldn't move for fear. The rope was horribly high.

Already he'd seen two other lovers try for the prize, and both had come to grief. One had been drunk and had fallen from half way up the ladder; the other had reached the rope and, after two steps, had fallen and broken his leg. His screams of agony still echoed in Piper's ears.

But Piper had been practising. He'd stretched threads across the storeroom floor and walked and walked till his feet never deviated by a hair's breadth. He'd—

"I'll 'ave a go at it, mister. 'Ere's me shillin'."

Even as Piper opened his mouth to speak, he was forestalled, and the worst thing in the world stepped up out of the crowd. It was the toad, the monster, the spoiler of his days; it was that filthy beast Shag!

He was even shorter and uglier on the ground than ever he appeared on his plank, and he stumped and strutted with a curious swaying motion, as if he were in danger of falling from the surface of the earth.

As usual, he was grinning his gargoyle grin, and Piper's hatred for him knew no bounds. He hated him with all his heart, with all his soul, and with all his might. It was a marvel that Shag never felt it. He grinned and grinned and paid out his shilling in pennies.

The Princess Betty watched the money, then dropped a faint curtsey and turned away. Shag blew her a kiss and to cheers and applause began to mount the ladder.

"I hate you! I hate you!" whispered Piper. "May God strike you down!"

The higher Shag climbed, the dirtier and uglier he looked, till, by the time he reached the top and crouched over all, he was like Satan himself.

"Fall down! Fall down!"

Suddenly Shag stood upright, and there was a great silence in the tent, for the lad seemed to be balancing on nothing. Then a sound floated down, as of laughter, and Shag, with stumpy arms outstretched and jerking his hips and knees like a cockerel, began to walk the narrow rope as cheerfully as if it had been as wide as all Smithfield.

"With a one! And a two!
And a one! And a two!"

He snapped his head from side to side, looking each time, it seemed, at a rapturous nothing. His eyes were shining like newly minted coins.

This was, after all, Shag's only talent: his gift for balancing and his marvellous head for heights. He revelled in the exercise of it, and the tent was full of angels, singing, cheering, and shouting for more.

So Shag obliged the company with his well-known imitation of a boy about to fall. He tottered, he swung and swayed, he flailed the air with sawn-off wings, drawing forth shrieks from those beneath and creating hope in Piper's anguished heart. But it was no use; Shag walked upon goat's feet, even though he hid them in boots.

At length he came off the rope and down the Jacob's ladder. He stumped up to King Solomon with a look of impudence and pride.

"Well done! Well done, young lover!" said the king, while the crowd roared and shouted for him to be given his prize. The old man smiled and bowed. He took his daughter by the hand and then reached out for Shag, as if to unite the happy pair. Piper nearly died.

"I want the two pahnd!" said Shag loudly.

"What's that? What's that?"

"You 'eard, mister!"

The old man stared in amazement, and the crowd began to laugh.

"Two pounds? Two pounds, when you can 'ave me lovely daughter?"

"Garn!" said Shag, eyeing the gaudy trifle with baffled eyes. "What do I want wiv' 'er?"

"Ain't you got no soul, young lover?"

"I ain't a young lover, mister. I'm a 'ouse painter. Gimme me two pahnd!"

The laughter increased, the king fidgeted; only his daughter remained unmoved. She stared over the heads of the multitude as if to some fascinating place that only she could see. Her expression was at once remote—and intimate. It was curiously like the look that had been on Shag's face as he'd strutted along on high.

Piper's brain was melting—with heat, noise, and a sense of cruelty that made him ache. He was bewildered and profoundly, bitterly dismayed. His all-embracing hatred for Shag had turned, quite suddenly, against himself. He loathed and despised himself—not because he'd hesitated in taking up the challenge, but because he knew that, never in a million years, could he really have done it.

He looked and felt and understood that he was not of them—the creatures who flew. He was earthbound in his little green coat and his knee buckles and his master's little shop. He was strained and constricted; he was fettered and locked up in a prison to which only he had the key. The key was in his hand, but he could not use it. Each time he reached out his hand, someone came running, and it was he himself, the gaoler, who struck the key from his hand with a cry.

"You filthy beast in there!"

"What was that, lad?"

"I said, filthy beast," repeated Piper, half dead with dreaming.

"Why did you say that?"

"I—I meant him! Taking the money like that . . . and leaving her."

"Have a go yourself, then—if you think she's worth a shillin'!"

"Have a go! Go on, lad! Have a go!"

"Walk up! Walk up, young lover! Try yer luck and save me daughter's shame!"

"Get out of my way!" screamed Piper suddenly, though no one was impeding him. "Get out of my way and let me have a go! I'm coming out! I'm coming out, I tell you!"

He stumbled forward, and Shag, money in his fist, turned to stare at him. Though they were scarcely six feet apart, not even the Law of Gravity seemed to unite them any more. If dropped, one would have fallen up, and the other down.

Curious, Shag watched Piper pay his shilling; then he stumped off towards the door of the tent. Curious again, he paused and looked back. He watched Piper, mottled green Piper, climb the swinging ladder.

He saw him get to the top and sway and bend down in a panic to clutch at the rope. Shag saw with interest that Piper's face was as white as plaster and that his eyes were rolling as if he longed to come straight down.

Then, suddenly, the silk mercer's apprentice straightened up and, to loud cheers, set his foot upon the rope. Shag watched him take three steps, then a fourth; then it seemed as though an invisible hand had seized one of his ankles and was waving it in the air. Piper flapped his arms wildly, and suddenly he was dancing on air.

Shag grinned his gargoyle grin as he saw the bright apprentice fall, like a doomed angel, from the high rope to the ground beneath.

"Serves 'im right!" said Shag, and went back to Amen Corner, proudly clutching his two gold pounds.

Amen Corner was as quiet as the grave, and the scaffolding in front of Martlet and Peabody's cast a cage of black shadows under the riding moon. Here and there, below windows particularly, Shag's paintwork had dripped and run, so that it looked as if the establishment had been crying with thick, pale tears.

Shag himself, high up on his plank, stirred in his rag of a blanket and awoke from his gargoyle dreams. He looked inquisitively down the front of the building, then nipped along the plank and peered down the side. He scratched his head. He could see nothing; he could hear nothing. Piper had not returned. Shag shrugged his shoulders and went back to his blanket. He lay on his back and stared up at the moon. The moon grinned down—and Shag grinned up.

"Most likely 'e's wiv' 'er."

"Go and see then," said the moon.

"Why should I?" said Shag irritably. "It's no skin orf *my* nose."

"And what's your nose got to do with it?"

"Pokin' it into 'is business. That's what."

"Then go back to sleep."

"I will if you stop shinin' in me face."

"No skin off *my* nose!" grinned the moon; and Shag swore and came wearily down to the ground.

He stumped off through the streets with nothing more inside his head than ever there had been. It was a good head for heights, but depths never concerned it.

He trod happily in the rubbish of Giltspur Street, kicking it in the air and bending down to pick up anything smelly and offensive and posting it through the first open window he found.

He reached Smithfield by Pie Corner and tried all the shutters of the cook shops with an iron bar he'd wrenched off a barrow. He had no luck, so he stared across the wide emptiness of the Fair. Booths, platforms, stalls, and pennants stood engraved under the moon, and the ground was sliced with silver.

"All right, then, where is 'e?" inquired Shag.

"He might be dead," said the Fair.

"Garn!" said Shag contemptuously.

"Suit yourself," said the Fair.

Shag spied a moonbeam and began to walk along it.

> *"With a one! And a two!*
> *And a one! And a two!"*

With infinite caution, he avoided the blacks and came, by a series of dances, hops, and wild gyrations, to King Solomon's silent tent. Inquisitively he poked his head inside and, after a moment, followed it with the rest of him. He listened carefully and heard a sound of breathing.

"Is that you?"

No answer, so he crept forward into the reeking gloom.

"Is it you in there?"

It was King Solomon, his boy, and his radiant daughter, lying in a heap behind the tattered curtain. They all looked dead to Shag till the Princess Betty stirred and parted her moon-black lips and showed her silver teeth. She was having a good dream.

Shag sat back on his heels, frowning and grinning and rocking himself to and fro. If there were thoughts in Shag's head, they were total strangers and quickly got lost.

Suddenly he stood up. A most curious phenomenon had disturbed him. There had appeared, against the dark canvas walls of the tent, several misty images of moving lights.

Shag hastened outside. The lights were over by the sheep pens. Half a dozen linkboys, with torches burning low, were creeping about in search of dropped valuables. As they moved, they made little pools of colour . . . as if the great grey, empty Fair were remembering, in patches, its past madness and lost joy. Bright paintings of marvels and wonders came and went, and a flag flashed out in scarlet and gold. . . .

Presently one of the boys halted, whistled softly, and waved his torch to his friends. He was under the archway that led into Cloth Fair. All the high brickwork moved and shook with the torch, and windows flashed and winked.

Now the others joined him, and all the torches warmed and expanded the architecture of the night. The boys were looking down; they had found something.

"What are they on to?" asked Shag.

"Go see for yourself," said the night.

He stumped across the open space and strutted up to the congregation of lights. The linkboys had found Piper.

The silk mercer's apprentice lay huddled against the wall of the archway like one dead. Knocked senseless by his fall, he'd been carried outside, where he'd been set upon by the Bridewell boys. He'd been kicked, punched, stripped, and robbed and dragged through the filth of the slaughterhouses. It was not so much a miracle that he was still alive; it was, to Piper himself, a disaster.

The linkboys stared down at him with repugnance.

"Filthy beast!" said one.

"Serves 'im right," said Shag.

"Friend of your'n?"

"Garn!"

"There ain't no pickin's 'ere," said another boy, bending his torch low. " 'E's been done over by hexperts!"

"Serves 'im right!" repeated Shag forcibly. "Serves 'im bleedin' well right!"

"Wotcher doin' now?"

Shag didn't answer. It was perfectly plain what he was doing. He was bending down and heaving the dirty, stinking Piper onto his own broad shoulder. Anybody who couldn't have seen that must have been blind.

The linkboys watched Shag's efforts and then wandered away, leaving only one of their number behind. This child, rendered almost transparent by the torch he was holding, continued to watch Shag's efforts with a slight smile of remembrance.

"Far to go?" he asked as Shag secured his miserable, moaning burden.

"Amen Corner."

"Need any light?"

"Shove off!" said Shag. "I got all the light I needs."

He carried Piper back to Amen Corner and propped him up against Martlet and Peabody's side door in the alley. He knew that it would be opened at half past five. He looked Piper over for serious injuries but found nothing worse than bruises and scrapes. If anything had been broken, it certainly didn't show.

Shag stood up and vigorously scratched at his head, as if something were itching inside. He scowled and, reaching into his pocket, drew out his two gold pounds. He examined them carefully, as if for imperfections; then, apparently deciding that there was nothing to choose between them, he bent down and tucked one of them in Piper's feeble hand.

"That's my boy," said the moon.

"Garn!" said Shag, his face all wreathed in a gargoyle smile.

At seven o'clock Piper, or the ghost of him, took down the shutters and began to sweep the pavement with a broom that seemed made of lead. Dim memories of the night kept coming back to him, but he could make nothing of them. He had walked in the valley of the shadow—and come out of it with a bright gold pound. He looked up—and Shag looked down. Shag grinned and, taking careful aim, let fly with a brushful of paint.

"Thou anointest my head with oil!" said Piper ruefully. "You filthy beast up there!"

The gargoyle aloft hugged himself with glee and gave his well-known imitation of Shag, the house-painter's apprentice and bane of everyone's life.

THE
ENEMY

HOBBY THE YOUNGER, SON OF HOBBY THE JOINER AND COFFIN-
maker to Jessop & Pottersfield's of Little Knightrider
Street, was in love; he was in love with Miss Siskin, barmaid at
the Golden Goose at the corner of Harp Court. So also was
Larkins, of the cheesemonger's, just opposite.

Miss Siskin was a fair and friendly nineteen; Hobby and
Larkins were a grubby twenty-one—between them. Hobby was
ten and Larkins was rising eleven.

Now Larkins, in addition to the advantage of a year in age,
was able to make Miss Siskin modest gifts of Windsor, Cheddar,
and Stilton, nicked from his father's stock, whereas Hobby's pa
only had coffins, which were too heavy to nick and, in any event,
would not have been welcome.

So Larkins prospered in his love; which is to say that Miss
Siskin patted him on the back, pecked his cheek, and accepted
his gifts, while she told Hobby, with a charming smile, "Shove
off, nipper, or you'll get me hung!"

Hobby grew gloomier and gloomier, contemplated all manner

of terrible things, until one day, driven stark wild by his hope-
less love and the crying need to tell of it, he fashioned a pair of
turtle doves from mud in the street outside.

They turned out so real that if he'd clapped his hands, they'd
have flown away!

Tremendously uplifted and excited by this sudden evidence of
a gift, a talent, a divine spark, Hobby rushed to call witnesses:
first, his ma, and then Miss Siskin, who, after all, was chiefly re-
sponsible.

Unluckily, before anyone could come and see the wonderful
birds, Larkins trod on them. Purposely. Such was the demonic
nature of his love that he could brook no rival, especially that
coffin nail, Hobby.

Hobby was grief stricken; he was shocked and outraged. He
vowed that somehow he'd destroy Larkins, who was two inches
taller and wore boots like hammers. He wrote his name, in the
blackest of black chalk, on a coffin lid, and waited.

Larkins laughed his head off, and went to the side door of the
Golden Goose with half a pound of double Gloucester. Miss
Siskin pecked his cheek and said, "You naughty boy, you! You
shouldn't—you reely shouldn't!"

She took the cheese, and Larkins was in seventh heaven.
Hobby, on the other hand, languished in hell.

Being in hell, he had nowhere else to go but to the devil, and,
acting on advice received, he began to make, out of mud, a very
venomous likeness of Larkins. He laboured long and hard till
the likeness was so close it almost spat. Then he punched it in
the nose and squashed it flat.

Sure enough, next day Larkins came out in tetters all over his
face, and Hobby rejoiced and danced on the coffin from which
he'd been told to scrub Larkins' name.

Although it was a well-known fact that Larkins often came

out in tetters and black spots on the side of his nose and boils
on the back of his neck, the coincidence this time was too great
for Hobby not to feel that he had friends in dark places and that
the devil, no less than God, moves in mysterious ways.

After that, Hobby, enchanted with his new-found gift, made
many more things, not out of mud, but from clay his pa dug up in
the backyard. He made ducks and geese and owls that his ma
arranged along the dresser, where they slowly dried out and
crumbled into dust. But all who'd seen them agreed that the boy
had a natural genius and that it would be flying in the face of
Providence not to apprentice him to the modelling trade as soon
as maybe.

By this time Miss Siskin had faded from his heart (and the
Golden Goose as well, with a sailor from Wapping and a dozen
of the best-plated tankards, besides), but somewhere inside him
there remained a misty, rosy dream of a lovely lady for whom
he'd once made birds.

When he was fourteen, he was taken along to Naked Boy
Court and apprenticed, for the sum of twenty pounds, to Falconer's Figurines ("Every Piece an Heirloom"), where they made
pretty plaster chimney sweeps, cottagers, and beggar children that
sold at upwards of a guinea a time.

His ma blessed the gift that had elevated her son out of coffins
and kissed him tenderly; his pa shook him by the hand, in a
manly sort of way, and gave him a book, written by a Lord
Mayor of London and containing all the good advice needful
for an apprentice to make a success of his seven long years.

There were Religion and Truthfulness, Discretion and Affability, Faithfulness and Industry, Caution and Friendship, Silence
and Affection; and there were stern warnings against Quarrelling,
Bad Company, Drunkenness, Boastfulness, Dancing Schools, and
the Courting of Females, which, on an apprentice's pay, was

like calling a hawk without a lure.

Hobby, recollecting Miss Siskin and Larkins with his advantageous cheese, nodded. You certainly needed a lure. He marked the passage in the book and then fell to wondering about Dancing Schools and how much they cost, for there was no virtue in resisting a temptation if you weren't going to be exposed to it. But it turned out that so far as temptation was concerned, he was to have no need of Dancing Schools. . . .

It happened on his very first Monday morning. It was half past six and he'd unbolted the shop door to take down the shutters. He stepped out into the bright sunshine of Naked Boy Court—and there she was! She was twirling round and round in the middle of the Court with her green and yellow spotted skirts flying out like a Christmas bell.

It wasn't Miss Siskin, but someone younger and immeasurably more beautiful. Hobby gazed at her, utterly entranced. Then, remembering Affection but forgetting Caution, he went right up to her and said, "I'm Hobby. You can call me Jack, if you like, for short."

He'd picked up his courting round the side door of the Golden Goose, where things were inclined to be brisk and businesslike.

She stopped her twirling and down swung her skirts, giving off a faint perfume of cinnamon and burnt sugar.

"Now that's a queer name," she said, climbing up onto a pedestal where once a carved boy had fed carved birds till more durable children of flesh and blood had done for the child of stone and left only one broken foot behind. "Hobby's a very queer name!"

"Oh, no, it ain't!" he said, watching her two feet tread either side of the stone one and so make a kind of monster. "Everybody's got a hobby!"

She frowned in an effort to find a worthy reply.

"All right, then. I'm Linnet, from Linnet's Pies. You can call me *Miss* Linnet, for short."

"I didn't suppose you was wed yet!"

"And why ever not? Though I'm only a pie maker's daughter, I'm wonderfully full of good things!"

"But a bit on the underdone side!" came back Hobby, neatly avoiding Miss Linnet's right hand. "See you tomorrow?" It was wonderful how he could sparkle when he was not in Larkins' shade.

"Oh, life's much too serious for that sort of thing," said the pie maker's lovely daughter, bending down to scratch the stone toes that peeped from beneath her petticoat as if they were her own and itched. "Besides, I ain't got the time to waste on a silly *hobby!*"

She jumped down from the pedestal and skipped towards the pie shop, chanting as she went:

> *"Sing a song of sixpence,*
> *Pocket full of rye.*
> *Four and twenty blackbirds*
> *Baked in a PIE!"*

Hobby, wild with joy over such a beginning to his seven years in Naked Boy Court, sang back:

> *"When the pie was opened*
> *The birds began to sing.*
> *Now wasn't that a dainty dish*
> *To set before a 'prentice king?"*

Miss Linnet paused in her doorway and gave Hobby the strangest look, with brows that frowned and eyes that smiled. Then she waved and vanished, and Hobby went into Falconer's Figurines, where a million white sweeps and cottagers and beggar children turned to greet him with their plaster smiles.

He embraced them all with a gesture that all but did for a shelf-ful. He was so happy that his heart was almost bursting. He longed to make something for the pie maker's daughter. He wanted to make her the most beautiful thing in the world.

He furrowed his brows and thought, and misty memories returned. He'd make her a bird, not an ordinary bird, but a bird that, once she set eyes on it, would sing for ever in her heart. It would sing such songs as the sun sings, in woods and gardens where the shadows play.

The ghost of Miss Siskin sighed and withered quite away before this glorious blaze of the pie maker's daughter. It was not love at first sight; it was sight at first love, so freshly did Hobby see the world!

He simply had to confide all these fine feelings to Mr. Greylag, the journeyman, who came at seven and was so old and frail that Hobby couldn't help wondering if he might not do a stroke of business on the side and get Mr. Greylag to bespeak a coffin from his pa while there was still time.

Mr. Greylag put on his streaky canvas apron and said, "Ah. That chit from across the way."

Then he told Hobby to sweep the dust from the shop and Miss Linnet from his thoughts. Females were a snare and a delusion; they were the downfall of apprentices and in the gift of the devil.

"*And what shall it profit a man,*" he croaked, sitting at the bench and beginning to open up Saturday's moulds and take out the dead-white figurines, "*if 'e gain the 'ole world and lose 'is own soul?*"

Hobby couldn't honestly say. Mr. Greylag was very religious and earned a guinea a week with daily beer and pie, and so ought to know. He took up his broom and, as he swept, wondered if now was the time to talk of coffins, since Mr. Greylag's mind was plainly on matters eternal.

At eight o'clock sharp, for he was a punctual man, Mr. Falconer himself came down. He lived upstairs with Mrs. Falconer, who was always shouting for doors to be shut, as the drifting plaster dust made her sneeze.

Mr. Falconer was a huge, quiet man, with small hands and small feet. It was his imagination that had bodied forth the chimney sweeps and cottagers and pretty beggar children, all of whom also had small hands and feet. He created them out of clay, and Mr. Greylag turned them into plaster and finished them off with a narrow-bladed knife and the edge of his little finger, worn as smooth as marble. Then Mr. Falconer scratched his name beneath, and they ended up on mantelpieces all over town.

Soberly, for he was an abstemious man, he wished Hobby and Mr. Greylag good morning and, putting on his apron, began to show the new apprentice how to pummel and wedge up the wet clay and make it ready for working.

Hobby stood behind his master and gave him half of his attention, for we cannot always, at the drop of a hat, oblige with the whole of it. He'd noticed, through the glass screen that divided the workroom from the shop, that the pie maker's daughter was out in the Court again.

She was perched on the pedestal and, with her gown flowing round her, was holding out a handful of pie crumbs to the sparrows that hopped on the cobbles. She was a lovely sight. . . .

"Pay attention!" said Mr. Falconer sharply, for he was not a patient man.

So Hobby paid attention, and whenever Mr. Falconer didn't —which happened from time to time—he provided himself with enough clay to make Miss Linnet's marvellous bird.

He finished it that same day, and in spite of interruptions and having to push it into corners, it turned out so well that he couldn't resist showing it to Mr. Greylag, of whom he was determined, remembering Friendship, to make a friend.

"Ah," said Mr. Greylag. "And what might that be?"

"Why, it's a bird, of course! Can't you see? There's its head and beak, and—and here's its wings!"

"Ah. Well, now. So it's a bird," said Mr. Greylag, who was a solemn believer in learning to walk before you ran, let alone flew. "Now just let me tell you something, young feller-me-lad. In the beginning God created the 'eaven and earth. *And the earth was without form.* Even *'e* didn't start right off with birds!"

Hobby, more used to praise than criticism, scowled and took his bird away.

"Ah. Well, now," said Mr. Greylag, relenting. "Now I comes to look at it in a better light, it ain't all that bad. In fact, considering your newness to the trade, I'd go further and say it ain't half bad."

He'd really been quite touched by the apprentice's trust in him, and he went on to say that if Hobby let the object dry out to a real leather hardness, he'd make a plaster of it for Hobby's ma.

"But not," he added, taking off his apron, "for that chit across the way."

Hobby, remembering Discretion, but forgetting Honesty—for we cannot be thinking of everything at once—thanked Mr. Greylag kindly and wished him a respectful good night.

Next morning, cradling his bird (which had been practising in his dreams for its forthcoming concert in Miss Linnet's heart), Hobby unbolted the shop door and stepped out into the bright sunshine. He was brimming with pride and hope.

At the same moment, Linnet's Pies opened up and out stepped, not the pie maker's daughter, but—LARKINS!

Hobby nearly fainted. He stood stock-still, glaring wildly across the twenty cobbled yards. It wasn't possible! It was the aberration of an overexcited brain. It was a delusion—a nightmare!

While these explanations were going through Hobby's mind, Larkins, with his sleeves rolled up and wearing a smart green apron, began taking down Linnet's shutters as if he'd been doing it all his life.

"*Sing a song o' sixpence,*" he chanted melodiously, "*Pocket full o' rye. . . .*"

A window over the pie shop went up like a rocket and out leaned Miss Linnet, her brown hair flying.

"He's Larkins," she said needlessly. "New apprentice. Come yesterday."

"Them's lovely eyes you got, miss," said Larkins, with all his old gallantry. "If I didn't know they was your own, I'd swear you'd nicked 'em from the sky!"

"Though I'm only a pie maker's daughter," said Miss Linnet to the new apprentice reprovingly, "I'm not to be buttered up."

Hobby, feeling suddenly like a blown-out candle beside Larkins' bright sun, said nothing. Dazedly he set his bird on a projecting sill and began to take down Falconer's shutters.

"What's that?" asked Miss Linnet, leaning out of the window as far as she dared.

"Nothing," said Hobby gloomily. "A secret."

Miss Linnet pursed her bright lips and vanished from the window.

Larkins put his hands on his hips and smirked.

"I saw her first," said Hobby.

"Want a fight?" inquired Larkins, urging his superior height.

Miss Linnet came out of the pie shop and danced lightly towards the pedestal. The two apprentices converged upon her, as if drawn by wires. Hobby, who'd been carrying his bird, laid it down tenderly and offered Miss Linnet assistance to her perch. She ignored him.

"His pa makes coffins," said Larkins confidentially. "Creepy trade."

"His pa sells cheese," said Hobby. "Crawly, smelly trade."

"My pa made *me*," said the pie maker's daughter dreamily. "And everyone says I'm a dish fit for a king!"

"If them lips wasn't your own, miss," said Larkins, kneeling impulsively at Miss Linnet's feet, "I'd swear you'd nicked a pair of rubies from the king's own crown!"

Miss Linnet nodded thoughtfully and looked at Hobby.

"What's your secret?"

Hobby's hopes rose. He beamed up at the girl on the pedestal, then bent down to pick up his marvellous bird. NO!

Larkins had trodden on it. He stared down at the ruin in stark disbelief. It was Miss Siskin all over again. No! It was a million times worse! Tears of rage blinded him. He punched Larkins in the stomach—which he knew was his weak spot. Larkins kicked him on the ankle. Miss Linnet, on her pedestal, looked down with interest and wondered what was going to happen next.

"I'll kill you!" said Hobby.

"You and who else?" demanded Larkins.

Hobby thought for a moment. His rage was so enormous that he felt like picking up the world by a handful of forest and smashing it down on Larkins' head.

Silently he limped back into Falconer's Figurines, holding his lump of shapeless clay. It no longer sang of sunshine and shadows; it croaked of darkness and death. He laid it on the bench, where Mr. Greylag found it.

"Better is the ending of a thing than the beginning thereof," said the religious old man, by way of consolation.

Hobby, thinking of the ending of Larkins, agreed wholeheartedly, and set about sweeping the workroom floor so violently that he raised clouds of choking dust that forced the old man to retreat into the shop.

"I'll kill him!" said Hobby, panting, and sending up whole whirlwinds of plaster till the very workroom itself disappeared in the agitated obscurity. "I'll kill him!"

"*Them what sows the wind shall reap the whirlwind*," coughed and spluttered Mr. Greylag, reproachfully.

"I'll strangle him!" raged Hobby, wielding his broom as if it were a flaying iron and Larkins were under it. "I'll slit his rotten throat!"

"You and who else?" echoed Larkins' contemptuous words. Larkins was bigger and stronger and Hobby's superior in everything.

"I'll poison him! I'll push him in the river!"

"You and who else?"

In vain, Hobby glared into the gloomy whirlwinds of his own raising for some sign of supernatural help. But the devil sends no clerks to take instructions from apprentices driven frantic by love and hate; he simply wouldn't have had enough to go around.

"I'll choke him! I'll smash him in pieces! I'll—I'll—"

Suddenly Hobby stopped sweeping. Out of the dust had crept, not the devil, but an idea. It was a wicked idea; it was dark, deformed, and diseased. Yet, at the same time, it was haunting and tempting, and it clutched fiercely at the roots of his heart. Already it filled him with such an excitement that he had to bite hard on his lip to prevent himself from blurting it out aloud.

The tall columns of dust began to subside and settle, and Mr. Greylag came back for his apron.

"'*E maketh the storm a calm*," he croaked, blinking through the clearing air. Then he saw Hobby. The plaster had settled all over him.

"A whited sepulchre!" chuckled the old journeyman. *"Full o'
dead men's bones!* He—he!"

That night, when all the household doors were shut against
Mrs. Falconer's enemy, the all-pervasive dust, Hobby abandoned
himself, heart and soul, to his terrible idea. Remembering his
friends in dark places, and the strange success they'd once brought
him, he began to make an image of his enemy, just as he'd done
before.

He worked by the light of a single candle, first preparing the
clay and then, thumbful by thumbful, creating a shape of Larkins
out of the dull grey void.

He was going to make such an image that when he came to
crush it, so help him God or the devil, Larkins would surely
sicken and die.

He worked till long after midnight, when weariness made
Larkins' hateful image fade from his mind's eye. He could no
longer remember the shape of Larkins' nose or the height of his
detestable brow. So he hid his work away and resolved that next
morning he would look at his enemy with more than ordinary
care.

At half past six, after a night of troubled dreams, he rose
wearily and went out into Naked Boy Court. Miss Linnet
watched him from her window and saw that his eyes were dark
from lack of sleep.

On account of me, she thought with satisfaction.

She heard the pie shop open and saw Larkins come out. Hobby
stared at him and began to walk towards the middle of the
Court. Larkins frowned contemptuously, and did likewise.

They're going to fight, thought Miss Linnet with interest. On
account of me.

The two apprentices halted within an arm's length of each other.

Larkins looked Hobby in the eye; Hobby looked Larkins in the nose, the chin, the cheek. Neither of them spoke, so Miss Linnet, growing impatient (for we, none of us, have all morning to waste), dropped her handkerchief. It fluttered to the cobbles like a broken dove.

Both the apprentices saw it, but fearing a treacherous attack from the other, neither moved. So the pie maker's daughter, frowning heavily on the two marble youths, came down herself.

"I'm glad you two didn't fight," she said insincerely, and picked up her handkerchief with a deep blush.

"Oh, miss," said Larkins, "if them cheeks wasn't your own, I'd swear you'd nicked 'em from the queen's rose garden!"

Carefully Hobby noted the curl of Larkins' mouth and the lifting of one of his eyebrows.

And that's another nail in your coffin, he thought, and wondered if he might not drop a hint to his pa that the Larkins family would shortly be in the market for a boy-sized article in elm. He stalked back into Falconer's without uttering a single word.

"He's off his head," said Larkins.

On account of me, thought the pie maker's daughter proudly.

All that day Hobby was intensely preoccupied, and drew down on himself many rebukes from Mr. Falconer and even Mr. Greylag, who warned him that he might "fly away in a dream and not be found." Irritably he shook his head. He was trying to keep the details of Larkins' countenance in his mind so that, when the time came, he might transfer them to the clay.

He waited till the workroom was wrapped in the full secrecy of the night, and then he set to work again. With a feverish excitement he scraped and pressed and thumbed his creation in search of his enemy. At times he fancied the gloom was full of phantoms watching over him. He could almost believe that their pale hands were helping him, so uncannily did his own fingers turn and probe.

Already the likeness was quite striking. Hobby paused, and the grey head, shimmering dully in the candlelight, stared mutely back at its creator. Hobby marvelled, but at the same time he saw that there was much more to be done. It was in his mind to make so close a likeness of Larkins that his own ma would have kissed it good night.

He tried to continue, but once more weariness clouded his memory and he had to give up.

"Tomorrow," he muttered, "I'll have another look."

Next morning he studied Larkins with almost loving care. There was no doubt he'd got Larkins' features off amazingly well. But equally without doubt, there was something missing. It was Larkins' soul. He hadn't got it; and without Larkins' soul, all his labours would be in vain.

But souls, he soon discovered, don't come all of a piece. They come little by little, in the frown beneath the smile and the smile beneath the frown, and even, sometimes, in the strange blind look cast by the back of a head.

But more mornings than one were needed for study such as this, and looks so deep and penetrating that Larkins himself was abashed and became uneasy in the presence of Hobby.

Miss Linnet also was troubled by him, as he no longer seemed to have eyes for her. She wondered if he'd found another girl, but could not quite bring herself to believe *that*.

Hobby alone seemed tranquil, as, morning by morning, he carried away a little more of Larkins to feed the growing image in the night.

And there's another nail in your coffin! he'd say to himself as he walked away, and he'd give a smile as wicked as hell.

These were autumn days, when the sun in the sky was no

more than a golden mark left by the ingenious workman who'd made the spring and summer. A chill had begun to strike through the air and Miss Linnet took to coming out in a green worsted shawl and Larkins wore his sleeves rolled down.

At last it was Michaelmas Eve, when rents were to be paid and accounts to be settled in full. Hobby looked at Larkins as if for the last time, and Miss Linnet, more troubled than ever, went over and over in her mind a dozen possible rivals and wondered which of them could have supplanted her.

She climbed up on her pedestal and began twirling round, filling the air with her cinnamon fragrance and presenting the two apprentices with glimpses of white silk stockings embroidered with pretty cherry clocks.

"Tomorrow night," she said, turning all the while so that her words flew as much to Naked Boy Court as to the apprentices, "there's to be . . . a goose supper at the Nag's Head. . . . Lots of my friends . . . are going . . . with their boys." Round and round she whirled, extending her hands as if to catch the revolving air. "If you like . . . you can take . . . ME!"

She'd stopped like a fairground toy; she was staring at Hobby, but her hand had picked out Larkins.

"If I didn't know this little hand was your own, miss," cried Larkins, seizing it as if he meant to eat it, "I'd swear you'd nicked it from an angel!"

Miss Linnet waited for Hobby to betray her rival, but he never seemed to notice that he'd been passed over; he was watching the parting of his enemy's lips and the delighted widening of his eyes.

And there's another nail in your coffin, my friend, he thought. And it'll be the last!

That night he put in Larkins' soul—and heard the nightly

phantoms draw in their breath; as well they might, for the apprentice had made his enemy to the very life!

Or the very death, more like it, thought Hobby, as he walked round his creation, scarcely able to believe in what he had accomplished. He'd found such a likeness in the cold clay that Larkins' own ma would have wept and kissed it good night.

Clay Larkins, uncanny in the candlelight, gazed at his maker with parted lips and wonderment in his eyes. Clay Larkins, fashioned out of nights and days, out of love and hate, seemed to whisper, "Why—why did you make me?"

"To kill you, of course! To smash you into dust!"

"What a pity," said clay Larkins. "What a pity!"

"You should have thought of that before."

"So should you."

Hobby shrugged his shoulders. He touched the cold head and slowly moved his fingers down till he could feel the brow he'd come to know so well. He stroked the eyes and remembered, smiling, the pain they'd cost him and the joy he'd felt when he'd got them right. Ah, well, it was all over now. Nothing more remained but to destroy it. He raised his clenched fist.

"Good-bye, Larkins. I'm going to smash you now."

"You and who else?" whispered clay Larkins, gazing at his creator with all the wonderment and affection that had gone into his making.

Hobby looked round as if for some supernatural assistance, but the workroom was a solemn, lonely place. There was no one present but the creator and his work.

Slowly he lowered his fist and let it fall to his side.

"Tomorrow, then," he muttered. "I'll wait until tomorrow."

The truth of the matter was that he'd suddenly felt immensely sad at the thought of destroying what had taken so much labour to make.

He went to bed with the image on the floor beside him and stared at it, long and hard, through the gloom. He longed to show the masterpiece to Mr. Greylag, to his master . . . but he dared not. They were both too experienced in the making of images not to guess why he had fashioned such a likeness of his enemy in clay.

Half fondly, half bitterly, he stretched out his hand and touched Larkin's well-made lips—as if enjoining the clay to secrecy.

"If you don't say a word, I'll let them see you."

He shook his head. The very excellence of the work would betray him as surely as if it shouted from the housetops. He would be cursed and sent out from the shop and the trade for ever.

He groaned aloud as the irony of his situation overwhelmed him. He could neither show his masterpiece nor find it in his heart to destroy it. He had made it too well to do either. He felt that the devil had tricked him. . . .

He fell asleep and had the most extraordinary dream; that is, if it *was* a dream, for at no time could he *prove* to himself that he was actually asleep.

It began with his thinking that there was someone else in the shop. He sat up in bed and saw that he was not mistaken. There was someone else: another youth, dressed quite simply in black worsted and stained grey satin. He could make him out quite clearly, even though it was dark; this, surely, was evidence on the side of dreaming.

The youth was sauntering round the cabinets and shelves, examining the plaster sweeps and beggar children as if whiling away a few moments while politely waiting for Hobby's attention.

He had a rosy face and a flashing crimson smile; he might have been a lawyer's apprentice, such as one meets with gossiping with clients at the corner of Cliffords Inn and Fetter Lane. Yet, on closer inspection, his cheeks were not all that smooth; in fact, they were closely wrinkled, like worn morocco leather. He carried a wooden box that was a little too long for pistols and a little too short for swords.

"How did you get in here?" asked Hobby, wavering between dream and reality and trying to get the intruder to commit himself.

"Oh, I move in mysterious ways," said the elderly youth, leaning over the counter and flashing his courteous smile down at Hobby and the clay image by his side.

"If you don't go away, I'll call Mr. Falconer," said Hobby cunningly.

"All right," said the youth easily. "I don't mind."

Hobby, temporarily outwitted, thought again.

"We're shut," he said, determined to treat this dream with all the business of reality and so send it packing. "So whatever you want will have to wait till ordinary working hours."

"But it's not what *I* want."

He put his box down on the counter in the manner of a commercial traveller about to display his samples. It was fairly obvious that the dream was trying to beat Hobby at his own game.

"We—we don't buy goods here," said Hobby, clenching his fists under his blanket and wondering if he'd be a match for the intruder if it should come to blows.

"You were thinking, just before you dozed off, that you'd been tricked?"

"How do you know what I was *thinking*?" asked Hobby quickly. Surely, now he had the dream trapped!

"As I told you, I move in mysterious ways."

A very unconvincing answer, thought Hobby triumphantly.

"What have you got in your box?" he asked, pressing home his advantage with the skill of a practised inquisitor who darts from one thing to another in order to throw his victim into confusion.

The youth laughed appreciatively and came round to Hobby's side of the counter. He knelt down with a loud cracking of joints, which was, after all, evidence on both sides again. The sound was real, but, on the other hand, the youth was much too young to be rheumatic. He gazed admiringly at the image of Larkins.

"It's not for sale!" said Hobby quickly.

"I know that," said the youth. "But you must admit it's turned out rather well. You certainly do have the divine spark, don't you!"

And much good it's done me! thought Hobby bitterly, but certainly didn't say it aloud.

"Oh, I wouldn't say that," said the dream, thereby hopelessly betraying itself.

"I didn't *say* it!" pounced Hobby.

"I wouldn't say that at all. In my opinion, it's done you a power of good. My dear boy," went on the wrinkled youth—most unsuitably, Hobby thought, for he couldn't have been much older than Hobby himself—"you seem to have quite missed the point. You made this beautiful object for the sole reason of using it to destroy your enemy. That's right, isn't it?"

Hobby, unwilling to commit himself even to a dream, obstinately held his tongue.

"Exactly," said the youth, as if Hobby had answered, which he knew he hadn't. "And that's what your work will have achieved. You do see that, don't you! You haven't been tricked at all."

"And how do you make that out?" asked Hobby, intrigued in spite of his elaborate caution.

The youth fumbled in his waistcoat pocket; then, as if recollecting something, laughed and trotted off into the workroom.

"Come out of there!" called Hobby. "It's private!"

"I know," said the youth, hurrying back and kneeling once more beside Hobby.

"Here," he said, putting something down on the floor. "Do you understand now?"

Hobby's eyes widened in horror! The youth had fetched him Mr. Greylag's sharp, narrow-bladed knife!

"It'll be quite easy," said the aged lad. "You can do it to-morrow night. Larkins will have been drinking too much, and, as we both know, his stomach's his weak spot. He'll be no match for you. And, honestly, whether you do it in a dark alley at the back of the Nag's Head in Covent Garden, or here in the shop"—he patted the clay head—"it amounts to the same thing.

"The image you've made will have destroyed your enemy. *Now* do you see that you've not been tricked? You do see it, don't you?" went on the youth with a sudden earnestness, as if to convince Hobby of his desire to deal honourably.

"If you hadn't made it so marvellously well—and all credit to your divine spark!—you'd never have dreamed of smashing the flesh-and-blood Larkins just to preserve the Larkins of clay! Yes, my dear boy, it's been a certainty from the moment you put your heart and soul into it! One way or the other, this image will destroy your enemy. As I believe I mentioned, I move in mysterious ways."

He looked hard at Hobby, and then, with a shrug of his shoulders, he slid his box from the counter and brought it down to Hobby's level. He fiddled with the clasp, clucking with annoyance as it seemed to stick. At last he opened it.

"My credentials," he said, and displayed to Hobby a red velvet interior in which was fitted, very neatly, a pair of horns with brass screw fittings and a long black button-on tail.

Hobby awoke with a scream. Trembling, he got out of bed and looked round the workroom and shop for some evidence of his nocturnal visitor. Of course, he found none. He had only had a bad dream.

Why, then, did he sweat so much . . . and why did his eyes keep turning from side to side in dread? Because he had found, lying on the floor beside his bed, Mr. Greylag's sharp knife!

Over and over again he tried to persuade himself that he'd brought it in himself, in order to finish off some tiny detail of his work, but he could not remember ever having done such a thing. And all that came into his mind were the fatal words: "One way or the other, this image will destroy your enemy."

He picked up the knife and put it back in the workroom; then he went outside to take down the shutters. He saw Larkins —worse-than-ever Larkins—laughing and joking and boasting of the night to come with Miss Linnet as she leaned out of her window and brushed her long brown hair. Neither of them spared Hobby a glance.

Savagely he went back into Falconer's. There was no doubt that the very sight of flesh-and-blood Larkins drove him wild. He brooded on all the injuries Larkins had done him . . . of which the last was the worst of all. Because he was so hateful he'd forced Hobby to hide away the best work he'd ever done— his very soul—from the sight of an admiring world. Carefully he wrapped up his masterpiece and hid it among his bedding.

Mr. Greylag arrived, and Hobby cursed the hatred that now denied him the old journeyman's praise. At eight o'clock Mr. Falconer came down, and Hobby's curses were redoubled. Throughout the day, customers came and went, were charmed by this plaster sweep or that smiling beggar child . . . and went away without an inkling of the wonder the apprentice had created, and was too frightened and ashamed to show.

And all because of that swine Larkins.

At last Mr. Greylag hung up his apron, and Mr. Falconer, in company with his lady wife, went off to Michaelmas goose in Cheapside.

Hobby was alone. His feelings by now had passed through a furnace in which everything less than fireproof had been consumed. His dream—if dream it had been—had been true. The clay image, standing on the shop counter—now mysterious, now frightening, now inexplicable in its secret life—was doomed to destroy his enemy, just as surely as its smile of blind certainty declared that it could not be destroyed itself.

He gave his masterpiece a last deep look, in which pleasure and fear were equally mingled, left the shop, and hastened towards Covent Garden.

There'd been a smallish riot at the Nag's Head. Pies and spiced apples had flown like cannonballs and ripe plums had exploded against the walls. There'd been thunderous dancing on the long table, and the landlord, hoping to lay out the turbulent apprentices cold, had laced their beer with gin. But it had only made them worse.

Having demolished their roast goose, they'd set about demolishing the Nag's Head itself; the landlord, driven frantic, had shouted that he'd send for their masters if they didn't clear off and never come back.

They took his word for it, and tumbled outside in a heap, where the cool night air, acting on their heated brains, caused them to caper about with tipsy abandon and seize innocent passersby in ferocious attempts to dance.

Dancing was the order of the night, and though feet were

sometimes uncertain, spirits were as deft and nimble as mice.

Larkins was well away. He skipped and hopped in a blaze of hiccups and broken gallantries, while the pie maker's lovely daughter, wearing her ma's hoop, swung and chimed haplessly in his wake.

He clutched her by the hand, the waist, the neck—and sometimes lost her altogether, when he'd cry out: "Miss! Oh, miss! Come back or—hic!—was you always only a dream?"

And Miss Linnet, acting on the principle that the devil she knew was likely to be the better proposition, endeavoured to free herself from other hands and recapture her capering Larkins.

He wove in and out of the dark arches of the marketplace, tottering for support from column to column.

"Miss—oh, miss!" he called, stretching out his hand into the shadows.

"Larkins—oh, Larkins!" murmured Hobby.

He'd watched his enemy leave the Nag's Head and had followed him as softly and secretly as the angel of death. He reached out to grasp Larkins' hand, but suddenly it was snatched away as Miss Linnet dragged him off to join in the general dance.

Hobby cursed and waited . . . and sure enough, Larkins came weaving back.

"Miss—oh, miss!" he called.

"Larkins—oh, Larkins!" whispered Hobby, when again the hand was snatched from his grasp.

The apprentices had made a serpent—a long, tipsy serpent of linked arms, of swinging skirts and silken ankles and great brass buckles that jumped on the cobbles like firecrackers.

It rolled along by the arches, and then, on a confused impulse, for it was a serpent of many minds, it began to tug and pull away. With shrieks of laughter and snatches of song, it danced across the wide marketplace, leaving in its wake a mysterious fragrance of ghostly roast goose and phantom beer.

A dozen times the shadowy Hobby saw his enemy stumble and fall . . . and a dozen times he saw him gathered up and danced away. He bided his time, knowing that sooner or later his enemy would be delivered into his hand.

A linkboy, more needy than wise, darted forward and stood over the newly fallen Larkins, with torch uplifted and downcast, hopeful eyes.

"Light you 'ome, young sir? Light you 'ome for a penny?"

"A candle!" hicupped Larkins, looking up and seeing many more candles than one. "A candle to—hic!—light me to bed!"

At once the cry was taken up by his companions of Michaelmas night.

"Here comes a candle to light you to bed;
Here comes a chopper to chop off your head!"

The linkboy, with an inkling of disaster, backed away.

"Chop—chop—chop!" chanted the apprentices, making menacing arches of their joined arms.

The linkboy wailed and fled.

"Chop—chop—chop!"

The linkboy departed from the marketplace so rapidly that his torch was almost torn out. His passing was marked by a scribble of smoke and a blinking of sparks.

"Chop—chop—chop!" shouted the apprentices, streaming after the light.

Desperately the little linkboy darted along King Street. What would they do to him if they caught him? Would they really chop off his head? He vanished, like a fiery mouse, down an alley and into Three Kings Court.

"Chop—chop—chop!"

It was no use. His light had betrayed him and they'd followed it. They poured down into the court, chanting and stamping till the windows rattled and the doors shook.

The linkboy squealed in panic and fled from doorway to doorway. Then an old man came out.

He was a savage, unshaven old man—a sour-faced lamplighter whose beauty sleep had been shattered beyond repair. He roared out with his ladder and wielded it like a scythe.

"Chop—chop—chop!" he snarled. "I'll give yer chop—chop—chop!"

He made a rush at them—and the apprentices shrieked and fled. But Larkins remained behind. He lay in the alley in the old man's murderous path.

He'd danced too high and fallen too far; he'd twisted his ankle and could scarcely stand.

"Help me—help me!" wailed Larkins, seeing the shadows of the old man's weapon racing up the alley walls like the wings of death. "Save me—save me!"

A hand reached out and clutched at his, and arms helped him to his feet.

"Chop—chop—chop!" panted the old lamplighter, hobbling up the empty alley. "I'll give yer chop—chop—chop!"

He peered venomously into the darkness, like an ancient cat who had scattered a flock of birds.

"You saved me life!" puffed Larkins, halting painfully in a black corner off Henrietta Street.

"That's right," said Hobby. "I did."

"I'm much obliged to you, Hobby."

"Don't mention it, Larkins."

The pie maker's daughter gazed in bewilderment from one apprentice to the other.

"I'm glad you two have made it up," she said.

"But we've always been friends," said Hobby. "Really."

"Have we?" asked Larkins, bending to rub his injured foot.

"Oh, yes. I've always liked you, Larkins."

"Come to think of it," said Larkins, feeling it was called upon him to respond, "I've always rather liked you, Hobby. Old friend."

"By the way," said Hobby casually—as if it had just come into his mind—"I've done rather a fine head of you, Larkins. In clay."

"A head of me? What for?"

"Because I like you, Larkins. Because you're my friend."

The devil, thought Hobby, with a cunning smile, ain't the only one what moves in mysterious ways. His, Hobby's, ways were considerably more mysterious. He beamed. Now he could show to the world, not the image he'd made of his enemy but the marvellous likeness he'd fashioned of his friend.

Just as his dream had advised, he'd destroyed his enemy. But he'd destroyed him without either loss of blood or ruin of clay. He'd done it by turning him into a friend.

"And—and is it really like me, Hobby, old friend?"

"Oh, Larkins—dear Larkins! If them eyes and cheeks weren't your own, I'd swear you'd nicked 'em from me clay!"

The pie maker's lovely daughter held her peace. She found it hard to decide between two such suitors, one of whom was a marvel with words and the other, it seemed, with his hands. Oh, well, she thought, shrugging her tempting shoulders, she'd seven long years in which to make up her mind. . . .

There was a quietness all about Covent Garden—a quietness of held breath and watchful eyes. Then, from somewhere in the distance, over London Bridge way, a solitary church bell began to chime. One . . . Two . . .

"*Oranges and lemons*," came a soft voice, singing from one of the dark courts into which the Michaelmas apprentices had fled.

"*Say the bells of St. Clement's*," came an answer from an alley.

Three . . . Four . . .

"*You owe me five farthings*," chanted a thin voice, sweet as a starling, from Drury Lane.

"*Say the bells of St. Martin's.*"

Five . . . Six . . .

"*When will you pay me?*"

Seven . . . Eight . . . The lonely bell pealed on, and the chorus, ever growing, replied, "*Say the bells of Old Bailey.*"

Nine . . . Ten . . .

"*When I grow rich . . . when I grow rich . . . WHEN I GROW RICH!*" swelled the voices, from every alley and court, from every shop and workroom, from every bed and dream, and from every young heart all over the town.

"*When I grow rich . . .*"

Back in Three Kings Court, the old lamplighter leaned his ladder against the wall. The little linkboy, standing by his side, looked up at him and then to the stars. The chorus drifted down. The pair of them listened, and then the lamplighter scratched his greasy head.

"We give 'em light," he mumbled. "And what do they do with it?"

The linkboy shook his head, and turned away to hide his smile.

Eleven . . . Twelve . . .

About the author

LEON GARFIELD was born in Brighton, England. His brief art studies were interrupted by the outbreak of World War II, when he joined the army and served in the Medical Corps in England, Belgium, and Germany. After the war he worked as a biochemist until his success as a writer allowed him to devote himself to writing full time.

He is the author of several widely acclaimed novels including *The Sound of Coaches*, a Literary Guild selection, *Prisoners of September*, and *The Pleasure Garden*.

Mr. Garfield lives in north London with his artist wife and their daughter.